Christopher Reich was born in Tokyo and grew up in Los Angeles. He worked in the private banking department of a major Swiss bank in Geneva before joining the bank's department of mergers and acquisitions in Zurich. In 1995 he decided to pursue writing full-time. He lives in California and Switzerland and is the author of three previous bestselling thrillers, *Numbered Account*, *The Runner* and *The First Billion*.

Praise for Christopher Reich:

'Astonishingly powerful' *Daily Telegraph*

'An original and highly inventive thriller' *Mail on Sunday*

'*The First Billion* is a dynamite thriller that says a lot about investment banking, business in general, and greed in particular. This is Christopher Reich's big book' James Patterson

'Reich keeps things moving at breakneck speed' *Wall Street Journal*

'*The Runner* is a wonderful novel, a sophisticated story of conspiracy, treachery and political intrigue . . . Reich is a master of atmosphere and detail' Nelson DeMille

'Briskly paced thriller packed with genuine surprises . . . deliciously plausible' *Entertainment Weekly*

'If you want high-concept espionage, it doesn't get much better than this' *Booklist*

The Devil's Banker

Christopher Reich

headline

First published in Great Britain in 2003
by HEADLINE BOOK PUBLISHING

First published in paperback in 2004
by HEADLINE BOOK PUBLISHING

10 9 8 7 6 5 4 3 2 1

ISBN 0 7553 0626 0

Typeset in Palatino by Avon DataSet Ltd,
Bidford-on-Avon, Warwickshire

Printed and bound in Great Britain by
Mackays of Chatham plc, Chatham, Kent

Headline's policy is to use papers that are natural,
renewable and recyclable products and made from wood
grown in sustainable forests. The logging and manufacturing
processes are expected to conform to the environmental
regulations of the country of origin.

HEADLINE BOOK PUBLISHING
A division of Hodder Headline
338 Euston Road
London NW1 3BH

www.headline.co.uk
www.hodderheadline.com

To Bill, Helena and Jackson Reich
With love

Many members of the United States Law Enforcement community contributed to the writing of this book. Due to their positions and the confidential nature of their work, I find it best not to give their names. I can only offer my thanks. As well, I would like to extend my gratitude to the Department of the Treasury, the United States Customs Service, the Financial Crimes Enforcement Network, and the Internal Revenue Service. Dan Starer of Research for Writers in New York City was a huge help. He can be reached at Researchforwriters.com.

At Bantam Dell, my thanks to Irwyn Applebaum, Nita Taublib, Andrea Nicolay, and, of course, to my editor extraordinaire, Bill Massey.

At Headline UK, thanks to Martin Fletcher and his band of merry men for a great night in Zurich. Let's do it again!

At Arthur Pine and Associates, hats off to Lori Andiman. As always to my agent, Richard Pine, a very big 'thank you' for his enthusiasm, counsel, and unwavering support.

Finally, to my wife, Sue and my two wonderful daughters, Noelle and Katja, you make it all worthwhile.

Chapter 1

It is difficult to walk casually with five hundred thousand dollars taped to your belly. More difficult still when any of the men brushing past you would gladly slit your throat were they to suspect the king's ransom you carried.

The man who had chosen the warrior's name Abu Sayeed snaked through the alleys of the Smugglers' Bazaar, careful to check his impatient step. He was close now, but he could not hurry. To hurry invited attention. And attention meant trouble he could not afford.

Around him, shopkeepers leaned in open doorways, smoking cigarettes and sipping cups of tea. He could sense their eyes upon him as they studied his bearing, gauging its strength, deciding whether he was a predator or prey. Instinctively, he stood straighter and thrust his chin forward. But all the while he kept his pace relaxed, his face slack, even as the claws dug into him.

The money was divided into fifty packets, each containing ten thousand dollars, each wrapped and waterproofed in transparent plastic. The packets had sharp, cruel corners that chafed and cut his flesh. He had been traveling for thirty-six hours. His chest and back were flayed as if scored by a cat-o'-nine tails. Only by thinking of the operation was he able to continue. The prospect of the infidels' death invigorated him with the strength of the Pharaoh's army.

At four P.M., the summer sun was at its fiercest. Dust devils arose on the dusty road, swirled lazily, then spun themselves out. After a brief lull, the bazaar was rousing itself to life. Beneath fluorescent lights, shelves sagged with cartons of Dunhill cigarettes, Toshiba laptops, and Paco Rabanne cologne, all brought overland from Afghanistan to avoid duty and tax. Other windows displayed less mundane goods: Kalashnikov rifles, Colt pistols, and Claymore mines. Hashish, heroin, even human chattel could be had at the right address. If there was a free market on earth, mused Sayeed, it was here on the western outskirts of Peshawar, the gateway to the Khyber Pass.

Stopping to purchase a cube of diced sugar cane, he cast his gaze behind him. His depthless black eyes scoured the street, checking for the misplaced face, the averted gaze, the anxious dawdler. So close, he must keep his senses keen. He did not believe that the crusaders knew his identity. Still, he must be cautious. Members of the American Special Forces infested Peshawar as lice infest a beast. Most were easy to spot, with their Oakley sunglasses, Casio watches, and desert boots. A few even dared enter the bazaar, where foreigners were not welcome and Pakistani law held no sway.

The thought of the Americans brought a contemptuous smile to his lips. Soon they would learn that they could not run. The fire was coming. It would burn them in their heartland. It would scald them from within.

And for a moment, the claws loosened their grip. The pain subsided, and he basked in the glow of destruction.

Satisfied his trail was clean, Sayeed spat out the sinewy cane and crossed the narrow road. To look at, he was no different from any of the thousands of souls who eked out an existence trafficking the porous border that separated Pakistan from Afghanistan. His *shalwar kameez*, the baggy shirt and trousers that made up the local dress, was filthy and stiff with dried sweat; his black headdress smothered with red alkali dust. His beard belonged to the most fervent of believers, as did the AK-47 he carried slung over a shoulder and the bejeweled dagger strapped to his calf.

But Sayeed was not Pakistani, nor was he a Pashtun from the southern provinces of Afghanistan, or an Uzbek from the north. Born Michael Christian Montgomery in London, England, Sayeed was the bastard offspring of a cancerous British officer and a teenage Egyptian whore. His father had died while he was a boy, leaving him a polished accent and not much more. Unable to care for him, his mother returned to Cairo and gave him over to the *madrasas*, the religious schools that gifted him with an Islamic education. His childhood was brutish and short. It was a natural progression to the camps where he learned the creed of the gun, memorized the verse of violence, and worshiped at the altar of rebellion. And from there to the killing fields of Palestine, Chechnya, and Serbia.

At twenty, the Sheikh found him.

At twenty-one, Michael Christian Montgomery ceased to exist. It was Abu Mohammed Sayeed who swore the oath, accepted the mark, and joined Hijira.

Skirting a convoy of carts piled high with Korean fabrics, Tibetan rugs, and Panasonic televisions still in their factory packaging, he reached the Tikram Mosque. The doors were open, and inside the shadowy hall, a few men lay on prayer rugs, prostrate in worship. His eyes returned to the street. Scanning the intersection ahead, he felt a new pain lash his back. This time, however, it was not the jagged belt that provoked his discomfort. It was fear. He could not see the store. Somehow, he had taken a wrong turn. He was lost.

Frantically, Sayeed turned his head this way and that. It could not be. He was at the Tikram Mosque. He had seen the photographs. He had studied the maps. Despair washed over him. Others were waiting. The countdown had begun. Seven days. The thought of failure turned his bowels to water.

Terrified, he wandered into the street. A horn blared in his ear, loud, very loud, but from another universe altogether. Sayeed jumped back a step and a jitney lumbered past, passengers hanging from the doors, clinging to the luggage rack. In its wake, a cloud of rank exhaust choked the already oppressive air. He could not go on. He could not go back. Truly, he was damned.

The exhaust fumes dissipated and he saw it. The gold letters emblazoned on a black field. 'Bhatia's Gold and Precious Jewelry.' His despair vanished. In its place came joy. The light of a thousand suns.

'*Inshallah*, God is great,' he whispered, a bolt of piety swelling his heart.

Guards stood on either side of the doorway, Kalashnikovs to their chest, fingers tickling the trigger guard. Sayeed passed them without a glance. They were not there to protect jewelry, but cash, primarily US dollars, and gold ingots. Bhatia's reputation as a jeweler might be suspect, but his trustworthiness as a *hawaladar*, or money broker, was unquestioned. Faisan Bhatia had long served the local smuggling community as its agent of choice. He was the only broker in the region able to handle the large sums that Abu Sayeed required.

In Arabic, *hawala* means 'to change.' And in Hindu, 'trust.' Put simply, it was the *hawala* broker's job to effect transfers of cash from one city to another. Some of his clients were traders eager to repatriate their earnings after selling their haul in the bazaar. Others, simple folk wishing to send money home to loved ones in Karachi, Delhi, or Dubai. Both groups shared a distrust of the bureaucracy and paperwork demanded by the country's less-than-solvent banks. For them, *hawala* was a welcome alternative. A system built on trust, hidden from intrusive eyes. A system that had been in place when Arab traders plied the Silk Road hundreds of years ago.

Bhatia, a fat Indian with a streak of gray in his hair, stood imperiously behind the counter. As Sayeed approached, he eyed the customer's caked clothing and unwashed face with undisguised contempt.

'I would like to make a transfer,' Abu Sayeed whispered when he was close enough to taste the man's breath. 'It is a matter of some urgency.'

The Indian did not move.

'The Sheikh sent me.'

Faisan Bhatia's eyes flickered, but only for an instant. 'Come this way.'

Chapter 2

It was the most god-awful frightening place she had ever been. Some parts of Jakarta came close. Jakarta with its garish slums, oppressive pollution, and packs of teenage muggers giggling with hostile intent. Macao had a few dark corners where you didn't dare venture. And everyone knew about Rio, the gorgeous bad boys on motorbikes, streaking past with their razors at the ready. But here – the unremitting heat, the hostile stares, and worst of all, the *burqa* draped over her head and shoulders, baking her like a Christmas goose – this topped it all.

Her name was Sarah Churchill, operational designation: 'Emerald,' and through her black gauze veil, she watched the target advance across the intersection. She could see that he was in distress, trying not to limp, compensating by standing too straight and puffing out his chest. Two days she'd been tracking him, up and down the mountain passes, a distance of sixty miles. She was hurting, too, but she'd be damned if she'd show it. Her feet were raw and blistered in their leather sandals; her legs fatigued beyond measure. A little while ago, her lower lip had cracked and she could feel a trickle of blood, salty and strangely reassuring, on her tongue.

A trio of Indian women clad in red and orange saris scurried across her path, and she mimicked their gait. The 'second-class shuffle,' she called it – head bent, shoulders hunched, eyes fixed to the ground like a dog that's been beaten too much.

Drawing in her shoulders, Sarah made herself shrink beneath the full-length garment. Her horizons seemed to dwindle before her and she bridled at her training. *Blend in with your environment:* the first rule of tradecraft taught at Fort Monckton, where all good little English boys and girls go to learn to be spies. Ever the prize pupil, she kept her back hunched and continued to hug the inside of the street.

She was too tall. That was the problem. You didn't see many Pakistani women who stood five feet nine inches in bare-stockinged feet. Her height came from her father, a six-foot-four-inch Welshman. Her hair, a raven's black and cut to her shoulders, was her mother's gift, as were her sierra brown eyes. Her attitude, though, was all her own, and not subject to amendment or revision. She was determined, outspoken, and possessed of a dangerous temper she could not quite control. Five years ago at IONEC, the Intelligence Officer's New Entrant's Course, she'd set the women's mark for the fifty-mile hike, but when at her graduation ceremony her instructors called her their toughest recruit, she'd broken down and cried like a baby.

Her earpiece crackled with static. 'Primary still visual?'

'He's gone into the store,' she whispered. 'Bhatia's Gold and Precious Jewelry.' She spelled the name slowly, enunciating each letter just as matron had taught her at Roedean. 'It's the bloody *hawala*, all right. Time to call in the reinforcements.'

'Give us a GPS read.'

'Coming up.' She found the global positioning device on her belt and hit the locate/transmit button. Within a second, the stationary satellites that comprised the Central Intelligence Agency's proprietary GPS had established her exact latitude and longitude to within six inches of where she actually stood, and her altitude above sea level to within four. She'd been transmitting her location every hundred meters since she'd entered the bazaar. Taken together, the coordinates constituted a route marker for the cavalry, or in more dire circumstances, a path to get her the hell out of Dodge.

'Emerald, you are mapped. An A-team is moving in to clean up. ETA is twelve minutes.'

'*Twelve minutes?* He could be out the back and halfway back to Pesh by then. Damn it, tell them to hurry.'

The Smugglers' Bazaar encompassed an area as big as the City of London, with half again as many alleys, roads, and lanes. Few of the roads were marked, if they even possessed a name. There were certainly no addresses. It had sprung up as an informal 'gray market' trading in goods stolen across the Afghani border. Carts had given way to shacks, and now most of the stores were housed in sturdy concrete bungalows. A patchwork of dubious signs advertised the wares. Marks and Spencer. Maytag. Pringle of Scotland. Sony. And her absolute favorite: Sacks Fifth Avenue. Though wholly within Pakistan's borders, the bazaar was treated as its own autonomous region. Crime was rampant. Thieves, pickpockets, and worse roamed freely, practicing their trade on the weak and unsuspecting. It was up to the victim to catch the criminal. Once he did, the punishment was up to him, too. If there was any rule at all, it was the harsh custom of the Pathan tribesmen who made it their home.

'Maintain visual,' snapped the voice.

'How's the picture?' she asked. 'Getting what you need?'

'Reception's a little fuzzy. Keep still for a second. I need to reset the color balance.'

Sarah held still, staring out at the bustling street. Seven thousand miles away a technician was deciding whether the picture was too red or too green. The Sony microdigital camera embedded in her sunglasses was a gift from the boys in Langley. She liked to think of it as a 'welcome to our side of the pond' present given upon her secondment from MI6. The Yanks always had the neater toys. The camera's images ran to a transmitter in her belt that relayed both audio and visual signals to a spot station nearby. The spot station, in turn, sent the signals on to Langley. The boys at Langley had also given her a machine pistol, three spare clips of ammo, and a tab of cyanide tucked inside a neat little compartment where her wisdom tooth used to be.

'Give us a slow scan left to right.'

Sarah turned her head as directed, the camera capturing the same exotic imagery as her eyes: the mosque and its beautifully carved doors, the merchant stringing fresh offal in his front window, the gunsmith tooling a rifle barrel on the sidewalk, and finally, Bhatia's Gold and Precious Jewelry, where she could make out a tall, lean figure standing at the far counter. Abu Mohammed Sayeed. 'Omar,' for operational purposes.

But they couldn't get the smell. The acrid whiff of long-tended fires; the spiced scent of lamb on a spit; the eye-watering odor of men who toiled and sweated in the one-hundred-degree heat and had not bathed in weeks.

'Close enough?' she asked. 'Or would you gents like me to stick my head inside the store and say hello?'

'Negative. Just give us a walk-by. Nice and brisk. We can slow down the pictures on this side.'

Sarah crossed the street, dodging a howling Vespa, doing her best to keep to a walk. She was sure that somewhere in the Koran there was a *hadith* banning 'righteous women' from running, just as the holy lessons banned them from everything else, except catering to the whims and desires of 'righteous man folk.'

Stepping onto the raised walkway, she continued past the jewelry store, letting her gaze fall on the array of gold chains in the window. The doorway gaped beside her. Two guards with AK's stood at attention inside. Surveillance cameras stared down from the corners. A portly Indian was talking to Sayeed. There were no other customers.

'Confirmed. Omar on premises,' came the voice in her earpiece. 'Looks like he's got some muscle in there. Keep it moving.'

For a quarter second longer she watched, then continued her promenade. At that very moment, however, there was a flurry of movement inside the store, and she stopped. It was a clumsy, jerky halt, a dead giveaway. And there she stood for one second . . . two – a perfect silhouette frozen in the doorway.

'He's going in the back,' Sarah whispered. 'I mean the two are going together. So is one of the guards. Where are the bully boys?' she asked, desperation crowding inside her.

'ETA nine minutes. Do not jeopardize your cover. Proceed to the Tikram Mosque and continue surveillance from there.'

'Nine min—' Her rigid training cut short her protest. In her mind, however, she howled with frustration.

At the end of the walkway, Sarah stepped off the curb and stopped. The courtyard to her right was filled with automobile tires. Hundreds and hundreds of brand-new tires, stacked neatly upon one another, row after row, rising thirty feet in the air. Turning, she peered across the intersection toward the mosque. It would be safer to watch from there. An A-team was inbound. She knew what that meant: bullets, and lots of them. Abu Sayeed was not the type to turn himself over to the authorities and say, 'Okay, Officer. I'll come along quietly.'

'Emerald, this is Ranger.' A new voice sounded in her ear, calm, authoritative. *Ranger*. The DDO himself. The deputy director of operations. 'Go on into the store. Take a look around.'

'*Go in?*'

'We wouldn't want him to sneak out on us, would we? Not before the party starts. It's a jewelry store,' he went on. 'Have a look at a necklace. Buy whatever you like. Call it my treat. You can put it on my expense account.'

'I don't think they take American Express,' she answered blithely, knowing that the banter was to relax her, to deceive her about the peril of his command. And make no mistake, it was an order. He was asking her to flit by her lonesome into a shop with the biggest underworld financier on the northwest frontier and a hardened terrorist associated with a group so secret, so rife with all manner of rumor, that no one even dared whisper its name – if it even had one – because until now, no one had wanted to acknowledge its existence. One supreme evil commander was enough for the world these days.

Across the street, a fierce-looking man was staring daggers at her. He wore a black headdress and a black *dishdasha*, and his beard hadn't been cut in a decade. An Imam, she guessed. An Islamic cleric. The man refused to avert his gaze, lips trembling, eyes afire, his entire being a vessel of hate. Through the veil, she met his accusing glare, and from his obduracy, his anger, his bewildering disrespect of the superior sex, she drew the courage she herself lacked.

'Roger last,' she said. 'I think I'll have a look at some of Bhatia's tat.'

'Good girl,' said Ranger. And Sarah thought that if he ever called her that again, she'd slug him in the jaw even if he was a crip. But by then it didn't matter. She was moving, not thinking. She dodged the curtain of sparks sent up from the gunsmith's forge. She grimaced in her private netherworld as she passed the coils of lamb intestines dangling from the butcher's hook. Then she was inside the store, admiring Mr Bhatia's mediocre wares as if they were the Crown Jewels.

* * *

The money sat in a pile on a table in Bhatia's private office. The Indian opened each packet with a barber's straight-edged razor, then handed the bills to an associate to count. When he was finished, he grunted. 'Five hundred thousand dollars, as you claimed.'

'The Sheikh does not lie,' said Abu Sayeed. A bountiful rain had doubled the poppy harvest. One ton of raw opium was Allah's gift to Hijira: his benediction upon the holocaust to come.

'It is not easy to move such a sum,' said Bhatia. 'How quickly do you need it?'

'Immediately.'

'Today?'

'Now.'

Bhatia's grave features registered concern. 'Where is the money to be sent?'

'Paris.'

'Hmm.' Bhatia's eyes narrowed, and he mumbled a few words to himself, shaking his head. Sayeed knew it was a ruse, the Indian figuring how large a fee he might get away with. 'It can be done. However, the cost for such a transaction is two percent.'

'One percent.'

'Impossible! No one keeps such cash on the premises. A bank will have to be involved. There will be borrowing costs. Overnight at least. Maybe longer. It cannot be avoided. And, of course, the risk. One and a half.'

Sayeed disliked negotiation, but in some cases, it was necessary. Five thousand dollars was a small fee to ensure swift delivery of money to Paris. Small, indeed, compared to the damage it would wreak. 'One,' he repeated. He had his orders. 'The Sheikh will show his appreciation.'

'How?'

Abu Mohammed Sayeed clamped his hand over the Indian's, allowing his eyes to deliver the threat.

Four hundred and seventy miles above the Indian Ocean, an Intruder Geosynchronous SIGINT (signals intelligence) satellite, tasked by the National Reconnaissance Agency to monitor mobile communications in the Pakistan-Northern India-Afghanistan triangle, responded to an emergency override command. In the freezing infinity of space, guidance boosters fired for a half second. Rectangular electromagnetic phased array panels minutely altered their attitude. In an instant, the satellite's field of surveillance or 'footprint' shifted forty miles to the north and twenty-two miles to the east, and centered on code name Emerald's last relayed GPS coordinates.

Several minutes later, the satellite intercepted an open-air cellular transmission based in Peshawar with a respondent in Paris. Along with two thousand three hundred and twenty-nine other calls it had concurrently captured, the satellite's transponders relayed the signal to a ground-based listening station at Diego Garcia, maintained by the US Air Force's 20th space satellite group. In real time, the listening station directed the signals to the National Security Agency in Fort Meade, Maryland, where the conversation was analyzed by a team of parallel-linked IBM supercomputers for any of a thousand 'keywords' in one hundred languages and dialects. In .025 of a second, the supercomputer determined the call was of 'strategic or military' value, coded it 'urgent,' and forwarded a digital copy of the conversation to an analyst at the Central Intelligence Agency's headquarters in Langley, Virginia.

The analyst, realizing he was in possession of 'real-time intelligence,' or information of an immediate strategic concern, phoned the deputy director of operations and requested a crash meeting.

'Sixth floor. CTCC,' said Admiral Owen Glendenning. 'Get up here on the double and bring me a copy of the call.'

'So,' trumpeted Faisan Bhatia, reentering the office after a fifteen-minute absence. 'Everything is arranged. The money can be picked up at Royal Joailliers. It is located at the Place Vendôme in Paris. Do you wish their address?'

'Of course.' Abu Sayeed smiled secretly. The Sheikh had informed him that Bhatia would use Royal Joailliers. Royal called itself an *'haute joaillier,'* meaning that nothing in its satin-lined showcases sold for less than ten thousand dollars. The cartels were their best clients – Colombians, Mexicans, Russians – and it was their practice to keep unconscionable sums of cash on the premises. When Sayeed had written down the address, Bhatia inquired if he would like to provide him with the recipient's name.

'That is not necessary,' said Sayeed.

'Very well. The recipient must use a password to identify himself. In this case, a dollar bill will do nicely.' Bhatia slid a worn US banknote across the table. 'You will take it with you. As soon as possible, I advise you to transmit the serial numbers on the lower lefthand side of the bill to the recipient. When he presents himself to Royal Joailliers, he must give them the identical numbers in sequence. Only then will he be given the money. There can be no mistakes. It is agreed?'

Sayeed knew the rules of *hawala* well. The Sheikh had made use of the informal banking system for years to funnel funds to his operatives. 'It is agreed,' he said.

'May I offer the use of my telephone?'

'I have my own.'

'Very good then. You will join me for something to eat. If I may say, you look rather done in.' Bhatia clapped his hands, barking an order to an unseen consort. A moment later, his wife entered carrying a tray with two porcelain cups and a china teapot. A younger woman followed, bearing a goat's head upon a silver platter. In the cloying, ninety-degree heat, flies swarmed the tray, attacking the staring, gelatinous eyes.

'Please,' said Bhatia, extending a hand toward the Pakistani delicacy.

But Sayeed was not interested in food. Glancing at the monitor that broadcast the interior of Bhatia's showroom, he watched as a woman clad in a full-length *burqa* examined a tray of jewelry. She had been there the entire time he had been with Bhatia. The picture grew fuzzy as if losing reception, then snapped back into focus. A tinge of unease soured his stomach. The clock read 4:45. It would be 12:45 in Paris. He wanted to leave. He wanted to make the call. His brother would be waiting.

Abruptly, he stood. 'The monitor,' he said, lifting his finger toward the screen. 'It is a closed-circuit system?'

'No,' answered Bhatia proudly. 'Wireless. New from Japan.'

Sayeed stalked from the office without another word.

Chapter 3

Admiral Owen Glendenning sat at the rear of the Counter-terrorism Command Center on the sixth floor of the Agency's headquarters in Langley, Virginia, digesting the latest information. It was too soon to hope, but he had no intention of ignoring the first flush of optimism that reddened the back of his neck and had him tapping his cane on the floor.

'Keep on him a little longer, girl, and we're there,' he said to himself. 'Just a little longer.'

Projected onto a ten-foot screen, a live feed from Pakistan broadcast Sarah Churchill's point of view as she examined a selection of gold chains. She raised her head, and Glendenning came face-to-face with a frantic jewelry sales-man blabbing the usual nonsense about high quality and best price. A simultaneous English translation ran across the bottom of the screen.

A second screen broadcast the footprint of the Central Intelligence Agency's spy satellites on a political map of the globe. A shaded area indicated each satellite's footprint. Some shadows remained stationary; others crept across the map with the turning of the earth.

The seal of the CIA highlighted against a navy blue background lit up a third screen, currently unused.

At seven A.M., the Counterterrorism Command Center

was fully staffed and humming. Three rows of analysts occupied the gallery of the auditorium-sized command room. All enjoyed brand new workstations, the latest flat-panel displays, and state-of-the-art ergonomic chairs that cost twelve hundred dollars a pop. It had been a long time since the Company had enjoyed such generous funding, but with the war on terrorism running at full bore, the spigots were wide open. To his frequent visitors from Capitol Hill, Glendenning liked to joke that his op center looked like a movie set – the way Hollywood imagined the espionage community operated. Lately, though, his audience had been less enthralled. Briefings that had once been little more than secret check-writing ceremonies had lately taken an adversarial turn. Where were the results Glendenning had promised? the more daring senators demanded. A few hundred million dollars in confiscated accounts was fine and dandy, but what about the terrorists behind it? Warm bodies, not frozen assets, were the order of the day.

They'd get their terrorists, Glendenning promised silently. A little patience would be nice.

Suppressing the grunt that came with the pain of standing, he pushed himself to his feet, then took hold of his twin bamboo canes and shuffled across the back of the op center to the glassed-in enclosure that served as his office. Owen Glendenning was sixty-one years old, thin and balding. People remarked on his resemblance to Franklin Roosevelt. They said he owned the same patrician bearing, the great politician's indomitable smile and easy charm. He knew they were lying, that his looks made people nervous. As a young SEAL lieutenant in the Vietnam War, he had been gravely wounded leading a nighttime incursion behind enemy lines to capture suspected VC cadre. The mortar rounds that had mangled his legs had also disfigured his face. His right cheek and jaw were concave, as if someone had hit him very hard with a spading tool. The mission, however, was a success, and for his part in it, Glendenning had been awarded the Medal of Honor. He might have looked like FDR once, but now the only things he had in common with the great man were a steely self-reliance, a hatred of sympathy, and a refusal to be patronized.

Picking up a phone, he dialed the Foreign Terrorist Asset Tracking Center (FTAT) two floors below. 'Get me Halsey.'

Strictly speaking, FTAT was a Treasury operation. Treasury funded it. Treasury supervised it. But when the scope of the investigation into worldwide terrorist financing had become clear, all involved had decided to move FTAT's operations to Langley.

There was a time not too far back when the very idea of the CIA contacting Treasury to share information was practically a jailable offense. There was law enforcement and there was intelligence, and never the twain shall meet. But the events of September 11, 2001, had changed all that. With the passage of the Patriot Act, communication between the United States' varied and multiple law enforcement and intelligence agencies not only was permitted, it was encouraged. The old concept of 'stovepiping,' or keeping information inside the particular agency, or, as was the case with the FBI, inside the individual department that had discovered it, was thrown out the door. Concerns about infractions on civil liberties and personal privacy were quickly dismissed. If you weren't stepping on someone's rights, you weren't doing your job, Glendenning liked to say. The threat beyond the country's borders took pre-eminence and was far greater than anyone could be told.

'This is Halsey,' answered a deep, gravelly voice.

'Don't you have a home either?'

Allan Halsey, chief of the Foreign Terrorist Asset Tracking Center, gave a shallow laugh. 'Not according to my wife.'

'We nabbed the call,' said Glendenning. 'The money's being moved as we speak. Come on up and we'll run it from here.'

'How much?'

'We're guessing five hundred grand or five million. Either way, it's the real deal.'

'I don't like it,' said Halsey. 'Risky to move so much.'

'I couldn't agree more. Something's about to pop. Who's running your team in Paris?'

'Adam Chapel.'

'Don't know him. A new guy?'

'Treasury pulled him in after the WTC.'

'Military?'

'God no,' said Halsey. 'A quant jock all the way. Kid was on the fast track at Price Waterhouse. Partner at twenty-nine. National audit manager.'

'Sounds like a real killer,' said Glendenning. 'Ought to have 'em quaking in their boots.'

'Come on now, Glen. He's the new kind of soldier. You know, brains instead of brawn. Different war we're fighting this time.'

'That's what they tell me. In the end, though, you still have to shoot the bad guys.'

'Don't worry about Chapel,' said Halsey, his voice quieter, more confident, as if vouchsafing a secret. 'He can hold his own.'

Midmorning traffic was light as the canary yellow postal van accelerated across the Place de la Concorde. Jaw clenched, Adam Chapel leaned close to the windshield, willing the van to go faster. *Finally*, an anxious voice pleaded inside his head. *Finally*.

The tires hit a stretch of cobblestones and Chapel jostled inside the tight cabin. Looking out the driver's window, he was afforded a clear view up the Champs-Elysées. Rows of oaks lined the boulevard, giving way to wide sidewalks and an array of stores and restaurants. The Arc de Triomphe rose at its head. The sun broke from the clouds, and the monument to France's fallen warriors glimmered like an ivory tower.

'How much faster can you go?' Chapel asked the hulking black man behind the steering wheel.

'This is it, my friend,' said Detective Sergeant Santos Babtiste of the French Sûreté. 'Any quicker and we'll blow the tires off. Be happy – the average speed around town these days is ten kilometers per hour. You're better off taking the Métro, even if you are the police.' *Zee poleece.* Gingerly, he kissed two fingers of his right hand and touched them to the photographs of his children glued to the dashboard. '*Dieu nous benisse. Aujourd'hui, nous avons de la chance.*'

'We'll see about that,' answered Chapel, shifting in his seat, eyes to the fore. Luck scared him. It was work that yielded results.

Chapel was not as big as Babtiste, but like the French detective, he looked cooped up and uncomfortable in the cramped cabin. There was something about the roll of his shoulders, the striated muscles around the neck that suggested a caged restlessness, a quivering, explosive ambition. His black hair was curly and cut close to the scalp; his skin pale, an army of stubble visible beneath the hollow planes of his cheeks. He wore what he always wore, a pressed white Polo button-down, Levis, and a pair of handmade loafers from John Lobb of Jermyn Street. Perched on the edge of his seat, he had the haunted, lonely look of a skipper who'd been at sea too long, his whiskey brown eyes scanning the horizon, willing land into sight.

A stone's throw away, the Obelisk passed in a blur. He was thinking the sights should stir him more. Inspire him, even. But he was too nervous to award them more than a passing glance. It was his first command as team leader and he was determined not to screw up. The sights could wait. He was busy mapping out the job at hand, rehearsing his responsibilities, and calculating the odds of nabbing his first honest-to-god terrorist.

Two weeks earlier, a pair of Treasury agents he'd trained with at Quantico had gotten the call in Lagos, Nigeria. A sale of diamonds in the old town. Cash only. High six figures. Seller was thought to be a player. It was a 'wait and watch' job, just like today. Their bodies were discovered five hours after they'd failed to report back. Both had been shot in the head at close range. Someone else had been waiting and watching.

That was the first time Adam Chapel had heard the name 'Hijira' mentioned.

Today, it was his turn. Somewhere between five hundred thousand and five million dollars was being transferred to Paris. *Now. At this minute.* He wondered if the transfer belonged to the same network that had killed the men in Lagos.

The jump team had hit Paris three days earlier. Like the other teams that had landed in Frankfurt, Hamburg, Rome, Milan, Madrid, and London, it had a mandate to contact the local 'cop shop,' target probable points of currency entry, and if possible, set up visual and electronic surveillance on said location. Paris's large Arab population – more than fifty thousand French Algerians alone lived in the capital – coupled with the jump team's limited personnel, precluded any stakeouts. It was just as well. While there were over one hundred registered money-transfer businesses, better known as *'hawalas,'* operating in the city, Royal Joailliers was not one of them.

'Con!' roared Santos Babtiste, ramming his enormous palm into the horn, letting it ride for a while as he jerked the wheel hard to the right. An ancient Citroën Deux Chevaux

flashed across the windshield and was gone. Chapel held his breath as the van braked, then lunged forward, asserting its place in the five-lane circus.

'Take it easy up there!' came a voice from the rear of the van.

'That you griping, Santini?' asked Chapel. 'What's the problem? You got a weak stomach?'

A glance over his shoulder revealed four men seated on the metal floor, knees to their chests. All guarded the same hardened expression, and they reminded him of a stick of paratroopers ready to jump into combat. Ray Gomez and Carmine Santini from Customs. Mr Keck from the Agency. And a very small, taciturn Frenchman with a cloudy affiliation to the Sûreté named Leclerc.

Leclerc, who rubbed the slim wooden briefcase between his knees, as if he were calming a pet.

Chapel was certain he knew what was inside.

'Weak stomach?' called Santini. 'You got the wrong body part, mister. It's like getting a jackhammer up your ass back here. Someone hurry up and tell our hosts a road's supposed to be smooth.' Frowning, he looked at Leclerc, seated next to him. 'Haven't you guys ever heard of shock absorbers? Now I know why you don't sell any French cars in the States. No Peugeots. No Citroëns. Like getting it in the ass all day.'

Leclerc looked at him for a second, then smiled thinly and lit a cigarette. 'Pussy,' he muttered through a cloud of blue smoke.

'What'd you say?' Santini demanded, then to the others: 'What'd he say, the little prick?'

'Pussy,' said Keck. 'You heard him.'

'Called you a pussy, Carmine,' chimed in Gomez. 'How 'bout that?'

Santini considered the remark, his back coming off the rear wall, shoulders rising like he was going to ratchet things up a notch. At six two, one-eighty, he had it over the

Frenchman in height and weight. His eyes fell to the brief-case, to Leclerc's indifferent eyes, dull as a shark's, and he sank back. 'Ah, fuck the bunch of you,' he said half-heartedly.

Leclerc lofted a perfect smoke ring across the cabin. Shaking his head, he began rubbing the wooden case again.

'How long till we're there?' Chapel asked Babtiste.

'Two minutes. A miracle, I tell you. A sign. We're going to get this man, you will see.'

Looking over his shoulder, Chapel asked, 'What about Royal? They on our radar?'

Ray Gomez was online with TECS, the Treasury Enforcement Computer System's database, checking for references to Royal Joailliers. 'Turned up once as a possible accomplice in a money laundering case we were working against the cartels,' he said, looking up from his laptop. 'No charges filed. Owner is Rafi Boubilas, Lebanese national.'

'They are dirty,' said Leclerc. He had a folksinger's lank dark hair and the three-day stubble to go with it. 'Boubilas, he runs a big coke ring in town. You know how he gets the money out? His partners in Bogota grind up old bottles of Seven-Up, green glass you know, then import the pieces as uncut emeralds. This man, he has many friends. He is rich. He is well connected. No one looks too closely. The invoice says five million. No problem. Boubilas, he takes all his coke cash and sends it back to his masters to pay for the phony stones.'

'Why don't you take him down?' Chapel asked.

Leclerc made no reply. He was suddenly busy looking out the rear window, humming.

The postal van leaned hard into a left-hand turn. Build-ings rose on either side of them. Shadows drenched the cabin as they advanced the length of the Rue de Castiglione. Ahead, the buildings fell away, and the road gave onto a grand square. Place Vendôme.

Another left turn. A flood of sunlight. A decreased tempo. A courtly circuit of the square. Rising like a giant roman candle in its center was the monument to the Battle of Austerlitz, smelted from the twelve hundred cannons Napoleon had captured on the field that day in Germany. Colored awnings advertised the world's most famous luxury goods. Chanel. Repossi. Van Cleef and Arpels. And passing to their left, the blue welcome carpet of the Hôtel Ritz, their destination.

Babtiste turned into an alleyway and parked the postal van outside the service entry.

Chapel threw an arm over the back of his seat, his eyes going from one member of his team to the next. He thought about telling them to keep their heads up, their eyes and ears open. What was the point? Between them they had fifty years' experience setting up stings, going on stakeouts, taking down *narcotrafficantes* with shields out and pistols blazing. He was the new guy. They knew better than he did what to do.

A team of hotel security waited. Quietly, they guided Gomez, Santini, and Keck to the service elevator. Babtiste followed, swinging the stainless steel case loaded with eighty pounds of A/V gear as if it were a lunch box. Leclerc took the stairs with Chapel. Entering the opulent suite, he shot the American a challenging glance. 'You look nervous,' he said.

'I am,' Chapel answered.

Six months, Sarah had been chasing the shadow. Six months shuttling between Kabul, Kandahar, and the Khyber Pass, chasing down leads like an errant fielder. One week she was a UNICEF relief worker, the next, a clinician from *Medecins San Frontières*, and the next, an administrator for the World Bank. She spent as much time building her legends as she did working her sources.

The first whispers had reached her at her desk in London, though by wildly different routes. A field officer had buried a mention in his report of some rumors he'd picked up at a party at the Indian consul's in Kabul, the kind of boozy affair frequented by aid workers, diplomats, and the local gentry, in this case a few of the tamer regional warlords. Then there were the first-hand snippets delivered over a tepid lunch at Fortnum's by a wallah from agriculture just back from a tour of the area: something vague about a new poppy farmer in the southeast taking control of the large fields near Jalalabad. With the Taliban gone, the Afghanis were hell-bent on reclaiming their place as the world's largest suppliers of raw opium. Word was, however, that the seller wasn't a local, but an Arab-Afghan like bin Laden, a devout Muslim from the Gulf who had fought as a Mujahadeen during the Soviet invasion of Afghanistan. There were rumors of an important sale. Several tons of product coming to market.

Both times the word 'Hijira' came up.

'Hijira,' as in the journey from Mecca to Medinah undertaken by the Prophet Muhammed in the year A.D. 622 to escape persecution. Or more important, 'Hijira,' as in the date from which the new Muslim calendar began.

To Sarah's seasoned ears, it could not be a coincidence.

Marshaling her evidence, she'd marched downstairs to Peter Callan's office and demanded an immediate posting in country. When he demurred, she blew her stack. Wasn't CT what it was all about these days? Counterterrorism. Intelligence's desperately needed raison d'être borne on silver wings in what everybody had to agree was the barest nick of time. When he hesitated still, she built his argument for him. Arabic speakers were in demand. Those who spoke Pashtun were particularly prized. Sarah, who'd taken a first in Oriental languages at Cambridge, trumped them all, with Urdu, French, and German under her belt as well. The question wasn't why she should go to Afghanistan. It was why she wasn't already there! Callan had grunted something about a budget and called Langley.

Four days later, she was packed aboard a commercial flight to Dulles for a one month's crash course in the culture of the American intelligence community. From there, it was on to Karachi, and by overland route to Kabul.

Her brief was simple: Keep an ear to the ground for the bad guys. 'Players,' the Yanks called them. She was to cultivate sources, debrief agents in place, and establish her own network.

'Follow the money' was her maxim, and it led to the gold souks of Gilgit, the vaults of the Afghani central bank, and Kabul's bustling black market for medical supplies.

While she never found the Arab-Afghan, she did run across one Abu Mohammed Sayeed, wanted by nearly every Western intelligence agency for barbarous acts too numerous to mention, as he scurried to and fro across her radar arranging to sell his mother lode of opium.

Follow the money, she repeated silently, staring at the gold chain in her hand. She had, and the money had led her here, to Faisan Bhatia's jewelry store in the heart of the Smugglers' Bazaar.

'No, no,' she remonstrated the clerk. 'The quality of the links is terrible. Look: this is not solid gold. It is electroplated.'

'Yes. Twenty microns.'

'Ten at most,' she countered. 'I can scratch it off with my fingernail.'

She'd been in the store for twenty minutes, and her every sensor was telling her to get the hell out. One of the surveillance cameras was pointed directly at her, and she could imagine Sayeed in the back room, glancing up at the monitor and asking, 'Is she still there? That's a bit long, isn't it?'

She dropped the chain on the counter and pretended to spot a bracelet that captured her fancy.

'There's been a delay,' said a voice in her ear. 'A traffic jam.' It was Ranger and he no longer sounded so calm and authoritative. 'The A-team will be there in five minutes. If Omar comes out, you need to stop him. Once he's in the bazaar, he's got the advantage. We need him penned in.'

Stop him? The reply choked deep in her throat. Damn it! She knew they wouldn't make it in time.

'Are you with me?' asked Ranger. 'Just nod.'

So, it had come to this, thought Sarah. With all their satellites and uplinks and GPS, it had come back to the same old thing. Put your body in front of the bullet.

She would do it. She never considered saying no. Not with a daddy who'd gone ashore with 2 Para at Goose Green in the Falklands and a brother who'd done thirty missions over Baghdad. The Churchills were bred to fight. And they had the coat of arms and the professional soldier's proud penury to prove it.

She just hadn't thought it would be hers to do alone.

Swallowing, she found her throat dry as a chalkboard. It was the heat, she told herself.

She nodded.

'I'd like to see the red one.' To her surprise, Sarah realized that she was asking the salesman a second time to see the bracelet and that he wasn't responding. She heard a rustle behind her, the creak of a door opening, hushed voices. The salesman's eyes were pinned to the men emerging from the back room. Against her every instinct, she turned so that Langley could see what she was seeing, so that they would know that their vaunted A-team, their bare-chested macho superstars, were too late, and that Omar was going to get away unless she tackled him right then and there.

Sayeed was talking on a cell phone, his words rushed, urgent. She caught a string of numbers, a pause, saw his mouth widen to utter an arrogant laugh. As he slid past her, she caught his ripe scent.

Stop him, Glendenning had said.

Sarah took a step back. The collision was stilted and orchestrated. Sayeed grunted and spun, immediately on the defensive. And even as she turned to apologize, and the futility of her cause overcame her, she knew that, at least for a moment, she'd accomplished what she'd been told, and that her father, the general himself, would be proud.

Abu Sayeed lifted his arm to brush away the woman, his eyes drawn into a distasteful grimace. Until she had backed into him like a clumsy ox, he thought he'd been wrong to suspect her. Her *burqa* was immaculate. Her posture at once respectful, yet with the right amount of pride. She revealed no part of herself. She was a righteous woman, not a street whore eager to prey on a man with a little money in his pocket.

Abu Sayeed believed in the law of *Hijaab*, or 'concealment.' He believed that women had no place in public. They belonged at home, caring for children, tending to their household. Only in this way could their dignity be upheld, their purity protected. Should they have to venture out, they must cover their figure in deference to the Prophet. The smallest piece of exposed flesh was as provocative as a woman's pudendum.

Now he knew it was a sham. Her adherence to *Hijaab*, a lie; a ploy to rid an unsuspecting male of a few dollars. It was common enough practice. You could barely pass a diamond merchant without spotting the women waiting outside like jackals. After all, if a man had a few hundred dollars to spend on a precious stone, he might be willing to part with a good deal less to sate his baser desires. He'd been mistaken. The cloudy reception on Bhatia's TV was from her pager, no doubt. They all carried them, anxious to meet their customers' beck and call. Carrion birds, they were. Vultures. And laden with as many diseases.

Still, Sayeed was unable to look away. The sun shone through the window, silhouetting her breasts. He imagined that beneath the full-length garment she possessed an exquisite form. He was tempted to take her to his safe house and have his way with her, but the current of lust was swept aside by waves of self-righteousness. Years of education demanded to be heard. He was talking before he knew it, speaking as if the Prophet himself commanded his tongue.

'Harlot,' he said. 'Do you think every man is corruptible? Do you think you tempt me even for a moment? You are a disgrace to Islam and to the Prophet. Do you not follow the holy teachings?'

The woman did not respond.

'Speak when you are addressed!' he bellowed.

'Excuse me,' came the voice, timid and repentant. 'I did not mean to run into you. It was an accident. I did not realize I was of offense.'

'Of course you did. How else can your actions be taken? Why else have you been waiting so long in the store? Do you think I do not know what you wish of me?'

Sayeed grasped the woman's arm and pulled her along with him. 'Stay on the street, where you belong. Or better yet, inside your house of ill-repute.'

Her upper arm was muscular. She was strong. He had known women like this, in the camps, and in America.

He pushed her through the doorway and into the street.

'Away,' she cried, struggling. 'You have no right.'

'I am a man. I have every right.'

He heard her exhale, and then she was upon him, striking him with the ferocity of a wildcat. A fist swung at his face. Stepping away, he deflected the blow, keeping a grip on her arm.

'A fighter, eh? Is that where you built your muscles? Hitting men and stealing their wealth when they are weak and sated?'

A dozen men had stopped to gawk at the struggle. Quickly, a circle formed around Sayeed and the woman. Voices offered all manner of advice, a precious few even calling for Sayeed to let her go.

'Away,' she yelled repeatedly, the fear of retribution pinching her voice. 'Let me go. I shall call the police.'

'Call them,' he seconded. 'Be my guest. Here, the Lord God is judge. We require no other authority.'

He tried to swing her around and get her arm locked behind her, but suddenly she slid inside his reach. His jaw rocked. His mouth filled with a warm, salty fluid that he knew was blood. It surprised him, nonetheless. She had hit him. The whore had hit him. Clenching his fist, he swung at the veiled face, holding back nothing. A cry escaped as she collapsed to a knee.

A cheer erupted from the crowd. The spectators closed in, fifty of them at least, more rushing in every second. Their voices were raucous and hungry, the confrontation awakening an ancient taste for savagery.

Sayeed lifted the woman to her feet. Dust coated her *burqa*. Rivets of blood dotted the ground beneath her, some black, some violently red. Yet, as she rose, he felt something hard and angular rub against him. Something that felt very much like a gun.

'Who are you?' he asked, raising his machine gun to port arms, pulling the firing pin and slipping a finger inside the trigger guard.

'I know who she is,' came a cracked and rusted voice. 'I have seen her watching.'

Sayeed spun to face an old man, dressed entirely in black, emerging from the ring of spectators. 'Yes, Imam,' he addressed the mullah. 'Tell me. Tell us all.'

The Islamic cleric raised a gnarled finger, his voice shrill with the fury of a thousand years. 'A crusader!'

Chapter 4

With two fingers, Adam Chapel inched back the Flemish lace curtains and peeked at the Place Vendôme. A steady stream of vehicular traffic flowed clockwise around the square. Flocks of tourists strolled its perimeter. Some window-shopped arm in arm. Others kept a businesslike pace. Raising a pair of binoculars to his eyes, he spotted Carmine Santini strolling past the Armani boutique. Rucksack hanging from one shoulder, camera and document holder strung around his neck, he looked every inch the gawky American tourist, right down to his cargo shorts, sickly white legs, and scuffed basketball shoes. A hundred yards along, Ray Gomez, dressed more conservatively in blazer and slacks, queued up to withdraw some cash from an ATM.

Chapel's eyes skipped back and forth across the cityscape, selecting, evaluating, analyzing. Is it the pretty blonde woman in the flower print dress? The taxi driver loitering too long after dropping his fare? The harried executive with his mouth glued to his cell phone? Chapel had no idea who would be sent to pick up the transfer or when they might arrive. One fact kept his nerves from fraying. Unlike other stores housed in the seventeenth-century arcade, the jewelry shop boasted a single point of entry, and it was right in front of his eyes.

Next to him, Leclerc sat on the carpet with his legs crossed, cigarette dangling from the corner of his mouth, as he meticulously assembled a sleek rifle.

'You know it?' he said, without looking up. 'The FR-F2. Seven-point-six-two millimeter, semiautomatic.'

'Sure,' he answered, lying. 'It's a nice piece. Real nice weapon. Real solid.' He watched the Frenchman ram a cartridge into the stock, then work the bolt back and forth.

'What do you carry?' Leclerc asked, bringing the rifle to his cheek, sighting along the barrel.

'Me?'

'Yes, you.' Leclerc dropped the rifle into his lap and stared at him.

Chapel blinked repeatedly, needing a second to answer. The truth was that guns unsettled him. A pistol's cold, dead weight, the seductive curve of its trigger, left him queasy with dread and apprehension. Shooting for score on the range at the Federal Law Enforcement Training Center in Glynco, Georgia, he'd managed an eighteen out of fifty, with two bullets missing the target altogether. He argued that this ineptness grew from his being an accountant, not only by trade, but by nature. He preferred the precision of a balanced ledger, its promise of fiscal transparency, its devotion to a world defined by generally accepted accounting principles, to the wild, terminal justice of a hollow-tipped bullet. Chapel knew the cardinal rule about guns. You couldn't own one without wanting to use it. He'd learned the fact firsthand. Alone among his team, he didn't carry a weapon.

'I guess I like my MBA four-point-oh from HBS the best,' he said. 'But I also keep a CPA and a CFA handy, you know, just in case. And, oh yeah, in my sock I got a nifty little MPA – that's a master's degree in public accounting. Absolutely essential when you're in close and things get a little hairy.'

Leclerc swung the rifle up to the windowsill and took aim on a provisional target. 'You're a funny guy.'

Chapel laid a hand on the barrel. 'We want him alive, Mr Leclerc. He doesn't do anyone any good dead. You're just here for emergencies.'

'Bang!' said Leclerc, pulling the trigger on an empty chamber, watching Chapel jump from the corner of his eye. 'See, I am funny, too.'

'Yeah, a barrel full of monkeys.'

Chapel walked to the center of the suite where Keck had set up the video monitors on a lacquered mahogany table. One of the six-by-six inch screens showed the façade of Royal Joailliers. The other two offered wide-angle views of the east and west halves of the square.

'So far so good,' said Keck. 'Transmit A-OK. FaceIt is online. We are operational.'

A wireless relay transmitted all three video feeds to the Foreign Terrorist Asset Tracking Center at Langley. There, FaceIt, a sophisticated and rapidly evolving biometric software program manufactured by the Identix Corporation, would pick out all visible faces, digitally enhance them, and compare each on the basis of fifty-three distinct characteristics with an FBI database containing photographs and artists' composites of several thousand known and suspected terrorists.

'We getting this on tape?'

'Not tape,' Keck said testily. 'On disk.'

'I don't care if it's super-eight film, as long as it records.' Chapel slipped on a communications headset. 'You there, Mr Babtiste?' he asked, pulling the slim microphone close to his mouth.

'*Ch'uis la.*' Babtiste had accepted a temporary position as a hotel doorman. He stood downstairs at the hotel portico clad in one of the Ritz's trademark blue topcoats, greeting arriving guests with a touch of his cap and the flash of his dazzling smile. 'I'm making some decent tips. If our man does not show till afternoon, I'm paying for dinner at Maxims for *nous tous*.'

'If he doesn't show, I'll hold you to it,' said Chapel, but even as he permitted himself a smile, a new voice barked in his ear. It was Halsey, and the strident edge to his voice made him shiver. 'Adam, we've intercepted a second communication. It was a little garbled, but we're betting it was Omar sending the code to his correspondent on your side. The number dialed had a Paris area code. Looks like this thing is going down now. Your team in place?'

'Affirmative,' Chapel answered, rolling on the balls of his feet.

'Good. We'll be watching with you.'

Hawala.

Two years ago, Adam Chapel had never even heard the word, let alone known that it constituted an underground banking network that transferred more than fifty billion dollars a year around the world. The Chinese had called it '*Fei Qian*,' or 'flying money,' but, in fact, the money never went anywhere. Today, a broker in New York asks his counterpart in Delhi to deliver five hundred dollars. Tomorrow, it would be the other way around. If, and when, accounts between the two needed balancing, some gold might change hands. But no one kept any papers. No chits, no receipts, no nothing. In the event of a dispute, *hawaladars* consulted human 'memorizers,' trained and kept on staff to mediate.

Hawala, however, was far more than a simple means of sending cash from one person to another. It was also a convenient mechanism to evade taxes and duties. Vendors provided importers with lower prices on their invoices and got the difference via *hawala*. In the late sixties, the first large *hawala* networks emerged to circumvent official restrictions on gold imports in Southeast Asia. Once the gold smugglers had perfected the system, it wasn't long before other criminals followed suit: drug traffickers, money launderers, and more recently, terrorists.

'Bachelor number one, come on down,' said Carmine Santini from his position at yet another fashion boutique. 'Male, twenty-five to thirty-five, approaching Royal. Navy blazer, tan slacks, and oh, look at that shirt. Could be Italian. Definitely Mediterranean. Enjoys dinner, dancing, and moonlight walks on the beach. Got him, Kreskin? Signor Romeo with his nose to the window.'

Santini the joker. Always ready with a name for everyone. Chapel had earned the nickname 'Kreskin' (after the famous mentalist) when five minutes after sitting down with a slippery Lebanese businessman to discuss his company's balance sheet, he'd figured out the guy was scraping ten percent off his pretax profits and sending the cash to the bad guys. Chapel had explained that it was an accounting issue entirely, the man listing the cash as a charitable donation but not taking the write-off. Three hundred grand a year was too much to forget about. But there was more to it than that. The truth was that a balance sheet was like a glimpse into a person's soul. The way someone kept their books – if they padded expenses, front-loaded revenues, took advances on salary . . . *or didn't* – told you everything you needed to know about him. Chapel was no mentalist. He was just good at finding the man inside the numbers.

'Yeah, I got him.' Chapel nudged Keck. 'Let's get up close and personal.'

The camera zoomed in and the back of the man's head filled the monitor. Black hair cut short, a little greasy kid stuff in it to give it some pizzazz. Pink checked shirt. *Turn around*, Chapel ordered the image. *Let me get a look at you.* The head turned, but only for a second, then it was back to studying the rings in the window.

'Did he give you enough of a profile?'

'Sorry,' said Keck. 'I need a full frontal shot.'

'Stay clear,' Chapel ordered Santini and Gomez. 'Carmine, take a minute at Boucheron, and a minute at Facconable. Ray, ditch that line and move to twenty yards.'

'Yo, Kreskin,' said Santini. 'You're getting good at this. Pretty soon you're going to ditch that desk and come into the field full-time with us.'

'Doubtful,' said Chapel, but for the first time the idea appealed to him.

Santini moved on to the next boutique, his eyes glued to the window in front of him. Gomez made a show of checking his watch, then shaking his head in frustration as he set off toward the jewelry store. Both had woven themselves into the human fabric of the square and were invisible to the watcher's eye.

Leclerc had slipped the barrel of his rifle through the curtain and laid it on the windowsill. Still as a cat, he crouched, cheek pressed to the gun's wooden stock.

'Well,' said Keck as he stared at the figure on the monitor. 'Either the price of the ring's too high or he's having second thoughts about the girl. Come on, buddy, make up your mind. Go inside or move along.'

Romeo broke off from the window and continued down the street.

'False alarm,' said Santini.

'Patience,' said Babtiste.

'Damn,' said Chapel.

'Crusader! Crusader!'

Sarah Churchill peered in horror at the seething crowd encircling her, reading hatred and blood lust in their eyes. 'Crusader' was the spiteful label slapped on any Westerner, civilian or combatant, who defiled the land of Islam. The voices grew louder and she sensed an evil animus rising among them. No longer were they just a bunch of curious onlookers. They were a force. Willful. Intent. United in unholy purpose.

'Crusader! Crusader!'

It's medieval, she told herself. *Any minute, they're going to send out the Imam himself. He's going to declare me a heretic, and they're going to put me to the stake. Saint Joan, redux.*

No, she corrected herself, *this is Pakistan. The Hindu Kush. They do worse things to you than burn you at the stake. They stone you. They chop off your hands and legs and tar the stumps. They run bulldozers up and down your body, and if that doesn't do the trick, they topple a stone wall onto you.* They hadn't given her the cyanide so she wouldn't talk. They'd given it to her to avoid this. Zionist crusaders merited the most gruesome of deaths.

Dirt fell from her fingers as she struggled to remain standing. The punch had caught her squarely on the cheek, knocking the sunglasses from her face. Blood pooled in her mouth. Her vision was a mess. She was dizzy. Either the bruising or the heat made the world dip and twirl, even as she fought to stand still.

God, the heat.

'Bit of a mess here, boys,' she spoke into her mike. 'Wondering if that A-team you mentioned is due anytime soon.'

With a start, she noticed the microphone was no longer there. White noise hissed in her earpiece. A hand fell to the transmitter, got tangled in the *burqa*, then found it. She pressed the reset button, but nothing happened. Damned thing must have broken when Sayeed knocked her to the ground.

Bit of bad news, dear, she informed herself in her Aunt Gertie's deliciously arch tones. *I'm afraid the A-team won't be coming today. Not in five minutes or fifty. No point in kidding yourself. There's no way an all-terrain vehicle can make it through the bazaar's tight lanes. Bloody donkey carts have enough trouble as it is.*

The A-team. 'A' for absent.

She'd been quick to spot the Special Forces boys out and about. In Kabul. In Jalalabad. In Peshawar. She had wanted to chat them up, if for no other reason than to remember what it was like to speak to a man who didn't value a donkey, or a yak, or whatever the indigenous beast of burden was around here, more than a woman.

'Crusader! Crusader!'

Look at their eyes. They're on fire. Sarah turned in a circle. Hot. It was so damned hot. Sod this *burqa*. She had to get the thing off. She needed some air. She needed to breathe.

Grasping the top of the garment with her left hand, she ripped off the veil and flung it to the ground.

The gun was in her hand now. The Glock 18, thirty-three rounds of nine-millimeter Parabellum ammunition, another three clips at the ready. She held it as she'd been taught, one hand for the breech, the other on the trigger.

You must stop him, Glendenning had said, and his voice rang like a battle cry in her ear.

'In the name of the United States,' she called out, 'and the government of Pakistan, I am placing you under arrest for conspiracy to commit terrorist acts.'

Abu Sayeed gestured towards the automatic weapons pointing at her, then lunged at her with the snout of his machine gun. 'Under arrest? I think it's the other way around.'

A man in a brown turban began to ululate, the terrible shriek the Pathan tribesmen utter to build up their courage. Others took it up, a war cry penetrating to the four corners of her sanity. The unearthly warbling grew louder. A siren song of death. She was no longer frightened. She was beyond that. She was defeated. Utterly, unabashedly defeated.

Turning, she did a mental count of the Kalashnikovs aimed at her heart. She stopped at thirteen, which was unlucky, so she found one more to add to the collection.

'May I?' Sayeed asked, and his gentleman's Mayfair accent stunned her as much as his rock-hard fist had moments before. Gently, he freed the gun from her hands. She did not resist. How many would she have gotten, anyway? Would she even have slain Sayeed? Half of these men were battle-hardened soldiers. The moment she'd made a move to fire, Sayeed himself, or any one of the others, would have cut her to ribbons.

Stop him.

She'd tried, damn it.

Sayeed had exchanged his rifle for a knife. A curved dagger big enough to thresh wheat. Slowly, he approached, with the Mona Lisa's smile and a hypnotic cast to his eyes. Her hands were lead. Her feet, too. A prayer escaped her lips.

'*Father . . . Into Your hands I commend my spirit . . . Forgive me my sins . . .*'

And as she recited the words, her tongue found the porcelain compartment that hid the cyanide capsule. With a trained flick, she opened it. The capsule was round and dry and lolled on the center of her tongue. Positioning it neatly between her rear molars, she congratulated herself on her bravery. Expedience was more like it. Anything had to be better than being cut with that evil blade.

Sayeed was talking to her, but she didn't hear his voice. Strangely, all was silent. She was aware only of the heat, the drafts of warm air rising from the ground, bathing her in an arid current, luring her into a soporific trance. The blade rose in a great arc. She met his eyes and saw how very young he was beneath the beard and the dirt. Beneath the hate.

She bit down on the capsule.

A great gob of blood showered her face and suddenly, Sayeed wasn't there any longer. He was on the ground, eyes wide open, staring in indolent horror at the splinter of bone and flesh where his forearm and hand used to be. There was a scream, and she saw that the bullet that had taken off Sayeed's hand had continued right through and very messily blown the head off of a man standing a few feet behind him.

Tat tat tat.

Gunfire crackled in the air. The dry mechanical cough of a machine gun. Loud. So incredibly loud. An amplified voice was shouting in Urdu. 'Disperse immediately. Leave the area or you will be arrested.'

The hood of a Dodge four-by-four broke through the circle of men, scattering them like bowling pins. Twin thirty-caliber machine guns peered over the cab and the gunner fired a burst into the air. Someone shot at the truck. Bullets ricocheted and she winced at the bent notes. The machine guns dipped and spat fire and she heard a sound very much like someone striking a hollow pumpkin with a cricket bat. A knot of men fell upon themselves, their chests savaged, cartilage and viscera gleaming like ripe fruits.

She spat the capsule onto the ground and bent double, hawking the saliva from her mouth. God save her, she hadn't bitten all the way through.

A soldier was standing next to her. For all the world, he looked like one of the Pakistanis who'd been taunting her. The dirt, the beard, the brown skin. She flinched at his touch. Blue eyes, she noticed dreamily, and realized she must be in some kind of shock.

'Help me get him into the truck,' the soldier was saying. 'We've got about thirty seconds before Ethan Allen and the Green Mountain Boys here build up their courage and all hell breaks loose.'

But as far as Sarah was concerned, hell had already

broken loose. A blur of men and women ran in every direction. Every few seconds, the thirty-cals fired for effect. Cordite, dust, manure, and the ever present army of horse-flies swirled together and rose in a dense yellow fog. And still the amplified voice instructing the locals to leave the area, like Dante guiding the damned.

A spooked donkey trotted past, teeth bared and braying, dragging a pullcart stacked high with DVDs and video-cassettes.

Sayeed writhed on the ground, eyes nailed to his ruined limb. He screamed in irregular spurts, a vain and tortured caterwaul that, frankly, pissed her off. 'Where did you send the money?' she asked, kneeling beside him. 'Why are you doing this?'

'My hand,' Sayeed was shouting. 'Where's my hand?'

'Get me a tourniquet,' she ordered the soldier.

On the ground next to him were a packet of TicTacs that she suspected held amphetamines rather than breath mints, a dollar bill, and a cell phone. *Get the phone*, she told herself. As she reached for it, a pair of soldiers frog-marched Bhatia out of his store. 'Can't find the money,' one was saying, apparently to Sarah. 'It's nowhere.'

Sarah looked up. The guards lay dead near the entry, as did the salesman who'd so badly wanted her to buy a chain. 'It doesn't mat—' she began to respond.

It was then that Sayeed moved. Drawing his legs to his chest, he kicked her in the stomach, sending her sprawling into the dirt.

'Hey!' shouted the American soldier, simultaneously shouldering his weapon and lowering it to Sayeed's chest.

'No,' Sarah said weakly. 'We've got to talk to him.'

But it was already too late. Sayeed had found his thresher's knife. In a single whipsaw motion, he buried the blade into the outstretched tendons of his neck and slashed his throat.

'No!' she screamed, as blood fountained from his neck and his head collapsed onto the ground.

Only when they had cleared the bazaar and she was staring at the Karakoram's blue-gray dreamscape far in the distance did she realize she had forgotten the cellular phone. Momentarily, she rose in her seat and thought of ordering the driver back, but she knew it was too late. Even if a second incursion were to be tolerated, the phone was already gone.

Finders keepers.

Chapter 5

'Romeo's back.'

Santini's hushed voice sent a current through Chapel. In an instant he was at the window, binoculars to his eyes. The same well-dressed man they'd observed thirty minutes earlier dawdling in front of Royal Joaillier's sparkling store windows had returned. At first, Chapel was convinced that he'd stroll right past. He walked purposefully, one hand in his trousers, the other smoothing his hair. Just a guy coming back from a coffee break, he'd decided. A stockbroker stoking up his courage to make another hundred cold calls or a sales clerk taking five to iron the wrinkles from his smile.

Then Romeo stopped, and Chapel's heart stopped with him. Directly in front of the entry to Royal Joailliers, Romeo did a little stutter step. For a long second he turned, which left him facing the jump team's third-floor suite. Time stood still.

'Tell me you got the head shot,' said Chapel *sotto voce*.

'I got it,' said Leclerc from his assassin's post at the window.

'I wasn't talking to you.'

'Got it.' Keck froze a close-up of Romeo and transmitted the still image to Langley for identification.

A dozen people had lit up their radar since they'd taken

up their positions. Most had been women stopping to take a snapshot glance at the five-carat diamond rings, time enough for a wish, a glimpse of another life, before the less glittering pressures of the real world called. There'd been an older man with a dog who'd played with entering the store, and a young couple who seemed to be daring each other to take the plunge, but not a one had actually gone inside.

Staring at the screen, Chapel silently urged the man to enter.

An instant later, Romeo threw open the door to Royal Joailliers and disappeared from view.

'He's in,' said Chapel. If he'd expected to feel relieved, he was mistaken. His stomach tightened and his heartbeat kicked up a notch. 'Ray, did you get a look?'

'Went right by me,' said Gomez. 'I'm guessing Lebanese, but he could be from anywhere in the Gulf. He's no gutter rat, either. Wearing an eighteen-carat Rolex Daytona and his fingernails look like they've been spitshined by a Marine.' Gomez was an Aramco orphan, the son of an oil executive who'd grown up in the cloistered compounds that foreign oil companies maintain inside the Kingdom of Saudi Arabia. He was wiry, dark, and scruffy, and he spoke Farsi like a native. 'He's our guy,' confirmed Gomez. 'He's got the eyes, man. Burning a hole in everything around him. Listen, I'm outta here. Romeo gave me the full once-over. I'm charred.'

'All right, then. Come in, but nice and slow.'

'Adam, we've got a FaceIt confirm on your man.' It was Allan Halsey, and his voice was taut. 'Checks out as Mohammed al-Taleel, native of Saudi Arabia, naturalized an American citizen in 1993. Mr Taleel is wanted in connection with a 1996 London car bombing, the Khobar Towers case, and the murder of two Russian nuclear physicists in Damascus in '97. Funny thing though: Our records indicate that he drowned in a ferry accident crossing Lake Victoria in Kenya in 1999.'

'Then it must be his ghost that just walked in that store.'

'He's our man. Take him down.'

Chapel stared at the storefront, at the throngs of tourists crowding the sidewalks. 'Not yet,' he protested. 'Let's see where he takes the dough.'

'No chance,' said Halsey. 'We can't risk his getting away. We're enforcement. We're paid to arrest the bad guys. You've got a major player trapped inside a store two hundred yards away. I said take him down.'

Chapel bridled at the order. He thought of Khobar Towers, where a truck bomb had killed nineteen American servicemen stationed in Saudi Arabia and wounded several hundred others. He didn't want Taleel to escape his just rewards. Add to that the London attack and the slaying of the Russians. Taleel was a nasty piece of work, all right.

'Do we have any word from Glendenning?'

'He's shut down the operation on the other side. Now, do as I say.'

'Did we get him?'

'Adam, do as I—'

'*Did we?*'

'No,' admitted Halsey. 'No prisoners were apprehended.'

Chapel choked back his frustration. It wasn't good enough. Not after busting his hump to get inside the Islamic alternative remittance network. Not after sniffing the shorts of every halfway questionable charity in the United States. 'Disrupt and dismantle' were the task force's watchwords. So far, they'd arrested a dozen moneymen and frozen over a hundred million dollars in questionable assets. It was good work to be sure, but as yet they had no proof they'd impeded the functioning of an active terrorist cell. Finally they had a certified player in their sights, one caught with his hand in the cookie jar, and they wanted to take him down before they could put a finger on his associates or clamp down on his cell.

'Follow the money, Mr Halsey. That's the rule. Stop him now and we got nothing. One more smartass who won't talk.'

'A bird in the hand, Adam. With the proper inducements, I'm sure Mr Taleel will be most cooperative.'

'Arrest him and we've got no idea what he's up to. Intel says he's set to pick up five hundred G's or more. Something's got to be hot to risk that kind of transfer. Let me follow him. We'll tag and mark him. He's ours.'

'You need three cars and five or six guys on the street not to spook him. You telling me you can follow him in a city of six million people? All he has to do is take off his jacket and he's gone. I won't tell Glen Glendenning we've lost a major player.'

'Arrest him now,' said Leclerc, in his gravedigger's voice. 'I promise you I'll find out everything you need to know.'

Chapel glared at him. 'We don't do things that way.'

Leclerc glared back. 'Ah, you will, *mon ami*.'

'What's he doing with the money?' Chapel demanded of Halsey. 'Tell me that and I'll arrest him. It's like nine-eleven. You think if we stopped Atta the day before the attack, he would have told us what was going to happen? You think they would have canceled their plans? He'd have told us to go to hell and we'd have had no choice but to respect his rights, get him a lawyer, and wait until the goddamn towers went down to get after him. I say we wait. I say we see who Taleel's delivering the money to. We can't stop short on this.'

Suddenly the suite was too small. The ornate furnishings pressed in on him like a bad migraine. You could toss a football across the salon, but you couldn't go two feet without bumping into some Louis XV chair, a froufrou sofa, or an antique oak secretary. Every nook had a Chinese vase. Every shelf, an ormolu clock. Every wall, a rustic oil painting. A chandelier hung in the entry and another dangled over the dining-room table. And all of it – the couches, the carpets, the ashtrays, and artwork – was color coordinated in a sea of navy blue and ivory, with just a touch of maroon to remind you that the French still loved their royalty, even if they had led them to the chopping block in a tumbrel cart.

'Mr Chapel?' It was a new voice that he recognized as Owen Glendenning's. 'Are you telling me that you can hang on to Taleel in all that mess?'

'Yes sir, I can.'

'Those are pretty big words for your first time out.'

'I've got some good guys with me.'

'They trust you to run this?'

Chapel looked at Keck, who was listening to every word of their exchange. Keck raised a thumb and nodded his head. 'You da man, Mr C.'

'Yes sir,' replied Chapel. 'I believe they do.'

'All right then. We lost one player today. Don't lose another. Ghosts don't make a habit of turning up in the same place twice.'

'Yes sir.' And then Chapel was doing five things at once. 'Ditch the coat and bring round the van,' he ordered Santos Babtiste. 'And call in a second tail car.

'Get to the service entrance, PDQ,' he commanded Ray Gomez. 'Carmine, circle the other way. Calmly, now. Calmly.'

'Go, Kreskin,' cheered Carmine Santini.

'Keck, put your system on automatic pilot. You'll ride in the second car. Be ready to hit the street at my mark.

'And you,' Chapel said very quietly to Mr Leclerc of the Sûreté, first name unknown, 'Where I come from we like our prisoners alive, so please put away that peashooter and get on your feet.'

But the last word belonged to Keck. Keck with the spiky blond hair and elfin stature. 'Hey, dude,' he said as they filed out of the hotel suite. 'Three words.'

'Yeah, what?'

'Don't fuck up.'

Mohammed Al-Taleel, aka Romeo, emerged through the tinted glass doors of Royal Joailliers fifteen minutes later. In his hand, he carried a scuffed leather briefcase, the tried companion of attorneys and academics around the world. He left the square along the same path as he had entered it, walking with the same brisk gait that Chapel had remarked on earlier. One more man about town in the world's most cosmopolitan city.

'All right, Carmine, move in. Put a smear on Romeo. One chance, my man. Do not mess up. Tag him.'

'Tagging' referred to the act of depositing a trace of tritium on a subject's person. Though invisible to the naked eye, the mildly radioactive substance could be tracked by a sensitive Geiger counter at distances up to five hundred yards.

Santini closed in on Taleel. As he passed, he nudged him ever so slightly, a shoulder glancing against the back, nothing more. Taleel never felt the applicator brush his trousers. *Bingo*, thought Chapel, *you're ours.*

From the Place Vendôme, Taleel walked up the Rue de la Paix, turning left on Rue Daunou and passing Harry's Bar, one of Ernest Hemingway's favorite haunts when he'd lived in Paris in the 1920s. Keck followed at twenty yards, with Leclerc shadowing him ten yards farther back on the opposite side of the street.

By the time they reached the Madeleine, the sidewalks pulsed with a vibrant, swarming humanity. Chapel decided that blue blazers and tan slacks were a kind of French national uniform. From his position in the passenger seat of the postal van, he counted seven men wearing a similar outfit crossing the intersection at the Boulevard des Capucines. A small metallic box similar to a Magellan GPS rested on his lap. The backlit display showed a map of Paris. The blinking red dot above the Madeleine Métro station represented Mohammed al-Taleel.

'He's hitting the Métro,' said Santos Babtiste. '*Merde.*'

'*Ligne douze. Mairie d'Issy,*' said Leclerc, already underground.

'Keck, pull back,' Chapel ordered. 'Leclerc, it's your turn to play shadow.'

'*D'acc,*' replied the Frenchman.

'I'm going in,' said Chapel, flinging the tracking device onto the seat.

Crossing the street, he hit the stairs to the Métro at a run. The underground was crowded and hot. White tiled tunnels led in four directions. It was a labyrinthine steam bath. The sign for Ligne 12 pointed to the right. Not stopping to buy a ticket, he jumped the turnstiles and dashed down the corridor toward the platform. At least he'd picked up one worthwhile skill growing up in Brooklyn. Hustling down another flight of stairs, he rounded a corner to find the platform deserted and the door to the train closing.

'Damn it,' he muttered under his breath, even as he rushed toward the train. As if by a miracle, the doors wheezed open and he slid into the car. At the next doorway, Leclerc retrieved a foot from the entry. Taleel sat ten feet away, paying the briefcase between his legs no concern.

A pro, thought Chapel, as he took a spot towards the rear that positioned Taleel in his line of sight.

Concorde. Assemblée Nationale. Solférino.

The stations passed in turn. Chapel swayed with the train's rhythmic swagger. Don't look at him, he repeated over and over, reciting the lines from his training manual.

Live your cover. *You're a tourist from New York. You know better than to stare.*

As new passengers came and went, the cars grew neither more nor less crowded. More than once, he felt Taleel's eyes sweep over him. When the train pulled into the station at Sèvres-Babylon, Taleel stood and walked to the door. Chapel stood, too, taking up position inches behind the man. He smelled the Saudi's cologne and noticed that he'd recently had a haircut. And yes, Gomez was right: Taleel's fingernails were shined to perfection.

The doors rattled open, and Taleel stepped out and walked down the platform toward the exit. Chapel followed. From the corner of his eye, he saw Leclerc's diminutive form slink past and shuffle up the stairs.

And then Taleel did an odd thing. He stopped. Dead in the center of the platform. A rock in the midst of a fast-flowing stream. The exiting passengers walked past him, and Chapel had no time to react, no choice but to follow them. In a moment, he was ascending the escalator, sure he had blown the assignment, the light of day as punishing as his own tortured conscience.

'He's staying put,' he said to Babtiste. 'He's still on the platform.'

'*Montez.* We have a clear signal.'

The van idled at the corner. Chapel climbed in and a second later, Leclerc followed suit. The three huddled close to one another, all eyes on the beacon. A minute passed. Then another. A tremor shook the van. A new train had pulled into the station beneath them.

'Which way?' Chapel asked, his eyes moving from Babtiste to Leclerc to the illuminated screen. Suddenly, the red spot began moving.

'*Salaud,*' said Leclerc. 'Just waited for the next train in the same direction.'

They drove. The city took on a grittier feel. Gone were the

monuments, the grand boulevards, the chic boutiques and the pricey cafés. This was the old Paris. The Paris of artists and immigrants and the hopeless poor. The streets were narrow and unloved, the buildings painted black with soot and grime. Every once in a while, Chapel caught a glimpse of the Tour Montparnasse, the tallest building in the city, looming before them like a mystical glass tower.

'End of the line,' said Leclerc as they pulled to a halt at a red light. Beside them in a beat-up blue Renault, Keck and Gomez nodded hello. Spurts of men and women exited the Métro as trains came and left. The red dot stopped moving. Taleel's train had arrived. A few people trickled out. At their tail came Taleel. He crossed the street without looking around him. His gait slackened, the briefcase dangling at his side, and Chapel guessed he was on his home turf, relaxing, congratulating himself on a job well done.

'We're close,' he said. 'Let's not spook him. We follow him in, let him get comfortable, count all his dough.'

'If he's going home,' cautioned Babtiste.

It was Leclerc on the street, Santini playing his shadow. Gomez and Keck followed a block up and over, Chapel and Babtiste keeping in the rear. The city changed its clothing once again, the urban grit yielding to leafy roads lined with pleasant apartments. This part of town was called the Cité Universitaire, and true to its name, it housed thousands of students doing their coursework at one of the French capital's many outstanding academic institutions. Taleel turned down a broad avenue. As Babtiste edged to the corner, Chapel had a clear view down the road.

It was a landscape by Renoir. Century-old elms lined the street, the tallest branches providing a verdant canopy through which determined rays of sunlight penetrated, each marvelously accented, defined in shades of orange, yellow, and gold. Halfway down the block, a park began. Rolling grass hills cradled a fountain that shot a plume of water into the sky. Somewhere, a dog was barking, and for a moment, it all seemed to blur together in a collage of beauty and hope and the infinite possibility of a glorious summer's day. Chapel knew that he'd been right to follow Mohammed al-Taleel, that his gamble had paid off, that they would capture Taleel, and maybe his associates as well, and that *they* – meaning the law enforcement communities of the Western nations allied against the new scourge of Islamic terrorism – stood a good chance of learning what Taleel was up to, and stopping it, then and there.

He heard the first shrill notes of the siren, and at first, he didn't understand. He thought it was an ambulance passing a few blocks behind them. Taleel checked over his shoulder, a little nervously. But the acoustics and the Doppler effect were playing tricks on both of them. The source of the siren was in front of them, not behind. The assonant wail grew louder. At the end of the street, a French police car hurtled into view, shrieking to a halt at the next cross street. A second car followed, then a third, doors flying open, uniformed officers forming a phalanx, weapons drawn. Incredibly, Taleel ran towards them.

Chapel opened his door and jumped to the ground, even as he shot Santos Babtiste an uncomprehending glance. 'You bastard,' he said. 'You screwed me.'

'Never,' protested Babtiste. 'I swear it. I told nobody!'

Chapel was running, Santini at his side, Gomez and Babtiste a step behind. Twenty yards ahead, Taleel cut across a strip of grass, the briefcase tucked under an arm, jaw pressed forward in divine concentration. He leaped a hedge, landed, and made toward the front entrance of an apartment building.

The battered Renault flew past, turned hard onto the sidewalk, and slid to a halt inches from the dorm entry.

Keck half fell out of the driver's side, picked himself up, and dashed towards the door in perfect position to cut off Taleel. Steps away, a frightened bystander hurried to escape the scene, his Scotty barking madly.

'Keck,' shouted Chapel. 'Heads up!'

'What?' One hand in his jacket going for his gun, Keck collided with the pedestrian full-force and the two tumbled to the ground, the terrier on Keck in an instant, growling and nipping at his arms.

Taleel hurdled the two men, his foot catching Keck's shoulder. Hitting the ground, he stumbled, his loafers slipping on the sidewalk, losing a second before he regained his balance and charged ahead.

Skirting Keck, Chapel saw his chance. Five feet separated him from Taleel. He wanted the Saudi outside, on the ground, where he could be subdued without the force of arms. With a last terrific stride, he threw himself at the Arab. His outstretched hand found a hip but his fingers closed too early. The hand slipped to the calf, Taleel still running, looking behind him, grunting as he kicked off Chapel's advance, a loafer coming free as Chapel skidded across the sidewalk.

Flinging open the dormitory door, Taleel disappeared into a murky half dusk.

Chapel was there a second later. Pulling open the door, he slowed a beat, checking to see who was behind him. He met a straight-arm that propelled him against the exterior wall. 'Not you, Kreskin,' puffed Carmine Santini. 'This is the real thing. No guessing this time.'

'Fuck, man, you had him,' cursed Gomez, sliding in behind him.

Babtiste and Keck ran inside. A gunshot rang out. Stunned, Chapel drew a breath, needing only a second to decide that Santini was wrong, that he was ready for the real thing, too, whatever that was. He was inside an instant later, taking the stairs two at a time, his eyes trained above him.

'*Arrêtez! Police!*' Babtiste's voice echoed through the stairwell.

The abrasive sound of wood splintering crashed through the hall, then a tremendous thud. The door was down. Chapel crested the stairs and took off down the hallway.

'*Arrêtez! Bougez pas!*'

Christ, they had him, thought Chapel.

'Jesus, man, shoot him! Kill the fucker!' said Ray Gomez.

'*Ne fais pas cela, mec.*' Babtiste's resonant baritone. Don't do it.

Reaching the door, Chapel had a clear view down the abbreviated hallway. Mohammed al-Taleel stood in the center of a neatly kept living room. A desktop PC sat on a laminate table. A window was open and a gentle wind caressed the curtains. On a far table, a television was on, broadcasting a bicycle race, and he thought, *Who keeps the television on when he goes out?* His eyes ticked to the right, taking in a poster of Madonna and the French singer, Jean-Jacques Goldman.

All this he saw in the blink of an eye, before he fixed on the curlicue wire running from the briefcase Taleel held in one hand to the pistol grip he held in the other.

They were all around him. Babtiste, Santini, Gomez, and Keck.

'*Du calme,*' pleaded Santos Babtiste, hands patting the air, teeth bared in an excruciating grin.

Santini turned and saw Chapel. 'Get back, Kreskin. Get the hell out!'

Taleel looked past him and met Chapel's eye. His expression registered nothing. Not fear, not surprise, not anger. He was already dead.

Adam Chapel stepped back.

Then there was light, more light than he had ever seen, or knew could exist, and he was hurtling through the air, the searing wallop of a gargantuan's punch striking him squarely in the chest. He was aware of being upside down, of smashing his head, of a tremendous weight falling upon him.

Then darkness.

Chapter 6

Trails of dust scattered from the Fiat's tires as it sped through the back alleys of Tel Aviv. The driver hunched over the wheel, hands at eleven and one o'clock, not so much steering the car as willing it with his body language. He was fifty-seven but looked ten years older, a hunted, gray figure with close-cropped white hair and beard, and mournful brown eyes that had seen too much for one lifetime. Too much hate. Too much sorrow. Too much death.

The day was hot even by the taxing standards of an Israeli summer. The car possessed no air-conditioning, so he drove with the windows rolled down. The wind rushing in smelled of dried fish and lamb on a spit and billowed his pale blue shirt like a jib in a changing sea. Even so, he was sweating profusely. The perspiration ran down his cheeks and pooled in his beard. He had lived in Israel his entire life. He was used to sweltering summers. It was not the heat that provoked his sweat.

He checked the rearview mirror.

The taxi was still there, maintaining the watcher's distance. 'A hundred meters or a half a city block,' read the manual. The Sayeret were good boys, he thought appreciatively. Nothing if not studious. He was used to being followed. It was procedure; a safeguard for a man in his profession. His eyes fell to the infantryman's rucksack sitting on the floor by the passenger seat. The pack was empty but for one item. It was not procedure today.

He had chosen the back route because he wanted to lull them. He could have reached the old port by any of a dozen quicker routes. He might have stayed on the Dereh Petach Tikva until it fed into Jaffa Road, or driven down to the coast and taken Hayarkon Street past all the tourist hotels – past the Hilton and the Carlton and the Sheraton – Israel's own Croisette. But the familiar anarchy of the old town ensured their pursuit. There would be no traffic jams, no detours, just a slow, methodical game of cat and mouse.

He had forgotten how lamentable the roads had become inside the city. Even when driving carefully, he was unable to avoid all the potholes. The Fiat lurched into a crater and he swore. It was beyond him why a technological and industrial powerhouse like Israel was unable to keep its roads better maintained. Or, for that matter, bury its telephone wires underground next to the miles of fiberoptic cable the telecom companies had insisted everyone needed, and now did beautifully without. He stared too long out the windows, as if taking a last look at the place and making his farewells.

Tel Aviv was a seething, vibrant, violent contradiction. Skyscrapers and shanties, discos and delicatessens, *shwarma* and *slivovitz*, synagogues and mosques. The old and the new shoved into an urban blender, stirred and spilled onto a sun-bleached cityscape with a joyless and seemingly random abandon.

Crossing an intersection, he entered the Shalma Road and began the short climb to the old town. He checked his watch. It was nearly four. He had begun his run three hours and twenty-seven minutes ago. By now, the theft had been confirmed. The border patrol, the airports, the militia had all been put on alert. The prime minister had been informed and a war council convened. It would be put forward that Mordecai Kahn was their man. No one else had the access. No one else the means. Only the motive would baffle them. Kahn was, after all, a patriot, a staunch member of the Likud Party, a decorated veteran of Mitla Pass who had lost a son and a daughter to the country's defense. Finally, they would decide that it made no difference. The order would be given.

Kahn smiled ruefully. It was all a dance. A wonderfully choreographed *pas de deux* whose principals had rehearsed their steps a thousand times.

A left turn conducted him past Clock Tower Square. The elegant spire of Mahmoudiyeh Mosque pierced the sky. Beside him, the sidewalks pulsed with humanity. Old men sat around iron-legged tables playing chess, drinking coffee, dreaming of peace. Jaffa counted as one of the oldest functioning ports in the world, and in its time, had been ruled by Greeks, Romans, Turks, Christians, and Arabs. Today, it was the Jews' turn.

Peter had raised Tabitha from the dead here and gone to live with Simon the Tanner. Richard the Lionheart had raised the Crusaders' banner fifty yards out to sea on Andromeda Rock. But Kahn found the city's modern history more compelling. Throughout the first half of the last century, Jaffa's docks had welcomed the worn and sturdy multitude that had sworn to remake the Holy Land in its own image. As a boy in 1946, he himself had trodden the wooden piers, a refugee from Hitler's malice.

Today, he would make use of the pier again. He had come to the country by sea, and by sea he would leave it.

Reaching a stop sign, he put the car into first gear and glanced out his window. Nearby, two men, an Arab and a Jew, turned their faces to the sky. One shielded his eyes, while the other shook his head and looked away.

Kahn knew the helicopter was shadowing him. He had

caught the rotor wash twice already. The bird was an Apache, and flying low today. When the order came to fire its Hellfire missiles, the pilots did not want to miss. A military radio tuned to their frequency was jammed into the glove box. Kahn believed in precautions.

The radio squawked as the men from Central Command issued their impotent instructions.

'Now,' a voice crackled amid a haze of white noise.

Kahn sat straighter, seized by doubt. Years had passed since he'd donned a soldier's uniform. He had certainly never been trained for something like this. He had no business embarking on such a dangerous and doubtful enterprise.

You are a human being, a voice scolded him. *And a Jew. You have every right.*

Two blocks ahead, two cars entered the intersection from opposite sides and collided with one another. Glass shattered. Metal twisted. The drivers flew out of the cars, arms waving, hands gesticulating angrily. Kahn narrowed his eyes. The performance had begun. They hoped to catch him quietly, with a minimum of fuss and as little notice as possible. They would not wish to explain why their policy of targeted assassination had been turned on one of their own, or what drastic circumstances had demanded it be carried out in one of the more historically sensitive areas of the city.

He would give them no choice.

The taxi was closing behind him.

It was time.

Kahn wrenched the steering wheel to the right and punched the accelerator. The ancient Fiat hurtled the curb, the back wheels spinning free for a moment, before catching the dusty asphalt and screeching in submission. He only had a block to go. Images passed in a blur. A boy on a bicycle. Workmen digging a ditch. A vendor hawking oranges from a wooden bucket.

The voices on the radio barked like rabid dogs. *Do you have him in sight? Close the distance. Requesting order to fire. Negative. Hold. We can take him on the ground. Unit Two move in. Unit Four take Al-Ashram Road south two blocks.* Confusion. Panic. Then a change of tack. *Arm missiles. Lock on to target.*

The helicopter hovered behind him. In the rearview mirror, he spotted a sniper seated in the open bay, legs dangling into oblivion, his rifle raised, its stock pressed to his cheek.

Faster. He must drive faster.

He skirted Jaffa's main square, the site of an ongoing archaeological dig. The ruins descended three levels, showcasing successive Hellenic, Roman, and Moorish buildings dating from the third century B.C. In 231 B.C. the Greek king, Pompus, had housed his soldiers here. Wary of an attack by land, he had tunneled three hundred feet through the limestone cliffs to the harbor below to guard his retreat.

A tour bus was parked across the street. Students dressed in clean blue and white uniforms paraded to the ruins. He sped past them, pulling into the opposing lane of traffic. At the corner, he braked hard and pulled the wheel to the left. The car skidded and came to a halt. A curio vendor's canopy shaded the driver's side and the hood. The helicopter was no longer in view.

Kahn grabbed the rucksack. 'Fire,' he spat at the radio. 'Give the order, now!'

They were too scared. Too confident of his ineptness. He cursed their indecision.

Picking up his officer's revolver, he shoved the snout out his window and fired a volley of shots into the air. The curio vendor scuttled into his shop. Across the street, the students scattered. He thanked God for the well-practiced survival of his people.

'Fire, missile three,' said a voice on the radio.

A scarlet sizzle burnt the air as a Hellfire missile dropped from its carriage and sped towards Mordecai Kahn's car. The missile penetrated the rear window and exploded on impact with the dashboard. The force of the detonation lifted the car ten feet in the air and engulfed it in a billowing fireball whose core temperature exceeded three thousand degrees Fahrenheit.

The watchers surrounded the car a moment later. Several tried to approach the inferno. They wanted to confirm their kill. But the fire burned too hot, and they kept their distance.

Sailing a fisherman's skiff across the diamond-kissed waters of the eastern Mediterranean, Mordecai Kahn watched the plume of smoke snake into the bleached sky. He prayed the missile had not damaged the excavation site. Archaeology was his first love. Before he discovered numbers. Before the numbers turned on him and made him their captive. A stiff wind filled the mainsail and the boat picked up speed. He looked at his feet, where the rucksack lay on weathered wooden slats. He unzipped a pouch and took out a bottle of water, a bag of gummy bears, and a long-billed cap. Popping a few of the gelatin candies into his mouth, he turned his eyes to the sea.

He had bought himself three hours and not a minute longer. To a man who lived by the most precise calculations, it was more than enough time.

Chapter 7

In a leafy Paris suburb, a warm wind gusted through the burned-out remains of Mohammed al-Taleel's apartment, sending a curtain of fine dust dancing through the air. Lifting himself off a knee, Sergeant René Montbusson of the French Sûreté's evidence recovery unit turned his nose into the breeze and breathed deeply. He was happy for the relief. Eight hours after the explosion, the crime scene still smelled of seared flesh and scattered viscera, and it sickened him. As he looked around what had been the living room, it seemed that every square inch was coated with the victims' remains. Medical technicians had removed the larger body parts, but scraps of flesh and muscle, and Montbusson didn't know what, hid beneath every concrete fragment and hung from the walls like tattered pennants.

The blood – it was everywhere.

Montbusson sighed. Twenty years on the force and he still wasn't accustomed to the sights, the smells, the textures of death. Frankly, he hoped he never would be. At mass each Sunday, he thanked God for the love of his wife and his two daughters, asked forgiveness for his sins, and prayed for the strength to make it through another week on the job. Tonight, however, the work was particularly grim, and he knew that if he stayed at it much longer, he risked losing his humanity.

Five men blown up in such a small, contained space. There were no words to describe it. He kept asking himself the same question: Where was God in this place? Though he thought himself a pious man, Rene Montbusson could find no response.

A flutter of white at his feet caught his attention. A piece of paper, hardly larger than a few postage stamps. Kneeling, he took a pair of tweezers from his pants and bent towards it. The tweezers dropped to the ground and he saw that his gloves were too smeared with blood to hold them. After changing the translucent, polyurethane gloves, he managed to pick up the paper. One side was white, the other, at first glance, multicolored. The edges were charred, but otherwise it was in good shape.

The same couldn't be said for the apartment. The charge had destroyed every piece of furniture in the living room, blown out the windows and curtains, and blasted a hole in the floor as well as through the drywall separating the living room and bedroom. The first persons allowed on the scene, besides medical technicians, were the structural engineers. An examination of the building proved it to be sound. As a precaution, the engineers installed eight floor-to-ceiling braces in the apartment.

The ordnance experts had come and gone hours ago. A swab of the walls subjected to a handheld ion mobility spectrometer confirmed the presence of RDX and PETN, the two principal ingredients of plastic explosives. The vapor detection device also found the presence of ethylene glycol dinitrate, a chemical marker that identified the explosive as being 'Semtex,' a product of the Czech Republic. The ordnance team estimated Taleel had used about a half-kilo of the professionally manufactured, and all too easily available, plastique to blow himself to kingdom come.

Standing, Montbusson raised the paper so that the light from one of four industrial-size paint-drying lamps brought in to illuminate the crime scene caught it squarely on its face. It was a map – that much he could tell right away. He could see the horizontal lines that denoted streets, a comma of green that indicated a park, and a ribbon of red and white that probably meant a section of freeway. He had more of a problem making out the letters. Dropping a hand into his jacket pocket, the forty-five-year-old crime scene investigator fished out his bifocals and balanced them on his nose. ' – nt St. De'. Here the paper ended. A narrow expanse of blue curled across the bottom left-hand corner of the paper. Running through its center were larger, well-spaced, letters – 'm a.'

Carefully, Montbusson retraced his steps to his collection tray and laid the paper in a plastic folder, pasting a number onto it, and cataloguing the piece in his notebook as 'Remnant: city map. America???' On a hand-drawn site map of the apartment, he placed a dot where he had found it, along with its corresponding evidence number.

A check of his watch showed the time to be eleven o'clock. Montbusson sat down. He felt tired, older than his years. Through the window – or rather the gaping maw where the window used to be – he viewed a chain of headlights negotiating the roadblocks and moving rapidly up the street. Strobes atop the cars spun blue and white. Mercifully, the sirens were silent. No doubt it was the American FBI's own bomb blast specialists come to the rescue. He'd been told to expect them at any moment and to show them the utmost courtesy.

Montbusson stood, brushing the dust from his jacket. To think that the Americans called the French arrogant. The FBI acted as if they were the only competent law enforcement organization in the world. Fired by a sudden, passionate desire to do his job as well as he knew how – call it what you will, pride, patriotism, or a healthy sense of competition – he set about sifting through the rubble landscape with a demon's eye. He had found little of interest. There were no clothes in the closets, no papers in the desks, no food in the refrigerator. Either the terrorist was planning on leaving soon or he used the apartment as a safe house. The only items of any intelligence value Montbusson had salvaged were a computer whose CPU looked like it had been run over by a Mack truck, a cellular phone crunched to the width of a stick of gum, and a few fragments from a handwritten notebook.

Step by step, he walked through the apartment, carefully lifting bent and mangled pieces of furniture, moving slabs of debris. Outside, a bevy of doors opened and closed. A chorus of loud, optimistic American voices rose towards him. He supposed he'd better go and greet his counterpart. Determinedly, he fixed a welcoming expression to his face, smoothed his mustache, and pulled his shoulders back. The Americans always stood so damned straight.

That was when he glimpsed it. A triangle of silver winking at him from the floor below. Curious, he advanced towards the 'seat' of the blast, the exact spot where the terrorist Taleel had been standing when he had detonated the bomb, and looked through the hole into the apartment below. Only a cursory examination had been made of it, and a blanket of white dust coated the furniture. Squinting, he saw the swatch of metal again. It looked like an old transistor radio wedged into the wall. Hurrying from the room, he descended a flight of stairs and entered the lower apartment. Crossing to the sofa, he jumped onto the cushions and lifted himself on his tiptoes. It was a video camera. A very small Sony digital number. The viewfinder was missing, the lens was cracked, and the severe heat of the explosion had warped the casing so that it bent like a banana.

'Jean Paul!' Placing his fingers in his mouth, he whistled for his assistant to join him. In a matter of minutes, the two men had pried the camera from the wall without causing the device any further damage. Montbusson turned the camera around in his hands, seeking the on switch. A toggle controlled the apparatus's actions. Switching it to VCR, he was surprised to hear the camera power up. He put an eye to the ruined viewfinder and pressed 'play.' Immediately, a mélange of colors played across the screen, and though he was unable to make anything of it, he was thrilled nonetheless.

Cradling the camera, he left the apartment, only to walk squarely into the broad chest of Frank Neff, the FBI's legal attaché to the American Embassy.

'Hello, René. Did you find anything?' Neff asked.

Montbusson displayed the camera. 'It still functions. There is a film inside.'

Neff glanced dismissively at the camera. 'That's fine and dandy,' he said. 'But what about the money? The five hundred grand?'

Rene Montbusson looked from Neff to the cluster of pale, expectant faces behind him. He had a terrible sensation that everyone knew something except him. Something very, very important.

'What money?' he asked.

Chapter 8

A faint blue light glowed in the office of General Guy Gadbois, chief of the General Directorate for External Security. Gadbois, a barrel-chested paratrooper, forty-year veteran of Algeria, the Congo, and too many brushfires to mention, lit another cigarette and stared at the blizzard of gray and white snow swirling on the television screen a few feet away. Though the tape had finished fifteen seconds before, he couldn't shake his eyes from it.

'Again,' he said dully, rubbing the bridge of his nose with his thumb and forefinger.

'*Oui, mon général.*'

Gadbois sighed as his assistant rewound the digital tape. Though it was two A.M. and well past normal working hours, three other officers of the French intelligence service were also present. Two of the men came from the Arab Department, known inside the service as the 'Midi Club,' as it handled information concerning Spain, Morocco, and the erstwhile French colonies of Algeria and Tunisia, as well as the Middle East. They were here to translate and to offer opinions that Gadbois knew in advance he would disagree with.

The third man came from the operations directorate, or the DST, the crazy bastards who had bombed the

Rainbow Warrior, Greenpeace's protest ship, in Auckland Harbor fifteen years back. It was he who had lifted the digital film from the evidence locker at the Sûreté's headquarters. He was short and thin, and looked like he weighed less than a fully loaded pack. But he was tough, thought Gadbois, for whom 'tough' was the highest accolade. Anyone who was still on his feet after such a blast, let alone operating with his faculties intact – well, he must have a head like pig iron. If only he'd cut his hair like any self-respecting soldier.

Without preface, the dark screen came to life. Fragments of binary data flashed on the screen in colorful erratic patches. Fifteen seconds passed before the first clear image appeared.

'Stop!' Gadbois pounded his meaty fist on the table.

The image froze. A male figure clad in the Palestinian freedom fighter's de rigueur getup of olive drab combat jacket and red-checkered *khaffiyeh*, or headdress, stood in front of a generic Islamic flag – crescent moon and star against a field of forest green. What wasn't de rigueur, however, thought Gadbois, was the pair of mirror sunglasses.

'Print a picture,' said Gadbois. The digital VCR player whirred and a moment later, he had a snapshot of the freedom fighter. 'Go on.'

The image remained clear. The man began to speak.

'Americans, Zionists, and your sycophantic allies, I address you in the name of Muhammad, peace be unto him, and in the name of everlasting peace between all peoples. Today our battle has reached your shores . . .'

The picture sputtered, dissolving into a chaotic digital patchwork, before regaining clarity. Gadbois watched for another three minutes, jotting down the words he was able to pick up, stopping twice more to ask his assistant to print a photograph. Finally, the picture crapped out altogether. Gadbois grunted again. 'Anything else on the tape?'

'No sir.'

'Well?' he asked. 'What the hell is it? A martyrdom message?'

'Certainly not,' declared Berri, one of the Arabists. 'At no time did he offer himself to the "Lord, Allah," as is customary. At least not that we saw. It is simply a claim of responsibility.'

Gadbois agreed. This was something different than the trash that had been coming out of the Middle East the past few years. He was reminded of the time in the mid-seventies when every week had seemed to bring similar messages from the Red Army Faction, the Baader-Meinhof gang, and Black September. *But this* – Gadbois grimaced, as his stomach rumbled, souring with acid reflux. This looked like it might be on a larger scale than a kidnapping or a car bomb. He looked at the man from the DST. 'And so?'

'They are planning an attack,' said Leclerc, sitting forward to meet Gadbois's pouchy stare. 'That much is apparent. We have some idea where and we may assume it will be soon. They do not make these tapes until shortly before the attempt is carried out. That is all, except for one small thing.'

'*S'il vous plait, Capitaine.*'

'They are quite certain that they will succeed.'

General Gadbois stood, signaling the meeting was over. For the moment, he didn't need to know anything more. When the room was empty, he picked up the telephone. 'Get me Langley,' he ordered.

Waiting, he lit a cigarette and exhaled a thick stream of blue-gray smoke towards the ceiling. A familiar voice answered, and Gadbois said, 'Hello, Glen. I have some news that might require disturbing the President.' He wanted his colleague's full and undivided attention.

Yet even as he related the contents of the tape he had just watched, a most uncharitable and unprofessional thought crossed his mind: Thank God, it wasn't going to happen in France.

Chapter 9

'*Get up!*'

In the intensive care ward of the Hôpital Salpetitpierre, Adam Chapel shuddered, his body lifting from the bed as if juiced with ten thousand volts. The voice echoed across the recesses of his memory, dragging him from the darkness like a prisoner to the executioner's block. Chapel ordered his limbs to move, his head to rise from the pillow, but the drugs that numbed his body had left him as frozen as his fear had twenty years earlier. Consumed with dread, he lay still, hearing his father's voice, recoiling at the cruel, mocking melody of his childhood.

'Get up!'

The voice was not directed at him, yet Chapel flinched all the same. In the swirling crucible that was his mind's eye, he saw himself, a pale, chubby ten-year-old boy with tousled black hair, sitting at his desk in his cramped bedroom. He can smell the meat loaf his mother is making for dinner and knows that there will be pears and Hershey's chocolate syrup for dessert because pears were on special at Mr Park's grocery store.

The door to his room is closed and he looks at himself in the full-length mirror hanging on its back. *Get up*, he tells himself. *Go help her*. Several times he begins to stand, only to fall back to his chair. He wants to go to her, but he can't.

He's too scared. Only the shame weighing on his shoulders, the shame that shrinks him to a tenth his size, is worse than the fear.

'Stay down,' he whispers to her. 'Stay down and he'll leave you alone.'

But his mother is a stubborn woman. Through the paper-thin walls, he hears a chair scrape the linoleum floor as Helen Chapel claws her way to her feet.

'About time,' bellows his father. 'Aren't you going to make your son some dinner?'

'Robert, please . . . Adam'll hear . . .'

'Let him hear. I don't want him to think his father allows a woman to speak to him that way.'

'I'm your wife. If your commissions drop, I have every right to ask why. If you're having trouble with the new line, let's talk about it. Maybe I can help.'

'Help? Business is lousy. There, I told you again. People are buying loafers and we're selling lace-ups. You want Adam to hear that, too? Do you want him to know that his father can't hustle enough shoes to pay off his wife's charge at Alexander's? Let him hear. The boy's a freakin' genius. You think he doesn't know what's what? He's going to earn big money someday. Important he knows enough not to get stuck with some nag who never stops whining. Who else is going to teach him?'

Hurriedly, Adam turns the page of his algebra text and throws himself into his homework. Numbers are his refuge. Among the figures and equations and theorems, he can lose himself like a shadow in the night. Cheek pressed to paper, he asks himself question after question as the solutions spill from the tip of his Ticonderoga No. 2 pencil − 4 (X − 2) = 8. Answer: 4. 3X + 8X = ? Answer: 11X.

'Let go of me, you bastard. Let go!'

Let her go! Adam closes his eyes so tightly, his cheeks ache. Angrily, he wipes away the tears as he recites the quadratic equation, the Fibonacci sequence to a thousand, pi to the twenty-second digit, which is as far as he's memorized it so far, but he promises to go higher, to thirty, even fifty. Anything to block the images of his father grasping his mother's long, graying hair, lifting her off the floor to give her a few pointers about 'the world out there' as he knows it. Adam has listened to the drunken soliloquy so many times, he has the words memorized. 'American-made products don't sell anymore. The Pakis are undercutting us by a dollar a pair. They're dumping the stuff to get share; selling at below cost. It's illegal, but no one gives a shit. It's all about price, Helen. You have to fight for every cent. Scrap for every dollar.' And then the wider lessons about life. 'The only thing that means anything is money. Hear me, Helen? Money buys you respect. Money buys you position. Money buys you a better class of friends. You don't have money in this world, you don't have a life. Sooner Adam learns that, the better.'

Afterwards, his mother comes to him as she always does.

'Your father isn't a bad man. Do you understand?' his mother asks as she dabs away the perfect red pearl resting in the corner of her lips.

'Yes, ma'am.'

'He's frustrated, that's all. Things aren't going as well as he'd like.'

'Mom, he knocks you around like he's Jimmy Connors and you're a tennis ball. Look at your mouth. Let's get out of here.'

His mother grabs his shoulder and gives him a shake, as if he were a television on the fritz. 'Don't talk about your father that way.' Cowardice has made him his father's accomplice. Any slight against his dad is taken as a slight against himself. 'We have your education to think about. Bishop Manulis is a fine school. You're such a good student.

We can't jeopardize that. It's your career that matters now. Your father's right. With your intelligence, you can make a lot of money.'

'Come on, Mom. You can get work somewhere. You've got a degree. You're a CPA.'

'What's important is *you*. You're our star. You're going to take the world by storm. Earn yourself a million dollars by the time you're thirty. I know it. Now, come on, let's get cleaned up. After dinner, we'll walk down to the ice cream store.'

'With Dad?'

'Of course. Your father adores his mocha nut.' She squeezes him to her and meets his eye, demanding his cooperation. 'Did you know that they serve ice cream every night in those fancy dining clubs at Harvard?'

The lights dim. Adam drifts to the sounds of Atlantic Avenue on a summer night. A boom box plays Michael Jackson singing, 'Billie Jean is not my lover . . .' Kids shout and screech, playing stickball in the street. A siren whoops in the distance. From the living room, J.R. accuses Sue Ellen of conspiring with Cliff to steal Ewing Oil from beneath him.

'What do you want to do with yourself, son?' his father asks him. 'You know, when you get out of school.'

'I'm thinking of joining the police force.'

'A policeman? What? Are you kidding?'

It is an idea that Chapel has nurtured for a year. 'Yeah. A detective. I want to help people.'

A smile to console the misguided. 'You know what a cop earns? Twenty-five thousand dollars a year. How're you going to support your family on that? How do you plan on buying your boy a Rawlings Reggie Jackson mitt? Or a Walkman? A Polo shirt . . . all that Ralph Lauren stuff your mother's always picking up for you?'

'I'll make do. Besides, I'm not planning on getting

married. Police work's interesting. You're doing a service to the community. Solving crimes, murders, and stuff. I'd be good at that.'

'Nah. It's a crummy idea. No cash. They're always on the take. Looking for a little extra on the side. Bunch of crooks, really.'

'But, Dad—'

'Ever seen a cop's shoes, Adam? Florsheim's at best. Cheap brogues with rubber soles and Dr Scholl's inlays to kill the athlete's foot. That isn't the way to go. Not for you. You're too smart. You're going to wear Lobbs. John Lobb of Jermyn Street, London, England. Nothing finer on the planet. Custom fitted. The best leather. Topstitching on the vamp and sole. Soft as a baby's bottom. Fit you like a glove. Make you look like a million bucks.'

'But, Dad, policemen need practical shoes because they're running all the time. Lobbs are great, but you'd ruin them in a second. Policeman need—'

'No buts!' his father shouts, saliva speckling his face, the breath thick with Marlboros and Maalox. 'You – you're going into business. Hear me? And I don't mean to pull down a commission check like me. Unh-unh. I'm thinking Wall Street. A young man with your brains – you're going right to the top. You'll be pulling down a mil a year easy in no time. Right up there with Felix Rohatyn.'

'It's not just about money. There's other things in—'

The cuff comes from out of nowhere, a glancing blow that takes him on the ear.

'What do you know about money? Nothing. Not a godamned thing. Listen to me. Money is the only thing that matters. Money comes first. Wife, family, friends – all of that comes afterwards. Get your priorities straight. No kid of mine is going to be a policeman. Got that?'

'Yes sir.'

'Good boy. Now what do you wanna be?'

'A businessman.' Adam corrects himself immediately. 'I mean a banker.'

'What kind of banker?'

'An investment banker.'

'That's right, kid. You're aces all the way.' Tenderly, Robert Chapel touches the red spot where he struck his son. 'Better lose some weight, too. You don't see too many fatsos in the executive suite. No wonder your friends are always making fun of you.' He taps his boy on the cheek. 'Who knows? Might help you get a date.'

His father's image fades. The noises die off.

A new image forms itself in Adam's mind . . . a single gunshot punctures the darkness.

Adam sees the body sprawled in the easy chair, the legs splayed, but the Lobb brogues are sparkling, and over the whiff of cordite and blood, he can smell his father's Kiwi polish.

It is the day Adam Chapel made partner at Price Waterhouse.

The memories faded.

The past disappeared.

Hating himself for having met his father's exacting standards, Chapel allowed himself to drift towards a healing light.

There was only now and he was floating.

'Monsieur Chapel, wake up, please. Wake up. We must check your vital signs.' A hand tapped his cheek. 'How are you feeling?'

Adam opened his eyes and saw that the doctor was a woman. 'All right, I guess,' he said, starting to sit up.

'No, no. Better to stay still for a while. My name is Dr Bac. I took care of you when you arrived yesterday afternoon. Your ribs, they are bruised. If they were broken, you would feel something, even with the drugs we give you.'

Forcing the world into focus, he saw that she was pretty in an academic kind of way. Not a trace of makeup. Frameless glasses. Pale skin, and if hospital doctors were treated anything like they were in America, overworked. She wore a purple blouse, blue jeans, and white clogs. Were it not for the stethoscope around her neck, he would have taken her for a political activist, not his attending physician.

Bending slightly, she pressed a button that commanded the head of the bed to rise. Adam held his breath, waiting for the pain to arrive, but mercifully, he felt only a general soreness, as if he'd worked out particularly hard the day before.

'If you don't mind . . .' Dr Bac opened his gown and placed the stethoscope on his chest. 'Good,' she murmured. A hand gently took his wrist. 'Your pulse is forty-four. You are an athlete?'

'I run a little bit. Swim. Bike. You know.'

'You do the triathlon? We have one in Nice a week ago.'

'I used to do it for fun. I don't have so much time anymore. Why? You a runner, too?'

Dr Bac gave him a brittle smile. 'I run from patient to patient. You'd be surprised at how fit it will keep you.'

Chapel wanted to laugh, but he could see something dark shifting behind the lady's eyes.

'How is your hearing?' she asked. 'Some bells? Some ringing, perhaps?'

'A siren's more like it.'

'Your eardrum on this side. It is ruptured. You are lucky to hear anything at all. Your shoulder has been badly burned. Mostly second-degree, but a small patch that is very bad.'

He had come to briefly as he was being wheeled into the emergency room. Lifting his head, he'd noted with a punch drunk's surprise that the bomb had blown his clothing more or less completely off his body. One leg of his blue jeans was gone. The other was in tatters, as if someone had taken a knife and cut it into fine horizontal strips. His shirt was missing, except for a cuff on his right hand. The same hand had immediately ventured south, making sure he was intact. It was only then that he'd glimpsed the red, blistered pulp that was his shoulder. A moment later, a doctor – maybe it was even Dr Bac – had stuck a two-inch needle into him and he'd been out ever since. A clock on the wall read 9:15. Eighteen hours, more or less.

'Excuse me,' said Chapel, grasping her forearm.

'Yes?'

'What about the others? Keck, Gomez, Monsieur Babtiste? You know, the men I was with. Who else is being treated in this hospital?'

Dr Bac drew up a rolling stool alongside the bed and sat down. 'Mr Chapel, you were in an enclosed space with a man who detonated a pound of plastic explosives on his person. You are a policeman, *non*? Surely, you know what this material can do. When you place four walls around such a blast, it is like multiplying the force by ten.'

'What about Carmine Santini? Big guy . . . going bald . . . could lose ten pounds around the middle?' When she didn't answer, he said, 'Is Keck okay? Skinny, blond, looks like he's about twelve.'

'I'm sorry.'

'One of them's got to have made it out. Please.'

'Unfortunately . . .' The words trailed off as Dr Bac formed a smile of infinite sadness.

'No,' said Chapel. 'It can't be. They can't . . . God, no. One of them at least. I can't be the only one.'

'The only reason you are alive is that another man shielded you from the blast.'

'Who was it? Which one of them saved me?'

'I have no idea. They tell me you were pulled from beneath a body. Actually, I'm not supposed to discuss these things with you, but I see you are –' She hesitated, her intelligent eyes crinkling as if looking at something odd or mysterious. 'You are *different*.' She stood suddenly, fixing a strand of hair behind her ear, shoving her stethoscope back in her pocket. 'There are some men waiting for you outside. They are from the FBI. They showed me their badges. Very impressive. I told them you are weak, that you should remain in my care another two days, minimum, and then that you should rest another seven days at home. They would prefer to take you with them. I leave the choice to you.'

'No one made it out?' Chapel searched her eyes for a new answer. A better answer.

Dr Bac shook her head slowly. 'Come see me tomorrow. Ten A.M. sharp. I have to change your dressing. I will tell the men to come back in an hour. I think you need the time.'

'No. I'm all right. Send them in.'

'You are sure?'

Chapel nodded, and her expression darkened. Looking away, she shook her head as if to say, 'Of course, he's sure.' She was disappointed. She had been wrong about him.

Chapter 10

It was early morning, and as Sarah Churchill strolled the grassy strip overlooking the Bay of Bengal, she marveled at the sapphire sky, the emerald sea, and the hordes of tiny fishing craft bobbing like pearls as they made their way into port after a night's work. It was beautiful. All of it. She smiled crazily – giggled, even. It was a natural reaction – a rebound high from yesterday's events in the Smugglers' Bazaar. She couldn't have controlled it if she'd wanted to.

Leaving the Hotel Midway House in the grounds of the Karachi International Airport, she'd decided it was to be a day of superlatives. Never had she walked beneath so blue a sky, on so beautiful a day in so beautiful a city. If the tuk-tuks screaming past showered her with a foul spray of dust and exhaust, she chose not to see or hear them. In her world, it was Mozart playing 'Eine Kleine Nachtmusik,' and Monet doing the landscapes. For a few hours, she wanted nothing more to do with the CIA, the Secret Intelligence Service, or their battle to root out the seemingly inexhaustible scourge of terrorism.

Her first debrief had ended at midnight. Step-by-step she'd dissected the past three days, reviewing each leg for ways to improve her skills, to blend in more seamlessly, to penetrate the psychological guise of her target. The only question left unanswered was the one everyone was afraid to ask: Why hadn't she surmised that Sayeed would take his own life rather than be captured? Still, they'd tracked the money to Paris, and that was her primary goal. If her masters' smiles weren't all they should be, it wasn't her fault. What happened in France didn't concern her. Sad? Yes. A tragedy? Absolutely. But it was Treasury's op, and if their failure rankled her, she was to keep it to herself. Sarah's side of things was graded a success. An A-plus. If a few innocents got shredded in the process, the collateral damage was within acceptable limits. She was being put up for a meritorious conduct medal and could expect a warm reception when she made it back to England – which wouldn't be too soon. The Agency had adopted Sarah as one of its own, and wanted her back in the field within a month.

Pending her return to Washington (and the more extensive debriefing that would follow once she arrived at Langley), she'd been posted off duty. She had a day and most of the night in front of her to walk the city, see the sights, and keep her nose out of trouble.

Sarah turned in a semi circle, exchanging the blue of the ocean for the sun-bleached limestone of the city. The *burqa* was long gone. They could burn the damned things as far as she was concerned. In its place she settled for a pair of old 501s, a faded pink Polo button-down, and some Tod moccasins as soft as butter. A pair of Ray-Ban aviators had replaced her decidedly unfashionable commo gear. If her hair needed a trim, a shampoo, blow-dry, and some Sebastien mousse had done nicely in the meantime. In the war of cultures, America could claim her as another victim, and for the moment, that's exactly how she wanted it. She was a lone tourist doing one last tramp around Karachi before catching her flight home. If she got up the guts, she'd even try the local McDonald's.

Once, Karachi had served as Pakistan's capital, but to Sarah's eye it still belonged to the Raj. Monuments to Britain's rule beckoned at every corner. The broad, grass-lined boulevards, the Victorian architecture of the High Court and the Legislature, the local population's precise, polite English. Forty years ago, the capital had moved inland to Islamabad, to a spot deemed more central to administering the country's far-flung frontiers. The army had insisted on the move. It preferred the country's elected officials to be closer to Central Military Command, where rational minds might make themselves heard. Three coups later, a general once again ruled the land.

From the port, she ventured into the heart of the city. Turning down Club Road, she found herself looking at a tall, modern hotel, painted the brightest of whites. A large 'S' adorned one wall, and she recognized it as the Sheraton Hotel where in May 2002, a car bomb had killed fifteen French engineers shipped in to help Pakistan's submarine development efforts. Quickly, she turned the other way and headed back towards the diplomatic quarter.

Walking had always been her therapy. She'd grown up in the country on a family estate that grew smaller with each passing generation. Somewhere back in Wellington's time, a cavalry general on her father's side had been awarded a nice chunk of Shropshire farmland in exchange for doing some rather gallant and (she'd later learned at Cambridge) beastly things to Napoleon's army at Waterloo. By the time Sarah was born, The Meadows, as home was called, was down to forty acres and had taken to boarding horses for urban equestriennes, whom her father described as women who liked to ride without getting any shit on their boots.

But Sarah had always preferred lone treks across the

rolling countryside to the care, saddling, and endless grooming that went with riding. Slipping out of bed at dawn, she'd pull on her Wellingtons and rain slicker and disappear for hours on solitary reconnaissances of the surrounding meadows, trudging through marshes, dashing up hillocks, and navigating her way through dense woods, thick with thistle and pine. Returning at dusk, she'd sit at the table, quietly sipping her tea, resisting her mother's and brothers' entreaties about where she had been. 'Out,' she would say with a secret smile, and savor their ignorance.

But when Daddy, home for one of his all-too-brief leaves, inquired, she would share her adventure with him from the first footstep beyond The Meadows' immaculate white fences, and leaven her tales with nuggets of scurrilous information about their neighbors. She was first to know that Ben Bitmead was growing pot plants in the middle of his father's corn plot. (The police found out a year later, though not from her, and Ben spent six months 'on vacation,' as her Daddy told her.) She caught Ollie Robson siphoning the petrol out of Mrs McMurtry's pickup on two occasions, and this time, she'd called Mary McMurtry to tell her, or at least her father had. On the matter of Mrs Milligan, and why her Mini-Cooper was parked behind Father Gill's parsonage at six in the morning three days running, her father had pledged her to secrecy. Every human being needs a little love in their life, he'd said. Leave it at that, kitten. And tousling her hair with his broad, callused palm, he'd hauled her up on his shoulders and carried her to the kitchen singing, 'Too-ra-loo-ra-loo,' the Royal Marines' anthem.

Even then, Sarah had been a clandestine agent with a divided loyalty.

She'd also learned that silence often led to tragedy, and that the hardest job was not collecting intelligence, but in knowing who to tell it to, and analyzing it afterwards for meaning.

She was thinking of Mr Fenwick, the village grocer. Day after day, she'd spied him in his bedroom measuring the distance from his dresser to a rocking chair she recognized as Mrs Fenwick's, who'd passed away only a month before. He'd walk from the dresser to the chair, sit down, have a long stare straight ahead, then get up and set out the distance with a yardstick. Then one day, there was an ambulance parked in his drive, and Sarah found out that he'd laid a shotgun across the dresser, tied a string to the trigger, and taking a seat in his wife's favorite rocker and making things right with the Lord, he'd blown himself to kingdom come.

It was hardly a surprise when Sarah joined MI6, fresh out of Cambridge with her first in Oriental languages and a rowing blue. She had the brains and the brawn they were looking for, and God knew, the ambition to top her brothers, two of whom were military men, in the battle for her father's accolades.

Already six years, she thought, stopping at a corner for a red light, and Daddy gone four of them. A melancholy breeze swept over her, and she found herself whistling 'Too-ra-loo-ra-loo,' and wanting more than anything else to share this latest and most dire adventure with him. Not exactly Goose Green, but she'd cut it close just the same. She'd been blooded. 'Not bad, kitten,' he'd say succinctly, but his hidden smile would give her all the satisfaction a devoted daughter could ever want.

The day had grown hot and muggy. In the space of ten city blocks, the blue sky curdled to gray. Mozart had taken five, and the only music playing in her head was the choppy, unmelodious rhythm of her own humming as she trod to keep her head above water. The giddiness was gone, vanished as quickly as it had arrived. A dark menace lurked behind her every thought. And so she hummed louder.

It was when she decided her mouth tasted funny that the panic came on full-force. It was the cyanide. She'd had a peroxide rinse to clear out the poison, but suddenly she was sure the stuff was still in her system. Hurrying to the side of the road, she bent over, spitting repeatedly until her mouth was parched, her breath coming fast and her heart beating madly. Lowering herself to a knee, she struggled to calm herself down. *You're just a little in shock,* she told herself in a rational voice. *It's to be expected. You've suffered a 'traumatic event'* – as if watching a man cut his throat from ear to ear and bearing witness to the pulverization of a half dozen others, all after preparing your unwashed soul to meet your maker, could be made to fit into two words.

That was how they found her: on a knee, catching her breath, the color just beginning to return to her cheeks. It was a black Chrysler from the consulate.

'Miss Churchill,' asked a clean-cut man she recognized as a junior counselor. Bill or Bob or Brian. 'Are you all right?'

'Hello,' she said, waving, putting on that irrepressible grin, the one that said, *You know us Brits, we never give up, never complain. Cheerio, and all that bleeding crap.* 'Brian, isn't it? Yes, yes, I'm fine. Must've eaten something dodgy.'

'Brad,' he corrected her, the smile firmly in place. 'I'm afraid we've been asked to bring you back to the embassy.'

Straightening, she knew immediately that Brad and the local driver had been following her the entire route. *Cui custodiet custodian.* Who spies on the spies? Now she knew. The other spies. She just hadn't expected them to be from her side.

'But my flight doesn't leave till two this morning,' she said, a little unsurely.

'Change of plan, I'm afraid. There's a plane waiting for you at the airport right now.'

'To Washington?'

'No, ma'am. To Paris. Admiral Glendenning's orders.'

Chapter 11

'You can't unload this position now. You'll get killed. Do you have any idea what kinda hit you're gonna take unloading that size block? A point at least, maybe more. A hundred grand still means *something*. You're down what? Thirty percent. Hang on a little longer. Let me work the market. Better yet, wait. We'll sell into the next rally. It's overdue. All you need is a little patience. Patience and timing. Twenty-six years I've been trading. I know when we're due, and we're due. The market's going to turn any day now. Too much money's sitting on the sidelines. Fund redemptions are down. Pension plans are overfunded. All the leading indicators are up: consumer confidence, the Purchasing Managers Index, the Conference Board. The PPI's flat. Inflation's in check. Interest rates aren't going anywhere anytime soon. This is a market that's waiting to explode. We're sitting on a powder keg. You hear me, a powder keg? Twelve months from now we'll be testing new highs. Forget eleven thousand. Think twelve. Twelve five, even. This is not the time to be a spectator. You hear me? This is the time to keep both feet in the water. You cannot unload this position now.'

In his office overlooking the Eiffel Tower, Marc Gabriel distanced the phone from his ear. The problem with private bankers, he was thinking, was that they confused their own

THE DEVIL'S BANKER 89

welfare with that of their clients. His broker wasn't upset that by liquidating more than four hundred thousand shares of blue chip stock, his largest client was realizing a loss of over ten million dollars. He was scared that his own career might be in the shitter should Marc Gabriel and his company jump ship.

'Peter,' he said, tapping his sterling silver letter opener on the crease of his trousers. 'I do not need a lecture on the merits, or lack thereof, of selling in a difficult market. The stock's not performing, so we're getting out. It's that simple.'

'Dumping those shares isn't getting out. It's abandoning ship. We're due!'

'So is Father Christmas, world peace, and the second coming. Really, the decision's been made. Save your breath.'

Gabriel, forty-five years of age, was chairman and chief executive of Richemond Holdings, S.A., an internationally active investment firm with interests in equities, precious metals, and strategic shareholdings in a number of diverse companies. He did not like to be badgered. Running a hand along the back of his neck, he urged himself to remain calm. As usual, the building's air-conditioning was not functioning. The office was hot and stale, but despite the heat and the insistent nagging, Gabriel looked unfazed.

'Jesus, Marc, I don't like to see you get hurt like this,' the man in New York was saying. 'I mean, Christ, it's a bloodbath. Hang in there for another month or so. The stars are getting in alignment.'

'Wire the proceeds to my account at Deutsche Internationale Bank. I'll expect the funds by the end of business today. Frankfurt time.'

But the banker would not give up. 'What is it?' he demanded, unable to hide his desperation. 'You know something I don't? You boys start cleaning house, people are going to ask questions.'

A smile on your face guards the smile in your voice, Gabriel reminded himself. The last thing he needed was attention. 'The group is reconfiguring its portfolio. Nothing more. Nothing less,' he said, in a singsong way, his cheeks aching with the weight of the smile. 'The equity markets haven't been performing as we've liked. We're moving into real estate and commodities in hopes of increasing our returns.'

'*Commodities?*'

'Yes, yes, I know they're risky,' began Gabriel, as if asking for permission.

'I wouldn't say risky, so much as—'

'Get me some information on pork bellies,' Gabriel interrupted him. 'Take some time. I'll be in New York next week, then we'll talk. Lunch at Le Cirque? Make sure Sirio knows I'm coming.'

Gabriel hung up the phone, his face slack, a mask of hate. He was sick of the meaningless chitchat. If all went well, he would never have to speak to the foolish man again. Gabriel's problem was that he was too polite. Sometimes he really should forgo his manners, especially when there was so much that needed to be done.

Cardboard moving boxes littered the spacious office and sat bunched in groups near the credenza, the filing cabinets, and the antique Indonesian bookshelf that had displayed his personal vanities. Gabriel slid from one to the next, checking that each was full, sealing it with tape, marking the proper address in two languages. He was a compact man, trim and athletic, with a graceful economy of movement. Even with his sleeves rolled up, his Hermès cravat loosened, he never appeared rushed or in the least bit stressed. Panic was not a word in his vocabulary. Discipline. Self-control. Focus. There were his touchstones.

A cap of wavy dark hair framed a shadowed, angular face. As he worked, he kept a faint smile to his lips, and the smile along with the sparkling brown eyes lent him a wily, seductive air. He looked like a man who knew a few things about life. A man not afraid of the world's darker corners. A man who could keep a secret.

Standing, Marc Gabriel checked his watch. It was three o'clock, and he still had to call his bankers in Milano, Zurich, and Frankfurt, and order them to liquidate his portfolios. He was selling it all: Fiat, Olivetti, Fininvest, and Benetton. ABB, Julius Baer, Nestlé, and Credit Suisse. Bayer, Daimler, BASF, and Dresdner. There would be more arguments, more pleas to leave the money in the market. Again, Gabriel would explain his decision as a simple reconfiguring of his portfolios. Again, he would arrange meetings he had no intention of making. He would be sure to leave a million or two in each account, while asking that the proceeds of the share sales be wired to a web of numbered accounts in Dublin, Panama City, Vaduz, and Luxembourg.

And then he would sell again.

He would sell like he had never sold before.

Needing to stretch, Gabriel made a short parcourse of his office, stopping as was his custom by the window. Across the Seine, the Eiffel Tower soared into an unadulterated blue sky. It was a million-dollar view, and he knew that when he was gone he would miss it. A half mile distant, the tower appeared closer, within his very grasp. His eye locked on an elevator climbing the steel latticework and he thought the tower timeless – every bit as modern, as impressive today as when it had been built over a hundred years before to grace the opening of the 1889 International Exhibition of Paris.

This afternoon, however, he was more interested in the goings-on in the street below. Craning his head out the window, he took a long look around. Two buildings farther up, a liveried chauffeur was polishing the Qatari ambassador's three-hundred-thousand-dollar Porsche GT Turbo, though he was not so engrossed in his work not to notice the long, gamine legs of two women strolling past. A few children chased one another, shouting and screaming, as was every child's privilege. Monsieur Gallieni, the proprietor of the corner cafè, paced in front of his establishment smoking and looking to buttonhole an acquaintance to argue about the government's latest policies. Otherwise the sidewalks were deserted, as they always were in midafternoon.

Gabriel thought of the events of the past days. He knew that when they came, he would not see them.

He returned to his desk.

Yes, Gabriel decided, he would miss the Eiffel Tower. But he would miss nothing else about Paris; not its decadent nightlife or chichi bistros, its ungodly traffic and rancid pollution, its drippy autumns and frigid winters; and certainly not its flamboyant love of self. The rot was everywhere.

Picking up the phone, he punched in a number and began his second round of calls.

'Hello, Jean-Jacques. An order to sell. We're getting out of Citroën, Saint-Gobain, and L'Oréal. Yes, all of it. Every last share.'

Chapter 12

The Ford Mondeo carrying Adam Chapel and Admiral Owen Glendenning passed through three checkpoints before entering the courtyard of the American Embassy. Concrete caissons spaced five feet apart constituted the first line of defense. Next came the French police, three pairs standing abreast of squad cars parked directly before the embassy gates, all dressed smartly in sky blue shirts and navy pants, Legionnaire *casquettes* worn correctly, submachine guns strapped across their chests. Last came the Marine security detachment. Posted at the watch house that had once governed the entrance to the Chancery, they were no less vigilant because of the added measures.

'You'd think we're at war,' said Glendenning as the car slid to a halt and he opened the door. 'They've got the streets cordoned off for four blocks in every direction. Snipers on the rooftops. We've uncovered two plots to blow this place to kingdom come. God knows how many more are being fomented right now.' In an awkward ballet, he lifted his legs one at a time out of the car, thrust his canes out the door, and struggled to his feet, all the while ignoring the chauffeur's outstretched hands. 'Pardon me,' he called over a shoulder. 'Do you need help getting out?'

'Thank you, sir, I'm fine,' said Chapel, touched by the man's consideration. His shoulder was as numb as an iceberg, thanks to the painkillers Dr Bac had insisted he take prior to signing him out of the hospital. The last traces of shell shock had vanished on the ride over. Glendenning's words were as bracing as a slap in the face.

'Here's our problem,' he'd begun without preamble as they'd cleared the hospital grounds. 'Taleel never got the money from Royal Joailliers.'

'How's that?' asked Chapel. 'We had him red-handed entering the jewelry store and exiting two minutes later with a satchel that he didn't have before.'

'Be that as it may, we did not find a trace of a single US dollar bill, let alone enough to constitute the five hundred thousand or more that was supposed to be in that bag he took from Royal. Now, a bomb will destroy a lot of things. But it will not obliterate a few thousand hundred dollar bills. The greenbacks should have been fluttering around the place like confetti on a New Year's Eve. The only thing Taleel had in that satchel was a mess of Semtex.'

'I don't see how—'

'As I recall, there was a minute or two when you had to abandon visual contact.'

The Métro, Chapel thought, when Taleel had stopped short on the passenger platform. He stared at Glendenning longer than he should, trying to figure if the man was apportioning blame. His complexion was gray, his eyes hooded behind the thick lenses of his glasses. He looked owlish and unexceptional, and Adam thought he liked it that way, cultivated it, even, and that it was a uniform that required as much care and attention as his naval dress blues. The blandness coated him with a kind of emotional Teflon. He wasn't a man in the midst of a nasty divorce, a father with one son a recovering alcoholic and another at Harvard Law. He was an instrument of his government. Objective, dispassionate, and ultimately, Chapel imagined, divorced from the personal repercussions of his decisions.

'What about Boubilas?' Chapel asked. 'The owner of the jewelry store – did you pull him in?'

'General Gadbois has him at Mortier Caserne.'

'*Gadbois?* Isn't he with the DGSE? I thought we were working with the Sûreté on this thing?'

'The boys you were with yesterday were with the Action Service, part of the DGSE, not the police. Babtiste headed up their counterterrorism squad. Leclerc's in on the messier side of the business. Gadbois doesn't like to advertise their involvement in domestic matters if he doesn't have to.'

'So I wasn't in charge?'

'Did you really think you were?' Glendenning frowned, as if he didn't have time for such childish squabbling. 'You were in charge as much as anyone is in this type of affair. Babtiste was there to whistle you down if he thought you were making a wrong move. As for Boubilas, he swears he never got the call. "*Hawala?* What's that?" he asked. "A new dance?" Claims he'd never seen Taleel before in his life.'

'He's lying.'

'Of course he is. As far as we know, the transfer from Pakistan was legit. We fell for the three-card monte. We had our eye on Taleel while someone else picked up the dough . . . either in that store or on the Métro. That's where you come in. You're going to find who took that money. You see, Mr Chapel, we didn't come up totally empty-handed. We did manage to find something. A digital recording made by Taleel and his buddies.'

'A tape?'

'Yes, a tape. It makes for interesting viewing.'

Glendenning hadn't whispered another word during the rest of the drive. And thirty minutes later, as Chapel passed through the black iron gates and mounted the stairs to the embassy, he shivered with anticipation as once again, he wondered what could be so important to have brought a deputy director of the Central Intelligence Agency across three thousand miles of ocean in the middle of the night.

It was called the 'Quiet Room,' and it was located on the embassy's second floor, deep on an interior corridor as close to the building's heart as possible. Sheets of lead embedded in the walls locked all sound inside the room. Electronic bafflers provided backup. Twice a day, monitors swept the room for electronic eavesdropping devices. Neither cry nor whisper could escape. France might be America's oldest ally, but of late, it was to be distrusted like anybody else.

The end of the Cold War had seen the DGSE, France's espionage service, redirect its efforts towards industrial targets. Its agents traveled the world seeking to purloin trade secrets, hijack intellectual property, and 'borrow' proprietary technology. Its 'main adversary' was no longer the Union of Soviet Socialist Republics, but the United States of America. And no more eloquent testimony could be found than front page headlines proclaiming the arrest of French spies caught *in flagrante* attempting to steal trade secrets from Microsoft and Boeing. On this hot, sunny August morning, however, bygones were bygones. Peace, not profit, was once again the utmost priority. With the two countries united by a common foe, all disagreements belonged to the past.

A long, glossy conference table filled the narrow room, pitchers of water, glasses, and bowls of pretzels set out at even intervals. Photo portraits of the sitting US President and the ambassador to France provided the only decoration.

Glendenning lifted his arm towards a squat, barrel-chested man with grizzled hair wearing an ill-fitting blue suit. 'Meet Guy Gadbois. Runs things for the DGSE.'

Gadbois grunted a hello, but made no motion to stand or shake hands.

'I believe you know Captain Leclerc,' Glendenning said.

A square of gauze marking the Frenchman's cheek was all he had to show from the bomb blast. He wore a tailored gray suit, his white shirt open at the collar. His hair was combed neatly and tucked behind his ear. But there was no mistaking the distrustful cast to his eyes. Leclerc looked at everyone as if they were a suspect.

'Yes,' said Chapel. 'Glad you're all right.'

Where had *he* been when Taleel blew himself up? Chapel wondered. Vaguely, he recalled Leclerc following him up the stairs, shadowing him down the hallway. But after that, he wasn't sure. The events were all of a piece, melted into one another in some psychedelic, nonlinear way by the trauma of the blast. In his mind's eye, he conjured up Babtiste, Gomez, Keck, and of course, Santini. The only person he hadn't seen inside the apartment was Leclerc.

'And you?' asked Leclerc. 'You are all right? A quick recovery, is it? *Tant mieux.*' He averted his gaze, but not before Adam caught the veiled admonition, its hint of duty unfulfilled, or worse.

Before he could respond, Glendenning was motioning past Leclerc towards the sole woman in the room. Standing crisply, she extended a hand along with a sympathetic smile. 'Sarah Churchill,' she said, before Glendenning had the chance. 'I heard what happened yesterday. I'm dreadfully sorry, Mr Chapel.'

She was nearly as tall as he was, dressed in dark slacks and an ivory silk tank top that highlighted her tanned arms and face. She kept her black hair pulled off her forehead and bundled into a thick ponytail that fell below her shoulders and shone in the fluorescent light like Chinese lacquer. She wore no makeup – no eyeliner, no lipstick, no mascara. Her eyebrows were thick, her eyes brown flecked with gold and narrowed with suspicion, and for a moment, Chapel wondered if despite the accent, she wasn't English but Middle Eastern – Egyptian, Lebanese, or even Turkish.

'Miss Churchill's on loan to us from our British cousins,' said Glendenning, as if in answer to Chapel's question. 'She's a military brat like me. It was Sarah, running the other side of the operation.'

'I guess it was a bad day for both of us,' said Chapel, grasping her hand, finding the grip cool and firm.

'Rather,' she said, the smile souring just long enough for him to question her goodwill.

'Let's get this show on the road, shall we, folks?' said Glendenning. 'All those present are to consider themselves members of joint counterterrorism task force Blood Money. All information discussed in this room is subject to the highest security clearance, classification Whirlwind. Is that enough of the bullshit, or do I have to give it to you in writing? Mr Chapel, Mr Leclerc,' he continued. 'I want to thank both you gentlemen for making the effort to be with us today. Miss Churchill, likewise. If you've got any jet lag, I can guarantee you that the film you are about to see will keep your eyes wide open.'

The lights dimmed. A nervy stillness fell over the room. A video screen four feet by four lowered from the ceiling. Chapel leaned forward in his seat, tasting a sour bile in his throat, as his heart drummed faster. The tape began. A man dressed in a fatigue jacket, Arafat's red-checkered *khaffiyeh*, and mirrored sunglasses filled the screen.

'Americans, Zionists, and your sycophantic allies, I address you in the name of Muhammad, peace be unto him, and in the name of everlasting peace between all peoples . . .'

The language was English, spoken with a colloquial American accent. The man was either native-born or a gifted linguist. Glancing around him, Adam noted that everyone had assumed his own posture of stiff anticipation. Everyone except Leclerc, who stared at the screen with undisguised nonchalance.

'In your holy book, David rose up and slew Goliath with a stone. And with a stone we have slain those who oppress us, who force an unjust peace on the land of Abraham, and who occupy the Land of Two Holy Places. The time of humiliation and subjugation is over. On this day, a new history has begun, and its first pages have been written in the blood of the Zionist Crusaders. Feel our hate, for it is yours. Know our desperation, for it is yours. Choke on our rage, for it is yours. It is time for the hypocrites to leave and take their reign of false values with them. The light of Islam shall sear every trace of Western corr—'

Abruptly, the tape dissolved into a stuttering patchwork of black and white lines, interrupted by stretches of darkness.

'From here on out, the picture quality is quite poor,' said General Gadbois, pulling his muscled forearms more tightly around his chest. 'The original is at our lab. They tell me that it is unlikely we shall be able to recover anything further.'

The images regained clarity, but it was clear that this portion of the tape had been damaged by the blast. The speaker moved jerkily. His words were garbled. For the next sixty seconds, Chapel was unable to make out more than a phrase here and there, a few stray syllables. 'Struggle has come . . . land . . . attack . . . 'tember morning . . . die . . .'

The audio cut out, and a moment later, the picture began to deteriorate. Color bled from the images. Darkness peeled across the screen. As the figure faded to obscurity, Glendenning froze the picture.

'Look at him,' said Glendenning, and for once, Chapel heard real malice in his voice. 'Smug bastard. He's smiling. Thinks he's pulled one over on us.'

Chapel scooted forward an inch. Yes, the bastard was smiling, and for a shocking moment he reminded him of Leclerc, that smirking, know-it-all look he wore to beat back the world. Then he saw something else. 'Hold it,' he said, barely containing his urge to shout. 'Keep it there.'

Chapel walked to the screen. 'There!' he declared, his index finger touching the mirrored lens of the speaker's sunglasses. 'That's a reflection of someone else in the room.'

'Probably Taleel,' said Leclerc. Despite his dismissive tone, he was pulling himself out of his chair, craning his neck towards the screen.

'Maybe,' said Chapel. 'Maybe not. This figure looks like it's on the other side of the room.'

It was hardly a figure, more an hourglass pastiche of red and blue.

'No, no, Mr Chapel's got something,' said Sarah Churchill. Rising, she walked to the screen, a silver-dollar smile to move him aside and allow her a closer view. 'I'd be inclined to agree that it's a human form,' she announced after a few seconds.

Glendenning offered Gadbois a tired, disappointed glance that summed up the history of the two nations' relations. Cooperation without trust. Friendship without affection. 'Let's get a copy to our boys in DC. They can blow up the image to a hundred times that size, manipulate the pixels and lighting. If someone is there, they'll be able to tell us their height, weight, and what they ate for breakfast.'

'We can do the same,' said Leclerc.

'Then do it!' chided Glendenning, with an angry turn of his head.

Overhead, the panels of fluorescent lights blinked to life.

'We have no idea who this man is,' Gadbois announced with evident frustration. 'Or who filmed him, though we are assuming that since the tape and camera came from Taleel's apartment, he was the cameraman. Let's hope our respective photographic laboratories can shed some light on the question. Until then, we are working with the Sûreté to canvass the area. They are going door-to-door with members of your FBI showing Taleel's picture. Give us a few days. We'll have something about him and his friends.'

'Excuse me,' said Chapel, tentatively. 'Is that it? Is that all there is to the tape?' To his eye, it appeared that the speaker had been cut off midsentence. He felt puzzled. While the threat was sobering, it was hardly specific enough to warrant the DDO flying to France at the drop of a hat. There had to be something more. 'Seems like he's got something else to say. Is that really the end of the speech or was the tape damaged at that point?'

'That is the entire speech,' said Gadbois, turning his bulk towards Chapel, his bullfrog's glaring eyes and blemished features all but telling him to shut the hell up and stop making waves. 'We're lucky we got it at all.'

'Of course,' said Chapel, sinking back into his seat. 'I'm sorry.' *Exception noted*, he mused sourly.

'Miss Churchill's been closer to the case than anyone,' said Glendenning. 'She's the one who first posited the existence of this group. "Hijira," you call them. Why?'

'From what I gather, it's what they call themselves,' Sarah answered. 'Hijira marks the beginning of the new Islamic calendar and dates to the time Muhammad fled his persecutors.'

She was back in the debater's corner at Cambridge, first affirmative making her team's argument. She didn't know why she felt so nervous. She'd done the same thing often enough with the analysts back at Legoland, which was what everyone called MI6's new modernistic headquarters on the south bank of the Thames. She kept her voice even, her eyes passing from one man to the next, mustering support, always ready to deploy a smile when necessary to bring the doubters to her side.

'Who are they? Why have we heard so little of them until now? And do you mind if I ask just exactly what new era it is that they hope to usher in?'

It was Chapel, and behind the polite demeanor she sensed a challenge. Another 'newbie' not content with being low man on the totem pole.

'Pan-Arab nationalists,' she explained. 'One more group sick and tired of Western cultural and political hegemony. You heard what he said about allowing "the light of Islam to sear every trace of Western corruption." He wants a solution to the Palestinian question, and the Yanks out of Saudi Arabia. Saudi's what the man in the video called the "Land of Two Holy Places." He was referring to Mecca and Medina, the two holiest cities in the Muslim world. As Admiral Glendenning hinted, until a few days ago, pretty much everything we'd gathered about Hijira was supposition, if not speculation. Their primary focus appears to be generating income to support their operations. They're into drugs – cocaine, heroin. That's nothing new. Al Qaeda's up to their neck in the poppy trade. Bin Laden doesn't have half the money everyone likes to believe, and he spent what he had ten years ago. Hijira's taken it a step further. More than once we've picked up chatter that they're involved in more sophisticated enterprises: gold smuggling, software piracy, conflict diamonds.'

'To what end?' asked Chapel. 'Any idea what kind of operation they're going after? Who their primary adversary is?'

'Not until today. We do know this: They're operating in Afghanistan, Pakistan, the UAE –' here she hesitated as a shadow crossed her face, 'and, now, in Europe. If they're in Paris, we can assume they've got cells in other cities on the continent, as well. We believe they're headquartered in the Middle East – Yemen, the mountains of Oman, or Saudi's Empty Quarter. They appear to be a close-knit group, quite small. Judging from communication patterns, we reckon there are between six and eight key operatives.'

'One was killed yesterday,' Glendenning cut in. 'Abu Sayeed. At one time or another, he was tight with Hezbollah, Islamic Jihad, and Al Qaeda. We don't know why or when he crossed the fence to Hijira.'

'Sayeed was the man killed yesterday?' asked Leclerc, shaking his head as if his death was a bungle.

'It was a messy takedown. Our boys were a little late to the party. Sarah did a fine job keeping Sayeed until we could get to him.'

'Another corpse to interrogate,' said Leclerc. '*Super.*' *Soop-air.*

Biting back her contempt, Sarah pulled her notes closer, and ran a broken nail over the words. 'I think we'd all agree that the man we've just watched is no ordinary player. He's smooth, this one. Someone very special. Very frightening. He's educated, probably in the West. Hardly your run-of-the-mill *jihadi*, is he? They're usually younger, poorer, and for the most part illiterate. As to an objective, I can't offer anything, other than what he obviously stated. "The struggle will come to you." As he was addressing "Americans and their sycophantic allies," I think we can take it that means the attack is to occur on US soil. A few other observations, then I'll be finished. First, he mentions " 'tember morning." I heard that as September. Anyone think he may have been saying November or December?'

'It is September,' said Leclerc, unequivocally. 'I have watched the tape a dozen times.' Lifting a hand, he motioned for her to continue, and even graced her with a smile. 'Please, go ahead.'

Sarah nodded diplomatically, scolding him from behind frozen eyes. The pompous, misogynist prick. *Eet ees Septemburr*. 'It's tempting to take this as a date of the attack, but we can't be sure. What puzzles me is his saying "'versary.'" Is that "anniversary"? If so, should we be looking at an anniversary in September as a possible date of the attack?'

'Nine-eleven's the big one,' said Glendenning.

'True,' she said, 'but September is chock full of important dates in Middle Eastern affairs. The Yom Kippur War started in late September of seventy-three.'

'The twenty-eighth, actually,' Chapel added, a little too assertively for her taste. 'But it's called the "October War." It's hardly the kind of event they'd want to commemorate. It was a resounding defeat for the Arab states. Israel took the Golan Heights from Syria, territory from Egypt, and destroyed the armored capabilities of their three neighboring states. Maybe that's the "humiliation and subjugation" the freedom fighter wants to rectify.'

'Maybe.' Sarah looked closer at the Treasury agent. He was some kind of monetary specialist and Glendenning had told her they would be working together. He didn't look like a quant jock. Too rough around the edges. More of a brute than a finesser. Here it was only twelve o'clock and he needed another shave. She reminded him of one of Daddy's enlisted men who muscled his way into the officer ranks. All energy and good works, but God help you once he got his pips.

'I have one question,' Chapel continued, and she felt as if he were grilling her and she didn't like it one bit. 'You mentioned that when our friend on the tape used the term "the land of two holy places," he was talking about Saudi Arabia, right? Mecca and Medina?'

'Yes,' she replied. 'It's similar to what bin Laden liked to talk about, except that bin Laden was referring simply to the presence of US soldiers on Saudi soil, whereas this man seems to be referring also to US influence. I guess he doesn't want his MTV.'

To her mind, the Kingdom of Saudi Arabia was one of the

most repressed countries in the world. It had one TV station, two newspapers, several state-sponsored radio networks, and the government controlled all of them with an iron hand. Less than ten percent of the female population had attended school at any level. Travel into and out of the kingdom was frowned upon and required a rigorous vetting process. Oil workers were confined to company towns. The Al-Saud family had done everything but hermetically seal the borders to keep out the 'traces of Western corruption' the madman on the tape had talked about.

'So then, since he's calling his group "Hijira," can we take it he's Saudi?' Chapel asked. 'I mean, that's where the flight of Muhammad took place. Do you think his aims might be closer to home?'

Sarah decided she'd had enough. It was time to put the probationer in his place. 'We haven't the slightest hint that this is anything but an anti-Western group. One more Salafist Muslim organization that sees it as their holy duty to eradicate Christianity from the Ummah, the community of countries united beneath the Islamic flag. I'm afraid, Mr Chapel, it doesn't matter if he's a Saudi or a Palestinian, or a Frenchman. He's a Muslim, and whatever he plans on doing, it's to further what he believes is the cause of Muslims and Islam around the world. No, I do not think his aims are closer to home.'

Chapel pursed his lips and sat back, his eyes flashing real anger. Sarah wondered if he was trying to intimidate her. Another tongue-tied bully? Perhaps she'd been too hard on him. No, she decided. She hadn't. There was no point in letting their investigations get sidetracked before they'd even started. Hijira was her baby. She would point. He could dig.

Silence crowded the room as Glendenning made his way to the head of the table. 'What we have on the table is a threat to the United States of America,' he said quietly.

'Nothing more. Nothing less. We have all of us gathered in an effort to find the man who delivered that message and stop him and his associates from carrying out whatever assault they have in mind. We can't afford any more of yesterday's snafus. No more jumping the gun.' He paused, and it was clear that he was addressing the comment to Gadbois and Leclerc. 'We have to lock down this investigation and keep its true focus known to only a few people. There will be no leaks. There will be no discussion of our real purpose outside of those here today. For the public, for the press, and for the police, we are engaged in a murder investigation with Middle Eastern overtones. A suspected terrorist killed four agents resisting arrest. End of story. There will be no mention of the tape and no mention of a plot. The defense minister has agreed to grant special police powers to all members of the Blood Money task force. Taking into account your expertise and experience, you are to use any and all methods at your disposal to find this man.'

Glendenning stopped speaking long enough to acknowledge all those present. 'And if I'm not sufficiently clear, let me share with you the wishes of the President of the United States, as well as his close friend and ally, the President of France. You are to shoot first, and ask questions later.'

Chapter 13

'How long?' Adam Chapel asked, raising his head towards Sarah. 'How long before the act do these guys make these tapes?'

'Hours,' she said. 'Days. Longer if they have to travel some distance. At least that much is in our favor. If they are planning on hitting a target in America, we can assume they'll need a little while to get there.'

'Why?' demanded Leclerc, bolting to attention. 'They might have boarded the plane this morning. For all we know, they could be in Manhattan as we speak. How do we know they are not already there? Just because the tape was made in Paris, it doesn't mean that the people who will execute the plan are also here.'

'Doubtful,' said Sarah. 'They needed the money for a reason. And they needed it in Paris. They took a chance by sending so much through a *hawala*. If it cost them one of their men, you can bet it was bloody important. You can also bet they made sure they got the money here in plenty of time, and that the operation isn't going to take place until they've spent it.'

Only the three of them remained, and they'd gathered at one end of the table, alternately shaking their heads, smiling disconsolately at the ceiling, and silently ruing their luck, like a group of students who'd just been given a murderous assignment. Despite Sarah Churchill's protests and an illuminated sign on the wall to the contrary, Leclerc was smoking, lobbing a parade of smoke rings toward the ceiling. He was their 'babysitter,' Glendenning had told them. There to watch their backs, shine a light down the dimmer passageways, and provide the oil necessary to grease some of the rustier wheels in the French law enforcement community.

It was a tall order, thought Chapel. Asking them to put an identity to an unknown face, to track down and apprehend a culprit who no one confessed to knowing the first thing about, other than that he was an associate of Mohammed al-Taleel, and thus a member of Hijira.

A minute ago, Guy Gadbois had left the room in urgent conversation with Glendenning. Together the DGSE, the Sûreté, and the FBI promised to shake as many trees as possible, to call in their favors from the street, in Paris and in the States. To help them with their task, they had a single photo of Taleel five years out-of-date that didn't look a damned thing like the man Chapel had followed across the Parisian cityscape. And that was all.

Leclerc leaned across the table, sweeping a strand of hair out of his eyes. 'I have an appointment to see Mr Boubilas later today. Perhaps he can shed some light on the situation.'

'I understand he's not talking,' said Chapel.

'He will talk to Captain Leclerc.'

Sarah rolled her eyes, and Chapel said, 'Just leave a piece of him for the next guy, if you're not as successful as you hope. In the meantime, if we want to start building a trail on our man, I need to know who Taleel was renting the apartment from.'

'Azema Immobilier,' answered Leclerc. 'One eight-five Avenue George V. He was using the alias Bertrand Roux. There are seven other men in Paris with that name. We are checking if Taleel acquired any types of government identification under that name: driver's license, passport, national employment card.'

'Try credit cards, too,' Chapel added. 'The more places we know he frequented, the easier it will be for us to get a picture of who his associates might have been.'

'It is being done.'

'What about his apartment?' asked Sarah. 'Have they turned up any of his personal effects? Anything at all?'

'There was very little to find,' explained Leclerc. 'No food. No clothes. No books. The place was either deserted or he was moving out soon.'

'Not totally, it wasn't,' complained Chapel. 'I saw a TV in there and a PC sitting on his desk.'

'Ruined, I'm afraid. Maybe we can recover something from the hard disk. There is still a team over there, sifting through the rubble. It will take weeks to figure out what exactly we have. After talking to Rafi Boubilas, I'm going over to Sûreté headquarters to see what they've turned up.'

Every criminal left a particular scent; every organization, its own signature; and this one, Chapel realized, was sophisticated, wily, and expert. For two years, he had been investigating all manner of groups and organizations suspected of even the remotest involvement in the financing of terrorists and terrorist activities. He'd cut his teeth on the *hawalas* sending money to Iraq in violation of the US embargo, and from there moved to charities funneling contributions to Hamas and Hezbollah, and then to legitimate businesses cutting checks from their bottom line to rebels in the Philippines and in Indonesia. Earlier in the summer, he'd taken down a sixteen-year-old Saudi prince who was secretly selling his father's American equities and wiring the proceeds to a bank in Grozny to support the Muslim Chechen freedom fighters. But that was as close as he'd gotten to the enemy.

Increasingly, he was frustrated by the feeling that he had been confined to the periphery of the fight against terrorism. His was a bureaucrat's game involving endless court appearances, demands for subpoenas and search warrants, uncounted hours studying balance sheets, P&L's, and the tedious minutiae of monthly bank statements.

In law enforcement, there is an intoxicating myth that one man can make a difference, and that it is through effort alone that he does or does not. At some point, Chapel had decided to be that man. Like a snake molting its skin, he'd shed layer after layer of his personal life to devote more time to the job. He'd given up the weekend bike rides to Annapolis and afternoon swims at the Y. He'd cut his morning runs from six days to four, then to two, and now was lucky to hit the road even one day a week. He'd forsaken his addiction to Monday Night Football, his terminal rereading of John le Carré, and his love of five-alarm curry. His relationships with women, never his strong suit to begin with, had dwindled to monthly dinners with coworkers before stopping altogether. He took his shirts to the dry cleaners regardless of the cost. He gave up making his bed. He traded oatmeal and fresh orange juice at breakfast for a cup of coffee and a day-old Danish on the drive to Langley. Nutritious sit-down dinners of diced chicken breast and steamed garlic broccoli gave way to orgies of stuffed crust pizza and Coca Cola at his desk.

All in the name of the myth.

Adam Chapel would make a difference.

Lately, though, he had begun to doubt the result of his efforts. Too often, after a twenty-hour stretch logged on to a computer terminal, he'd look at his bloodshot eyes in the mirror and ask, 'Why?' and wonder whether he would ever actually stop a man from committing an act, whether he was a soldier in the line or a reserve trying to fight a rainstorm with an umbrella. Selfishly, he wondered if he'd given too much of himself for an elusive cause, if he had to find the answers to his questioning heart somewhere else.

And then, in the space of a day, everything had changed. The enemy was no longer a mirage taunting him from the end of the highway. The enemy was here. He was in Paris. Chapel had stared him in the eye and by the grace of God escaped his terrible commitment. Stung by the death of three friends and a man he was only beginning to know, he realized that his efforts had not been trivial and that his ethic was rewarded in the form of a greater challenge.

'Azema Immobilier,' repeated Leclerc as he wrote down the address and slipped the paper to Sarah. 'It is near the Champs Elysées,' he said pleasantly to her, as if she were the only other person in the room. 'Mr Chapel will be pleased to know there is a Métro station quite nearby. He won't have to walk far, though there are a few flights of stairs.'

'What did you say?' Chapel asked.

'You won't have to walk far.'

'No. No. What did you *say*?' he repeated.

Leclerc's face remained blank, his dolorous brown eyes darting to Sarah, then back to Chapel. He was guessing how far to push. Chapel could see it in the way his lips trembled, the little stutterstep his fingers danced on the armrest.

'You heard me,' Chapel said. 'Now, answer.' It was a whisper balanced on the razor's edge of control.

'I said you don't have to walk far.' Leclerc chuckled joylessly and the tautness went out of his shoulders. 'I was thinking about your leg. There's something wrong with it, *non*? First you miss grabbing Taleel. Then you're the last man into that building. I hear you run marathons. I thought you could have caught up to him. That's all. What happened, anyway? You pull a muscle or something?'

'Nothing happened,' said Chapel. 'I missed him, that's all. I thought I could tackle him. I came close. I just—' He broke off and looked away. There was no reason he should explain to Leclerc. Yet, he couldn't stop. He needed to say the words, if only to forgive himself. 'Those were my friends in that room. I worked with them every day for two years running. I'm the godfather to Ray Gomez's son. I brought Keck over from the Agency, spent twenty-four seven with him until he was up to speed. We were a team. A unit. I got there as quickly as I could. I tried so hard – are you listening?' The pressure at the back of his neck was building. Each second, he found it harder to remain seated. 'I asked you a question.'

At some point, Sarah Churchill had come closer, and suddenly, Chapel was aware of her hand on his good shoulder. 'Mr Chapel,' she said softly. 'I'm sure Mr Leclerc meant nothing by his comments.'

'It's *Captain* Leclerc, don't you remember?' Chapel said. 'And where were *you*, by the way?' he said to the Frenchman.

'Ahead of you,' Leclerc answered, eyes locked on Chapel. 'In the back bedroom. I was just lucky, I guess.'

'You *both* were,' said Sarah Churchill. 'Enormously so. Now then, Azema Immobilier, is it?' she asked, reading from the slip of paper. 'Are they expecting us?'

Leclerc smiled diplomatically. 'I am sure they will be the model of cooperation.'

Needing fresh air, Adam Chapel stood from his chair and walked the length of the table toward the door.

'You really think you will find them that way?' Leclerc remained seated, making a show of gathering his papers, eyes never leaving the desk.

'What way?'

'By tracking the money. They say an Indian can track a horse over rock, too. Me, I never believed it.'

Chapel paused in the doorway, a hand on the frame. 'I'll let you in on a secret, *Captain* Leclerc. All the stuff you guys gather from your informants is, by definition, suspect. Just look at who gives it to you. It's the product of treachery, deceit, bribery, and interrogation. Money is incorruptible. Audit trails don't lie. In the end, they're the diary every terrorist keeps, even if he doesn't know it.'

'If you say so,' agreed Leclerc, but to Chapel's ears, the words were a challenge.

Prove it. And fast.

Chapter 14

Admiral Owen Glendenning paid off the taxi and made his way into the cool recesses of the Hotel Plaza Athenée. The lobby was an oasis of marble. Marble floor. Marble columns. Marble counters. The tinkle of a fountain softened the noise of traffic drifting in from the Avenue Montaigne. A colossal spray of gladioli and white geraniums decorated a table in the center of the atrium. Except for the very slim, very chic women sauntering through the place, Glendenning found it more like a mortuary than a five-star hotel. He'd been thinking a lot about death lately.

At the front desk, he inquired where he might use a telephone.

'Down the corridor and to the left, sir,' answered the clerk.

'*Merci*,' said Glendenning, though the clerk had spoken to him in perfect English.

Walking to the bank of phone booths, he caught his cane on the transom separating the marble floor from the carpeted corridor. He stumbled, but caught himself. He was hurrying . . . that was the problem. He flushed with shame, and then with anger at his vanity. You'd have thought that after being stuck with the lousy sticks for thirty-five years, he'd have grown used to the deflected glances, the impromptu hushes that crowded his wake. The fact was that he'd never gotten over being a cripple.

There was honor in a face that had seen battle, but the scarred, useless legs were an embarrassment. A sign of weakness. He'd tried everything to regain full control of them. Exercise. Therapy. Surgery. Nothing had worked. In the end, he'd decided it was a failure of the will and tortured himself for his weakness.

Inside the booth, he sat down, arranged his canes, and picked up and folded his legs so that he could close the door. Through the window, he caught a boy staring at him. Glendenning smiled, but the boy ran off with a frightened expression. Glendenning's smile faded. It wasn't the physical inconvenience that bothered him most, or the ever present pain. It was being the bent, shuffling reminder of what could go wrong in this life. Any way you looked at it, it was a damned high price to pay for capturing four low-level slopes who didn't know jack shit.

Turning his back to the window, he picked up the phone. The hotel operator answered. '*Oui?*'

'An international call, please,' he said. He gave the number and waited as the operator dialed. His heart was beating very fast and he thought he'd lost his taste for clandestine ops.

'*Allo.*'

'Hello,' he said, trying to sound calm, dispassionate. 'It's me.'

'Where are you?' The voice belonged to a woman. She was concerned. 'You sound next door.'

'In Paris.'

'Should you be calling?'

'Probably not, but I had to talk to you.'

'It's too risky. Hang up now.'

'Don't worry,' said Glendenning, glancing over his shoulder, a hooded eye scanning the lobby. 'No one followed me. First time I've been alone in days.'

'You're in France? Couldn't you have given me any warning?'

'I didn't have a chance. We had to play it fast. Went from the office right to the plane. People are watching me every step of the way. I had to sneak away just to call you. Said I was getting a souvenir for my nephew.'

'Is it that tight?'

'Yep. And you? Are you ready for the event? Ticket, passport, the special papers you'll need?'

'Everything's in order. I am a professional, after all.'

'Just checking. Security will be tight. The timing of this couldn't be worse. We don't want anything to go wrong. It will be enough of a scene already. So you're ready?'

'I said I was. You're making me nervous.'

'Don't be. The only way to get through this is by guarding our nerves. Anyway, we'll talk later.'

'But Glen—'

'Yes?'

'No more risks. We're too close.'

Chapter 15

'Roux, Bertrand. Yes, yes. I have it right here. Pays by check the second of every month.' The keyboard clicked as Jules Ricard, office manager of Azema Immobilier, scrolled back in time through Taleel's rental record. Abruptly, he stopped, and pressed his damp, gray face closer to the monitor. 'Incredible, really. Sixteen months and always on the second. "Like clockwork," you say in English, *non*?'

'Yeah,' said Chapel, without the verve. 'Like clockwork.'

The office was small and cramped and windowless, and like most offices housed in a nineteenth-century building, without the luxury of air-conditioning. In deference to the heat, Ricard had turned off the lights, so that even though it was only three P.M., the room had the fusty, melancholy pallor of an abandoned classroom. Thumbing open the top button of his shirt, Chapel billowed the fabric to get some air.

The place was a pigsty. Strips of paper were taped to every free square inch of Ricard's monitor, each bearing an abbreviated message punctuated by a quiver of exclamation points. *'Appelez P!!'* *'20:00 Chez FB!!!'* *'Payez C!!!'* Ashtrays filled to overflowing decorated his desk and credenza, while piles of magazines lay toppled and scattered across the floor. Chapel shuddered at the sight. He was a 'neatnick' of the first degree, the kind of guy who kept his desk clear of everything but what he was working on at the time and who regularly checked his shelves to make sure the spines of his books were properly aligned. He enjoyed filing. The mere act of organizing calmed him. How anyone could work in such squalor was beyond him.

'Any problems with him?' Sarah asked. 'Complaints from neighbors? Parties?'

'None,' said Ricard. Dapper as dapper can be, he was attired in a crisp poplin suit, his thinning ginger hair pasted neatly across his scalp.

'A lot of guests coming and going at odd times?'

'Not that I know of.'

'No roommate?' asked Chapel.

'No.'

'You're sure?' In his mind, Chapel guarded a clear picture of Taleel's apartment. He was sure there had been a television set broadcasting a bicycle race. Who in the world walked out of their house with a TV on?

'Absolutely not,' said Ricard gruffly, rolling his chair back an inch and lifting his jaw, as if his dignity had been impugned. 'It is a one-bedroom apartment. We are strict. We must be, or else the students would have five or more people in every flat. Especially the Africans. You have no idea! Mr Roux, never a problem.'

'If only *all* your tenants were so good,' offered Sarah Churchill.

'I was just going to say the same—' Ricard caught himself, and his voice went as gray as his face. 'I am sorry,' he said. 'Really, I had no idea who this man was. A terrorist, the paper said. It scares me. An Arab. Taleel?'

'You've never met him?' asked Chapel. Pushing aside an enormous hidebound ledger, he cleared a space to lean against a waist-high cabinet.

'Me? No, never.' Ricard consulted the screen, tapping the eraser of his pencil on the appropriate spot. 'Antoine

Ribaud was the leasing agent. He showed Roux the apartment.'

'Is Mr Ribaud available?' Sarah asked, fanning herself with a folded copy of *Le Monde*.

'On vacation. Paris in August . . . everyone is away. Except the tourists, of course. And me.'

'Where's he gone?' Chapel was hoping somewhere nearby – Nice, Sardinia, Rome. A phone call from Leclerc, a forty-five-minute flight, and by morning they'd have Ribaud in the hot seat.

'Guatemala,' answered Ricard. 'Chichicastenango. To see the Mayan ruins. Or is that in Honduras?'

'Guatemala,' said Sarah, and when she looked across the room at Chapel, he knew they shared the same thought. Ribaud couldn't have gone farther away if he'd known they were coming. Ricard seemed to sense their frustration and was quick to offer an apology. 'Even so, it would make no difference. The company owns thirty-seven buildings in Paris. Over four hundred flats. We only remember the tenants who pay late, or not at all, or those who cause problems. Mr Roux, he is perfect.' Again, Ricard looked aghast at his choice of words. But Adam thought his reaction justified. He was certain Taleel wouldn't have wanted it any other way.

'Do you have his banking information?' he asked.

'Yes, yes. Of course. Mr Crissier telephoned before you came.' Crissier was Leclerc's work name. A few keystrokes yielded what Adam and Sarah had come for. 'His account is with the Banque de Londres et Paris.' Ricard scribbled a nine-digit number on a piece of notepaper and handed it to him. 'You are all right, *monsieur*?' he asked, his face wrinkling with concern. 'May I get you a glass of water? You would like to sit, perhaps?'

Chapel caught a glimpse of himself in a gilt-framed mirror. He looked wan and pallid, sickly. One eye drooped lazily. *It's the heat*, he told himself. He needed some fresh air. 'I'm fine,' he said, rising from the cabinet too quickly, pulling his shoulders back. Too late he remembered his bandaged and blistered skin. The pain was vivid and overwhelming. He sank to his place at the cabinet, his vision bleeding white as if he were staring at a giant sun. 'It's nothing,' he said. 'Just a little . . .' Letting the words drift off, he stood more carefully and swallowed a breath. 'Ready to go?'

Sarah took the paper, thanked Jules Ricard, and asked him to call should he remember anything that might be useful about 'Bertrand Roux' or his associates. But as they descended the stairway, Chapel wasn't thinking about Ricard or Taleel, or the investigation at all, for that matter. He was counting the hours until his appointment with Dr Bac the next morning. He wasn't sure if he could make it that long.

The Renault sped over the Pont D'Orsay, over the Seine tumbling and sparkling in the afternoon sun like a sea of warring emeralds. Gold-leaf Apollos atop triumphant columns saluted their passage. His window open, Chapel drank in the cooling breeze as the bite of the river's fresh-water brine tickled his nose. He felt better now that they were moving. The sights, the sounds, the smells of the city distracted him from his own discomfort. More important, the dash through the Parisian streets proved a psychological tonic. To move was to act, and to act was to succeed. However long the odds, however remote the possibility, as long as he was moving, anything was possible.

Upon leaving Ricard's office, Chapel had called Leclerc and asked him to contact the Banque de Londres et Paris and use his juice to have Roux's account records ready for examination. Leclerc agreed, and went on to say he had some news of his own. Mohammed al-Taleel had, in fact, obtained a driver's license in Roux's name, and given his address as the ruined apartment in the Cité Universitaire. Jotting down the number on his notepad, Chapel enjoyed the first precarious intimation of progress. In addition to a permanent address, government-issued identifications were a must when opening any type of credit account; with banks, utilities, phone, finance companies. It was his experience that money launderers relied on two or three documented aliases to conduct their business. Taleel's driver's license number would give them an extra and invaluable tool in spotting his financial footprints.

Ahead, the traffic lights flashed yellow, then green. Maneuvering into the left lane, Sarah guided them in an arcing turn onto the Quai D'Orsay. Shifting into third, she gave the pedal a little muscle and the Renault took off like a jackrabbit.

'You're sure you're all right?' she asked, her concern looking a lot like aggravation. She didn't want Chapel slowing her down. 'For a moment back there, you looked like you might keel over.'

'My shoulder was burned pretty badly. I just have to take care when I move it.'

'Maybe you should have stayed in the hospital.'

Chapel looked at her sharply, but kept quiet. *And do what?* he wanted to ask her. *Let someone else go after Taleel. Cede the promise he'd made to his murdered friends to someone they didn't know. Someone who couldn't possibly care about nailing their killer as much as he did. Someone who wasn't as good at his job.*

'No way,' he said finally, and sat up straighter to show her that he was okay, that she didn't have to worry about him, even if it did cause his shoulder to hurt like a sonuvabitch.

They were approaching the cathedral of Notre-Dame. Isolated in its own medieval fief between the left and right banks on the Ile de la Cité, its blunt towers resisted the summer's charm, standing gray, stern, and stoic. Someone had come up with the idea of making the Seine into an urban beach. Parasols and lounge chairs lined the concrete walk bordering the river. A sand volleyball court had been set up and two teams played fiercely in front of a bikini-clad throng. A cheer erupted, and its bubbly frivolity lent the day a sense of unreality.

'So you're the money man?' she asked, without taking her eyes from the road.

'Is that what Admiral Glendenning told you?'

'You don't call him "Glen," like everybody else? An American who prefers formality? I don't know if I should believe you.' She laughed sarcastically, then said, 'You're an accountant, is that right?'

'That's right. I was at Price Waterhouse.'

'Long time?'

'Six years.'

'How far did you climb?'

Chapel looked at her out of the corner of his eye, not liking the questions, the feeling that she was checking for any inadequacies. 'Partner.'

'Impossible!' she cried, and her surprise almost made the years of misplaced effort worthwhile. 'You must have worked yourself to the bone. I know, you see. My oldest brother works in the City for one of the snootier investment banks. He's a partner too, from what I understand. I haven't heard from him in ages, except for his dreadful Christmas cards. Sends them unsigned. It's his wife I feel sorry for: three children and no daddy, to speak of. She makes do with the paycheck, I suppose. He makes loads of money. Practically prints it, I hear. Then again, you can't cuddle a pound note, can you? Oh well, we all choose our sacrifices. Still, I am impressed, Mr Chapel. And now you've gone and traded one eighteen-hour-a-day job for another. Pity about the cut in pay.'

'No pity at all, actually,' said Chapel. 'Money—'

'Next thing, you'll have me believe you're a patriot.'

When did that become a four-letter word? 'And you?'

'Me? Oh, I do it for the travel ops. You know: Voyage to faraway places, meet exotic people, and—'

'And kill them.' Chapel finished it for her, remembering the old bumper sticker that had popped up after the Vietnam War.

'Actually, I just talk to them, try to get them to see things our way, turn them to our side. I like to think I'm a sane advocate of my country's foreign policy.'

'And a patriot?'

Sarah took a moment to answer. 'Once in a while,' she said slowly, deliberately, as if he'd seen a side of her she didn't like. 'And how are things going at FTAT? That's who you're with, right? Foreign Terrorist something-or-other?'

'It's a mouthful,' said Chapel.

'Well,' she said, after a second. 'Go on, then.'

'We had some big wins up front: a few major league money-transfer agents and *hawalas;* some charities ostensibly set up to send money to the Middle East for schools, food, medical care. All told, we froze around a hundred million in assets in those first eighteen months.'

'A hundred million's not bad.'

'It is and it isn't. People always talk about how it only cost the hijackers five hundred thousand dollars to mount the operation that resulted in nine-eleven. That might be true, but it takes millions to finance the system that bred those guys. The schools, the camps, the propaganda machines they've got turning twenty-four hours a day. Some of the bigger *madrasas* need a hundred grand a year to keep their doors open. And there are hundreds of those schools in Pakistan alone.'

'Expensive to brainwash an entire generation, isn't it?'

'What gets me is that when we get inside these organizations and look at their books, we see that a lot of the money – and I'm talking five, ten million dollars – was going to medical supplies, relief funds, to building a hospital here and there. Legitimate works. But the rest was going to the Hamas regional security office or to the Al-Aqsa Martyrs Brigades to buy TNT for suicide bombers or AK-47s for the next generation of *jihadis*. You have no choice but to freeze it all.'

She was looking at him strangely, her head cocked, eyes scrunched up, a determined set to her lips. She was the cat who'd cornered the mouse and was deciding whether to eat it.

'What?' he asked.

'Why, Mr Chapel, it sounds like you have a conscience.'

'So? That against the law these days?'

'It is in this profession.'

The car was fitted out for undercover work, equipped with a two-way radio, a Heckler and Koch 'street sweeper' twenty-gauge racked beneath Adam's seat, and a dashboard siren hidden inside the glove compartment. Sarah drove confidently, with attention and foresight, as if driving were her job and she was determined to be good at it. She barely took her eyes from the road, and Chapel used her bouts of sustained concentration as an excuse to take a good look at her. In the harsh sunlight, lines of wear spread from her eyes and her mouth, hinting at an inner tension. She was wound tight. Her cool and confident act didn't fool him a bit. He could see it in the way she sat, too – back barely touching the seat, jaw jutting a half inch too far forward, eyes nailed in front of her. When she'd spoken at the embassy, her voice wasn't just crisp, it was near military in its inflection. Even in the car, her hand movements belonged to a general delivering a briefing to his commanders. But a while ago, she'd asked him what he did for fun, and when he said train for marathons, she'd burst out laughing. With a supple hand, she'd freed her ponytail and stared at him, for the first time really looking at him, and her eyes had come alive with mischief and merriment and all the qualities she was not allowed to exhibit as an officer of British intelligence.

Only now did he realize that her manner was designed to camouflage what she'd learned to be a professional liability. She was a natural beauty, and she knew, as Chapel had seen firsthand in the business world, that beauty was not equated with smarts, savvy, or any of the positive traits she needed to get ahead in her profession. More than anything, she was competitive, and her diligently veiled ambition frightened him.

'And you?' he asked. 'How'd you get him? I mean Sayeed. Or am I allowed to ask?'

Sarah considered his request. 'A bit like how you get your bad guys, I suppose. Looked at where the money was going. Problem is, though, in Afghanistan there isn't any banking system, I mean not like how we know it. It's still nineteenth century over there – paper ledgers, doing sums on an abacus, the whole works. Audit trails may not lie, but what if there's no trail to begin with. So you ask questions. You rely on people, even if they are deceitful and untruthful. When you've got to find someone in a hurry, I'd take a live source anytime.'

Chapel knew a lecture when he heard it. 'And who was yours?'

'Who wasn't?' she replied, like he'd asked a dumb question. 'Information's the national currency over there. No one's got any money, but everyone's got just the story you want to hear. In this case, we came across some reliable information that a lot of field workers were heading to Jalalabad to help harvest poppies for a foreigner, an Arab-Afghan like bin Laden. When ninety-nine percent of the population is destitute, someone who's throwing money around like confetti sticks out like a sore thumb. Then we got lucky. We learned about a Pakistani banker, a former big shot with BCCI, in from South America who was heading to the same area. He couldn't pass through town without letting his old buddies know that he was up to something big. He insulted a lot of Qaeda fighters, calling them ill-focused. I heard that he used the word "scattershot" twice, and called their attacks pointless.'

'How did you know he was hooked into Hijira?'

'We tracked him to Sayeed's village in Jalalabad. No coincidences, Mr Chapel. Not in this game.'

'Did you pull him in?'

Sarah shook her head and he could see the muscles working in her jaw, a tightening around the eyes. 'We lost him at night,' she said with palpable disgust. 'Place is like a sieve.'

Bringing the car to a halt at a red light, she thudded a hand against the steering wheel. 'Anyway, that's where we stand. Hijira's about money. About focus. Of course, we've learned something new. They won't let themselves be captured alive.' She looked at him, and when she spoke, her voice had dropped a note and was stripped clean of artifice. 'Tell me, Mr Chapel, what are they planning that they'd rather die than tell us?'

Chapter 16

It was a King's fortune. Two hundred and seventy-one million four hundred and fifty-nine thousand dollars and three cents. He had sold his last share of stock, covered his last call, closed out his last option. For the first time in two decades his portfolios stood empty. The three screens on his desk broadcasting real-time account information blinked like a barren New Age triptych. For a few minutes anyway, the sum total of twenty years' obsessive effort rested in his cash account. Every last cent.

Marc Gabriel stared at the numbers, feeling nothing: not contentment, not pride, not avarice. Long ago, he'd acquired the professional trader's ice-cold objectivity. If anything, he relished the coming challenge, and the warrior's daring flared in his eyes. Money was the ultimate weapon. Everything had been a prelude to this moment.

Two hundred and seventy-one million dollars.

He could have used it to buy a yacht in Antibes, a two-hundred-foot Suncruiser with a helicopter deck aft and a crew of ten. He could have purchased a *finca* in Ibiza, a chalet in Zermatt, and an estate near Chenonceau, and had enough left over for lavish parties, the finest clothing, a lifetime of waste. Gabriel wanted none of it. He owned something far more valuable already. A cause.

Pushing aside his *pain baignat*, he slipped his earpiece

into place and murmured to himself, 'Two seventy. Let's see what we can do with it.

'*Gruezi*, Heini,' he said to his banker in Zurich, his Swiss-German dialect nearly perfect. 'New strategy. Don't be shocked and don't ask why. Richemond is going short big-time. Got a pencil? Short ten thousand IBM, ten thousand 3M, ten thousand Merck, ten thousand Microsoft . . .' he went on, listing the industrial stalwarts of the United States before traveling round the globe to visit his dooms-day doctrine on Britain, France, Germany, Japan, and Hong Kong. In every country he picked only the most heavily traded issues. He shorted consumer goods, electronics, drugs, and paper products; financials, insurance, entertainment, and lodging. He avoided only one sector: defense.

When he finished with Zurich, he called Madrid, and did it again. And when he was finished with Madrid, he called Dublin, Frankfurt, Mexico City, and Johannesburg.

'We're shorting this market,' he said, over and over again, but when pressed, offered no explanation for his pessimistic view, other than to say that prices were 'overvalued.'

To 'go short' meant to sell a stock you didn't own in hopes its share price would decrease and you could buy it back at a lower level. The idea was to sell at a hundred, wait for bad news to drive the price down, then buy it back at fifty, giving yourself a fifty-dollar gain. Shorting was just buying and selling in reverse.

It wasn't quite that simple. Officially, you had to borrow the stock. If the stock's price increased – if it 'moved against you' – you could be forced to buy it back from the true owner at the higher price. (But only if he wanted to sell it then and there, and if there were no other shares for sale that could be substituted.) Dividends were also your responsibility and were debited to your account. These were technicalities, however. What mattered in the end was that, even if you didn't officially own the stock, you got to keep the proceeds of the sale.

Mostly, you needed three things to short a stock. Balls, good credit, and information. It was up to the trader to supply the first. Brokerage houses were generous in extending the second. Financial firms were as greedy as any other for-profit business in the Western world, and they liked to give their customers ample rope with which to hang themselves. A good client like Marc Gabriel with his Richemond Holdings was allowed to sell a hundred dollars of stock for every twenty-five dollars he kept in his account. A margin ratio of twenty-five percent. As for information, Gabriel didn't have any nasty secrets about any one particular company hidden up his sleeve. No news about a pending lawsuit, a deal gone sour, or a failed technology. He was privy to a more violent brand of information. News that would adversely impact every stock in every market around the world.

An hour after he'd begun, the screens buzzed with life and showed his accounts to be valued at just over one billion dollars.

Nine zeroes.

Gabriel steepled his fingers thoughtfully.

He had begun in 1980, a twenty-one-year-old neophyte out of the London School of Economics with a degree in finance, a convert's zeal, and a kitty of four million dollars, equal parts his father's pension and donations from like-minded friends. He almost lost it all several times, and the recollection of those early white-knuckle trades, the endless weekends with open, unhedged positions, the sleepless nights with bankruptcy looming overhead, was enough to bring on a nervous sweat.

Then came the nineties, a ten-year bull run in the West and the destruction of the Nikkei in the East. He bet big with Soros against the pound, and rode the back of the Japanese market all the way down on its suicide leap from 36,000 to a quarter that level. Meanwhile, he'd bought IBM at 50 and sold at a split-adjusted 200.

The boom in Internet stocks was the capper, and to his pious eye, all the indication he needed that God was on his side. Yahoo, Netscape, Inktomi, and Akamai. He rode them up, up, up. If his analyst's eye told him the stocks were overvalued, his trader's logic steadied him. 'The trend is your friend' was the rule of the day, and he followed it as devoutly as he did his religion. He also knew the meaning of a 'stop/loss,' and when to use it.

Along the way there were other deals, ventures into businesses legitimate and otherwise. Inteltech in Paraguay. Gropius Gems in Nigeria. The Allen Victor Metal company in Kazakhstan. He had vowed never to tamper with his capital, and the steady revenues generated by ongoing concerns were necessary for other more interesting sidelines.

Finished with the calls, Gabriel walked to the kitchenette and poured coffee into a chipped porcelain cup. As he sipped the strong dessert brew, he lit a cigarette and stared at the blinking screens, at the scuffed briefcase sitting next to the desk, and at the rest of his abandoned office. Drawers yawned from the polished teak filing cabinets. Gilt-framed oils stared down from paneled walls. Most were still-lifes, sterile depictions of fruit, fowl, and fish purposely chosen to reveal nothing of his tastes or background. They would stay. He hated them, anyway. Photographs of smiling children, a lovely blonde wife, and a pair of Yorkshire terriers, adorned the credenza and a visitor's coffee table. They would stay, too. The subjects were complete strangers. He didn't know one of them. Except the dogs.

Setting down his coffee, he walked to the printer next to

his desk and snatched a sheaf of paper. The top page showed the layout of a building. He skipped past the first floor, the second floor – ah, here it was – he slipped the page showing the third floor on top, and took a seat. Running a nail across the page, he quickly located the burn unit. Consulting his notes from an earlier conversation, he jotted down a few names, then added the most crucial information: Room 310. 10 A.M.

He shook his head, a little bewildered at the speed of events.

It was all moving so fast now.

The phone had rung at four-thirty that morning. Gabriel had been awake, showered and dressed in business attire, seated in his private study at his home in the leafy, upmarket quartier of Neuilly. He was listening to the BBC World Service broadcast news of the death of one Abu Sayeed, a high-level member of Hijira, a heretofore unknown Islamic extremist group. He was wondering who had tipped off the Americans.

'Yes,' he answered.

'I shall be arriving in Paris, the day after tomorrow. Sometime in the afternoon. Do you have the cash?'

Gabriel winced at the hard Israeli accent. 'Of course. Do you have the package?'

'I do.'

Gabriel swallowed. The world had begun to spin on a new axis. 'Do you need a place to stay while you're here? I can arrange something.'

'I'm quite capable myself, thank you.'

'Shall we set a time to get together?'

'That would be impractical.'

A baby's cry broke the morning still. Gabriel turned his head towards the noise. It would be Fayez, his seventh son, just a few weeks old. Suddenly, he wanted very badly to sit with his wife in the darkness and watch as she nursed the boy.

'I will contact you in forty-eight hours,' said the caller. 'If you do not hear from me, presume I've been taken. I am not a brave man. I will talk. I do not know your true name, but you may wish to take precautions.'

'Good luck,' said Gabriel, hanging up.

The professor was on his way.

It was five o'clock. Gabriel had one last item to take care of. He sat at his desk, a commander of one. His eyes fell to his notepad. The name 'Gregorio' was circled crazily, reflecting his own frustration. He picked up the phone and dialed the ten-digit number. A cheerful, Spanish-speaking woman answered. 'Inteltech, *buenos días.*'

'*Buenos días,* Gloria,' said Gabriel, his own Spanish very good, but not fluent. 'I would like to speak to Senor Gregorio, if you would be so kind.'

'Senor Gregorio is not in—'

'Gloria,' Gabriel cut in, steel in his voice. 'Pass me to Senor Gregorio. Immediately.'

'*Si, Jefe.*'

The faint hum of Latin Muzak tickled his ear and he wondered why no one thought of broadcasting something uplifting instead of this insipid fare. A minute passed, and to his horror he discovered he was humming the tune. Disgusted, he bit his lip. It was insidious. The rot was everywhere. Even in a backwater like Ciudad del Este.

'Gregorio speaking.'

Marc Gabriel hunched forward and spoke. 'Ah, I'm happy to have caught you, Pedro. There's been a small misunderstanding.'

'Hello, Marc. A misunderstanding? What in heaven's name are you talking about?'

'I am talking about the sum of twelve million dollars. The

sum that you had promised to wire to our partner's account last week. I'm certain it's an oversight.'

With annual revenues of nearly seventy million dollars, Inteltech was a leader in the sales and distribution of over-the-counter software to the rapidly growing markets of Southeast Asia, South America, and Eastern Europe. Last year, the company had shipped more than one million copies of Microsoft Office, Lotus Development, and Corel WordPerfect. It was a lovely business. Gross margins of eighty percent. No marketing costs. No advertising expenses. After the cost of goods sold, the largest below-the-line item constituted 'official gratuities,' which Gabriel knew better as bribes to government officials. Every last copy Inteltech sold was a pirated, or 'bootleg,' edition reproduced with the company's proprietary counterfeiting technology. Richemond's ninety percent stake in the company accounted for one of the holding's largest investments.

'An oversight on the bank's behalf,' said Gregorio. 'I can tell you I was on the phone screaming bloody murder. It's terrible here. You have no idea. They have a completely different conception of time.'

'I can imagine,' said Gabriel agreeably, as he toyed with his letter opener. It was Gregorio who was the problem, however. Gregorio, who had an excuse for every occasion. Gregorio, who'd honed his lying skills as an executive at BCCI, the Bank of Credit and Commerce International, the Pakistani financial institution whose spectacular flameout in the early nineties had earned it the moniker the 'Bank of Crooks and Criminals Indicted.'

Gabriel continued, 'Be that as it may, your primary responsibility is to see that our funds are transfered as directed.'

'Apologies, *Jefe*. I will call the bank immediately and see that it is carried out as soon as possible.'

'Not as soon as possible,' said Gabriel, pressing the point of the opener into his leg. 'Now. This very instant. We no longer have use for this enterprise. Our energies are required at home. Your travel documents are in order?'

Again, Gregorio said yes.

'Very good. Go in peace.'

As Gabriel hung up, he could not ignore his lingering suspicions. 'Senor Gregorio' could not be trusted. He'd been too long in the jungle, too long away from his people. The rot had consumed him.

Gabriel stood, adjusting his cuffs, tightening the knot of his tie, counting the days until he could be rid of the constricting clothing. The twelve million dollars was necessary, a crucial component to the lie. It must come from South America. It took him only a few moments to decide.

The professor was due in forty-eight hours.

There was time.

Before going home, he booked a flight for that evening to Buenos Aires with onward connections to Fozdo Iguaçu, returning the next day, then reserved a motorbike, something nimble to negotiate the knotted traffic.

As he walked along the Rue Kleber, passing from the shade of one elm to the next, he carried the briefcase casually, letting it bang against his leg. A stiff wind had come up, and women were fighting to keep their dresses down and their hair in place. He checked the sky. Dark clouds were on the march from the north. Almost unconsciously, he checked over his shoulder. He saw nothing. It was Sayeed that was bothering him. Had he talked before dying? When had his death actually taken place? Facts were still sketchy. Gabriel had too few people on the ground, and news reports were unreliable.

He whistled a tune to distract himself. It took him a moment to recognize it as the same unpleasant ditty he'd heard while on hold to Gregorio. He stopped. Fishing in his jacket, he found his sunglasses and put them on. Hidden behind the mirrored lenses, no one could see the worry in his eyes.

Chapter 17

To be alone was to stand out.

To be alone was to be vulnerable.

To be alone was to be a target.

He had left Athens an hour ago. The bustling, chaotic city lay behind him like the memory of a warm bed. The coast highway had narrowed to two lanes. He followed its undulant, graceful curves halfway up a steep mountainside. Whitewashed villages crouched among copses of pine and thistle to his left. The endless expanse of the Aegean spread to his right. The water was coursing with activity, ferries, tugs, and fishing boats scratching white trails across the azure surface. The bigger vessels, the cruise liners packed with sun-starved tourists, the supertankers that belonged to the scions of Onassis and Niarchos, the mile-long cargo ships loaded with the Orient's bounty of cars, televisions, stereos, and computers, had docked at Piraeus. He was patrolling the old Greece, the territory of the partisans, the hills of Pan and Apollo, and the invasion route of the Huns.

For the moment, he saw no other cars on the highway. His rearview yawned empty. The road ahead beckoned, an untrammeled pathway to a glorious future. At the wheel of his sparkling gold BMW 750iL, he was just another transnational tourist traveling Europe's unmatched highways.

He drove the speed limit – no slower, no faster – though the muscular automobile begged to be given its reins, like a racehorse on an early morning run.

By now, the efforts to track him would have gathered a critical mass. He was sure they'd worked up a good story, something urgent, but hardly an emergency. Something along the lines of a Palestinian spy who'd escaped with some marginally important data about troop strength on the West Bank. They'd confine their inquiries to the local level. They liked to work quietly and would not wish to attract undue attention. If they contacted the state police, if the whole affair went federal, it would be only a matter of hours until the Americans started asking questions.

America: *the world's policeman.*

Mordecai Kahn allowed himself a rare smile, a raspy, mean-spirited laugh.

There was no way the Americans could be allowed to know. Not about this.

The Unit would be in charge. They always got the messy stuff: the operations that were either too politically sensitive or too difficult to execute for anybody else. Their official name was Unit 269 of the Sayeret *Matkal*, or the general reconnaissance staff. They'd made their name at Entebbe and in Beirut. Their history was colored with the blood of their adversaries, rarely their own.

By now, they'd questioned his wife, searched his offices at school and the lab, grilled his coworkers, his secretaries, his teaching assistants. They'd braced the base security officer, Colonel Ephraim Bar-Gera, with a view towards how a theft of this magnitude could occur. There'd be no general's stars for Ephraim. They'd checked and double-checked their sensors. They'd changed the codes. They'd convinced themselves it would never happen again.

But Kahn was by nature a cautious man, if not made paranoid by his work. He had no intention of being caught, or in fact, ever heard from again. He had taken care to modify his appearance. His skin was darker by three shades. His hair was dyed an inoffensive brown and his beard shaved off altogether. He wore a businessman's natty suit and had even remembered to snip the stitching holding his jacket pockets closed. He was nothing if not detail-oriented. He liked the horn-rimmed glasses best: Alain Mikli of Paris, slim, stylish, sophisticated. Either they took ten years off his age or they made him look like a queer clerk, he wasn't sure which. He was only sure that he looked nothing like Dr Mordecai Kahn, of late distinguished Professor of Physics at David Ben-Gurion University, director of Quantum Research at Haaretz National Laboratories, and consultant to certain unnamed divisions in the Israeli Defense Force, too secret to mention, if, in fact, they even existed. The camouflage was complete down to the lifts in his Bruno Magli loafers.

While part of his mind occupied itself with the chore of driving, another spent its time constructing his pursuer's investigation. His altered appearance would only go so far to shield him. The men seeking him out were determined and crafty. He did not know all their secrets.

He was certain that by now they had found the abandoned skiff and tracked his presence aboard the ferry to Cyprus. They would have had a harder time figuring which boat he'd taken from Larnaca, but through persistence, and maybe a break here and there, they would have learned that he'd boarded the tramp steamer *Eleni* bound for Athens. The locus of possible destinations multiplied at each point. And from Athens where? By train to Berlin? Budapest? By bus to Sofia? Another ferry to Crete or Italy? At each spot, the possibilities multiplied, the matrices grew more complex.

They knew only that with the package he could not fly.

The infinite array of his choices comforted him. If he kept to plan, if he followed the groundwork he had meticulously laid these last six months, he would be invisible. They would not catch him. The numbers did not permit it. Europe was too large a place, and the Unit too poorly staffed.

Yet, even as he drove, he could not rid his mind of the suspicion that somewhere or someplace during his rigorous preparation, he'd slipped up. He'd left a clue. It was a fear that kept him checking the rearview mirror when he should be looking ahead, the fear that had kept him awake all night on the rough transit to Athens, the fear that even now, traveling at 100 kilometers an hour on a sunny summer day, laid a track of goose bumps along his arms.

He would be safe once he reached Vienna. It was a twenty-hour drive through the underbelly of Europe – Bulgaria, Hungary, Yugoslavia. Across isolated roads and deserted countryside.

Until then he was alone.

He was vulnerable.

He was a target.

Chapter 18

It had been years since Adam Chapel had sat in one of the plush conference rooms where bankers and accountants met their moneyed customers, but with the rush of familiarity it provoked in him, the recognition of the de rigueur symbols of wealth and privilege, it might have been a day. Velvet drapes framed the windows; the lace inner curtains remained drawn, allowing daylight to enter, while rendering the heart-stopping view over the city a blur. A subdued, but nonetheless magnificent, Persian rug covered a shopworn carpet. Prints of gentlemen riding to hounds decorated the walls. The only furniture was an antique mahogany conference table with clawed feet and the four Louis XV chairs surrounding it. Looking around, he remembered the pride he'd felt meeting with his clients. It was a child's excitement of dining at the grown-ups' table, the worker's pride at gaining admittance into an elite club.

The door opened and a female executive entered, carrying a single accordion file. Petite, tight-lipped, wan brown hair pulled into a severe bun, she marched up to Adam and Sarah, offering each a single, deliberate shake of the hand. 'Good day. My name is Marie-Josée Puidoux. I am the bank's compliance officer. I have with me all the bank's records for the account in question. Naturally, we at BLP deplore terrorism and violence in all forms. We had no idea that Mr

Roux, as he called himself, was anything but a customer in good standing.'

The bank had expressed no qualms about turning over the private banking records of one of its clients without the proper court documents. The man was dead. He was a terrorist. Most important, in return for the bank's immediate and unconstrained cooperation, the French government had promised absolute silence about their dealings with the man.

'Naturally,' said Chapel. 'We're appreciative of your assistance. I'm sure it won't take long.'

Madame Puidoux set the file on the table. 'If there's anything else?'

'One thing,' he said. 'We recently came into possession of Mr Roux's driver's license number. Would it be possible to run a search of your bank accounts to see if any list that, or Roux's address or phone number, on the opening documents?'

'Of course,' the bank executive answered. 'If you'll provide me with the number, I'll see that it is taken care of right away.'

With a curt smile, she withdrew from the room.

Chapel began to stretch his arm across the table, then thinking better of it, sank back into his chair. 'Sarah, could you?'

Grasping the file, she untied the clasp, and removed a sheaf of papers the width of her thumb from inside. 'Not a lot for two years,' she commented, passing the papers to her right.

'We don't need a lot. We only need a mistake.'

The statements were in reverse chronological order, the most recent ones on top. Chapel threw his gaze around the room, drawing breath like a sprinter settling in the blocks. He had the same anxiety, too. The butterflies in his stomach. The quivering tension in his legs. This was the beginning. How they proceeded, the entire course of the investigation, would be determined by what they found in Taleel's account.

'Okay,' he said, selecting the uppermost page. 'Here we go. July of this year. Beginning account balance: one thousand five hundred euros – about the equivalent value in US dollars. Cash deposit via ATM on the first of July of five thousand euros. Next day he writes the check to Azema for fifteen hundred.' He dragged a nail down the page. 'Check clears on the eighth. What else? ATM, ATM, ATM. Withdraw seven hundred euros. Again seven hundred.' His eyes ran up and down the summary. 'Looks like every five days Mr Taleel helps himself to seven hundred euros. Probably his daily limit. A total of five withdrawals for three thousand five hundred euros. Ending balance, Miss Churchill?'

'Fifteen hundred euros.'

'Like clockwork.' Chapel raised his eyes to hers. 'Pros. No messing around. Next month, please.' He read from the top again. 'June. Beginning balance: fifteen hundred euros. Cash deposit via ATM on the first of the month of five thousand euros –' here he stopped. 'Sarah, ask Mrs Puidoux for a map of the city and a list of all the bank's ATMs. And see if it's possible to find out what time Taleel made the withdrawals.'

Sarah stepped from the room as Chapel recommenced his examination of the statements. Each month's statement read the same as the last. The initial cash deposit, the single check written on the account, the five cash withdrawals, each for seven hundred euros. The guy was a machine.

'She'll bring up a map in a few minutes,' Sarah said when she returned. 'We're to write down each ATM's unit number and she'll provide us with its address. She's getting on to records about the time of his withdrawals, but she doubts they'll have anything further back than a year. Anything new?'

'Nada. Here, take these.' Chapel handed her a dozen statements. 'Let me know if you see anything out of the ordinary. God forbid our man actually wrote two checks in one month, or better yet, received a wire transfer from somewhere.'

'He's good, isn't he?' It was a lament.

'Never steps into a branch. Lives on cash. Entirely self-contained. The trail begins and ends with the account. What did Ricard say? He's perfect.'

'The invisible client.'

Chapel's eyes flared, and as if challenged, he spun to face her. 'No one is invisible.'

Thirty minutes later they'd finished running through Taleel's statements. In twenty-four months, he'd varied from practice exactly twice. In March of the preceding year, instead of waiting five days between cash withdrawals, he'd hurried up and taken out the thirty-five hundred over five consecutive days at the beginning of the month. Sarah suggested he'd gone out of town and a surrogate was making the withdrawals for him. Neither of them, however, was ready to hazard a guess as to what the money was for. Carefully, Chapel noted the ATM codes for the March withdrawals.

The second exception was more recent. A month earlier he'd made two withdrawals for a thousand euros each.

If there was to be a surprise, he had hoped to find it on Taleel's initial account statement. If the opening deposit had been made via wire transfer, it would allow Chapel to see where the money had come from. A glimpse behind the curtain. From there he could establish a trail from bank to bank – a golden thread, as it were. Again, he was disappointed. The opening deposit was made via an over-the-counter money order, an anonymous instrument that paid the bearer. Worse, it was bank policy to discard hard copy records of checks after two years. The physical evidence of the money order had been destroyed thirty days earlier.

'Pretty paltry living allowance,' he scoffed as he gathered up the statements and slid them into the file. 'Five grand a month minus fifteen hundred for rent. Thirty-five hundred bucks in the big city doesn't take you far. It's hardly enough to keep your clothes cleaned and pressed.' Earlier in the week, he'd discovered that the cost for dry-cleaning a suit ran to twenty dollars. Shirts cost three dollars a pop, and slacks five. 'It certainly isn't enough for hundred-dollar manicures. No sir. I don't buy it. Not at all enough do-re-mi for Mr Eighteen Carat Rolex Daytona.'

Yet, he wasn't half so disappointed as his tone indicated. He hadn't expected Taleel to leave a clue behind. His quarry was better than that. In a strange fashion, he was pleased by Taleel's discipline. It was important that his friends hadn't been killed by a dime-store Charlie with his shoes untied. At the same time, he was beginning to get a feel for him, for his organization. Often, you learned more about somebody by what they *didn't do*.

'It's not his spending money,' declared Sarah. 'I'd wager that the withdrawals represent his operational expenses. The funding he receives to keep the cell running. He's following a schedule, making his meets, handing over their allowance.'

Cells, operatives, meets. The words belonged to Sarah's lexicon, not Chapel's. 'Maybe,' he said. 'From my end, it doesn't really matter. It all spells out the same conclusion. He's got to have access to more money. That means he's got to have other accounts in the city.'

The map lay sprawled across the table, an army of red, green, and blue dots indicating the locations of the ATMs Taleel had frequented. The green dots showed where Taleel deposited his monthly allowance. The blue dots where he made his withdrawals. And the red dots, of which there were only five, where he withdrew the money in the one aberrant month of March, a year earlier. While the blue dots (withdrawals) were scattered over the entire Parisian cityscape, the green dots (deposits) were bunched much more closely together – twenty within the sixteenth and seventeenth arrondissements, the area just north and west of the Arc de Triomphe; the remaining four near the Cité Universitaire, far to the west.

The five red dots showing where Taleel, or as Sarah suspected, his surrogate, had used the ATM were clumped more closely again, all of them within a ten-block radius inside the sixteenth arrondissement. One of the machines had been used not only to make deposits, but on three occasions prior to that March, to make withdrawals.

To Chapel's eye, it was a homing beacon.

There was a last piece of information to map. With a nail, Chapel flicked the top off a black felt-tipped pen and colored a dot at the corner of Rue Saint-Paul and Boulevard Victor Hugo, the Neuilly branch of the BLP – smack dab in the middle of that same ten-block radius in the sixteenth arrondissement – where on June 29, two years earlier, Mohammed al-Taleel, aka Bertrand Roux, had opened his account. Leaning over the table, Chapel drew a circle around all the dots in the sixteenth.

'Whoever was paying Taleel either lives or works somewhere inside that circle,' he said. 'And whoever that person is, he's the same guy who made the deposits a year ago March.'

'Why put cash into an account if you're only going to take it out a few days later?' Sarah had left her chair and taken up position directly next to Chapel, so that their bodies touched and he could smell her scent. No perfume, she wasn't the type, but he couldn't mistake the tart sniff of French milled soap and the hint of vanilla that drifted from her hair. Or miss the faint scar tracing the periphery of her eye. She'd lost some battles, too.

'Don't know yet,' he said. 'But there's a reason, you can count on it.'

Laying a hand on his shoulder for balance, she bent closer to the map. Her sleeveless T-shirt draped loosely from her chest, allowing him a glance at one full, perfect breast. He tried to look away, but he hadn't slept with a woman in a year. His eyes lingered, and he was unable to suppress the electric sexual current that warmed his body.

'Neuilly. That's where he lives, huh?' said Sarah. 'It's a nice part of town. One of the ritziest, actually. Can't you just see it? Taleel picks up his allowance. It's burning a hole in his pocket, so he deposits his loot as quickly as he can. One month he walks north eight blocks. The next, east. Then, west. He thinks he's being a clever boots. You need time and a bird's-eye view to discern the pattern.' Standing straight, she sighed with frustration. 'Now all we have to do is find every family of Middle Eastern extraction in Neuilly, bring them in for a quick once-over. Even if it were legal, it wouldn't be feasible.'

As Sarah finished her words, the door quietly opened. Entering the client room with a martial stride, Madame Puidoux handed Chapel a single paper. 'I'm afraid we show no accounts with the details you provided. However, we were able to come up with the times Mr Roux used the ATMs. Only for a year, but I hope you will agree that it is better than nothing. Go ahead. Look.' She waited, her shoulders pinned back, her chin held at attention, not so much a victorious smile etched on her face as an arrogant smirk, which in France probably qualified as the same thing.

Scanning the paper, he was pleased to find a listing of the exact times that Taleel had visited the automatic teller machines during the preceding twelve months. A pattern was immediately discernible.

'He made his deposits in the afternoons between and five and six,' said Chapel. 'And his withdrawals in the morning between seven and eight. Both are peak traffic periods. People mostly use ATMs on their way to work and on their way home. Looks like Taleel had a nine-to-five job.'

Again, however, Taleel's record was imperfect. Chapel pointed to the notation citing a withdrawal of a thousand euros at two A.M. on the thirteenth of June of that year. 'Madame Puidoux, can you tell me where this ATM is located?'

'La Goutte d'Or. Near Montmartre.'

'And this one?' The second of the thousand euro withdrawals.

'Also in Les Gouttes d'Or.'

Chapel knew the name vaguely as a haven for money-transmitting businesses. '*Hawala* heaven,' Babtiste had called it.

'Hardly the kind of place I'd want to be caught at two in the morning,' commented Sarah. 'It's a working-class area, mostly West Africans and Arabs. A lot of garment shops, jewelry stores. Head there at noon, it's like walking around downtown Lagos.'

Chapel massaged his temple. 'Lagos,' he said. 'Two of our guys were killed there in June. It was a diamond buy. We still have no idea what exactly happened.'

'We know this: The orders came from here.'

'So this is where they're based,' he said.

'It appears so.'

'No coincidences?'

'No coincidences, Adam. Not in this game.' She was staring at him and her gaze was forceful and inquiring. Was she challenging him? Appraising him? For a crazy moment, he thought she was seducing him, but then he knew it was himself, his own weakness.

Thanks were given. Documents collected. A few minutes later, he and Sarah were standing on the curb, surveying the parking lot that was Paris traffic at rush hour. They walked to the end of the street. In both directions, cars lolled in endless rows, bumper-to-bumper, engines conjoined in a miserable rumble, exhaust rising in the narrow urban canyons and forming a mustard-tinted cloud.

'It's like they saw us coming a mile away and covered their tracks,' said Sarah when they'd reached their car.

'What did you expect to find? A neon sign pointing the way to his accounts?'

'Call me an optimist, but I wouldn't have minded one nine-digit account number at a bona fide banking institution on any one of seven continents. At least we'd have a trail to follow.'

But instead of being put off, Chapel found himself seized by a prickly anticipation. He was basking in the glow of unfettered access to a suspect's banking records. He could forget the rigamarole of subpoenas and writs, the constant wrangling with magistrates and judges. He could kiss the dreaded MLAT good-bye – the Mutual Lateral Assistance Treaty used to request information from a friendly government under which responses never, ever came back in less than ten days, and in most cases three times that long. Not only had the French government promised their cooperation, they were delivering.

'We know Taleel was making weekly payments to someone,' he said, 'most probably the other members of his cell. We have a map of the ATMs he was using. You said there were between six and eight principal members of Hijira.'

'Of whom two are dead.'

'Maybe so, but someone picked up the money from Royal Joailliers. I'm betting it was the person who was sharing Taleel's apartment. Damn it, Sarah, someone was watching TV before he came in. Tell Leclerc to have his boys set up round-the-clock surveillance on the ATMs inside that circle and to put a man here at the bank. If anyone tries to access those accounts, we'll know in real time. We can take him down.'

'Do you really think so? They're smarter than that. Smart enough to figure out that your jump team was on to them. If they can outwit you, they certainly aren't going to access a compromised account. That would be tantamount to turning themselves in.'

'Look,' he went on. 'They're here, Sarah. They're operating in this city. We can hazard a guess that their paymaster's holed up somewhere in Neuilly, and that the guy's a wee bit complacent.'

'He sure as hell isn't going to be complacent anymore. Not after losing two of his lieutenants and learning that the CIA had practically crawled up his posterior and infiltrated his organization. No, Adam, he will not be the least bit complacent.'

'Even so,' Chapel went on, 'Taleel had to have opened more than one account in Paris. Ask me, I'd say he was working at least ten accounts at ten different banks. Maybe more. There's no way he had ten aliases, ten different addresses, and ten driver's licenses. I've never seen it. We've got the guy's address, his driver's license, his home phone. Somewhere he's left behind his mark.'

'He knew better than that.'

'I'm betting otherwise.'

'And then?' Sarah threw her arms up, exasperated. 'All this information about his moving money from place will take us only so far without someone to tell us why he's doing it. We need flesh and blood, Adam. Someone to lean on. The numbers are fine for establishing a pattern of behavior, maybe even to construct a predictive model. But we're past that. We're into the endgame. They've made the tape. They're not planning any longer. They're doing.'

'People lie,' said Chapel. 'They deceive, they mislead. I'd take numbers any day.'

'Then you're a fool.'

The words stung more than a slap across the face. 'I'll prove you wrong.'

Sarah hid her disbelief poorly. Playing toss with the car keys, she shot him a loser's glance. 'What odds are you offering?'

'Odds?' He nodded towards the sea of traffic a block away. ''Bout the same that you can find a way around this mess and get us to the Finance Ministry in, say, an hour.'

'Address?'

'Twenty-three bis rue de l'Université.'

She chewed her lip. 'You're on.'

Chapter 19

The trip took them fifty-seven minutes.

Sarah drove with furious concentration, her lips issuing a string of silent commands. Twice they barreled down one-way streets. Once they mounted the sidewalk to go around a stalled Citroën, scattering pigeons but no pedestrians. No fewer than six times did she disobey a red light. Chapel refused to protest, and for her part, Sarah was too absorbed to explain. Time was not the only matter being contested.

'Call Leclerc,' she'd said as they crossed the Pont-Neuf. 'He's got to have found someone who knows Taleel by now. Between the FBI and Sûreté, they've a hundred bodies canvassing the neighborhood.'

'I'm sure we'd be the first to know,' said Chapel, surprised at her anger.

'Why are you fighting me?' Sarah snapped. 'Don't you want to put the finger on Taleel's friends? Or does it have to be your way? By the numbers?' She tossed him the cell phone. 'Just call him.'

She'd put her hair up into a bun, mumbling something about her neck being bloody hot. Her cheeks glowed with a dark warmth, but her eyes were cold and impossibly alert. At some point, a veil had descended around her, and Chapel felt as if part of her had left the car. He'd known her barely half a day, but a few minutes was all he'd needed to feel the power of her presence. When she was there, she was there. A force that would make any compass spin.

'Damn,' muttered Sarah. 'There's got to be someone who knew him.'

Chapel called Leclerc, who said they hadn't found a soul who knew Taleel as more than a passing acquaintance. Chapel then relayed the information about Taleel's propensity to withdraw money from ATMs in the seventeenth and eighteenth arrondissements, and Leclerc promised to have men at the addresses by midnight.

They arrived with a squeal of brakes, a wrench of the wheel, and thud of the tires as the car breached the curb. The brass plaque at the foot of the broad limestone stairs read 'Ministère de l'Économie, du Finance, et de l'Industrie.' A slim, earnest man in a pinstripe suit paced back and forth on the pavement. A chaotic wind played with his hair, but he kept his hands in his pockets, wrinkling his nose to keep his wire-rimmed spectacles in place. Seeing Chapel climb from the car, he dashed a few steps in his direction. 'Hello, Adam. I read about the bombing in the paper. Thank God you are all right.'

'I have. Many times,' said Chapel, shaking the man's hand. 'This is Miss Churchill. She's with our team. Sarah, may I present Giles Bonnard. Giles runs the shop over here.'

The shop in question was Tracfin, short for *Traitement du renseignement et action contre les circuits financiers clandestins*, or in English, Treatment of information and action against clandestine financial flows. Tracfin was not technically speaking a law enforcement entity, but an FIU, or financial intelligence unit. Its mission was to combat money laundering as a tool for drug traffickers, organized crime, and of late, terrorist organizations. To do so, it worked with the nation's varied financial institutions – banks, brokerage houses, money transmitters, to name a few – seeing to it they enforced the country's stringent money laundering regulations while gathering as much information as the law allowed them about their customers' banking habits.

'I believe we've met.' Sarah extended a hand. 'How are things, Giles?'

'Busier than ever.' Bonnard was unable to hide his curiosity. 'Have you been working with the Americans long?'

'A temporary assignment.' Sarah captioned her answer with a forceful glance. *Shut up, Giles*, it said. *You've been indiscreet before. Don't make the same mistake twice*. And again, Chapel got the feeling that there was nowhere he could go that Sarah hadn't been before. He knew better than to ask what they'd worked on in the past. But why hadn't she at least mentioned that she knew Bonnard, or that she'd worked with Tracfin before?

Because she's a spy, Chapel told himself. *She keeps secrets*. There was more, though he didn't care to admit it. *Because she doesn't trust you*.

'So, Adam,' Giles Bonnard said as they passed through the black double doors that led into the ministry. 'How can we help?'

'The terrorist that killed our guys had an account at the Banque de Londres et Paris. We looked at his records, but didn't find much.'

Bonnard widened his eyes, impressed. 'BLP, they show you the records already? Usually, you need one warrant to make them talk to you, another to get inside the door, and the police at your side to make sure they don't have any second thoughts.'

'Wasn't as hard as that,' said Chapel. 'They weren't too keen on being known as the terrorists' bank of choice. We need your platform,' he added, patting Bonnard on the back. 'I'm finally giving you the chance to prove that your database is everything you say it is.'

'That's why we are here. Our offices are upstairs. I show you the way.'

* * *

In the best of all possible worlds, Chapel would only have to plug Taleel's alias of Bertrand Roux, Roux's address in the Cité Universitaire, his driver's license, or phone number, into Tracfin's database to see if the same information had been listed by an account holder at any French bank or its subsidiary, in France or abroad. France, however, being a democracy, held an individual's rights inviolate, and his privacy equally so. The idea of a central database accessed by software that would allow Chapel to query the country's four thousand some-odd financial institutions was considered anathema and roundly denounced.

What he could look for was an account bearing Taleel's alias, or be given personal information, that had been written up as part of a suspicious activity report, known in the trade as an 'SAR,' or a cash transaction report, a 'CTR.' Whenever one moved large sums of money from one account to another, sooner or later, no matter how exacting his precautions, he would attract attention. If Mohammed al-Taleel had ever erred in this country, a record of his blunder would be in Tracfin's database.

As they zigged and zagged through the corridors, Chapel saw that Bonnard's pace had adopted his own urgency, and it pleased him. The fluorescent lights were terrible, half of them stuttering, the other half burnt out. Doors with drizzled glass panes slammed shut and rattled. The henna carpet was worn through in so many places that he wasn't sure which had come first, the carpet or the black-and-white checked tile beneath it. Chapel spotted a crack in the tiles, and another indeterminate flooring beneath it. The building was like a ruin. Dig down and you'd find the remnants of civilizations gone before.

To his right, he spied a large room crowded with carrels and PCs. Several men sat at the terminals, absorbed in their work. He guessed they were French officers come to the capital to plumb Tracfin's database in the hopes of gathering evidence of wrongdoing against suspected criminals, much as he wished to do against Taleel. Chapel had one advantage over these men. He did not have to build a case. He simply had to find a name.

After another left turn, Bonnard leaned his shoulder into a doorway and waited as Chapel and Sarah passed him to enter his private office.

'We do it from here, okay?' Bonnard said, his urgency momentarily absent as he removed his jacket, dusted the shoulders, then hung it inside his closet. Chore completed, he slid behind his desk, and motioned for Chapel and Sarah to pull up chairs on either side of him. A few keystrokes later, he had logged on to his computer. 'Give me what you have.'

Sarah recited the name, 'Bertrand Roux,' then began to give his address, only to be halted by Bonnard's outstretched palm. 'One piece of information at a time. First we start with his name. We wait for results, then we proceed to the next item. Roux, Bertrand,' he repeated, then hit the send key. 'He is French?'

'We assume so,' said Sarah.

Opening a drawer, Bonnard pulled out a packet of Disque Bleus and offered them around. 'It takes a few minutes,' he explained, lighting his cigarette after Chapel and Sarah had declined. 'The *Central des Données* was updated in ninety-seven using technology we bought on the cheap a few years earlier. They keep enlarging the memory, but the CPU stays the same.'

The specter of money laundering as a tool for organized crime had first demanded international attention in the late 1970s. With Colombian and Peruvian cocaine flooding the American and European marketplace, *narcotrafficantes* and their soldiers had to struggle, operationally and *physically*, to discover a means to dispose of the ton upon ton of Yankee greenback, French franc, German mark, and Spanish peseta their lucrative trade generated. In Miami and Marseilles, it was not uncommon to see certain olive-skinned gentlemen arrive at a bank's staff entrance and unload duffel bag after duffel bag of cash for immediate deposit into their accounts. On the documents they filed to open their accounts, they listed their profession as 'entrepreneur,' 'gambler,' or 'gentleman.'

The first legislation to combat such flagrant laundering required a bank's customers to fill out a 'cash transaction report' for every deposit or withdrawal over the sum of ten thousand dollars. The cocaine cowboys quickly found an easy way around the mechanism. 'Smurfing,' or what was currently referred to as 'structuring,' involved sending a few loyal soldiers to a legion of banks, each man depositing the sum of nine thousand nine hundred dollars. Flying low under the radar, so to speak.

Subsequent legislation placed the onus on the bank to know its customers. Efforts were made to train bank tellers to be on the lookout for activities that might tip them off to a client's criminal activities. More effective enforcement tools were constantly being invented. In instances where a rash of illegal activity was noted in a specific neighborhood, law enforcement agents were able to issue geographic transmitting orders, or GTOs, lowering the reporting requirements in that area to amounts as low as seven hundred dollars.

But Chapel had learned that drug traffickers and career criminals were easy targets. You knew who they were. You knew what they did, and when they did it. Mostly, you knew that sooner or later they had to use financial institutions to get at their dough.

A terrorist was much harder to find. The reason was simple. They moved their money *before* they committed the crime. Until then, they were invisible.

'Nothing on Bertrand Roux,' said Bonnard, after what felt like an eternity but was only two minutes.

Sarah read aloud Roux's address, his driver's license, and his phone number. Each time, the response came back negative.

'Reverse the phone number,' said Chapel. 'Read it off backwards.'

'Pardon?' said Bonnard.

'It's an easy trick. Guys do it all the time when they need to put down a fake number. Humor me.'

Sarah had lowered her eyes and a grim smile had taken control of her lips. He could read her mind as if it were his own. *The numbers won't lead us where we need to be. We need bodies. Warm bodies.* At that moment, Chapel felt a shiver of dislike rattle his spine. He wasn't certain what bothered him most. Her cool disdain. Her detached pessimism. Or just the way she was able to divorce herself from the events, while he hung on every word.

'*Eh, voilà!*' shouted Giles Bonnard.

Chapel rocketed from his seat, but Sarah had beaten him to Bonnard's side. 'You're bloody well kidding,' she said.

'I am not. Let's see here.' Bonnard pointed at the screen. 'A suspicious activity report filed June sixteenth of last year at the St-Germain-des-Pres branch of the Bank Montparnasse. The account belongs to Mr Albert Daudin. The telephone number listed on our documents is the same you gave me. I read you the teller's words. "Between nine and nine-thirty on the morning of Thursday, June sixteenth, Mr Daudin entered the bank three separate times. The first time he was a customer at my window and withdrew four thousand five hundred euros. The second time, I did not see him. Later, I learned from Geneviève Droz, my colleague, that he had withdrawn also four thousand euros. The third time, he came to Yvette's window (Yvette Pressy works next to me) and he withdrew again four thousand euros. When I spoke with my colleagues, we learned he had always used the same account. That is all.'

'What's the threshold for reporting requirements in France?' Chapel asked.

'Five thousand euros,' Bonnard answered. 'Clearly your man did not want to attract any attention.'

'Do we know what the balance of the account was?'

Bonnard searched the screen. 'Doesn't say. You'll have to speak with the bank.'

Chapel scratched his chin. He knew he should be pleased, but the actions didn't mesh with the discipline Taleel had shown before. Only an amateur would risk going into the same branch three times in a half hour. Bank Montparnasse had offices all over town. All Taleel had to do was jump a taxi ten blocks and he would have been safe. 'June sixteenth,' he said. 'What was going on then? Anything out of the ordinary.'

'Last year? June?' Bonnard shook his head with disgust. 'Of course, you don't remember. You don't live in Paris. Me, I remember. I live outside of the city. I don't have a car. It was impossible to get home. I had to sleep at the office three nights in a row.'

'What do you mean you couldn't get home?' Sarah asked, but as Bonnard began to explain, a light went on behind her eyes and she began to murmur, 'Yes, yes, yes.'

'A transportation workers' strike,' Bonnard was saying. 'The entire city was shut down. No Métro. No bus. That day the taxi drivers joined their brothers in solidarity. You have never seen such traffic. Your friend, Mr Daudin, or Mr Roux, or Mr Taleel, whatever he called himself, he was in a hurry, and he was too lazy to walk. Case closed. Hold on while I check the name Daudin, maybe we find him somewhere else.' Bonnard typed in the name, then sat back, hands locked behind his head.

The two minutes passed in agonized silence, all of them too keyed up to say a word.

'Nothing,' Bonnard announced to a chorus of groans. He printed out a copy of the suspicious activity report and handed it to Chapel. 'This helps?'

Chapel eyed the sheet, committing to memory the name of Albert Daudin and account number 788-87677G at the Bank Montparnasse. Was it another dead end? Another of Taleel's elaborately constructed Chinese boxes? Chapel didn't think so. This was the one no one was supposed to find. A mistake born of desperation. They had their golden thread. Now all they had to do was pull and watch Hijira unravel. 'Yeah, Giles,' he said. 'It helps. Big-time.'

Chapter 20

The doors to Mortier Caserne slammed behind Leclerc, and he swore audibly. *'Merde.'* He kicked the toe of his boot into the rutted concrete drive once, very hard. *'Merde,'* he said again, turning his head to direct the epithet at the massive oak doors.

Rafi Boubilas would not talk. The owner of Royal Joailliers had a lawyer, and the leftist bitch was promising to stay at her client's side until either he was charged or he was released. When Leclerc had told her to sod off, that she would stay with Boubilas as long as they allowed her and not a minute longer, she'd laid into him with a torrent of abuse. It was a screaming match, and as usual, the woman involved won. *'J'accuse!'* she wailed, a latter-day Zola with her red beret, Chanel bag, and cell phone at the ready.

It was nearly seven o'clock. Leclerc strode along the sidewalk beneath a row of century-old elms. The evening sunshine warmed the leafy canopy and dusted the air with a comforting, soporific hue, but did little to brighten his mood. If he had his way, they'd jail the loudmouthed broad with her client in La Santé and let her get a taste of real prison life. A six-by-nine-foot cell with dripping walls, a metal toilet that backed up every time you took a crap, and food that would sicken a cockroach. Leclerc would be free to speak with Boubilas as he saw fit, and that would be that.

His motorcycle sat parked a few yards away. Zipping up his leather jacket, he threw a leg over the silver and blue Ducati Monster S4R. He checked the choke and his hand came away greasy. The bike needed a wash. Just then, a thought came to him, and he was surprised he hadn't had it earlier. 'Shoot first, ask questions later,' Admiral Owen Glendenning had said. Fine. It was agreed. Leclerc would take him up on the offer. Target number one would be Monsieur Rafi Boubilas, owner of Royal Joailliers, drug dealer, conspirator of terrorists, and world-class scumbag. The bitch wanted him released. *Tant mieux*. Leclerc pulled out his cell phone.

'Edmond,' he said. 'Release our guest.'

'Boubilas?' asked Colonel Edmond Courtois, commandant of Mortier Caserne. 'You're joking. Let me work on him tonight. The lawyer won't stay much longer. She was just saying she'd sleep here to piss you off.'

'Trust me, *mon vieux*. Release him. I guarantee you that tomorrow he will wish that he were still your guest.'

'It is all right?'

'Call Gadbois if you want.'

Courtois laughed gruffly. The mention of the spy chief's name was enough. 'Need any help?'

'Have Schmid and Guillo meet me here at the caserne at midnight.'

'Should they bring any kit?'

'Their hands will do.'

Leclerc slipped on his helmet, lowered the mirrored visor, and started the engine. The Ducati growled magnificently. Goosing the bike, he turned toward downtown and headed into the city. Traffic was already thinning, and he needed only a quarter of an hour to reach Sûréte headquarters on the Rue Lamartine.

* * *

'What do you mean, I can't get into the bank?' Adam Chapel sat on the edge of Giles Bonnard's desk, arms raised in exasperation. 'It's barely nine o'clock. Someone has to be there.'

'It's not a question of time,' Bonnard explained. 'Their computers are down for the night. The ISM manager told me their central database is backed up each evening between eight and three. During that time, no queries can be entered. He can interrupt the backup, but it will take him longer to reset the system than if you just waited it out.'

An hour ago, Chapel had called Leclerc, and he imagined Leclerc had called Gadbois, and Gadbois, the minister of defense, and so on up the line until someone had called the president of Bank Montparnasse and informed him that his bank had given comfort and solace to a known terrorist who the day before had killed three American law enforcement agents and a member of his own country's espionage service. The bank president had thereupon pledged his immediate and total cooperation. The chain of command, precarious as it was in international investigations, had functioned perfectly. And now, all of it was being foiled by the very technology they were relying on to succeed.

'You're to go to the bank's admin center at six tomorrow morning,' Bonnard went on. 'They've promised to have all of Mr Daudin's records waiting for you then.' When Chapel didn't budge, Bonnard grew angry. 'Christ, man, be happy with what you've got. You picked up an important lead, and God knows, it's a miracle Montparnasse is cooperating with you. Adam, they are literally opening the doors for you. Three hours early, I might add!' He rolled back his chair and stood up. 'Sarah, I'll let you tell him that he looks like shit. Get some sleep, Adam.'

Bonnard stalked from the office.

Chapel shook his head at his colleague's behavior. 'We're the ones who should be pissed off.'

'He did his best and you didn't even say thanks.'

'Thanks? I'm supposed to say thanks? Oh, that's right, I'm in Europe. Excuse me, I'd best mind my manners.'

Sarah ambled towards the door. 'It's not just a question of manners; it's a question of class. Now come on, let's get something to eat. I'm famished.' In the hallway, she looked over her shoulder. 'You coming?'

Chapel hadn't budged from his perch on Bonnard's desk. 'Yeah.'

Sarah raised a finger and shot him a cautionary glance. 'This is Paris. Don't say you want a hamburger or I'll kill you.'

On the third floor of Sûreté headquarters, Leclerc ran straight into Franc Burckhardt; the beer-bellied Alsatian whose sworn duty was to misplace, falsely tag, or steal every valuable piece of evidence the police collected. He'd known Burckhardt for ten years, but he flashed his military identification all the same. It was procedure, and cunning pricks like Burckhardt thrived on it. 'I need to see the items from the Cité Universitaire.'

'Already taken to the labs for analysis.'

'I know, but I heard they'd left behind the computer.'

'A wreck. A husk. Half of it is melted. Worthless.' Burckhardt spat out his words like pistachio shells, with a little spit, to boot.

The Sûréte had one set of computer technicians, the prefecture of police another, and the DGSE, a third. Each thought its own group the most competent. Leclerc thought they were all a bunch of amateurs. He had his own resources and knew just the man to have a look at the PC. He offered Burckhardt a cigarette, but Burckhardt turned it away, as if he couldn't be bought by such cheap favors.

'Do you mind if I take it with me? The boys at the Caserne are drooling to have a go at it.'

'No problem,' said Burckhardt. 'Give me a four-oh-three and it's yours.' That was the official document number affixed to a transfer of evidence form.

'I'll go you one better.' Leclerc handed Burckhardt a sheet issued by the chief of the Paris police calling for all members of the force to offer their complete and unremitting support to all those investigating the bombing at Cité Universitaire.

'Impressive.' Burckhardt picked at his teeth as he read. 'Just missing one thing – a four-oh-three. Sorry, my friend. Nothing leaves without a paper.'

'Call Gadbois.'

'You call him. I'll call Mr Chirac, the President of the republic, and you still won't be any closer to taking the computer out of here. Four-oh-three. That's the magic number. I refuse to be busted in rank because a hotshot from the Action Service needs a favor. I'm sorry, Captain.'

Leclerc knew better than to be angry. The infighting and bureaucratic wrangling that went on inside the country's varied law enforcement agencies was old news, but something no one discussed aloud. If the public ever learned about all the fraternal competition, they'd fire the lot of them – the cops, the detectives, the spies – *all of them*, and start over from scratch. There was, of course, the option of actually obtaining a 403. First he'd have to find a form, then have the chief investigative officer sign off on it, then have the form countersigned by the chief of police, whose office was across town, before bringing it back to Burckhardt no less than twenty-four hours from now. Leclerc had other ideas.

'Mind if I take a look at it, at least?'

'You?' Burckhardt seemed to find this amusing. Shrugging, he opened the mesh gate and walked into the bowels of the evidence locker.

What remained of Mohammed al-Taleel's personal com-

THE DEVIL'S BANKER   165

puter rested on a silver trolley cart. It was a Dell desktop. Besides being charred and warped, it looked like someone very strong and very angry had taken a sledgehammer and beaten the living shit out of it. Leclerc circled it, as if eyeing roadkill. The CD-ROM drive protruded from the casing like an impetuous teenager's tongue. The housing was cracked, chunks missing helter-skelter, like one of the skulls the Leakeys had found at Olduvai Gorge. The motherboard was broken into a hundred pieces, much of it pulverized into a fine green dust. Maybe tech services had gotten it right for once.

'May I?' he asked Burckhardt, indicating he wanted to pick it up and look at it. The effort at politeness nearly killed him.

'Be my guest.' A buzzer rang, signaling the arrival of another client. Throwing his elbows around, Burckhardt saddled up his pants and offered an admonishing glance. 'But leave it here, eh? I'll be back to check.'

Leclerc nodded, suitably cowed. Finding a screwdriver, he opened the back of the computer, wrenched the casing off, and set it on the floor. The hard drive was destroyed, bent half in two, chips of the silicon memory disk falling into his hand, skittering onto the floor. He dropped them into his pocket, then tried slipping the rectangular disk housing into his jacket, seeing if it was noticeable. Right side. Left side. Either way, the bulge was too noticeable.

Leclerc made a note of the serial number. Odds were the unit was stolen or secondhand. All the same, he would have someone in intelligence phone Dell Europe and get the sales info on the unit. Dell computers were purchased online or over the phone, credit card only, and he wanted to know just whose had done the trick. Setting down the computer, he left the evidence locker, waving Burckhardt a disgruntled good-bye.

But to himself, he whispered, 'I'll be back.'

* * *

He needed a beer.

Leclerc trotted down the steps of Sûréte headquarters and crossed the street to the Café St-Martin. He hated the place, if only because its sole customers were cops, whom Leclerc did not generally care for, but there wasn't another café nearby and his head was killing him.

'*Pression*,' he said, taking a seat at the bar, lighting a cigarette.

The bartender set down a beer. Leclerc drank half in a single draft. He called Gadbois and spoke to the general's assistant, asking him to get onto Dell and get the sales information. Yes, Leclerc said, he knew Dell was based out of Ireland. Weren't they all one big happy family now? The vaunted EC? Leclerc stifled a laugh. The lousy micks should be happy to help out their French compatriots. If not, he'd phone the FBI and have them roust Michael Dell out of his bed in Austin, Texas. One way or the other, he meant to learn who had purchased that computer. And within twelve hours. No excuses.

'Another beer,' Leclerc signaled. 'And a Calvados, too.' Anything for his head.

It was Gadbois who was bothering him. Not the blast. Not the lack of sleep. Leaving the American Embassy, the old general had cornered him and forced him into one of the police service buses parked in front of the Chancery.

'A big case for us,' he'd said.

Leclerc knew enough to keep quiet. When Gadbois had something to say, he always did it where there were no witnesses.

'Terrible what happened, yesterday. You're lucky to be alive. You know that, don't you?' A pat on the shoulder. An appreciative glance. 'I like you, Leclerc. You're hard. Iron. Hmm? A tough son of a bitch. We could have used a few more like you in Algeria, more bastards ready to jump into the fire instead of running from it. We almost had it, you know. This close. This close, it was.' Fucking dinosaur had never gotten over having his ass kicked out of North Africa. Forty years later he was still getting fuzzy over it. 'Still, you were lucky. A bomb like that. Babtiste, the Americans. What a mess.' It was all bullshit, thought Leclerc. Preliminaries. Gadbois leaned close and he could smell the garlic on his breath. Gadbois was always taking garlic and ginseng and gingko biloba, chasing down the supplements with his morning tonic of brandy and black coffee. 'You're my eyes and ears, Leclerc. You do as I say and everything's okay. I want you to help the Americans. Whatever they need, you get it. Glendenning's a friend. One of us. Understood?'

Leclerc nodded, unable to keep a smirk from his face.

'Don't piss them off,' Gadbois continued. 'It's their show. *Our country*. But their show.' Gadbois's rock-hard gut pressed into Leclerc, his eyes narrowing, and for a moment Leclerc saw that, yes, once he'd been a real son of a bitch. 'You're to help,' Gadbois whispered. 'But only so much.'

'Pardon?'

'When I say stop, you stop. And don't you do one thing without telling me. Understood? Now get out of here. Find the bastards who killed Santos Babtiste.'

Tired and disenchanted, Leclerc caught a reflection of himself in the mirror as he sipped his beer. He looked lousy, even by his own low standards. What did he expect after twenty years in his country's service? Twenty years skulking in the shadows, dreaming up dirty tricks to keep the socialists from succeeding in their plan to make France a second-rate country. Katanga, Senegal, Ivory Coast. How many strongmen had he helped prop up? How many had he knocked down? And why? Oil. Diamonds. Natural gas. National security. Realpolitik. There was always a reason, but lately, he'd stopped caring. He had no say in it, either way. He was a soldier-cum-spy. A dagger to stick into someone's gut. He wondered if the eyes staring back at him had always been so vacant, and if it was time to start asking why.

Forget it, he said, twirling on his bar stool, staring out at the early evening assembly of notables. The usual gaggle of overweight, ill-shaven plainclothes cops crowded the walls and packed the corner tables. Someone dropped a euro into the jukebox and Jacques Brel sang, '*Ne me quitte pas, il faut oublier, tout peut s'oublier . . .*' A few cops joined in, not half-bad, actually, but Leclerc was captivated by other words.

You're to help. But only so much.

He lit a second cigarette from the end of the first. A small, insistent hammer was tap-tap-tapping at the back of his eyes, driving him crazy. The Calvados arrived. He picked up the snifter, swirled around the burnished liquid, sniffed it, then poured it down his gullet. The burn was to savor.

And if he had helped more yesterday? If he'd been a little quicker, as quick as Chapel, the glorified accountant still wet behind the ears? Leclerc had nothing to blame for his indecision. Not the jitters of a new command or an illness that garlic, gingkoba, or a half bottle of Remy Martin between sunset and sundown might cure. Leclerc had a curse. A stain.

Just then, the plump, disheveled form of Sergeant Franc Burckhardt, twenty-two-year veteran of the force, indispensable cog in the fight against crime, waddled down the stairs of Sûréte headquarters and disappeared along the street.

Leclerc paid for his drinks and left.

The length of duct tape was still stretched tight across the lock where he'd left it. Leclerc peeled it off, let the gate to the evidence locker close behind him, then walked through the maze of shelves to the trolley where Taleel's computer sat like a broken toy. You want courage? Drink a couple of beers, down a Calvados, and you'll have all the courage you need. Need a volunteer? Captain Leclerc is your man.

The hard disk didn't fit any better this time than it had an hour ago. Opening his jacket, he stuffed it inside, then yanked up the zipper. If anyone asked him what he was hiding, he'd pull a face and say a fuckin' Uzi, did they want to see it?

It didn't come to that. By nine o'clock the headquarters of the Sûreté were as empty as any other office – government or otherwise – in a country where thirty-five-hour work-weeks were considered the norm. Even if Burckhardt discovered that the hard drive was missing, Leclerc doubted he would say anything. Burckhardt was a survivor. He could be counted on to avoid initiating any actions that might steer trouble his way.

Leclerc stopped at the counter and pulled the evidence log out from the top drawer. Licking a thumb, he reviewed everything that had been accepted into safekeeping during the last twenty-four hours. He stopped when he saw René Montbusson's name. Montbusson, the evidence man at the Cité Universitaire. Sliding his fingernail across the page, he stopped beneath the word 'map.' *Zut!* No one had told him anything about any map being found in Taleel's apartment.

It only took a minute to find the shelf where Burckhardt had laid the evidence. The spot was bare. Leclerc looked above and below, to the left and right. The map would be in either a sealed envelope or a plastic slipcover. He saw nothing that fit the bill. Rushing back to the counter, he double-checked to see if someone had signed out the map, but the ledger bore no mark.

Someone had beat Leclerc to the punch.

* * *

It was a short ride to Clichy and a run-down apartment house. Leclerc rang the bell next to the name marked, 'Dupuy, Etienne.'

'Who is it?' a whiskey-soaked voice asked.

'A servant of your government. We need to call you back to the service in the name of the nation's security.'

'Fuck off.' The buzzer sounded and Leclerc entered the building.

Dupuy stared at the ruined disk. '*Mon Dieu*. What happened to it? Grenade go off near it?'

Leclerc didn't bat an eye. 'Can you put it together?'

'Put what together? There's fuckall of it left.'

'Humor me,' said Leclerc, though he wasn't smiling. 'You'll do it or I'll tell the general you're on the sauce again. You know how he feels about loose lips. For starters, you can count on your pension being cut. I should tell you, he's in a pissy mood these days. He never did exactly like you. A drunken queen fifty pounds overweight. Not the type he saw in the service. He might very well send someone like me over to effect a more permanent remedy.'

Dupuy scratched at his three-day stubble. 'I see you haven't lost your charm.'

'You bring out the gentleman in me.'

Dupuy lifted the housing with a finger, peeking inside. 'Can't tell you what I'll find. Don't expect anything.'

'If there's so much as a lick of information on that disk, I want to know it,' said Leclerc.

'*Jawohl, mein Kommandant*.' Dupuy threw off a *Führer gruss*. 'How long do I have?'

Leclerc thought what might be reasonable, then subtracted a day. 'Twenty-four hours.'

'Good,' breathed Dupuy. 'For a moment there I thought you wanted me to hurry.'

Chapter 21

In the gloom of his private study, Marc Gabriel sat on the edge of his glass desk and waited for his son to join him. His hands flitted to his chin, adjusted the knot of his Hermès tie (a habit he violently combated, as it darkened the fine silk with grease), and patted down his hair. It had been a tumultuous two days, but Gabriel had known the death of close ones and the terror of imminent discovery before. On balance, the day's news should have eased, rather than provoked, his concerns. The professor had made contact. In forty-eight hours he would be in Paris. Rafi Boubilas had been released from custody without divulging news of their relationship. A decision had been taken about Gregorio. Gabriel had yet to pack his bags, sort out his passports, and place a few calls to Ciudad del Este in advance of his flight to South America later that evening, but these were trivial duties. The fact was that when the sun set this evening, the family's dream would be closer to fruition than any of them might have dared imagine even a year ago.

At six o'clock, the two-story town house buzzed with the frenetic activity of his three bright and active children, his French family. Upstairs in the living room, Geneviève could be heard practicing a Chopin nocturne. The melancholy strains grew in intensity, then softened, not a note misplayed.

Just twelve, she was uncommonly gifted, and though she was afraid to tell him, he knew she hoped for a career in music. In two weeks, she was scheduled to play at a recital for the city's most talented young pianists at the Salle Pleyel. It was a shame she would not be in Paris to attend.

From the kitchen issued the sound of his seven year old, Arthur, demanding a sweet before dinner. Silently, Gabriel urged his wife to be firm, knowing all the same that she was powerless against him, as a proper mother should be toward her sons. Amina's sing-song voice was barely audible above the merry clamor of pots and pans. Lamb was on the menu, if his nose did not deceive him. One sound was pleasantly absent. The incessant jabber of TV. Television was not permitted in the Gabriel household.

'Amina said you wanted to see me.'

Gabriel rose from the desk, an arm extended in welcome. 'Ah, George, come in, come in.'

George Gabriel entered the room hesitantly, hands jammed in the back pockets of his Levis, eyes black as a well staring out of a strong, handsome face. He was a big boy, six feet two inches tall, with shoulders that put Atlas to shame and a forthright, uncomplicated manner. As usual, he wore the navy jersey of the French national soccer team. What wasn't usual was the newly razored scalp. 'Like Zidane,' his wife had forewarned him. 'It's important to him that you like it.'

'Come here, then. Let me have a look at you,' said Gabriel, swallowing his anger. 'Makes you look older. Responsible.' What it really made him look like was a muscle-bound hooligan. Brooding, angry, and a little too dangerous. 'Sit down. I feel like I haven't seen you in ages. How are your studies progressing? Finally getting the hang of derivatives? You'll have to master math if you want to become a doctor.'

'I'm past those. It's binomials that are tripping me up now. I have plenty of time to get the hang of them. The Bac's in June.' 'Bac' meant the baccalauréate, the national examination that determined which children would go on to university. In his final year at school, George Gabriel was an honors student as well as captain of the soccer team. He played center forward with a joyous ferocity that thrilled his father.

'I'm sure you'll do splendidly. Me, I was a poor student. You've already outshone me ten times.'

Gabriel ushered his son into the room, closing the door behind him. The study was a private enclave – no trespassing allowed – and George checked out the surroundings with a burglar's admiring glower. The décor was French minimalist: sleek bookshelves and lacquered Roche Bobois credenzas done in neutral tones. 'Have you got a game this weekend?'

'Just practice. Coach is sick. I'm taking over.'

'I hope you're not neglecting your other studies.' Gabriel regretted the words the moment they'd left his mouth. It wasn't like him to preach. No *dawah* from Daddy. That was the rule. He did not drink alcohol. He did not use foul language. He did not stay out late and carouse. He lived as he hoped his children would live and expected his example to suffice.

'No,' said George, sinking into a chair in front of the desk, balancing his muscled frame on the edge, a none-too-subtle indication he hoped the meeting would be brief. Small talk had never come easily between father and son. Gabriel didn't usually arrive home from work until eight P.M. By then, the children were either doing their homework or getting ready for bed. It might be a mother's job to tend the children, but the fact did little to ease his sadness at not knowing them well enough. He could not lie to himself that things would change anytime soon. If anything, he would soon be even busier.

Sliding into the chair opposite his son, Gabriel appraised him a last time. It wasn't a question of whether he was up to the task. He was. He'd spent six weeks at a camp in the Bekaa last summer learning the rudiments of a soldier's trade. Prior to graduation, he'd broken the arm and jaw of his hand-to-hand combat instructor. The boy was strong and capable. Still, camp was only a rehearsal.

And there was the other matter. The reason, he could now admit, for his anxiety. A subtle, but unmistakable, resistance had cropped up since the boy's return from the Middle East. Not rebellion so much as a guarded criticism of all around him. Gabriel could see it in his eyes, and in the reticent way his son carried himself inside the house, and in the newly acquired habit of taking Amina's side in disputes. The rot was seeping in.

'I am worried about one of the Americans,' he said. 'Someone who may hurt us. There is a question of his interfering with our plans.'

'Is he here in Paris?'

'Yes. One of those responsible for Taleel. We must take measures. So close, we can leave nothing to chance.'

Reaching into his pocket, Gabriel took out a ticket jacket bearing the Air France logo and placed it on the table in front of his son. George opened it, and studied the details. Round trip, economy class Paris-Dubai. His eyes flickered. 'By we . . . you mean me?'

'You're no longer a child. It's time you shared the family's responsibilities.'

George nodded, his eyes keenly focused as a new alertness came over him. 'I'm ready,' he said, and Gabriel noted that his son had tilted his head slightly to one side, and that he wore the vaguely self-satisfied air he put on after scoring a goal. *'Never cocky, just confident,'* his son liked to say.

'The prospect of killing does not frighten you?'

'Yes – I mean, no. I've taught myself to block that part of my heart. It scares me, but I'll be all right.' He thought a moment longer. 'This means I'm leaving – I mean, this is it – all that you've worked towards these past years.'

'We are all leaving.'

George shook his head in amazement. 'It's really happening? I mean, it's happening now?'

'This weekend.'

'So soon?'

Gabriel wondered if he'd said too much. Reluctantly, he explained. 'Abu Sayeed has been killed. It is not known whether he spoke before dying. This is our time. The time for our family to act.' He rose from the chair, and when his son rose, too, he hugged him. 'You have made me proud in so many ways. I wanted to give you the chance to make your name, to show your commitment so that all will recognize what you have done for our cause.'

'Thank you, Father. I'm grateful.'

'As for the Bac, I've made arrangements for you to take it at home. You'll sit for the exam at the French school in Jidda next May. Same day as in Paris, I've been made to understand. Just a different location.'

George Gabriel flipped open the ticket jacket and studied the flight details. A shudder passed through his sturdy shoulders, followed by a sigh that frightened his father. 'Tomorrow?' he asked.

'Yes,' said Gabriel. 'I am sorry that it must be so. Understand, son, that I would do this myself if it were at all possible. Unfortunately, I have a problem of my own abroad. I must leave this evening. At such a decisive moment, we can only trust our own.' He reached for his son's hands. 'Am I right to put the trust in you?'

'Yes, Father.'

He kissed his son on the cheeks, and when he embraced the boy, he was pleased to feel the muscled arms hug him in return. He put the sudden tremor, the uneasy sigh, down to nerves. He was, after all, asking a lot of the boy.

Gabriel gave him the details of what needed to be done, the location of the hospital, the name of the attending doctor, a layout of the burn unit. 'You'll be finished by noon. Your flight will depart at nine-fifteen. Someone will meet you at the airport in Dubai and drive you into the desert.' He patted his son's shoulders. 'Your grandfather will be more than proud.'

'Father, may I ask one question?'

'Of course, my son.'

George Gabriel narrowed his eyes, and his father knew he was already steeling himself for the task. 'From near or far?'

Gabriel clasped his son's neck and drew him close. 'From near. You will have the pleasure of seeing the *kuffar*'s soul depart his body.'

Chapter 22

By eleven o'clock, the sky had darkened to night and pressed down on the rooftops, a purple velvet cape fringed with a subtropical breeze. The wind was too warm for Paris, thought Chapel, as he strolled tiredly down the Boulevard St-Germain, the air humid, layered with garlic, exhaust and cigarette smoke. It pricked an unease deep inside him, a presentiment of violence, the threat of the unknown. Or maybe it was just the certainty that he was one step closer to his foe.

Taleel had slipped up big-time: three withdrawals from the same branch in one hour. What had driven him to assume such a reckless course of action? What had convinced him that he had no other choice? Chapel doubted he would ever find out, but at this point, it was the act that mattered, not the motivation.

'It's the golden thread,' he'd said to Sarah during dinner. 'If he withdrew twelve thousand euros in a day, there's no telling how much money he has socked away. The account at BLP never held more than seven thousand euros. He was religious about it.'

She'd chosen the restaurant, a sidewalk pizzeria she'd frequented during her year as an exchange student at the Sorbonne. She'd insisted he try the pizza puttanesca topped with Italian sausage, bell peppers, and onions. It was decent enough, but she wolfed it down as if she hadn't eaten for days. He wasn't going to say it didn't hold a candle to Patsy's in New York, not after her jibes about him being the boorish American.

'We've moved up the ladder a rung, I'll grant you that.' Sarah sat smoking a cigarette that she'd bummed from the next table, an arm slung over the back of her chair, eyeing him from behind her veil of smoke. 'Everyone smokes in Paris, Adam,' she'd offered, though he hadn't asked for an explanation. He already knew why. She was a chameleon. She couldn't help but change with her surroundings.

'Up a rung? This is a whole new ball game, lady. He wired in the money. Don't you see? Bonnard didn't pick up any cash transaction reports for the account. Any cash deposits over five thousand euros would have set off the alarms. Unless Taleel squirreled in the funds, he had to have transferred it in from another bank.'

'Or banks.'

'Just one will do for now. Let's not get greedy.' But to Chapel the discovery of a trail was only the half of it. 'We weren't supposed to see this account. The one at BLP was too clean. Sanitized. He ran that thing as if he expected someone to find it. *But this one . . .* this one's different. Too much money, for one. This one was his private stash.'

Stubbing out her cigarette, Sarah leaned across the table and laid a hand on his outstretched arm, settling him with a fond, sisterly gaze. 'Easy, Adam. Easy. You have that look in your eye like you're ready to storm a machine gun nest. Remember, it's not who wins the battle that counts, but who wins the war.'

'It's just my way,' he said, feeling defensive, tied to his chair when he wanted to be jumping out of it.

'I can't do it, myself. It's not wise to invest so much in every up and down. I'm just saying you have to take a step back.'

A step back. Impossible. Even if he could, he would refuse. Obligation. Duty. Friendship. Revenge. Love. He would carry the weight of these words with him every step of every day until Taleel's band of conspirators – *until Hijira* – was wiped from the face of the planet.

'Don't worry,' he said. 'I won't get burned out.'

'You have staying power, do you?'

'Yeah.'

'Endurance?' The sisterly look was long gone. Her eyes had narrowed, the brows raised in scrutiny, her lips puckered saucily.

'Absolutely.'

'Well then, Mr Chapel . . .'

It was then that he realized she was teasing him. 'Get outta here,' he said, sliding back his chair, freeing his arm from her touch as she broke up laughing.

An hour later, he was still embarrassed.

Fifty yards ahead, he spotted the awning for his hotel. 'Hotel Splendide' read the merry, cursive writing. Three stars and living on its glory. He imagined his room. Tile floors, a bed that sagged, and a shower you could water a houseplant with. The minibar, though, was first-class, and offered Jack Daniel's, Coke, M&M's, and Pringles, all for the exorbitant prices its clientele would complain about, but nevertheless pay. No one got homesick like Americans. He imagined the door closing behind him, the dead bolt sliding home, the miserable single bed staring at him.

Sarah walked next to him, arms crossed over her chest, her eyes distant, wandering. A couple passed between them, hand in hand, delighting at the boisterous voices that spilled from the nearest bistro, their smiles reflecting the restaurant's festooned fairy lights, and Chapel was struck by a desire to stand closer to Sarah, emboldened by a picture of them strolling arm in arm. Cover, she'd call it. He'd have to find his own word.

Inside the hotel lobby, a wilted chandelier burned too brightly.

'*Chambre cinquante-deux*,' he told the hotelier, his French passable.

'*Soixante-neuf*,' Sarah said a moment later, taking a place at his side. The hotelier turned and gathered the keys from their respective boxes. The lady received hers first, along with a friendly '*bonne nuit*.'

'You must be exhausted,' she said as they headed to the stairs. 'How's the shoulder?'

'It's there,' he said, defying the insistent, and increasingly uncomfortable, throbbing. His room was on the second floor. 'See you in the lobby at five-thirty,' he said as he left the stairwell and walked down the corridor.

'Five forty-five,' Sarah countered. 'At that time of the morning, we'll make it to the bank in five minutes.'

As Chapel inserted the key into the lock, he had a portrait of Sarah in his mind. The excited brows, the perky smile, the way she'd raised herself on her tiptoes and had given him the coyest of waves. Spinning on a heel, he looked down the hall, wanting her still to be there. Not to invite her in. Not even to say good night. Just to double-check the expression. He had no idea whether or not it was sincere.

Seated alone in the third row of the first-class cabin, Marc Gabriel sipped at his mineral water and stared out the window into the infinite black sky. Flying relaxed him as nothing else. The gentle, constant throbbing of the MD-11's Rolls-Royce engines lulled him into a pleasant, soporific state that allowed his mind to ponder his varied challenges, slipping from one to the other, taking the objective view and analyzing each without fear or rancor or the frenzied immediacy that his current situation demanded.

Closing his eyes, he saw the gritty, mud-coated streets of Ciudad del Este, tasted the infernal damp heat that he adored, sniffed the choking exhaust that was every third world city's curse. He was not worried about what he would find or that he would not be able to rectify the situation. He knew all the players and what they were capable of. One way or another, he would have his money. Absently, his hand rose to his jacket, feeling for his passport – an authentic Belgian issue listing him as Claude Francois, a forty-five-year-old resident of Brussels. It was the formalities that caused him concern. His mind ran ahead to the flight home, to the news of the US Treasury agent's murder, to his own meeting the next day with the Israeli professor and the divine moment when the package would be his.

Beneath his blanket, his fingers had found his cuff links. They were from Boucheron, gold with neat little batons of hematite or onyx or lapis lazuli that one could slip in and out. Delicately, he played with them, realizing how much he'd always loved them. There was no reason for it, other than that they had always seemed to him the pinnacle of Western fashion. In a few days, he'd have no need for them. His father abhorred Western dress. So had Marc Gabriel's oldest brother, dead these twenty-five years, and the one who had started them all down this road. He was the fanatic, the pilgrim, the puritan of the family.

So much death. So much sadness.

He allowed himself to mourn Taleel. His death was tragic, yes, but the transfer had been a priority. Withdrawing half a million dollars from a local bank was not a possibility. Notification would have to have been given days in advance; the funds wired in from one of the company's secure accounts; arrangements made to gather the American currency. Naturally, the manager would have insisted on meeting him. He shuddered, thinking of the trail he would have left. He might as well have sent the Americans a telegram asking them to meet him at the bank and to bring their most comfortable handcuffs.

No, Taleel, he explained to the man's departed soul. There was no other way. Your death was necessary, crucial, even. Your actions have brought us one step closer. To the brink.

A sad smile cracked his lips. He would not mourn. Every soldier knows that one day his name will be called. It is the price of duty, the stamp of honor. If anything, he reminded himself, it was a time for optimism. Twenty years' preparation was at an end. The day of celebration at hand.

'Sir, is everything all right?' An attractive stewardess with dusky brown eyes knelt next to his seat, her hand brushing his shoulder. 'May I offer you a glass of something?'

Gabriel realized he was crying. Sitting up, he wiped away the tear that had run down his cheek. 'Most kind,' he answered, 'but I think I will try to sleep a bit. Tomorrow promises to be a busy day.'

He knew he wouldn't be able to sleep. Still, Chapel moved around the room, going through the motions. He took off his shoes and socks. He washed his hands and brushed his teeth. With a nod to Giles Bonnard, and maybe even to Sarah and her aversion to American 'boors,' he took care to mind the crease as he hung up his trousers. His shirt was history – two tomato stains, a freckling of grease, and yes, even a clip of onion. He didn't have to worry about being a boor. He was a certified slob. Thou shalt not wear a white shirt to an Italian restaurant. It should be a commandment. Gingerly, he peeled it off, one shoulder at a time. A corner of the gauze bandage came loose, and for a moment he stared at the moonscape of burned flesh. It was another man's shoulder: ravaged, frighteningly red, and coated with a gelatinous ooze. Averting his eyes, he replaced the bandage and pressed his palm firmly on the gauze. The pain washed over him in waves, and as it crested, he sank to his bed and groaned. The shoulder was his, all right. He had oceans to cross before it would be healed.

His medication sat on the night table, arranged in a row.
Dr Bac had prescribed ampicillin to prevent infections,
hydrocortisone to arrest inflammation, and Vicodin to
combat the pain. There were stronger painkillers, but not
many, he thought as he shook loose a few tablets. He stared
at the pills lolling in his palm, then dropped them back into
the container.

Five minutes later, he was on the street in his jeans and a
T-shirt, the bandage visible, but no one paying it much
attention. He walked towards the river, his stride growing
until he found his marching rhythm and locked into step.
He passed the Café Aux Deux Magots, favorite haunt of a
lost generation, tables packed, white-aproned waiters navigating the throng, trays held on high. Across the way, the
church of Ste-Geneviève-du-Mont's four-square spire stab-
bed the sky's soft underbelly. A plaque informed him that
René Descartes was buried on the premises. *Cogito ergo sum.*
I think, therefore I am. No, thought Chapel. He had it wrong.
I act, therefore I am.

Crossing the square, he stared at the spire, at the narrow
refectory windows, at the sturdy wooden doors, built, at
least to Chapel's eyes, to keep people out rather than allow
them entry. In the morning, caskets holding the bodies of his
fellow jump team members were to be loaded aboard a US
Air Force jet and flown to Andrews Air Force Base, from
there to be dispatched to each man's hometown. Keck to
Falls Church. Gomez to Trenton. Santini to Buffalo. Which
God would their families pray to? The benevolent deity who
promised infinite kindness? The watchmaker who'd set the
world in motion, then turned his mind to bigger game? Or
the murderous mute who demanded belief in the face of
extraordinary barbarism?

A glance at the sky, the capture of a single sparkling star,
provided Chapel all the comfort he needed. Whoever or
whatever made that – and something did, you could bet on

it – would take care of him whenever the time came. It seemed to him that man ought to stop counting so much on God to look after him, and start relying a little more on himself.

The streets narrowed, grew quiet, a canyon of silence that suited him. For a block, he was alone, eerily so. A pair of footsteps not his own echoed behind him, and instinctively, he checked over his shoulder. A shadow blended into a doorway. Another late-night wanderer. He passed the *commissariat de police*, hitting the Quai D'Orsay two blocks later. More noise, but by then he didn't care. His ear was turned inward, listening to the rumblings of his own troubled conscience. Crosswalks in Paris can be a half-mile apart. Chapel ran across six lanes of traffic, pulled up at the esplanade overlooking the Seine as a *bâteau-mouche* slid past, lights blazing, one of the party boats – he could hear the bubbly chatter over the cars zooming past at his back. Over the thumping of his heart. He dropped a hand to his leg. Strong as ever. *'The office is near the Métro. Mr Chapel won't have to walk far.'* 'Fuck you, too, Leclerc,' he murmured.

He followed the river north, the Eiffel Tower his guide, breathtaking for the hundredth time, lit stem to stern, bathing the night in a warm, celebratory glow. He crossed at the Pont de l'Alma, and continued along the Rive Droite, leaving the Seine at the Palais de Chaillot, moving back into the city. The sixteenth arrondissement was largely a business district, the few restaurants he passed long closed, dark storefronts staring back at him. In their reflections, he saw the faces of his departed colleagues as he remembered them best. Keck configuring a surveillance system; Gomez slamming a fist on his desk and hooting after a judge had granted his motion for a search warrant; Santini cracking wise from behind the *Sporting News*; and Babtiste, a gentle giant who sought benediction not from God, but from his two children. Boys, Chapel had learned, seven and four, their mother taken from them by cancer the year before, now orphans. Who had told them their father was dead? Who had blotted the hope from their lives?

A wave of hate swept through him. He promised to exact a swift and terrible retribution for the deaths of his friends. He would be merciless. He would kill without compunction. He would avenge. Chapel laughed at himself. He was the only enforcement agent he knew who didn't carry a gun. He could never be an angel of death. Having grown up in a household where violence was an everyday occurrence, he had a built-in aversion to it. He was physically incapable of it. Yet, part of him knew that someday he might be put to that test. He tried to imagine pulling a trigger, actually shooting to kill. It was no good. He couldn't put himself in that picture. Then he saw himself stepping in front of a child, and this time, it worked. He could feel the trigger buckle under his finger, his arm reverberate with the weapon's kick. He told himself that if he had to kill, it would be for a different reason. To make sure that there were fewer boys left without a father, fewer children who spent their lives fruitlessly trying to fill the void left by sudden death.

Scattered lights burned on the upper floors. Sarah had said that Neuilly was a tony area; one of the city's ritziest neighborhoods. There was little clue to the fact. Few pedestrians were out, though that was to be expected at this hour. Traffic was so light as to be nonexistent. Otherwise, it was just another immaculate street in an immaculate city.

Finally, he stopped, his breath steady, his pulse eager, craving the order to move out. A blue and white lightboard high on the wall read 'ATM.' Next to it, a city placard showed the street. 'Rue Saint-Paul. XVIième.' On his city map, he'd inked three red dots and two blue ones at this location. It was the epicenter of Taleel's activity. Slowly, he turned, looking at the buildings around him.

'You're here,' he whispered to the mute facades.

'I'm going to find you,' he promised the drawn curtains.

'And then, by God . . .' and here words failed him. He wasn't sure what he would do.

Somewhere behind his accusing eyes, a chorus demanded answers to questions he would never dare ask aloud. Would the discovery of Taleel's trail really lead to his accomplices? Was there time to track them down? Would it be enough to thwart the attack on American soil the man on the videotape had spoken of? And deeper questions still. Was he up to this challenge? Did he have the experience to lead the investigation?

Time and again, the answer came back *yes*. He was certain Taleel's account at the Bank Montparnasse would yield information that pointed to Taleel's accomplices. From them, he would exact information about where and when the attack was to take place. And yes, he would have adequate time to stop them.

I believe, therefore I can.

To Adam Chapel, belief was an all-conquering force. Hesitation, doubt, ambiguity: these were words that brought a man nothing, words that led to failure, defeat, and shame. And tonight, as he stood alone beneath a flickering light in a section of the city he'd never visited before, he knew he must rely on his will alone to find Taleel's accomplices, to put a stop to their deadly plans, and to rescue his only chance at living a life free of torment.

Chapter 23

Chapel emerged from the Métro a little before one in the morning, bleary-eyed, exhaustion outrunning him. His mind had shut down. It was his body that was giving the demands. He needed a Vicodin and he needed it now. The Boulevard St-Germain was quiet and he crossed at his leisure. There is a calm that comes over a large city late at night, a hush that amplifies the slightest sound. Lifting an ear, he caught a familiar noise, a sweep whisking the pavement. Or the scuff of a leather heel. He'd heard it earlier, more than once. Turning a corner, he ducked into a doorway, pressing his body hard against the wall. He counted to ten. A shadow lengthened on the pavement. A figure approached, the step casual but steady. A mane of black hair filled the doorway. He recognized the white tank top, the sleek trousers.

'You shouldn't wear J.P. Tods,' he said, stepping into the street. 'At least, not the driving shoes. Those little round plugs tend to catch on the pavement and squeak. That's the third time I caught it.'

Sarah Churchill spun to face him, surprise, and maybe fear, widening her eyes. But only for a second, and Chapel made sure to remember the look. 'My mistake,' she said, too matter-of-factly. 'I'm tired and they're comfortable.'

' "Done in," I think you said earlier. Care to explain?'

Sighing, Sarah pushed the hair over her shoulders and shot him a world-weary glance. 'Got a drink?'

He poured Sarah a Jack Daniel's in a bathroom glass, popped a Vicodin, and downed it with a gulp of tap water.

'I'm not the enemy,' he said, stepping out of the bathroom. He handed Sarah her drink. He was too tired to be angry, too suspicious to be surprised. 'Why were you following me? Did Glendenning put you up to it? He's a sneaky shit.'

'No, no. Entirely my idea. Just something I do.' She might have been talking about her predilection for tiddlywinks. She lifted the glass. 'Cheers.' The Jack Daniel's disappeared in an instant. No shake of the head. No watering of the eyes.

'A little odd, isn't it?' he asked, taking a seat on the edge of the bed. 'One in the morning, playing hide-and-seek all over Paris.'

'Habit,' she answered. 'If it means anything to you, I only do it to people I like.'

'I'm flattered. What comes next? Mug 'em in a back alley, or do you just pounce on them and go for the jugular?'

'You don't understand.'

'I wouldn't presume to. Actually, seeing as I have no idea who you are, I don't think I could. Sarah Churchill. Is that even your real name? Mine's Adam Alonzo Chapel. Born November twelfth, 1970, in St Vincent's Hospital, Manhattan. Want my social security number? I can give that to you, too.'

'It's Sarah,' she said, her voice a whisper. 'Sarah Anouska Churchill. August the second, 1975. I'm a Leo, so we won't get along. Scorpios and Leos never do. My father was a paratrooper. A general officer. Mum's passed away, too. It was an accident. She fell asleep on the M1 motorway.

Luckily, no one else was hurt. I've got three older brothers. Two of them are in the service. I told you about Freddy. I joined MI6 out of university. Six years now.'

'It's gotten to you,' he said. 'Take a sabbatical.'

'Oh no,' she retorted. 'I was like this before. A nosy little brat. I used to traipse around the village. "Having a spy," I called it. You never really know a person until you see them alone. It's addictive.' She paced to the window, pulled back the curtain, scanned the sidewalk. 'I could see you were much too keyed up to go to sleep. Thought I'd just hang around and see what you were up to.'

'Where exactly did you think I was going?'

'No idea. Actually, I half wondered if you were one of Gadbois's boys.'

'I thought we were working *together* with the French.'

'We are. In fact, I've never seen such cooperation. That's what makes me nervous. Bending over backwards, aren't they? I mean, come on, this is the DGSE we're talking about. They're usually a pretty tight-arsed lot. Now they're being too damn chummy by half.'

'You thought I was Leclerc's teammate? Give me a break.'

'Lord, no. What I mean is that Leclerc wouldn't know that General Gadbois had recruited you. You think terrorists are the only ones who work in cells?' She pulled a chair from a stand-alone desk, turned it around, and sat down, her legs splayed, arms crossed on the backrest. Her interrogation was over. His was about to begin. 'Besides, why shouldn't you be working for the DGSE?' she asked. 'Industrial espionage is right up their alley. You've got experience at the highest levels of the private sector. Know your way around the Fortune Five Hundred. Solid contacts with the government. You can ask questions without raising eyebrows *and get answers*. But help me with something, Adam. You see, there's a piece of your puzzle I just can't find. Why did you leave Price Waterhouse? You didn't like the money? Eight hundred thousand a year not enough for you? Or was it a question of power? Had to be something. Come on, Adam, tell me. No one walks away after making partner at twenty-eight. Like winning the Olympics and forgetting about the endorsements. Simply isn't done. You had the entire package – looks, brain, drive. They were grooming you to run the whole enchilada. And then one day, you chuck it all and say, "Good-bye, I'm through. Take the parking space, the pension, everything. Adios, chaps. It's been fun." Come on, then. What?'

'It was eight-fifty,' said Chapel, grimly amused. 'The salary, that is. Might as well get your facts straight.' Of course, they knew all about him. It made sense that they'd briefed Sarah. He was the odd man out.

'And so?' she asked.

'Go on. I'm anxious to hear the rest.'

'Fine.' Sarah shrugged, as if she'd be happy to. 'So, you left PW and ran off into the sunset. Literally, from what I've learned. Practically swam, biked, or ran every minute of every day for the next two years. Not many people can finish an Ironman triathlon in ten hours and five minutes. Two-mile ocean swim, one hundred and ten miles on the bike, and then a marathon in case you're still feeling chipper. I tried it once myself. Crapped out during the run. Had the mind for it, but the legs wouldn't do it. I went down at mile sixteen. Never had the courage to try it again. What were you running from, Adam? That's what we're all asking ourselves. Never seen someone so dogged.'

Chapel bit back a rebuke. He'd never been big on introspection. He didn't like her in his face, asking him all the tough questions he'd been avoiding his entire life. He looked at her closely. She was damp from the walk. Strands of hair clung to her forehead. A rosy sheen flushed her cheeks. Her shirt hugged her breasts, the damp cotton revealing the shadow of her areolae, and he could see it turned her on, her secret knowledge giving her the jolt she needed.

'Finished?' he asked.

'Almost,' she said, cocking her head. 'Help me with something and we can stop. Piece of essential information, actually. Your father died right about then, didn't he? Shot himself, if I'm not mistaken. Excuse me for being blunt, but the profession frowns upon niceties. Was that the reason you quit? You, one of those poor chums who spend their life trying to measure up to someone else's expectations? When he checked out, you decided you were free. That it? Surprised you didn't kill yourself, too. Happens all the time, and with stronger men than you.'

'Think you're telling me something I don't know?' he said, trying to keep it light, ignoring the pressure behind his eyes. 'Give it a rest and save your sixty-second shrink job for someone else.'

'You can tell me, Adam,' she continued, her voice a silken ice pick. 'I know all about demanding fathers. I had one too. Only the best would ever do. Top marks in school. Best at the gymkhanas. Better win or not try at all. Was that it? Had to meet Daddy's goals. Do as he said. Be the man he wanted to be.'

'Enough!' Chapel shouted, the force of his voice firing the pain in his shoulder.

'Tell me!'

'Tell you what? That he was a failure? That he never stopped complaining? That he was upset about how the world treated him? That he thought that there was some kind of conspiracy to get him? Is that what you want to hear? You want to know if I lived my life trying to meet his expectations? Why ask me? You already have all the answers.' Chapel laughed bitterly. He hated discussing his past, his family, despised personal confessions.

Everything was so tawdry, so pat looking back. Life was about the here and now, not what was long over. 'Are you done now?'

But Sarah only sighed, shaking her head as she fixed him with a steady gaze. 'Then came September eleventh and you were saved. Your search was over. A cause. A reason. A grail. Treasury snapped you up in a second. Not many with the experience you had, or the brains. Finally doing something you wanted. Is that the way you saw it? Or were you just looking for someone else to make impossible demands of you?'

'I'm afraid it's none of your business,' said Chapel, finding his calm.

'I beg to differ,' Sarah retorted. 'I may have to count on you to look after me one day. I'd say that makes your past all of my business. If you're shaky, unstable, I want to know it now, not later. Wake up, man. You're not in the real world anymore. This is the netherworld. No one's who they say they are. Giles Bonnard's one of ours, if you want to know. MI Six. Surprised? You're a spook now, whether you like it or not. You're one of us.'

The words echoed like the reading of a jail sentence. 'Are you finished?'

'Not quite.' She approached him as she spoke, lowering herself to a knee in front of him. 'After all that, though, I must say I didn't know you until tonight. Not who you were. What made you tick. I thought all that stuff about duty and country might be a lot of bravado, the usual bluff. Wave the flag. See who follows. I was wrong, Adam. That's what I learned. Wrong to think you're one of Glendenning's boys. Maybe even to think you're like me.' Tenderly, she brushed his cheek with her finger. 'Look at you. Concussed, burned, traumatized by the loss of three of your best pals, and here you are working a double shift when you should be in a hospital bed sedated and sleeping for the next three weeks. Get out while you can. This is the real thing. You're not cut out for it.'

He met her eyes. 'That's what Carmine Santini said. You're both wrong.'

Her hands found his chest, massaging him gently. 'How's the shoulder?'

'It's killing me,' he admitted.

She kissed the sides of his neck, his chin, his cheeks. 'What are we going to do with you?'

Her lips brushed his. He met their touch, tasted her. Was this real? Did she care for him? Desire him? Or was it another of her ploys? Was she moving him around the board, a pawn in a bigger game? The questions dissolved in a rush of pleasure. Raising his hand, he ran his fingers across her cheek. At his touch, she closed her eyes, brought the fingers to her mouth, kissed them. He shuddered, his body weakening. It felt so good. Did she know that it had been a year for him? Of course she did. She knew everything else about him, why not that?

Equal parts confused and enraged, Chapel pushed her away and stood. It wasn't a seduction; it was a slaughter. 'You should go,' he said.

Sarah gazed up at him. Reaching out, she ran a hand up his leg.

He felt dizzy, his resistance waning. 'No, Sarah.'

'I can see it in your eyes, Adam. You need someone.'

'Maybe I do,' he said. 'But I'll be the one to choose who it is.'

She stood and kissed him again, moving her lips against his. 'We need each other.'

Firmly, he grasped her arms and stepped away. 'Go,' he said, and opened the door to the hall.

'You won't last a minute out there,' she said breathlessly, pausing in the doorway.

'Why's that?'

'You're too honest. Don't you see? You're the last good man.'

Sarah didn't look back as she walked down the hall.

Chapter 24

In the Grand Salon of No. 6, Rue De La Victoire, Rafi Boubilas, proprietor of Royal Joailliers, was celebrating his release from Mortier Caserne. A gathering of his best friends stood round him, drinking champagne, sampling canapés, delivering hearty pats on the back. Lit by a magnificent crystal chandelier, framed by floor-to-ceiling windows, they might have been actors on a stage. Crouching next to the wall at the rear of the enclosed garden, Leclerc had a perfect view of the eighteenth-century *hôtel de ville*.

The terrace doors opened. A man and woman stepped outside, accompanied by the snappy rhythms of a Brazilian samba. A joint was produced, a match lit and the sour-sweet smell of marijuana drifted into the night.

Leclerc waited until the two returned inside the house, then snapped his fingers. A moment later, a black-clad figure dropped to the ground next to him, then another. Guillo and Schmid.

'Six of them,' he said. 'The lawyer, too. It's time they went home.'

Guillo opened a cell phone and dialed the Boubilas home. A young woman strolled across the salon and picked up the telephone. 'Madam, this is the police. We have had some complaints from your neighbors about the noise. This is not the first time. Maybe it is time your party ends. Or would you prefer us to send a patrol?'

The woman answered the polite request with a not-so-polite instruction. Dutifully, she delivered the message to Boubilas along, it appeared, with an animated recounting of how she told '*les flics*' to fuck off. It was clear, even from a distance of twenty meters, that Boubilas did not share her sense of humor. Setting down his glass, he walked to his attorney and whispered a word in her ear. A few minutes later, the guests began to depart. As the bells of the St-Michel cathedral tolled the midnight hour, the lawyer adjusted her beret, offered Boubilas her cheek, and left. Only Boubilas and his companion, a young woman, remained in the house.

'Showtime,' said Leclerc grimly.

Pulling a balaclava over his face, he set out across the lawn. The three moved silently, shadows in a shadowless night. Reaching the terrace, they dropped to the grass and rolled to the wall. Leclerc lifted his head, eyes making a quicksilver scan of the salon. Glasses littered the tables. Ashtrays brimmed to overflowing. A miniature mountain of cocaine adorned a mirror on the coffee table. But he saw no one.

With index and middle finger, he motioned to the next room, then commando-crawled beside the wall until he reached the second window. Again he popped up his head. It was Boubilas's study, and the party boy himself entered as if on cue. Walking directly to a sturdy desk of polished oak, he picked up a silver straw and availed himself of a line of cocaine, throwing his head back and grunting like a sated pig as he finished.

The woman entered the room. She was too young, too blonde, and too good-looking for an overweight lounge lizard like Boubilas. Her eyes spotted the coke, and a plastic smile stretched her cheeks. Joylessly, she followed his example, wiping the residue on her finger, and rubbing it into her gums. Sashaying to Boubilas, she pressed herself against him.

Leclerc led the men back to the terrace. Vaulting the stone railing, he crossed to the door and tried the handle. Locked. Withdrawing a folding knife from his pants, he threw open the blade and worked it into the doorjamb. The lock was as old as the home. A flick of the wrist and it gave.

Inside, they moved like wraiths. Silenced Beretta in hand, Leclerc navigated the hall, secretly hoping to be discovered so that he might be forced to use it. Moans issued from the dimly lit study. A last step delivered him to the doorway. The woman was on her knees, her head bobbing like a jackhammer, but to no avail. 'It is okay?' she asked, after each bout.

Leclerc raised a hand and counted down on outstretched fingers. *Three . . . two . . . one.*

They were on him before Boubilas could react. The girl was pushed to the ground, hands bounds with plastic ties, a wad of cotton cloth inserted into her mouth, a strip of duct tape to seal it.

'Take her out,' Leclerc said.

Boubilas kept still as a rock, the snout of the Beretta pressed into the folds of his jaw. His pants had sunk to the floor and were bunched at his ankles. Leclerc glanced down. 'I knew coke made it hard to get it up. I didn't know it could make it disappear altogether.' And then he slugged Boubilas in the gut. Because he wanted to. Because he needed to get rid of his hate. Because it might prevent him from killing the worm later on.

'Bonsoir, Rafí. Know who this is?'

'Yes. Good evening, Captain.'

Boubilas sat on the leather couch. Guillo stood behind him, an encouraging hand laid on the jeweler's shoulder.

'Time for a heart-to-heart,' Leclerc said, kneeling down so that he faced Boubilas directly. 'I'll tell you up front that

I don't give a shit about a trial, about proper statements. I'm not here for justice. Just for answers. I am here to stop something from happening. Okay? Something bad. You give me what I want, and my friends and I will go. Everyone chums. If you decide to be the tough guy, then things will go badly. First off, there's that coke in there. What is it – an ounce? Not to mention your private stash on the table. What happened, the guests didn't deserve the good stuff? Tell me, if I look around, think I'll find some more?' When Boubilas didn't answer, Leclerc patted his cheek twice. 'All right then, we start with something easy. What do you say? Yes? No?'

Still no answer.

Boubilas was fifty and sallow, a pudgy, pear-shaped man with the dissolute scowl of a lifelong substance abuser. The few strands of hair left to him, he kept long and tied into a ponytail. Beads of sweat rolled down his forehead. He stank of fear.

'How much did you hand over to Taleel yesterday?'

'Five thousand dollars,' answered Boubilas.

'That right?' Standing, Leclerc wandered to the desk and picked up an open bottle of Taittinger champagne. He took a sip, pronounced it 'not bad,' then returned to his place in front of Boubilas. He wanted to give him a few moments to think about his answer, to reflect upon this last stretch of sanity. 'That's your first and last lie tonight, okay? Look, just think of me as an old friend. No secrets. Let's start again. How much?'

'Fifty thousand.' The eyes moved down and to the left. It was a rapid movement, quick as a blink, but Leclerc was trained to notice such things. It was a lie.

Swiftly, and with great skill, he acted. One hand flew to Boubilas's forehead and forced it back so it hit the couch. The other shook the bottle of Taittinger violently, a thumb over its mouth, bringing the bottle to Boubilas's upturned nose, where he released a stream of the agitated wine into his nasal cavity. As Boubilas began to scream, Guillo stuffed a towel into his mouth, and his body bucked as he sucked the liquid into his lungs. Leclerc had been made to understand that the process of drowning in plain air was most uncomfortable.

In the salon, the music still played. Leclerc tuned his ears to the lilting, upbeat rhythm of the samba. An abstract painting hung on the wall above an aubergine couch. He wondered what it cost to buy a house like this, buy the drugs, the women, the art, and why all that money hadn't brought Boubilas an ounce of common sense.

'Take it out,' he said to Guillo. The towel came out. Leclerc put down the bottle of champagne. 'How much?'

Boubilas gulped down the air. 'Five hundred thousand.'

Leclerc jumped to his feet, taking hold of the ponytail, yanking it. 'Five hundred thousand what? Euros? Dollars? Pounds?'

'Dollars.'

'Who was Taleel working for?'

'I don't know.'

Leclerc picked up the bottle. 'Who was Taleel working for?'

'Really,' Boubilas spluttered, his damp face contorting with fear. 'It's strictly a transaction between agents. Mr Bhatia and myself. I don't know who his clients are.'

'When someone tells you to hand over five hundred thousand dollars, you ask.' Leclerc shook the bottle. 'Now, who did he work for?'

The eyes squeezed shut and he shook his head. 'I ca—!' Leclerc forced his head back and sprayed the champagne up the man's nose. Standing above him, he alternately shook the bottle and sprayed, shook and sprayed, until the bottle was empty and he threw it on the ground.

'Please,' Boubilas managed, as he gasped for air. 'Please – don't make me – don't – I won't—'

Leclerc slapped him across the face and Boubilas shut up.

'No one knows I am here,' Leclerc said. 'As far as the rest of the world is concerned, you kept your mouth shut until your lawyer gained your release. You're a standup guy. Say anything you like. Just don't say *you won't*. If you don't talk to me, I guarantee you'll never say anything to anybody again. Who is Taleel with?'

Fear, worry, shame, hope: all these played across Boubilas's face as he struggled to find an excuse that would permit him to reveal what he knew. Leclerc pulled back his sleeve to check the time: 12:07. He had all night. 'Who?' he shouted, his face an inch from Boubilas.

'It was just business. With Michel – the one the papers called Taleel. I handled some rocks for him. Stuff from Sierra Leone, Nigeria, those places. I brokered their sale to the boys in Antwerp. Everything outside the cartels goes through there.'

The cartels. In this case, DeBeers and Russdiamant, not Medellin and Cali. The rocks he so cavalierly handled were known as 'conflict diamonds,' mined by the regional war-lords and sold off to fund their excursions into terror. Leclerc knew Africa well enough to be acquainted with their good works. The double amputations performed with the aid of a dull machete. The rape of teenage girls. The impressment of preadolescent boys into their private armies. And of course, murder. Murder and murder and murder. Leclerc felt his headache returning. The tap-tap-tap behind his eyes.

'It was Taleel, then, who brought you the rocks?' he asked.

'I knew him as Michel. Michel Fouquet, I swear it.'

'How often?'

'Maybe ten times. He would bring a few hundred carats of raw diamonds. Some of it good, some junk.'

Leclerc played back his conversation with Chapel earlier that evening. He recalled there had been a period when Chapel surmised Taleel was out of town. 'Always Michel?'

'Yes.'

Leclerc told Guillo to find some more champagne. A magnum, if there was one. 'One more chance.'

'There was another, but only once. I met him late at night. At the Buddha Bar. It's very dark inside. I saw him for maybe two minutes. He passed me the stones in a case, then I left. Even then I could tell he didn't like it. A handsome man. Short hair. Serious. He is somebody.'

'How old?'

'Forty. Forty-five.'

'When?'

'A year ago. April, I think.'

'Name?'

'Ange,' he gasped. 'Mr Ange.'

'And how did you pay him? The truth!'

'I wired the money to an account in Germany. Gemeinschaft Bank of Dresden. The Holy Land Charitable Trust. That was the name. My bank will give you the instructions. Credit Lyonnais. Ask for Mr Monaco. I'm not lying. You'll see.'

'This Mr Ange, he is with Hijira?' Leclerc threw out the name, but Boubilas's face registered no knowledge of it. The eyes stared at the ground, forlorn, abandoned.

'He is with Mr Ange.'

With a warrant, Leclerc could make Boubilas sit for an Identikit artist, but by then Boubilas would be in a less cooperative mood. *A warrant.* Leclerc laughed at himself for even considering such a quaint notion. It was his time at the Sûreté. An hour inside police headquarters and he was beginning to think like a cop. The truth was that tomorrow morning at nine o'clock, Boubilas would be standing in front of his lawyer, screaming his head off about the brutality he'd suffered at the hands of the French secret service. She, in turn, would ream Gadbois a new asshole, and Gadbois would come calling to Leclerc. The only warrant Leclerc would see would be the one with his own name on it. No one needed that shit. Standing, he took a last look at Boubilas. What a fucking waste product.

'Okay, boys, I'll see you outside.'

Schmid and Guillo left the room. Leclerc walked to the doorway. The pounding in his head was growing worse.

'That's it?' Boubilas asked, whimpering as he struggled with his pants. 'You finished with me?'

'What's wrong? It wasn't enough?'

Boubilas shook his head, cowing from a phantom blow. 'I know it's you, Leclerc. I recognize your voice. You can't do this to a man. Torture him, force him to answer your questions. It won't stand up, you know.'

'It doesn't need to. No court will ever hear of it.'

'Oh, they'll hear of it all right.' He was talking through his tears. 'Breaking into a man's house, hurting him. They'll hear of it. Where are your friends? Probably going at Lisette upstairs. Join them. I'll add rape to the charges.'

'*Charges?*' Something inside Leclerc snapped. One second, he was calm, disgusted by Boubilas, but ready to leave it at that. The next, he felt like he'd been the one tortured, and that it was his turn to seek retribution. Rushing across the room, he rammed the snout of his gun into Boubilas's neck. 'I wouldn't recommend telling anyone you had visitors tonight. No matter where you run, I can find you. Tonight you had a little bath. Think of it as a warning to get your life in order. If you make me come back, I'll break your neck. And you know the scariest part? I'll do it while you're sleeping. You won't even know I was there. Okay?'

Boubilas shuddered, nodding his head.

'Good,' said Leclerc. '*Alors, dors bien.*'

Chapter 25

George Gabriel closed the door to his room, kicked off his tennis shoes, and flung himself onto his bed.

'No!' he shouted, burying his face in his pillow, his fist pounding the mattress.

He was leaving Paris tomorrow. *Forever*. After what his father had ordered him to do, he could never come back. The thought of fleeing terrified him. He felt like a small boy. He wanted to hide. To cry. He wanted to appeal to someone that it wasn't fair, but there wasn't anyone to listen to him. Not Amina, his father's third wife. Not his real mother . . . *wherever she was*. Not his younger brothers or sisters. There was only Claudine, and she wasn't family.

Claudine. Calling her name to himself sent a melancholy shiver down his spine. *I won't leave you*, he promised with a teenager's violent passion.

Sitting up, he drew his knees to his chest and surveyed the densely furnished space he'd occupied for twelve years. Posters of Beckham, Ronaldo, Luis Figo, and the incomparable Zidane graced one wall; a single framed print of thousands of *hajis* circumambulating the Ka'aba, another. Twin chrome towers displayed his CDs. Pearl Jam and Creed were sandwiched between Nusrat Fateh Ali Khan and Salif Keita. Wedged against the wall was his prayer rug, neatly rolled up. An autographed photo of the 1998 World Cup winners occupied pride of place on his dresser, next to the desk where he'd studied countless hours to make the grades his father expected of him. When he'd made perfect marks three years running, his dad had rewarded him with a Bang and Olufsen stereo. More meaningful was the hug that came with it. The pull to his father's chest. The lasting embrace. The kiss on the cheeks. He would never forget the fierce light burning within his father's eyes, or the palpable outpouring of his pride.

Abandoning the bed, George Gabriel picked up a pair of fifteen-kilo dumbbells and began pounding out a set of curls. He could feel the eyes upon him, still prideful, but watchful, too. Commanding him. George was no longer a son, but a soldier, with the same responsibilities, and the same punishment for failure. His breath came harder, his arms swelling with fatigue. No matter what, he could not fail his father. It was unthinkable.

After thirty repetitions, he laid the dumbbells on the ground and looked at himself in the mirror. His biceps quivered. He checked that the door was locked, then rummaged through his armoire. His stash was hidden in a sock deep on the second shelf. He took out a pipe and filled the bowl. The window was open a crack, admitting a cooling night breeze. He lit the bowl and held the hit in as long as possible. When he exhaled, only a wisp of smoke left his mouth. He slipped the weed back into the sock, smiling. He was sure Amina knew it was there, just as he was sure she'd never say a word to his dad. They were friends. They shared secrets. She knew about Claudine. She'd asked how Claudine's father could allow her to date a boy she was not going to marry, and listened in awe as George related his girlfriend's plans to study medicine and become a cardiovascular surgeon. He'd even shown Amina her picture.

A hand groped beneath the shelf, peeling away the tape

until he freed the photograph. A glance at the door and he brought it into the light. She was blonde and intelligent, with a cat's green eyes. Born a Roman Catholic, at nineteen she was a devout atheist. On the back of the photo she'd penned the words, 'With all my heart to my forever man.'

There was no more dangerous contraband.

George smiled bitterly. Her 'forever man' was booked on a flight to Dubai in less than twenty-four hours. Disconsolately, he replaced the photo. There were still a few things he hadn't told Amina. He hadn't revealed that the touch of Claudine's hand made him happy for a week. Or that the hint of her smile filled him with an uncontrollable anticipation. He hadn't told her that they were sometimes making love two times a day, and that yes, he really did want to marry her. Some things even Amina wouldn't understand.

Not long ago, he'd spoken to her about a woman's rights. He told her she didn't have to stay inside all day long, looking after the kids, cooking all the meals. She didn't have to agree with his father's every pronouncement. Later that night, he'd overheard her tell his dad she would be going shopping the next day with a friend she'd made, a *kuffar* like Claudine, a lady not of the faith. Sweetly and excitedly, she'd told him that she wouldn't be home until later that evening, and asked if he might come home early to look after the kids and feed them their supper. There followed an ugly laugh, then a terrific slap that had made George wince. The ground floor shuddered when Amina hit the floor.

George had been too scared to go downstairs and check how she was.

Strangely, Amina had thanked him the next day. It was better that she knew her place, she'd said. She hadn't asked about Claudine since.

The room was suddenly quiet and he could hear his heart beating in his chest. The household was asleep. Not a sound lifted to him. He swallowed and found his mouth dry. He was smart enough to know that it was no ordinary case of cottonmouth.

'Hijira.' He whispered the word. *A new beginning*. George Gabriel had to pinch himself to remind himself he wasn't dreaming.

Yet, the word stirred him. How could it not, when he'd been hearing of it his entire life, living it day in, day out, eating it, breathing it, sleeping it? The moment was upon him: the realization of his family's destiny. And with it, the responsibility his father had thrust upon him.

The plane ticket lay on his desk, next to the dagger. It was an Italian blade, his father had told him. Made for the close kill. Unsheathing the knife, he caressed the tip. A bead of blood blossomed on his fingertip. He licked it, before spreading the plans of the Salpetitpierre Hospital out in front of him. Using the dagger, he traced his path from the parking lot to the third-floor burn unit. He found the exits and committed them to memory. He located the stairwells and the security stand and the nurse's station. Getting in would not pose a problem. The hospital was a sprawling complex covering three city blocks with a dozen entrances, none of which boasted so much as a security guard. There were no metal detectors on the premises, no secret surveillance devices. It would be a question of courage, of moxie, of having the courage to get in and do the job, and get out, quickly, neatly, and efficiently.

Pushing aside the map, he opened the ticket jacket and removed a photograph of the man that he was to kill. It looked like the reproduction of a passport shot. He was still young, but there was nothing boyish about him. The eyes were exacting. The mouth firmly set. The jaw wide. The neck well-muscled. He decided he would not want to fight this man, even if he had been badly burned by Taleel's bomb. A blow to his shoulder would incapacitate him, but George should not be worried. The American would be unsuspecting, an easy target if George moved quickly and did not hesitate.

Dagger in hand, George Gabriel stood from the desk. Assuming the fighter's stance, he executed the controlled movements he'd learned at the camp in the Bekaa, advancing, lunging, blocking, slashing, always grunting as he delivered the death blow. In the warm air, his bare skin glistened with sweat.

'I am a Utaybi,' he murmured to his reflection as he drove the blade home. 'Hijira is my destiny. I am a Utaybi. The desert is my home.'

But as he repeated the words, his conviction faltered, weakened by the sinful smile of a passionate young woman with hair of gold and a generous figure. Dropping his hands to his side, he froze, knowing then fully, and for the first time, that he was no longer certain of anything. His name. His destiny. Or his home.

Chapter 26

The weight of the Virginia dusk struck Owen Glendenning like a velvet hammer as he poked his head through the doorway of the Lear jet. It was just after eight. In the distance over the army of bridged oaks and the picket of weeping willows, the sun retreated below the horizon. They had taxied to a far corner of the runway at Dulles International Airport. As the roar of a departing aircraft faded, a bullfrog's contented croak reasserted itself in lovely counterpoint to a lazy cicada.

Allan Halsey was waiting at the base of the stairs. 'Welcome back, Owen. How are you feeling?'

'Trips are getting longer and the days are getting shorter. If that doesn't sum it up, try this: like shit.'

Halsey led the way to the waiting automobile, opening the rear door for Glendenning. 'I figured as much. I've got some chow set up for you in the war room. Sykes is in from the Bureau to take a look at the evidence you brought along.'

'If it's a steak, I want it well-done,' said Glendenning. 'Goddamn frogs gave me an entrecote for lunch that I swear was still alive and quivering. They call it *"bleu"* and sneer at you if you don't think it's the damn best thing since Escoffier created béarnaise.'

'How's chicken fried steak with buttered carrots and mashed potatoes sound?'

'As long as there's a mug of coffee to go with it, why, just about perfect.'

'A mug? I've got the Mr Coffee boiling over.'

'Maxwell House?'

'Nothing but the best.'

Glendenning chuckled for the first time that day. 'I knew there was a good reason we transferred FTAT from Treasury.'

The drive to Langley took fifteen minutes. After clearing security, the two men took the staff elevator to the sixth floor and proceeded directly to a conference room at the end of the east wing. The table was set with place mats, cloth napkins, and silver cutlery. Silver warming trays adorned a sideboard. A lone man waited inside, cleaning off his plate with a last chunk of cornbread.

'Hey, Glen,' said Sheldon Sykes, shooting out of his chair, wiping his mouth with a sleeve. 'Didn't know when you'd get here, so I went ahead and helped myself.'

Sykes was the Bureau's technical liaison to the Agency, half scientist, half bureaucrat, the kind of perpetually smiling face Glendenning could do without.

'No problem,' said Glendenning, though privately he was miffed at the Bureau man's piss-poor manners. 'You need to get moving anyway. Here's what we got.' Opening his briefcase, he removed a DVD and explained that it held a copy of the video found in Mohammed al-Taleel's apartment. 'At the end of the tape there's a chance these jokers inadvertently captured the image of a third party. It could be one of their buddies. As the speaker comes towards the camera, I want you to check his sunglasses. We're fairly certain that there's a reflection of someone standing inside the room. Enhance the images, do your magic, until you can tell me who or what it is.'

Sykes reached for the DVD, but Glendenning held it in his fingers a moment longer. 'This is white-hot, you understand me. You are to personally supervise the men examining this. Not a word of its contents is to get out.'

'Yes sir.'

'And Sykes? It doesn't do to keep the President waiting.'

As Sykes pulled on his coat and rushed from the room, Glendenning pondered the fact that his mere presence at Langley was a minor miracle. It had been a long time since the two agencies had worked hand in hand. As a result of the Church Commission's investigations in the mid-1970s into abuses by the FBI under J. Edgar Hoover, and an endless string of CIA provocations abroad, laws had been put on the books preventing the two from anything more than a vestigial collaboration. FBI was domestic. CIA was foreign. And never the twain shall meet. The Patriot Act had changed that, and with the creation of a department of Homeland Security, it looked like cooperation might be institutionalized in the form of a new agency for domestic intelligence, something akin to Britain's MI5.

When he was gone, Halsey took a seat on the edge of the table. 'You staying much longer?'

'Another hour or so. Got a powwow with the barons of the banking committee tomorrow morning. The good Senator Leach wants to cut our purse strings in return for some of that "soft money" we hear so much about these days from his benefactors at the money center banks. The old boy'll have a heart attack when he hears how much Blood Money is costing us.'

'He's serious about cutting back?'

'Serious? The man wants to halve our budget. Says the money's better spent with the frontline troops. The Pentagon or Homeland Security'll suit him and his pals just fine. They're against everything we're doing. Too much disclosure, they cry. Too much oversight. A violation of their customers' rights. Truth is, they don't give a damn about their customers' rights. They're just pissed about the extra cost of filling out all those SARs and CTRs. Don't want to admit it's their job as much as ours to keep an eye out for the bad guys.'

'You set 'em straight. Tell 'em to leave our funding alone. If Hijira turns out to be the pain in the ass I'm guessing, it'll cost Leach's money center banks a damn sight more than what they're forking over now.' Halsey turned to leave, but hesitated at the doorway. 'Say, Glen, mind if I ask you something? Off the record?'

'Shoot.'

'What the hell happened over there?'

Glendenning looked up uneasily. 'Don't know yet. On the surface, it looks like the Frenchies slipped up, called in the cavalry before the trap was set. Only one problem . . .'

'What's that?'

'Doesn't explain why Taleel didn't have the money.'

If Halsey caught a whiff of Glendenning's suspicions, he made no show of it. 'Hijira's a clever bunch, eh?'

The deputy director of operations for the Central Intelligence Agency felt himself drifting and strangely ill at ease. His eyes wandered the room, unable to settle anywhere for more than a second. 'Maybe,' he said. 'Maybe more than that.'

Finally at home and ensconced in the warmth of his study, a second brandy in his hand, Glen Glendenning picked up a telephone and dialed a number in Geneva, Switzerland. For once, he was not thinking about Adam Chapel or Sarah Churchill or any member of the Blood Money task force currently searching for Hijira. It was one A.M. It was his private time.

'*Allo*,' answered a graceful female voice.

'Morning, love. I trust I didn't wake you.'

'Glen – you are back already? I told you not to call me. It is too dangerous. Not now.'

'To hell with it, Claire. If Maggie's lawyers are going to tap my phone, let 'em. What are they going to discover that they don't already know?'

'But you are so close to the court date. It could make things much more complicated.'

'That's hard to imagine. She's already getting all my money, what there is of it, at least. I decided to say screw it. If the President doesn't understand, he can have my resignation.'

Glendenning closed his eyes, and pictures of Claire Charisse filled his mind and warmed his body as no amount of brandy could. She was French, a petite brunette of thirty-five possessed of a dancer's lithe figure, inquisitive black eyes, and a sarcastic smile. She was stubborn as a mule and could swear like a Marine. She knit him wool sweaters that were far too large and cooked him gourmet meals that would feed an army. '*Mais mangez, mon petit*,' she would urge him, scooting her chair next to his and watching his every bite like an adoring mother. Once Glendenning had asked her what a beautiful gal like her was doing with a broken-down racehorse like himself. She'd grown furious on the spot. 'I have the best man in the world,' she'd answered. 'I would settle for nothing less.'

'Did you make some progress while you were in Paris?' Claire asked.

'Not exactly progress, but we came up with some interesting stuff.'

'All of Europe is afraid. The security at the office was terrible. Seven years I worked for the United Nations. This morning they treat everyone at the door like they are terrorists. Another threat, they said. I say I have work to do. Medicine that must be shipped out. Children are waiting. *Today. This morning.* But no one cares. Security, they say. The queue was so long, I had to wait an hour to get in.' Suddenly, she broke off her speech. 'Oh, Glen,

I am so sorry to think about myself. Did you know these men?'

'Not personally, but it looks like—' he cut himself off. 'I'd love to tell you more, but you know I can't.' Rousing himself, he adjusted his frame so that he sat up straighter in the leather chair. A reading light burned over his shoulder, but the rest of the room was dark. He pulled a blanket over his legs to warm himself. 'Anyhow, I can't tell you how difficult it was to be so close to you and not be able to come see you.'

'I miss you, dear.'

Glendenning sighed, needing her. 'I miss you, too. How are you feeling?'

'Not so badly. We started the second round of therapy on Monday. I haven't thrown up yet, so I suppose that is good.'

'And the pain?'

'I will see Dr Ben-Ami later this week. He has promised me a miracle.'

'Three days,' he whispered. It was the countdown until he could hold her in his arms.

'Yes, my dear. Three days.'

'Have you chosen a dress? Remember, nothing too sexy. We don't want to shock our esteemed guests.'

'Anything above the ankle shocks them. They are savages.'

'Now, Claire,' he admonished kindly, even as a part of him agreed with her.

'Really, it's true. The way they treat women is *insupportable* . . . it isn't fair.'

'They're to be the president's guests, so we must treat them with all due respect.'

'I should come topless. How typically French, they will say.' She laughed deliciously at her own humor. 'Do you think they would let me in?'

Imagining her naked form, he repressed a decidedly ungentlemanly response. 'You'd cause a diplomatic stir, to say the least.'

'It would teach them a thing or two.'

'Yes, my dear, it would.'

'I'm sorry you couldn't stop over.'

For a moment, neither of them spoke, and the silence burst with the accumulated joys and frustrations of a long distance relationship.

'Three days, my love,' said Owen Glendenning. 'Be strong.'

'*Toujours. A bientôt, mon amour.*'

Chapter 27

The digital clock read 8:45 when Adam Chapel and Sarah Churchill finished examining the account records of Albert Daudin, aka Mohammed al-Taleel, at the Bank Montparnasse.

'Two steps forward, one step back,' said Chapel as he pushed his chair away from the table.

'What do you mean?' asked Sarah. 'You wanted a lead, you've got it. I thought you'd be ecstatic. It's the triumph you wanted. Paper over people. You even have me convinced. Bravo, Adam. You were right.'

'Germany.' He spoke the word with unabashed disgust. 'The money was wired in from Germany.'

'And what's wrong with that?'

'You've got no idea.' He shook his head, recalling the woes of a dozen previous investigations: the requests for information, the promises of cooperation, the neglected messages, the nasty missives that followed, the institutionalized lying. 'America's most closemouthed ally. We don't talk to them and they don't talk to us. Bilateral relations at their finest.'

'Come now, they're not as bad as that. I've worked with the Bundespolizei several times.'

'Things have changed.'

Rubbing his forehead, he stared at the pile of account

statements spread across the chrome and glass table. While the account had not proved to be the gold seam he'd hoped, it pointed an unequivocal finger in the right direction and brought them one step closer to Taleel's paymaster.

On the first of every month, a numbered account at the Frankfurt branch of Deutsche Internationale Bank, a world-class financial behemoth with assets in excess of three hundred billion dollars, wired Mr Daudin the sum of one hundred thousand Euros and no cents. The statements went back three years without an aberration. Always the first. Always one hundred thousand Euros.

As with Taleel's account at the BLP, the money in the Montparnasse account was withdrawn primarily by ATM, according to a set schedule. The maximum daily limit was higher, however, set at two thousand euros. Until two days earlier, the balance of the account had stood at a healthy seventy-nine thousand and five hundred Euros. Today, it wobbled at an anemic five hundred. The remaining balance had been wired back to the Deutsche International Bank. Hijira was closing up shop. Endgame, just as Sarah had said.

Sitting on top of the stack were the original documents filled out to open the account. Two items had piqued Chapel's curiosity. Daudin's nationality, listed as Belgian, birthplace Bruges, passport number included; and his date of birth, the thirteenth of March, 1962. Taleel, though, was twenty-nine and looked it. He could never have passed for a forty year old. The conclusion was inescapable. Taleel and Daudin were different people. Hijira had more than one operative in Paris. Was Daudin the man who had left the television on in Taleel's apartment? Was he the man who had, in fact, retrieved the cash from Royale Joailliers? The questions fired a new urgency in Chapel. Immediately, he had phoned Marie-Josée Puidoux at the BLP to ask if Roux, too, was Belgian, and if he had indicated his date of birth.

'We need to get Halsey on the line,' he said to Sarah.

'Don't be silly. Call Giles Bonnard's opposite number in Berlin.'

'Germany's not an Egmont country. They don't maintain a financial intelligence unit. They're real touchy about letting anyone look over their shoulders.'

In the early 1990s, despite the creation of many national FIUs, or financial intelligence units, it was clear that the specter of money laundering was growing in scope and sophistication. Criminals relied increasingly on cross-border transfers to spirit their booty from one corner of the globe to another. Too often, a single country working alone to isolate a criminal found itself unable to surmount the obstacles limiting the exchange of information between foreign law enforcement agencies. In 1995, leaders of the FIUs of five countries met at the Egmont-Arenberg Palace in Brussels, to systematize the exchange of information between them – or put it in vulgar terms, to do away with bureaucratic bullshit that let criminals use the law against them.

Chapel dialed the chief of the Foreign Terrorist Asset Tracking Center from a landline. Waiting for an answer, he met Sarah's eye and held it, daring her to reveal her true thoughts, her real emotions. She had dressed formally in a tailored navy suit and cream-colored silk top. Her hair fell loosely about her face, and she'd made a point of leaving it ruffled, a little wild. She might be a fashion editor who'd been pushing herself too hard or a socialite washed-out after a night out on the town.

Every glance awakened his frustrations with the slippery course their relations had taken. He wasn't sure who she was, or what he was supposed to expect from her, or how, even, he was supposed to treat her. Was she a colleague, a rival, a would-be lover, or just a spy doing her job?

'Adam, this you?' It was Halsey, and his voice was pained with exhaustion.

'Sorry to wake you, sir. We've come onto something that might need your soft touch.'

'The sledgehammer is ready. What is it?'

'We've moved up the ladder a rung. We've identified a second player operating in Paris. He opened an account at the Bank Montparnasse under the name Albert Daudin. It looks like Taleel was sharing the alias to draw funds from the account.'

'Daudin. I'll check out the name. What else can I do?'

'This guy, Daudin, was getting his money from an account at the Deutsche International Bank. A hundred grand a month's worth. We've got the account number, the dates of the transfers, all that stuff. I'd like you to grease the wheels, see if you can convince our friends in Berlin to have a quiet word with DIB.'

As Chapel spoke, the door to the room opened and Leclerc slipped inside, no hello, no nod, no nothing. Taking a chair opposite them, he kicked one of his boots onto the table and shook loose a cigarette. Chapel turned towards the wall, putting a hand to his ear, though the connection was as clear as if Halsey were next door.

'The Germans are pretty tough on this kind of thing,' Halsey was saying. 'Individual privacy's a big deal over there. They don't even let their own boys look at their citizens' accounts. It's *verboten.* I don't know what good it will do, but I'll have a word with Hans Schumacher and see if he can pull some strings.' Schumacher was a big shot in the finance ministry, a former commando with GS-G9 who was regarded as having his priorities straight, which meant that he followed the American line. Halsey coughed, and Chapel could imagine him padding from the bedroom to allow his wife her sleep. 'Anything else you want to tell me now that you've gotten me up at two forty-five? What's the FBI doing over there?'

'They're going door-to-door, but so far they've come

up empty. The guy's a ghost. Get me a name.' Chapel hung up.

'*Les boches*,' said Leclerc, eyes focused on the lighting of his cigarette. His damp hair hung in his face, accentuating his pale skin, the iron black circles under his eyes. 'We were too soft on them at the end of the war. We should have made them a worker state. An agrarian economy. No factories. No more army. Just cows, *wurst*, and beer.' He laughed thinly at his joke, exhaling flutes of smoke through his nostrils. 'You want a name, Chapel? I have one for you. The Holy Land Charitable Trust. They're in Germany. Berlin, if I'm not mistaken.'

'Who're they?'

'Friends of Taleel's. Maybe they do some business together at some point.'

'Are they funneling money to Hijira?' asked Sarah.

'You can say that.'

'Well done, Captain Leclerc,' she chimed. 'Thank God, something other than a lousy bank account. Who's the front man? Any idea?'

She's playacting, thought Chapel angrily. Kissing our French colleague's ass, even though she disliked the arrogant shit as much as he.

'No one has been found, Miss Churchill,' Leclerc said bluntly. 'We've got nothing on them, as far as I know. It's a name, that's all. Like I said, a group Hijira did business with.'

'Where did you get the info?' Chapel asked.

'Sources,' said Leclerc.

'*What sources?* We're on the same team. Maybe I'd like to ask him a few questions myself.'

Leclerc didn't bother to look at him. 'Sarah, would you be so kind as to explain to Mr Chapel that we are not playing cops and robbers. We do not bring our informants to the station.'

'It's not a question of me corrupting your source,' retorted Chapel. 'You traipse in here and drop a bombshell – you've located an organization that is doing business with Hijira – financing them to some extent, I presume – and you want me to leave it at that.' Before he was even aware of his actions, Chapel found himself out of his chair, advancing on Leclerc. 'Come on, we're waiting. Who, exactly, is the Holy Land Charitable Trust? What, exactly, is their relation to Hijira? And where, exactly, did you come by this information?'

Leclerc went on smoking his cigarette as if he hadn't heard a word.

'You have an obligation to tell me!' Enraged, Chapel plucked the cigarette from his hand, but Leclerc was up before he could drop it in the ashtray. Kicking the chair behind him, he shoved Chapel against the wall. 'Stay away. Understand?'

'I'm waiting for my answer,' Chapel said, grimacing as his shoulder cried out. Then it came to him where Leclerc had gotten his name. 'I thought Boubilas wasn't talking.'

Leclerc laughed bitterly.

'What else did he have to say?' Chapel pressed. 'You expect me to believe that the only thing you got out of him was the Trust? How was he involved with Taleel? Brokering gems for them? Diamonds, I bet,' he mused, remembering the murders of the US Treasury agents in Nigeria last month. 'What else does he know about Hijira? Did Taleel have any associates? Friends? Come on. Tell us.'

Leclerc's face darkened. Picking up his cigarettes, he walked to the door. 'Just check them out. They have an account at the Gemeinschaft Bank of Dresden. I don't know anything more than that and neither does my source. And by the way, I don't think you have to worry about the German authorities forcing them to open their books. Thornhill Guaranty purchased the bank a year ago. That makes it an American company.' He pointed to the clock. 'Hey, *mon ami*, you better get moving if you're going to make your appointment. Almost ten o'clock. The Salpetitpierre Hospital is at the other end of town. You don't want to be late.'

Without another word, he stalked from the room, leaving the door yawning behind him.

Leclerc threw his leg over the saddle of the Ducati, zipped up his jacket, and slid the key into the ignition. *Chapel*, he was thinking, *you* really *must learn to close your mouth*. He knew it was stupid to expect so much. Americans were a loudmouthed bunch in general, even when they spoke in whispers. A thought had yet to cross their minds that they did not feel obliged to share with the rest of the world. Turning the key, Leclerc started the engine, but a second later, he turned it off again. Inexplicably, he felt nailed to that very spot.

It isn't right, a voice from a long-silent corner of his soul repeated.

Leclerc scoffed at it, but answered nonetheless. 'I'm a soldier. I follow orders. That's that.'

A soldier who cowers in the stairwell when the others charge.

'A smart one,' he answered, amazed at his conscience's newfound temerity. 'One who does as he's told. I'm alive. They're dead. Don't confuse being foolish with being brave. Besides, who else could have found out about the Trust or Monsieur Ange?'

So why didn't you tell them about him? Surely they'd be interested.

Finally, Leclerc had no more answers. He mumbled something about Chapel being an ingrate, but his words lacked conviction. He was looking for ways to hate the American, only to keep from hating himself. Chapel, who ran into danger without a backward glance. Chapel, who had every right to ask what Boubilas had said. Chapel, the accountant, who was every inch the soldier Leclerc should be. Suddenly, he raised his fist and crashed it down on his leg. The pain was welcome, if only to distract him from the lingering burn of Gadbois's huge palm on his back. A swat on the back was the general's ultimate compliment.

'You can give them the Holy Land Trust,' he'd said when Leclerc had met him at five-thirty that morning to debrief him about the Boubilas interrogation. 'But that's all.'

'They need to know the other thing, too,' Leclerc had protested. 'You know, the other man. Maybe the agency has a line on him. He's the boss. They've got to know.'

'No,' said Gadbois. 'Ange is for us alone.'

'You know him?'

'Know *who*?' Gadbois shook his head, the old lion looking his age. 'There is no such person.'

It wasn't much, but it was something. When you were as thirsty as Chapel, as desperate for a lead, it looked like a long, tall glass of water. The Holy Land Charitable Trust. The Gemeinschaft Bank of Dresden. One more account. One more chance. He felt the currents tugging at him, yanking him east. Still, for a moment he resisted. Maybe because he disliked Leclerc so intensely. His unassailable confidence. His flagrant disregard for the rules of human conduct.

Sarah drove the Renault south through town, the traffic light, a cheery sun behind them. They crossed through St-Germain-des-Prés and dashed past the Ile de la Cité. A bag of croissants sat between them, filling the car with a buttery, inviting scent. The mention of the bank in Dresden was no coincidence. First the DIB, then the Gemeinschaft Bank. Hijira was hiding in Germany. They didn't just know the rules, they knew more. About the nasty interplay between governments. About the petty backbiting and adolescent uncooperativeness. Someone had made them privy to all the backroom secrets no one ever talked about.

Chapel was on the phone yet again, this time to a nondescript office building in Vienna, Virginia, home to the Financial Crimes Enforcement Network, another unsleeping crusader in the unsleeping war.

'Hey, Bobby. This is Adam. I need you to run a search for me double quick. The Holy Land Charitable Trust. Reporting financial institution is the Gemeinschaft Bank of Dresden.'

'Know them well,' said Bobby Freedman, a twenty-five-year-old analyst full of piss and vinegar even at three-thirty in the morning. 'Picked up by Thornhill Guaranty in an all-stock deal thirteen months ago, primarily to expand Thornhill's private banking operations in Europe. A clean operation. Very white shoe, or white boot, or whatever it is they wear over there on the Elbe.'

'The Trust is anything but. It's a conduit of funds to Hijira. Go all-out on this one. Even if the search comes up negative, get on to Thornhill and have them run up a set of account records along with the Trust's opening docs. Give me anything and everything you got. If they so much as blink, call Admiral Glendenning and have him read them the riot act.'

'Roger that.'

Chapel had barely hung up when the phone chirped again. It was Halsey. 'I got Schumacher on the horn. It's a nonstarter. The presiding magistrate won't hear about issuing a writ for the Deutsche International Bank without a hearing. We never had a chance. The judge is a lefty – a Green, no less. He sees a fascist behind every minister.'

'Didn't you tell him about the video? What does he think we want the information for?'

'You're going to show it to him yourself. He's deigned to fit you into his schedule this afternoon at three P.M. There's a flight leaving from DeGaulle at eleven. Frank Neff, the FBI legat, will meet you there and give you a DVD of the video.'

Chapel checked his watch and considered skipping the appointment with Dr Bac. Awakening, he'd been met with a ferocious headache. His shoulder had stiffened. The slightest movement exacted a terrific revenge. Even so, he'd forced himself to forgo another Vicodin. It was more important to have all his wits about him at the bank than to avoid the worsening pain.

'I can't make the eleven,' he said. 'I've got to see a doc here about my shoulder. It got fried pretty bad.'

'You sure?'

Damn you, Chapel thought. 'Yes. I'm sure.'

'Okay. Hold on and let me check. Lufthansa's got a flight at one that will put you into Berlin at two-thirty. We'll have a car waiting. Pray that the plane is on time. We can't afford to piss off this judge.'

Chapel hung up. 'Step on it,' he said to Sarah. 'We've got to be clear of the hospital by eleven.'

Sarah plunged her foot onto the accelerator. 'What's the occasion?'

'Get out your passport. We've got a plane to catch.'

Chapter 28

Traffic came to a standstill along the International Friendship Bridge linking the cities of Foz de Iguacu, Brazil, and Ciudad del Este, Paraguay. Seated on a peppy Honda 125, Marc Gabriel waited patiently. To his right, a string of laborers, traders, and Guarani Indians plodded along the narrow walkway. Most struggled beneath huge packages wrapped in newsprint. One by one they passed him by. The border checkpoint consisted of a metal cabin built in the center of the road. Three patrolmen lingered outside it, waving traffic past. Twenty-five thousand people crossed the decaying iron bridge each day. Few were stopped. Security was not an issue. In Ciudad del Este, the law was of secondary importance. Economics came first. People flocked to Ciudad del Este to make money, and the government didn't care how.

The cars inched forward, eight automobiles crammed into four lanes. A fissure opened in the crush, a disjointed line clear to the checkpoint. Flipping down his sun visor, Gabriel guided the bike across the bridge, revving the motor as he cleared the border. The guards didn't give him a second look. Ahead rose a smudged urban landscape: steel and glass skyscrapers, a few halted in midconstruction years ago; a collage of red-tiled roofs; a welter of billboards. All framed by the ever encroaching jungle.

Located at the heart of the Triple Frontier area, at the meeting point of the Brazilian, Argentinian, and Paraguayan borders, Ciudad del Este – the City of the East – had served for thirty years as a mecca for smugglers, counterfeiters, tax evaders, and gangsters. It was a filthy town. Overcrowded streets gave way to overcrowded alleys where tiny stores, *lojas*, some barely six feet by six feet offered everything that could fall off the back of a truck: car stereos, in-line skates, X boxes, even Viagra. Watch sellers, money changers, hawkers, and vendors of every stripe infested the sidewalks.

Gabriel had been coming to Paraguay for ten years. He felt comfortable amid the dazzling heat, the ripe humidity, and the permanent fog of exhaust. A ten-minute ride delivered him to the offices of Inteltech in the Las Palomas district. The low-slung warehouse had been freshly white-washed and fairly sparkled in the morning sun. Three cars were parked in the lot. All carried Brazilian plates. He didn't recognize any, but it had been six months since his last visit. Seventy percent of the cars in Ciudad del Este were 'hot' – stolen and imported from Brazil, Argentina, and Uruguay. It was not uncommon for residents to frequently change vehicles. They did not, however, frequently change a silver Mercedes 600.

He parked the bike at the rear of the whitewashed warehouse. Strolling through the packing line, he waved hello to a few familiar faces. Box after box stood on the conveyor belt. Most bore easily recognized corporate logos: Microsoft. Corel. Electronic Arts. Oracle.

He stopped in the rest room, using the last of the hand towels to wipe the sweat from his face. He spent a moment checking that the floor was clean, the toilet flushed. Raising a hand to the vent, he felt that the air-conditioning was functioning. He might pay his workers the local wage, but he made sure they labored in decent conditions.

Using his key, he opened the service entry to the executive

offices and strolled down the hallway, popping his head into the offices on either side of the corridor. Several men jumped to their feet. Most were programmers charged with breaking transcription codes on new and popular programs. *'Buenos días, Jefe,'* they repeated, one after another. With a smile and a 'Please, don't bother,' he waved them down.

'Ah, Gloria,' he said, as he reached the reception area. *'Cómo esta?'* She was a pretty girl, twenty, married with two children, unfailingly polite, but not too smart. She wore a pink rayon pant suit that did not flatter her hips.

'Senor Gabriel,' she said, placing a hand to her chest, rising from her chair. 'This is a surprise. Please, what may I bring you? Coffee? Tea? Perhaps with a little Cachaca?'

Music tinkled from the intercom. It took Gabriel a moment to recognize it as the same dreadful tune he'd listened to while on hold the day before. 'Mineral water would be fine.' Gloria rose, her smile stretched to the breaking point. As she circled her desk, he grabbed her wrist. 'Where is Senor Gregorio?'

Her vivacious brown eyes fluttered, weighing a lie, finding it too heavy. 'He has not arrived yet.'

'Surely, he called to inform you of his tardiness.'

'He said he would not be in today. He mentioned a trip.' She added quickly, 'He did not say where.'

'Bring me the water in his office,' said Gabriel, releasing her wrist and smiling. 'I am sure you will not phone him.' Over dinner at Café Iguana during the last visit, he remembered Gregorio boasting that he'd bedded the girl.

Gloria shook her head no, and hurried down the hallway. By the time she set the bottle of San Pellegrino on Senor Gregorio's desk two minutes later, Gabriel had located the company's financial records. He was surprised to see that Inteltech had recently moved its business to a new bank. The Banco Mundial do Montevideo. Inteltech moved on average thirty thousand units a month to wholesalers in

Panama, Bogota, and Marseilles. The bank statements showed a steady revenue stream of approximately nine hundred thousand dollars. The company boasted gross margins of seventy-four percent and booked a net profit each month of over five hundred thousand dollars. The figure was not entirely accurate. It was Gabriel's practice to over-invoice the cost of the compact disks and production machinery, wringing an additional fifteen thousand a month out of the company and sending it directly to an account in Germany.

Selecting the most recent statement, Gabriel called the number at the top, introduced himself as Gregorio, and asked to be connected to the vice president in charge of Inteltech's account. A short discussion ensued and Gabriel learned that the twelve million dollars was no longer in Banco Mundial's coffers. Pleading a clerical error, Gabriel asked where the money had gone. He hoped the answer would be the Bank of Dublin, as he had ordered. He was disappointed. Gregorio had, in fact, wired the money to a numbered account at the Bank Moor in Switzerland. Gabriel's hand shook as he drank the water.

Before leaving for the police station, he stopped briefly at the reception desk. 'I know you will not think of contacting Senor Gregorio,' he said to Gloria. 'You have two children. Pedro and Maria.'

The patrol boat was an old Boston Whaler, rusting at the gunnels, with a string of bullet holes in the port side. Four men sat in the bow. They wore jeans, sunglasses, and black T-shirts beneath new Kevlar vests. They carried AK-47s on their laps and sidearms on their belts. All were officers of the Paraguayan federal police. Colonel Alberto Baumgartner stood at the wheel, steering the boat through the placid, muddy waters of the Parana River. After an hour's ride, the river began to narrow. The banks grew closer. The jungle loomed over and around them. Baumgartner opened up the two Suzuki engines, calling out to Gabriel, 'Snipers. They like to take a few potshots at us to keep us honest.'

Gabriel didn't answer. He stared at the mass of vines and trees and scrub, too focused to remark on anything but his anger. Smoke from cooking fires rose above the tree line. Baumgartner pointed to a series of chutes, carved from the riverbanks. 'Smugglers,' he said. 'They slide bales of marijuana into the river, float it to the Brazilian side.'

Baumgartner was tall and blond with a slight paunch and not quite a square jaw. His father, Josef, an SS *Standartenführer*, had fled Nazi Germany for Paraguay in the last days of the war, and had served Alfredo Stroessner – the strong man who had ruled the country as a private fief for thirty years – as chief of federal police. His son would likely soon assume the same post.

A ten-minute conversation and a fifty-thousand-dollar bribe had enlisted his active support.

'How much this guy steal from you?' Baumgartner asked. He spoke a mix of Spanish, English, and German with a complete absence of emotion.

'Too much,' said Gabriel.

'*Klar.*'

The Parana River had narrowed to the width of a country road. Branches ventured over the muddy water and more than once, Gabriel saw the thin, writhing shape of a snake hanging near the water. He did not like snakes. At a bend far up the river, he made out the figures of two men waiting on a dock. The boat slowed and Baumgartner shouted to them in German. '*Bitte, werfen-sie uns die Seilen!*'

Two Toyota SUVs waited in a clearing by the river. 'We've got the house under surveillance,' Baumgartner explained as they climbed into the vehicles. 'The Mercedes is there and one of my men said he spotted Gregorio inside. Two women, too. Maybe he stay at home, have himself a fest.' Baumgartner handed him a pistol. A Beretta nine millimeter. Gabriel was surprised it wasn't a Luger. 'In case he's not so happy to see you. I'm afraid we can't kill him for you, too.'

Gabriel began to decline the offer, then had second thoughts.

It had been easy to track Gregorio to his country retreat. A note on his dining-room table informed someone named 'Elena' to meet him at his ranch. The line reminding her to bring a passport tipped Gabriel off as to his employee's intent.

The road was a dream, a faultless asphalt expressway leading into an infinite nowhere. More evidence of the Germans' enlightening presence. The jungle had disappeared, and they sped across expanses of dried marshland, scrub, and chaparral. El Chaco, they called it, an area that stretched for hundreds of miles to the north and west. After fifteen minutes, they turned onto an unmarked dirt road and met up with a squadron of Land Cruisers, similar to their own. Gabriel didn't know how Baumgartner had mustered them so quickly. The police conferred among themselves. Baumgartner reported back a minute later. 'You say he's not a violent man – we'll take your word. He's still inside. He has some music playing. Why not we drive to the front door and let you two boys have a word together? *In Ordnung?*'

'*In Ordnung,*' said Gabriel.

Gregorio lived in a sprawling ranch-style house at the end of the road. It was an oasis of civilization in an otherwise barren spot. Palms, a rolling lawn, a swimming pool, and oddly, a basketball net, fronted the house. The convoy numbered six vehicles. Baumgartner approached the house slowly, parking near a tiled fountain. Leaving the lead vehicle, he adjusted his hat, then walked to the door and knocked. Gregorio himself answered. All smiles and an unctuous welcome. Gabriel stepped from the car and Gregorio's eyes opened as if he'd seen a ghost.

'Hello, Pedro,' Gabriel said after Baumgartner had retreated down the walk. 'I'm in a bit of a hurry, so let's keep this quick, shall we? I know you transferred the money to Switzerland. I must say, though, I've never heard of the bank. Bank Moor? Maybe you can teach me something, after all. All I need for you to do is to call the bank and transfer it to a more convenient location. It's only three in Zurich. Plenty of time.'

Gregorio had two choices. Either he could resist and play dumb, in which case after much unpleasantness, he would admit his folly and transfer the money. Or he could pretend it was all some sort of misunderstanding, plead embarrassment, and transfer the money immediately. In both cases, his death was certain.

'Let the girls go,' he said.

'Of course.'

Gregorio disappeared inside the house. A few minutes later, two local women, dressed as if for a day shopping on the Faubourg-St-Honoré, hunkered out of the house, each lugging a Louis Vuitton suitcase – fakes, like everything else in Ciudad del Este – and continued past the knot of federal officers down the gravel road. Gabriel watched them go. The nearest village was thirty miles away. Where were they headed in their high heels and designer dresses?

Wrapping an arm around Gregorio's neck, he led him inside the ranch house. 'Come now, Achmed, I'm sure this is all a mix-up. Let's put it down to cold feet and forget about it. I don't care who or what is responsible. First, we'll straighten things out. Then we can discuss your plans for our central bank's policy – the liberalized loan requirements I'd mentioned.'

I'll be doing him a favor, Gabriel thought to himself. *Rescuing him from the rot. Saving whatever chance he has left of seeing Paradise.*

Gregorio, whose real name was Achmed Haddad, smiled uncertainly. 'I've drawn up a proposal I think you'll like.'

'Wonderful.'

The two men made their way to Gregorio's private office. In a moment, Gregorio had the Bank Moor on the line. 'Where do you want the money wired?' he asked.

This question had caused Gabriel a good deal of thought on the boat ride. It was his practice to wire the funds to several different banks, then spread the money out further before moving it to the pooling account. The measures took days, if not a week, and time was no longer his to spend freely. Tomorrow, Gabriel would meet the Professor. The whirlwind would begin. He would be hard-pressed to shepherd the twelve million dollars to a safe account.

'To the Gemeinschaft Bank of Dresden. Leichlingen branch. Account 47-20833S. In favor of the Holy Land Charitable Trust.' The Trust collected donations from around the world. Twelve million dollars from Switzerland would not raise any eyebrows.

Gregorio repeated the information. 'Done,' he said, hanging up the phone. And turning, he lifted his hands and began to beg forgiveness. 'I can explain,' he began. 'Yes, I was gree—'

'Sit,' Gabriel demanded.

Gregorio sat down on the couch.

'For the past two days, I've been asking myself how the Americans got wind of our brother in Afghanistan,' said Gabriel. 'For years, Sayeed operated there without any problem. A Brit, for God's sake, and none of the locals breathed a word about him to the authorities. Suddenly, Sayeed is followed and captured. What, I asked myself, had changed in the intervening time? Do you know?'

Gregorio shook his head. He was a slim man with a very large, bald head and unattractive eyes. His underlings called him the 'Mantis.'

'I know,' said Gabriel. 'Because now I realize it was my mistake. You visited Sayeed. You and your big mouth. You and your greedy ideas. You and your lack of faith in my family's plans. Somewhere along the line they picked you up. They've a woman on their team, I understand. She followed Sayeed for two days. I don't fault him for failing to realize it. She's a professional. I fault you.'

'But I said nothing . . . I—'

Gabriel waved away the excuse. 'And now, you are running. What better proof could I have? Where did you think you could go that I would not find you? Under what rock did you plan to hide? In a week, I will have the resources of Croesus at my disposal. Did you think that I would forget you?'

Gregorio took a moment to answer. 'I did not think you would succeed.'

Anger was building inside of Gabriel, a virulent rage that swelled inside his head like a molten dome. Taking the gun from the waistband beneath his shirt, he threw it at Gregorio. 'Do it.'

'I cannot.'

'Do it,' Gabriel repeated, his cheeks burning, lips stretched tightly over his teeth. Moving closer, he slapped Gregorio across the head. 'You are one of us. You swore the oath. You know our code. Do it.'

'I cannot.' Gregorio looked at the gun, then at Gabriel. 'Please,' he pleaded. 'You—'

But Gabriel had no intention of easing the man's burden. Dropping to a knee, he grabbed Gregorio's chin and stared into his eyes. 'Do it. I command you,' he shouted, so close that his spittle sprayed the man's cheeks. 'Do it!'

With surprising adeptness, Gregorio picked up the pistol

and pressed it against Gabriel's chest. 'Leave me. You have your money back. Every last dime. Now go in peace.'

Gabriel laughed. 'Kill me, and another will take my place.'

'Leave! I am the one making the decisions. Go now!'

Gabriel pushed his face closer, so that their foreheads almost touched, and he stared into the other man's soul. 'You are already dead,' he whispered.

Gregorio blinked. A defeated breath left his mouth.

The blast of the gunshot deafened Gabriel, the hot, deflected powder stinging his cheek. Standing, he took out a handkerchief and wiped his face. He checked his watch. If he hurried, he would still make his plane to Paris.

Chapter 29

At the Financial Crimes Enforcement Bureau's headquarters in Vienna, Virginia, the introduction of the Holy Land Charitable Trust of Germany into their proprietary SQS, or suspicious activity query system, set off a string of alarm bells. The suspicious activity query system drew on a database of more than ten million suspicious activity reports and cash transaction reports filed by American financial institutions over the past ten years, and included all reports filed by banks, savings and loans, brokerage houses, cash-transmitting agencies, and more recently, casinos. Additionally, the SQS combed the Treasury Enforcement Computer System, NADDIS, and the Internal Revenue Department's proprietary database.

Utilizing an artificial intelligence program, the SQS was able not only to search for precisely defined keywords, such as 'Holy Land Charitable Trust' or 'Gemeinschaft Bank of Dresden,' but to sift and evaluate the descriptive portion of each report – the two or three paragraphs written by the teller who had actually witnessed the criminal activity – for catchphrases, partial names, and possible references to the account or individual being interrogated.

At .36 seconds, the first hit appeared on Bobby Freedman's screen. It came from TECS, and stated that during a year 2000 investigation conducted by the United

States Customs Department into software piracy, the Holy Land Charitable Trust had been linked to Inteltech, a registered Paraguayan corporation thought to be engaged in the illegal copying and wholesaling of software patented by American software concerns. The Trust's name was listed as a beneficiary of a German account said to be a conduit for Inteltech's funds. Due to a lack of cooperation by the Paraguayan government, the investigation was shelved.

The second hit arrived at .78 seconds. The Trust's name was found in a suspicious activity report filed by the Gemeinschaft Bank of Dresden stating that the account frequently received multimillion-dollar transfers from high criminal activity points, including Brazil, Colombia, Panama, Dubai, and Pakistan. Again, no action was taken.

Freedman studied the reports. With Chapel's words echoing in his ears, he phoned the head of compliance at Thornhill Guaranty at his home in Manhattan at 5:21 A.M. Stating that the terrorist who two days earlier had blown up three American law enforcement professionals had been discovered to have ties to the Holy Land Charitable Trust's account at Thornhill's Gemeinschaft Bank subsidiary, he requested them to supply – of their own volition, naturally – all pertinent account records.

At 7:01, a forty-six-page e-mail chronicling the Holy Land Charitable Trust's entire banking history at the Gemeinschaft Bank of Dresden arrived in his mailbox. At 7:08, Freedman called Allan Halsey at FTAT and advised him to log on to his computer and to have plenty of paper ready for the download.

It took Allan Halsey one hour to find the connection – the irrefutable link that Chapel had been begging for. When he saw the numbers, and ran them past the ones Chapel had given him five hours earlier, and noted that 'yes, they were the same, by God,' he felt as if he'd been hit in the stomach by a line drive.

For the past eighteen months, the Holy Land Charitable Trust of Germany had regularly received money from the same numbered account at the Deutsche International Bank that was funneling money to Albert Daudin at the Bank Montparnasse in Paris.

Immediately, Halsey contacted the Office of Foreign Asset Control (OFAC) and requested that the Trust's account be frozen pending an IEEPA edict. IEEPA stood for the International Emergency Economic Powers Act. It was the sledge-hammer Halsey had promised, a broad, all-controlling measure granted to the executive branch of the United States government to deal with any unusual or extraordinary threats to the country's national security, foreign policy, or economy.

A flurry of phone calls ensued.

OFAC called the White House. The White House called FTAT to confirm that OFAC's IEEPA request was legit, then followed up with a call to the under secretary of the Treasury for Enforcement to double-check. The under secretary called the secretary of the Treasury and suggested he might want to contact the chairman of Thornhill Guaranty to let him know that his bank was about to be put in the same bed as a celebrated terrorist. He then dialed Admiral Owen Glendenning, and said, 'Wasn't the Patriot Act a great thing? And it was nice working with you, too.'

The chairman of Thornhill Guaranty, however, was not so cheery. A generous donor to the ruling party, he phoned the White House to request that Thornhill's name be left out of it, and that only the Gemeinschaft Bank of Dresden be mentioned. In soothing tones, he was informed that the President was otherwise engaged, but that his comments would be passed along with all due haste. It was the truth. At that moment, the President was closeted with his press secretary, communications chief, and foreign policy czar, figuring a way to work the news into the day's public addresses at a UAW rally in Saginaw, Michigan (easy), and a luncheon for the National Midwives Association in Hannibal, Missouri (hard). All were agreed, though, that it would be a marvelous theme on which to base his after-dinner comments at the state dinner honoring King Bandar, the new ruler of Saudi Arabia, being held Saturday evening.

Decision taken, the White House called back OFAC and signaled their accord.

At 8:21, a provisional freeze was put on all assets of the Holy Land Charitable Trust of Germany held by the Gemeinschaft Bank of Dresden.

Chapter 30

A filthy white Peugeot 504 sat parked across the street from his house. It was a ten-year-old sedan, with a dented front fender, a Radio 24 bumper sticker, and Paris plates, identical to thousands of others trawling the French capital. The door was unlocked, the key in the ignition. Climbing into the front seat, George Gabriel adjusted the seat and checked the rear- and sideview mirrors. He was dressed in khaki pants, a white cotton shirt, and a loose-fitting black blazer. His cordovan loafers carried rubber soles that promised stealth as well as comfort should he need to run any kind of distance. Though he had hardly slept, he was more awake than he'd ever been in his life.

He started the car, and for a moment the hum of the engine, the kick of the accelerator lessened his anxieties. He was a city kid. He hadn't driven enough to lose a teenager's thrill at piloting his own automobile. '*This is it*,' he murmured, looking at himself in the rearview mirror. 'This is your last chance.' But it was his father's eyes that stared back and crushed his defiance.

Carefully he pulled into traffic and began the drive to the Hopital Salpetitpierre in the southwestern-most part of the city. He was careful to confine his hands to the steering wheel, the radio, the air-conditioning system. The trip took twenty minutes. At 9:32, he entered a public garage on the

Rue Danton. He parked the car at the rear of the fourth underground floor between a Renault minivan and another Peugeot. Using a handkerchief, he wiped down the dashboard and the steering wheel. After he closed and locked the door, he took care to swipe the door handle, too.

At the elevator, he held the door to allow an elderly woman and her toy poodle to enter. Any doubts about his appearance were erased by her lingering smile and countless thanks. If he could pass for a good Samaritan in the gloom of a parking garage, he'd do just fine beneath a hospital's fluorescent lights.

Outside, the streets crawled with traffic. The sun seemed brighter than usual; the everyday din of the passing cars louder than he remembered. He ordered himself to walk slowly. Yet, his calf muscles felt tight, ready to cramp.

At 9:40, the trauma entrance at the east side of the hospital was practically deserted. A single ambulance loitered in the emergency bay. The sliding glass doors were open to allow a cooling breeze. He walked past the reception, studiously ignoring the admitting nurse's inquisitive smile. The corridors yawned in front of him, white tile hallways smelling of bleach and linseed oil, decorated with childrens' crayola drawings. Doctors, patients, relatives, and custodians moved through the halls at a plodding pace. No one looked twice at the six-foot-two-inch visitor with the shy eyes and relaxed gait. He needed five minutes to find Hallway B, Corridor 7.

The door to the surgical changing room was marked 'Private – Staff only.' A splinter of wood dangled from the lock guard. Others had preceded him. George Gabriel pushed it open and stepped inside. A neatly folded white lab jacket waited on the shelf. Removing his blazer, he stuffed it in the bottom of the laundry bin, then put on the white coat. A stethoscope lay coiled in the pocket. Freeing it, he slung it around his neck. The staples of a first-year resident filled his breast pocket: pens, notepad, tongue depressor, and a penlight. Instinctively, his fingers delved into his sleeve. The dagger slept in an oiled sheath strapped to his left forearm.

He left the elevator on the third floor. At the crossroads joining the hospital's two main buildings, he paused to get his bearings. Right took him to the oncology department. Left to radiology. He needed to go straight. He reminded himself that his primary exit was two floors below and would leave him at the Rue Poitiers. From there, he could either catch the Métro at the Place D'Italie (the Number 5, 6, or 7 line) or walk two blocks to a taxi stand. Under no circumstance was he to return to the Peugeot.

It was difficult to keep his eyes fixed in front of him, to stop from glancing in every direction like an escapee from prison trying to figure out where exactly he was. He could in no way appear unsure about his surroundings. He must mesh with the landscape. He continued until he saw a sign with the words 'Burn Unit/Intensive Care,' and an arrow beneath it pointing the way.

The time was 9:50.

Stopping at a water fountain, he dared a look down the corridor. This part of the hospital was busier than the rest. The halls bristled with doctors, nurses, and orderlies. Most had serious expressions on their faces and walked briskly, with grim purpose. Every second person appeared to be of West African or Algerian descent.

Taking a deep breath, he straightened up and readied himself for the run in.

A heavy hand fell on his shoulders.

'Young man, can you help me? I'm afraid I am lost.' It was a doctor, gray-haired, pasty-skinned, with a flinty gaze beneath the polite manner. George Gabriel wiped the water from his mouth, but not the residue of anxiety. 'Of course, sir. Where do you need to go?'

'I'm here for the lecture on interventional radiology. The Pasteur Operating Theatre. Dr Diderot's talk about stents.'

Gabriel nodded his head, managing a sour smile. While studying the hospital's layout, he had come across the Pasteur Operating Theatre ... *But where exactly?* Panic welled inside him, gnawing at his gut like a starving rat. 'It's ... um ...' He blinked and he realized that his hand was shaking. He ordered his foot to move, but it didn't respond. He was frozen. And then it came to him. 'You're in the wrong building,' he blurted, causing the visiting doctor to retreat a step. 'You have to take the elevator up to Level Four, and find Corridor D. You should see plenty of signs. If not, just ask. We're all very excited about Dr Diderot being here.'

The doctor frowned. 'You're not coming?'

'No. I'm doing my cardiology rotation. Thanks anyway.'

'But Diderot is a cardiologist,' he exclaimed. The doctor stepped closer, placing his hands on his hips and staring up at George as if he were inspecting a simple foot soldier. 'Just what do you think stents are for, anyway? Come on. Tell me. The Diderot stent. Surely you've come across it in your studies.'

Gabriel stared into the doctor's eyes, and the idea came to him that he should kill him there and then and make a run for it. Forget Chapel. Forget his father. Forget Hijira. He'd make a run to Claudine's and hide out there until the trouble died down. A hand wandered into his sleeve. His fingers touched the dagger. Claudine would understand, he told himself. She understood everything. The thought of his girlfriend calmed him, and with a start, he realized that he knew what a stent was, after all. Claudine had raved about them one afternoon as they were studying together. Yet another of the medical miracles that would prolong their lives together.

'The Diderot stent is used as an alternative to coronary bypass surgery to force open arteries leading to the heart,' he said as his fingers released the dagger's cold grip. 'There are two types – coated or uncoated. Both—'

'All right. That's enough,' said the doctor. 'But you really shouldn't miss the lecture. It's not often that Diderot gives these talks. Why do you think I drove all the way from Lyons?'

'Thanks all the same, but I've got rounds.' Gabriel pointed down the hall. 'Level Four. Corridor D. You can't miss it. Thanks again.'

'Thank *you*,' the doctor said, starting off. 'Oh, young man?'

Gabriel looked back over his shoulder. 'Yes?'

'You are . . .'

Gabriel checked the impulse to see if he was wearing a name tag. 'In a hurry,' he said, not missing a beat. 'Good luck.'

The doctor waved a distracted good-bye.

But George Gabriel winced. He'd been marked.

'Keep it running,' said Adam Chapel as he opened the car door and extended a leg to the sidewalk. 'It shouldn't take long.'

'You sure you don't want me to come up?' Sarah was leaning over the passenger seat, her face lit with expectation.

Chapel hesitated. All morning, they'd been playing it as if last night had never happened. They were two professionals doing their job, both of them too engrossed in the onslaught of detail to pay attention to the other. On the way over from the Bank Montparnasse, though, he'd noticed a change of temperament. A warming of the air, so to speak. Maybe it was the fact that she was smiling a little or that she was humming to the music on the radio. Each time she went to shift, he was sure she was going to put her hand on his leg. At first he'd tensed, unsure how he would react. But as he got used to the idea, he decided he wanted her to touch him, and he relaxed his leg, allowing it to sway towards her hand.

It reminded him of that silly grade-school game where you passed your hand through a candle flame to see if it hurt, and kept going slower and slower until you got burned. Sarah was the flame. She was alluring. She was dangerous. She was impossible to resist. And in the end, he knew, she burned everything she touched.

'No,' he said. 'Wait here. You don't want to hear a grown man cry.'

'Be brave,' she said. 'And no flirting with the doctor. We've got to be at the airport by noon.'

The burn unit occupied the westernmost section of the third floor. Entry was controlled. Visiting hours tightly enforced. Fear of infection demanded that a minimum of persons be allowed near the patients. George Gabriel presented himself to the nurse on duty. 'I'm here to see Dr Bac. I've got her patient's charts. Mr Chapel. The American hurt in the bombing the day before yesterday.'

'Of course. Room 323.'

'Is he here yet?'

The nurse answered without looking up from her paperwork. 'Not yet.'

George walked briskly down the hallway. Even numbers were on the right; odd to the left. Few patients were to be seen. An odd quiet filled the air. There were no drawings of bright suns and frolicking children on the wall. The air smelled sharply of ammonia. He looked behind him. He could still leave. His presence here violated no codes. A new and undefined life beckoned. He kept walking, pushed along by his father's prideful gaze, his ruthless expectations.

He stopped in front of the door to Room 323. He reached a hand toward the door handle, then pulled it away. He shook his head and retreated a step. Just then, the door opened. An older man shuffled out, his hands swathed in gauze bandages. Now, certain of what he must do, George slipped into the room as the door closed behind him.

Jeannette Bac stood with her back to him, hunched over a counter furiously scribbling notes into a manila folder. She had long, kinky brown hair and a trim figure. Over her shoulder, he caught a triangle of her pale cheek and the corner of her glasses. He stepped closer and caught traces of lilac and vanilla. She wore a faded pink shirt and he could see the links of a gold necklace through the strands of her hair.

'There,' she said, punctuating her report with a flourish of her pen. Abruptly she turned, nearly bumping into Gabriel. 'Oh, God!' she exclaimed, a hand flying to her mouth. 'You scared me. I thought I was alone.'

The blade slid from the sheath and he held it against his leg.

'I'm sorry,' said George Gabriel, the smile coming easily to his cheeks this time, a rush of power swelling his chest. 'You've got nothing to be afraid of.'

At the main reception, Chapel asked directions to the burn unit. The nurse explained in perfect English that he should walk down the corridor, take the first bank of elevators to the third floor, and follow the signs. An elevator waited, its doors open. He rode alone, eyes on the panel, watching the blinking lights. For all that had happened, things weren't going too badly. He had high hopes that the Financial Crimes Enforcement Bureau might uncover information about the Holy Land Charitable Trust that would lead him a step closer to Albert Daudin – or the man who was using his alias. Though pleased the ball was back in the American court, he was no less driven. The memory of the ruined videotape remained fresh in his mind. At any time he expected to receive news of a terrible explosion, a host of deaths. Or worse.

The light advanced to the third floor and Chapel moved forward. The door opened. Stepping into the hallway, he heard an anguished shout echoing down the hallway.

'*Arretez! Vous, la! Arretez immediatement!*'

Somewhere a tray hit the floor and clattered violently. A glass shattered.

Chapel rushed towards the source of the noise. As he turned the corner and stepped into the main corridor, he was hit full-force by a running man and thrown to the ground. The man fell on top of him, scrambling to right himself even as he bounced off of Chapel's chest. 'You!' he said.

He was young and brawny, his dark eyes electric with fear, his mouth open, perfect white teeth bared as he desperately sucked in his breath. Their eyes met, and for a split second, Chapel felt the man hesitate. He could sense a decision being made behind the frightened gaze. A fist crashed into Chapel's shoulder, once, twice. Chapel screamed in agony, as his vision darkened and stars burst behind his eyes. As quickly, the man was up, attacking the hallway with a sprinter's high step.

'*Securité!*' someone yelled as Chapel struggled to his feet. For a moment, he remained bent over double, winded, shaking off the pain. A male nurse ran to him and asked if he was all right.

'What happened?' Chapel asked in his schoolboy's French.

'Him – this crazy man – he tried to hurt the doctor.'

Something clicked inside him. 'Dr Bac?'

'Yes, Dr Bac.'

'Get to a desk,' Chapel said. 'Call security. Tell them to lock down the hospital. Shut the doors. Now!'

And then he was running, too, taking off down the corridor with all the speed his thirty-year-old legs could muster. The man had been after Bac. *That means he was after me*, thought Chapel.

A roadmap of stunned faces and startled onlookers marked the man's path. Rounding a corner, Chapel burst into a trio of nurses gathered closely together, holding open the door to an internal stairwell and peering into the dusk.

'He went down there?' Chapel asked, catching his breath.

All three nodded in unison.

He took the stairs two at a time as visions of Cité Universitaire flooded his mind. Santini rushing past him, Leclerc helping him to his feet, the last sighting of Taleel. He felt the fireball singe his face, and his entire body jolted involuntarily. At every landing he paused. The rapid-fire patter of footsteps slapping the concrete far below rose to him. Glancing over the railing, he caught a fleeing shadow. A door opened two floors beneath him. A crescent of light lit the stairwell. Less than a minute later, Chapel emerged into the first-floor hallway. Four sets of glass double doors marked the hospital's main entrance. A white lab jacket crumpled into a ball lay on the floor a few feet away. There were no stunned faces to mark the terrorist's passage, only the ebb and flow of patients and physicians on a calm Wednesday morning.

On the sidewalk, Chapel rose to his tiptoes, searching for the clean-shaven scalp, the broad shoulders. He ran several steps up the street, then back the other way. The pavement teemed with pedestrians. He saw nothing to alert him.

Taleel's associate had escaped.

Jeanette Bac sat on an examining table, a fellow physician dabbing at a wound in her chest, when Chapel entered the room. 'Did you find him?'

Chapel shook his head. 'He was too fast. He made it out the front doors before anyone could stop him.'

She smiled bitterly.

'You okay?' he asked.

'He wanted you.'

'I figured that.' Chapel looked at the angry weal contrasted against Dr Bac's milk-white flesh. 'What happened?'

'He couldn't do it,' she said.

'What do you mean?'

'I had just seen a patient. I turned and he was there. On top of me. He was smiling, but as he pushed the knife into me, his face changed. He grew frightened.' She brushed away the attending physician's hand and showed Chapel the wound. 'Look at the placement – between the second and third ribs. Perfect. All he had to do was push a little harder. The blade slips in very nicely and pierces the heart. I am dead even before I can scream. It takes practice to find this spot.'

'I'm sure he had plenty of it,' said Chapel.

'Then tell me. Why did he stop?'

Chapter 31

Mordecai Kahn was traveling north by northwest on a two-lane macadam road through the killing fields of Bosnia. A while ago he'd skirted Srbenica, where seven thousand Muslims were led to slaughter inside of a week, their bodies dumped in shallow burial pits, sprinkled with quicklime and covered with just enough dirt to withstand a summer shower. Somewhere under the rolling hills ablaze with saffron, the tilled meadows, the dense pine glades were more bodies – hundreds, thousands, who knew?

Kahn was tired beyond any normal measure. Forty-eight hours had passed since he'd enjoyed any meaningful sleep. It was a different exhaustion than he'd known before. He missed the aching joints, the grotesquely red eyes, the stiff neck that followed all-nighters in the lab or at the testing ground. This was a new clear-burning fatigue that brought clarity of purpose, a renewal of ardor for the task at hand, a confirmation of his moral rectitude.

'We must put an end to their indignant cries,' the man from Paris had said. 'We must discredit them in front of the world.'

Kahn remembered the smiling eyes, the pained smile, the sense of purpose that flared inside the man like an oil fire. The two had met at a meeting of *Kahane Chai* in Bethlehem. *Kahane Chai*, or Kahane Lives, the messianic group founded by the survivors of Rabbi Meier Kahane, the man of God who preached the annihilation of all Palestinians from the land of Israel and foretold that the advent of the Messiah must be preceded by wide-scale bloodshed.

Dropping his eyes from the road, he searched for something to eat. Candy wrappers and discarded soft drink cans littered the passenger seat. He rummaged through them quickly, finding a half-eaten bag of gummy bears. Deftly, he emptied the bag into his palm and brought the soft candies to his mouth. The tart cherry flavor made him smile. They'd always been his children's favorite.

'It is time we pay attention to the Torah,' he had whispered. 'As we all know, there are no human rights for goyem in the Torah. We must therefore deal with Palestinians the same way Joshua the Prophet dealt with their ancestors.'

'Kill them?' Kahn had asked, sharing the man's zeal, feeding on his hatred.

'Kill *all* of them. But first we must discredit them.'

'How?'

'A single barbaric act.'

The words thrilled Kahn's ear like a lover's kiss. It had been three years since he had lost his son to a suicide bomber. The boy, an army conscript in the second year of his national service, was stationed at a checkpoint near Ramallah when the bomber struck. Afterward, they had sent a tape of the attack. Smiling crazily from the front seat of his car, the Palestinian bomber had offered a thumbs-up before crashing his vehicle into the iron shed and detonating over one hundred pounds of TNT, nails, studs, bolts, and washers, and obliterating every trace of Corporal David Kahn from the face of the earth.

A single barbaric act.

His daughter, Rachel, had died from a sniper's bullet, bringing medical supplies to a family in a disputed settlement on the West Bank. Rachel, who played the violin like an angel and made her father *kishkes* and soup. Rachel, his baby.

A single barbaric act.

Mordecai Kahn knew the precise meaning of the words. Yet something bothered him. *No more innocents*, he'd said. *I have suffered enough for all families.*

Only the deserving will perish. You will not shed a tear. Can you help?

Yes, Kahn had said, and he remembered the moment as the beginning of his freedom. *But I could never go back. There is a price.*

No price is too high for such an unselfish act.

Kahn enjoyed the memory. He was only doing a citizen's duty. Kahn and his father had turned a desert into a marvel: an agricultural, economic, military, marvel. The fact that they had succeeded while Israel had been under near constant attack made the accomplishment that much more satisfying. Wars had wracked the country in '48, '67, and '73. The past four years had been like a state of siege. Yet, every time, Israel had beaten back its aggressors. If the country had expanded its borders, all the better. It was but a temporal ratification of God's favor.

Kahn was mulling over the justice of it all when he noticed the car behind him. It was a black Mercedes sedan whose caked-on mud was an affront even at one hundred yards. The headlamps were mismatched; one yellow, one transparent. A rifle barrel lolled out of the passenger window.

Immediately, he consulted the GPS onboard navigation system. The nearest town was Pale, nine miles away.

'Pale,' Kahn grunted.

Population: 2,500. No UN garrison, only a local constabulary to adjudicate local disputes. He wondered if he'd been wise to exchange the safety of highway travel for the anonymity of back-country roads.

A moment later, a light truck rumbled into view, crossing his field of vision from left to right, braking hard in the center of the junction a few hundred yards ahead.

It was Tel Aviv all over again, and for a second, he dared to wonder if it might be the boys from the Sayeret. A look at the Mercedes in the rearview mirror killed the notion. The Sayeret moved as quickly and silently as a snake through the grass. You weren't likely to see them coming. They certainly didn't advertise themselves with a beat-up sedan and an AK-47's notched barrel.

Kahn's eyes wandered over the open landscape. Meadows of summer grass bled into gently rolling hills and untended countryside. There wasn't another vehicle in sight.

'Turn right in two hundred meters,' commanded the baritone voice belonging to the onboard navigation system, and Kahn flinched.

Flipping open his glove box, he removed a nine-milli-meter pistol. His officer's sidearm had last seen action in the Sinai in 1967. Come to think of it, he hadn't fired it then. He'd been too busy mustering his men, directing a counter-attack against Egyptian tanks that had cracked the Israeli line. Kahn considered his options. If he could get around the intersection, he could easily outrun the hijackers' two vehicles. And then? He had a feeling the men would phone ahead. There would be another roadblock, maybe one manned by the Pale constables themselves. A man in a gold BMW was easy to find. He'd underestimated the region's poverty.

He asked the navigation system for an alternate route.

None.

Well, then, he mused, stealing the pistol into his lap and chambering a round.

Two men were climbing out of the truck ahead, waving their arms across their faces, signaling for him to stop. Kahn braked. Using a turn signal, he brought the car to the side of the road, coming to a halt a hundred meters from the junction. He waited for the Mercedes to pull up behind him, his eyes trained on the rearview mirror. He was shivering and had to clench his jaw to keep his teeth from chattering.

The Mercedes' doors opened lazily.

Kahn slipped the gear into reverse.

Feet swung onto the ground. Combat boots. *But, of course.*

His heel rammed the accelerator. Tires squealed. The BMW rocketed backwards. Metal crumpled as the car shuddered violently.

The two men rolled on the side of the road, having thrown themselves clear of the Mercedes.

Scared out of his wits, but acting with a blooded soldier's calm, Mordecai Kahn stepped from the car, raised the pistol, and shot one of the men in the chest, pulling the trigger twice in rapid succession. Walking toward the jackknifed trunk, he spotted the second man struggling with his assault rifle, banging the clip into the stock, clumsily knocking the fire control with his fist. He was swearing, his dark eyes flitting desperately between the weapon and Kahn.

Kahn fired twice, and the Slav twisted about his waist as if his feet were nailed to the blacktop.

A single barbaric act.

The words played over and over again in his mind, a violent and cacophonous symphony, as he climbed back into his BMW and accelerated towards the pickup truck. Kahn would show them a barbaric act.

Directly ahead, one of the men was frantically rummaging for something in the front seat of the truck. The second man was shooting at Kahn, but either he was a poor shot or he had a weak pistol, because none of the bullets were finding their mark.

The speedometer read thirty kilometers an hour.

A hail of iron rained on the car. For a second, he made out the driver firing from his hip with a machine gun, but then the front and rear windscreen disappeared in a downpour of glass and he couldn't see anything.

The needle hit fifty. Kahn struck the rifleman, crushing him, and plowed into the truck. The momentum sent the vehicle tumbling off the road and rolling down a berm into the field. The BMW's front axel thumped once as the car ran over the second man, then it lumbered to a halt, its airbag inflated.

Kahn knocked away the airbag and opened the door. Steam hissed from the engine. The hood was a mess. He opened the back door and retrieved an overnight bag. He had no need to check its contents. The package would be in perfect working order. It had been engineered and constructed to withstand radical impacts and violent changes in velocity up to three thousand g's.

Sliding into the front seat of the Mercedes, he checked his watch.

He had twenty-four hours to get to Paris.

He would travel to Belgrade and purchase a new car. From there, it was ten hours to Frankfurt, and five more to the French capital. It would be tight.

Chapter 32

The fields of France passed beneath them, a patchwork quilt of golds and greens. They were flying east. The sun hovered overhead. The shadow of the MD-80 aircraft defined a bullet piercing rivers and valleys and plains of summer wheat. They had a row to themselves. Chapel took the window, Sarah the aisle. Since takeoff, they'd been huddled over the center seat, whispering like thieves in fear of their lives.

'He knew I'd be there,' said Chapel. 'He was waiting.'

'You can't be sure of that.'

'He slugged me in the shoulder, Sarah. He knew where I was burned. How much more sure do I need to be? Think about it. They had me pegged to be at the hospital at ten o'clock. They knew the time of the appointment. They knew I was going to see Dr Bac. Christ, Sarah, they even knew what I looked like. He'd seen a picture of me. Where in the hell did he get that? It's not like I'm on the cover of *People*.'

But Sarah persisted in her stubbornness. 'Why did he run, then? Why didn't he kill Dr Bac? If he'd waited another minute, he'd have had you all to himself.'

'I don't know. Maybe something spooked him. He was young. Twenty or twenty-one. I could smell the fear on him. Maybe he just couldn't do it. Anyway, it doesn't really matter why.'

Sarah took a moment to answer. The determined furrows that cradled her eyes relaxed, 'I suppose not.'

'They're inside, Sarah. Hijira's penetrated Blood Money.'

'Who?' she asked angrily, frustrated by their predicament. 'Give me a name.'

But neither of them was willing to hazard a guess.

An honor guard awaited them at Berlin Tegel Airport.

A covey of the local Bundespolizei, smart in their short-sleeved summer uniforms and wan green caps, lined the gate area. In its midst stood a chubby American who introduced himself as Lane, the FBI's legal attaché to Berlin. He presented the formal writ requesting Germany to turn over all information pertaining to Deutsche International Bank account 222.818E to Adam Chapel, designated representative of the US Treasury Department, then escorted the pair through passport control, past baggage claim, to a waiting black Mercedes 600. A blond driver nodded courteously as he slammed the door after them. Lane climbed in the front seat. 'The courthouse is in the new Federal Square near the Potsdamerplatz,' he explained. 'Hermann, here, is with the local cop shop. He informs me that he'll have us there in seventeen minutes.'

The Mercedes left the curb like the shuttle from the launch pad. Sinking into his seat, Chapel hoped the German government's accommodation might extend past prompt limousine service.

The German capital was a city of the living, a vibrant metropolis on an unending construction binge. Cranes chopped the skyline into hundreds of vertical slabs. Any building that hadn't been newly constructed in the last two years had at least been renovated, repainted, sandblasted, or steam-cleaned.

Abruptly, the cityscape ended. A sparse forest combed

with trails and dotted with ice cream vendors pressed in on them. The Tiergarten was Berlin's answer to Central Park, or to be historically correct, its antecedent by three hundred years. The car barreled down the Avenue of Third of June. The Siegessaule passed in a blur, Apollo's chariot perched high on the victory column. Ahead stood the Brandenburg Gate. They slowed as they passed around it. Chapel glimpsed the Hotel Adlon, stomping ground of the Third Reich's rich and famous, restored to its five-star glory. Another burst of acceleration delivered them onto the Unter den Linden, once Berlin's most fashionable street, where Goebbels had ordered its famed oaks to be chopped down to make way for winged swastikas perched on stone columns.

The federal courthouse stared out over the Alexanderplatz. It was a large government building, one of Schinkel's neoclassical masterpieces, complete with the imposing Doric columns, the monumental plinth, and the esplanade stolen from the Parthenon. Lane led them inside. An elevator took them to the second floor. The floor was radiantly polished, hewn from Italian Carrara marble. The snap of their heels sounded every ambitious attorney's charge. Lane opened an unmarked door and held it for Chapel and Sarah to pass by.

'He's a piece of work, this guy,' Lane said. 'Good luck.'

Without another word, he motioned them across the antechamber and into the judge's chambers proper.

'Hans Schumacher told me all about the tape,' complained Judge Manfred Wiesel as he shut off the DVD. 'He didn't say it was this bad, though.'

'I'm glad you were able to see the threat,' Chapel said, buoyed. 'It's clear he's talking about—'

'The threat?' Wiesel cut in. 'Good lord, no, I wasn't talking about the threat. I was talking about the quality of the recording. It's worse even than my rabid colleague described.'

Wiesel was the presiding federal magistrate, and as such the point man for official intergovernmental legal requests. His chambers were straight out of Faust, an oppressive symphony of polished wood, dark velvet curtains, and lead-framed windows. 'Let me see the motion,' he said, all but snapping his fingers.

Chapel handed over the papers. 'I'm happy to report that the government has decided to freeze the Holy Land Charitable Trust's accounts.'

'Have they?' Freeing a pair of bifocals from a tangle of wiry red hair, Wiesel turned his attention to the writ. He was fifty, a thin, dissipated man with an irritating sniffle. Finished reading the writ, he grunted. 'This is it?'

'Yes,' said Chapel.

'All of it?'

Again, Chapel nodded.

Wiesel shook his head as if not only distressed, but disappointed. 'It is my job to determine the legitimacy of your demands with regard to German law,' he said. 'I am not a clairvoyant, nor am I an oracle. The court demands facts, and facts alone.' He thrust the papers at Chapel and rustled them. 'You tell me the man on that tape is making a threat. Personally, I think he is merely ranting. It might as well be an editorial broadcast on Al-Jazeera. While I can imagine that the tape might scare certain parties, I do not see it as a threat and I most certainly do not see what it has to do with the Holy Land Trust. Facts. Give me facts!'

Sarah stepped closer to Manfred Wiesel, offering him a schoolgirl's demure glance. The Agency's thumbnail sketch stated unequivocally that he was a womanizer. His court record favored female prosecutors over male nearly three to one. 'If you examine account records from the Bank Montparnasse, you'll see that the Holy Land Trust received money from the same account at the Deutsche International Bank that funded Albert Daudin. "Daudin" was an alias used by Mohammed al-Taleel, the terrorist who took the life of one French and three American law enforcement officers two days ago.'

'How can you be sure Daudin and Taleel are the same person?'

Chapel wasn't, but he had no intention of voicing his belief that Taleel and a second man – a man still on the loose – had both used the Daudin alias. What was important was that Wiesel be convinced that Taleel and Daudin were one and the same.

'Daudin listed the same phone number on his account as another of Taleel's aliases, "Bertrand Roux," ' she explained. 'Both accounts demonstrate remarkable similarities in the timing of deposits and withdrawals. It was in Taleel's apartment that we found the videocassette.'

'Correct me if I am wrong, *Fraulein*, but it says here that the digital tape was found embedded in the wall of the apartment downstairs.'

'By the force of the blast,' said Chapel, and Sarah shot him a killing glance.

'So you say.'

Chapel rose on his toes. 'Your Honor—'

Again Wiesel cut him off. 'There are no "Your Honors" here. This is a court of the common man. "Mister" will do just fine.'

'Judge,' Chapel began again, his effort at politeness costing him dearly. 'The apartment directly below Mohammed al-Taleel is occupied by two female theology students, both French citizens, currently in Spain on their summer holiday making a pilgrimage to Santiago de Compostela.'

'Could Daudin be Taleel's roommate?' persisted Wiesel. 'Is it not common for roommates to share a phone?'

Sarah waved Chapel down. 'Taleel had no roommate. Even so, if Daudin were a roommate, he would still be a material witness to the crime,' she argued persuasively. 'If nothing else, we would have every right to detain and question him. Given the nature of the crime and what we know about how terrorists operate, we'd look at him as a coconspirator.'

'Yes, but to what crime?'

It was too much. The purposeful obfuscation, the stubborn refusal to see the facts for what they were. 'The murder of four damned good men, that's what,' shouted Chapel as he threw up his hands. 'Being party to a plan to commit an act of terror on American soil. Just what the hell do you think we're talking about?'

'Supposition. Supposition,' Wiesel shouted back. His pale face flushed red, but his eyes were pleading, not angry. 'I ask for facts, and you give me theories. I am not a fool. I can connect the dots as well as the next man. I know the picture you are trying to paint. Do you honestly believe that I am averse to your efforts?'

'No,' said Chapel.

'But you cannot march into my chambers and on the basis of such scant and threadbare evidence demand that I order the Deutsche International Bank to open its doors to you and reveal the private financial history of one of its clients. This is Germany! We have a history of government intrusion into the private sphere. And I am not just talking about the Third Reich. You are too young to remember the seventies, but I am not. I was there. I lived them. Before Al Qaeda, and this group, Hijira, there was the Red Army Faction, the Baader-Meinhof Gang, the Brigadi Rossi. They bombed department stores. They robbed banks. They kidnapped industrialists and bankers, demanded ransoms, then shot them dead before they were paid, just to show they could. As terrorists they succeeded in one thing only – in terrifying the populace.

'The government mobilized its resources to catch them. Its goal was to establish a predictive model to help them outsmart and outguess the terrorists. To do so, they began this thing called "profiling" that is so popular today. A man named Horst Herold was the mastermind. He asked companies to open their databases to him. He searched travel agency records, heating bills, phone bills, petrol purchases. He set up cameras on the Autobahns to record license plates and entered every traffic ticket issued in the entire country into his all-seeing computer. He wanted to know how the terrorists traveled, where they stayed, what brand of car they preferred to steal – it was a four-door BMW, if you want to know – all to establish a "movement picture." It worked to a point. Horst Herold locked up the ringleaders. But people were uneasy. Herold knew too much about us, and I mean *all of us*. Citizens were being turned into *glaeserne Menschen*, glass people, into whom the state could look and learn all their secrets. The whole thing stank of the Nazis. Of the Gestapo. This was too much power in the hands of the State.'

Wiesel paused, circling his desk and settling into his chair. He drew a breath and fixed his eyes on Chapel and Sarah. His calm returned and with it his belligerent tone. 'I won't allow those days to come back again. We will have no more *glaeserne Menschen*. If you want me to show you the records, give me a concrete reason. Show me that a crime has been committed.'

Chapel took a chair and set a copy of the writ on the desk. He felt frustrated, thwarted by the principles he was striving to uphold. What did privacy matter when lives were at stake? Why did an exception threaten the rule? If you were innocent, you had nothing to worry about anyway. Doggedly, he raced through the papers. Wiesel wanted a crime, fine. If lending financial succor to a proven terrorist wasn't good enough, Chapel would find him another. He turned page after page, growing increasingly impatient. Suddenly, his eye tripped over a word and he went back a page. He read one paragraph, then another, and he realized the answer had been staring at him the entire time. 'Software piracy,' he said.

'Excuse me?' Wiesel sat chin in hand, eyes burning into him, and Chapel realized the judge had been rooting for him to succeed.

'The Trust's name first came to our attention in connection with an investigation into a Paraguayan company called Inteltech suspected of illegally copying, manufacturing, and distributing computer software. The company's records showed that they were funneling profits to the Trust's account.'

'Paraguay, the United States . . . when am I going to hear Germany's name in all of this?'

'At the time, the case was brought to our attention by Microsoft. But a cocomplainant was SAP, who I believe is Germany's largest software provider.'

Wiesel nodded reluctantly.

'By helping to pirate copies of SAP's software,' Chapel continued, 'the Holy Land Charitable Trust is committing a crime against a German company. In essence, it's stealing bread from the mouths of German workers. Piracy is a felonious offense, isn't it?'

'Most certainly.'

'Well, then. Tell Deutsche International Bank to show me which of their clients is doing business with the Holy Land Trust.'

'Hand me the papers.'

Chapel sifted through the pile and selected the relevant pages.

Wiesel examined them thoroughly. Drawing a pen from his robes, he executed a flamboyant signature on the writ and handed it to his assistant. 'Done,' he said. 'Theft of intellectual property is a crime we do not tolerate in this country.'

Chapter 33

'What time is the flight leaving?' Claire Charisse demanded for the second time. She held the phone to her breast, and motioned with her free hand in an emphatic manner for her assistant to hurry up.

'Two, I think,' he answered, flinching as if she were going to hit him. He was a shy, lumbering Liberian whose first name was Samuel and his last name unpronounceable. She hadn't meant to scare him, but it was either that or swear, and Samuel was a born-again Christian.

'I don't want your opinion,' she railed. 'I want a simple fact. Look up the schedule and tell me what time the flight is supposed to take off. Global Trans can't have too many cargo flights leaving Geneva for Angola on a Friday afternoon.'

Lips pursed in desperation, Samuel flitted through the flight company's brochure. They'd sent it along with the reams of documentation the World Health Organization was required to fill out when shipping medical supplies across borders. 'It is here, Madame Charisse. I am sure.'

'Look it up on the Net, damn it!'

Samuel froze as if he'd been slapped, and Claire was sorry that she'd lost her cool. It wasn't like her, but then again these were hardly ordinary times.

'Two forty-five,' came the proud reply, thirty seconds after he'd sat down and punched in Global Trans's web address.

'That's better.' Claire exumed the phone from the folds of her crimson pashmina wrap and placed it to her ear. She was petite and fine-boned, with skin the color of porcelain and raven black hair that fell in perfectly orchestrated layers to her shoulders. She had a temper and knew how to use it when necessary. She also had charm by the loads and knew how to use that, too. Both were requisite skills for her job.

'Hugo,' she purred into the phone, twirling a lock of hair with her finger. 'We've got loads of time. If you could manage to have the cartons at the Global Trans desk at Cointrin by one, that would be perfect. Really, I don't know how to thank you enough. Or Roche. You're both wonderful. You're saving lives and that's the point of this, isn't it?'

Claire hung up. Spreading her arms wide enough to embrace the entire world, she turned to face Samuel and the trio of secretaries huddled in the anteroom. 'Mr Hugo Luytens of Hoffmann-LaRoche has generously donated two thousand doses of Coartem to today's emergency flight. Who says the Swiss don't care about anybody else but themselves? Three cheers for Helvetia and here's to eradicating the last vestiges of malaria!'

Samuel applauded enthusiastically. The secretaries less so. Coartem was the newest and most effective antimalarial drug ever to combat the illness. Known as an ACT, an artemisinin-based combination therapy, the drug had recently been added to the WHO's essential medicines list. It worked by localizing and killing the malaria parasite rapidly, allowing the patient a prompt and side effect-free recovery. With any luck, the drug would go a long way to saving the lives of the eight hundred thousand children who died of malaria each year in sub-Saharan Africa.

Claire bowed from the waist, doing her Sarah Bernhardt bit. 'Isn't getting any easier, is it, dears?' She coughed loudly and pretended not to see the concerned faces staring back.

Opening a desk drawer, she snatched a cigarette and lit it. 'Every girl deserves a reward,' she offered.

But Samuel wasn't buying. 'Claire, you are not to smoke,' he said, plucking the cigarette from her mouth with his long, tapered fingers. 'Even you have to follow doctor's orders.'

'Oh, damn you,' Claire Charisse caught herself. 'Sorry, Sammy – *blast* you,' she said with the same mock despair. 'I hate it when you're right.' Instead, she handed her chipped coffee mug to him, the one her boyfriend had given her with the picture of the United States Capitol Building decaled on the side. 'Another cup, if you please. They've yet to prove that caffeine keeps your white count down.'

Claire patted Samuel on the back and retreated to her office, where she collapsed into her chair. The workload was enough to bow the shoulders of a coolie. Somewhere lost in the riot of memos, files, and Post-its was a plaque bearing her name and title: 'Director, Drug Action Program.' It was her job to keep in close contact with aid agencies in developing countries around the world and do what was necessary to see that they were able to maintain sufficient stores of what the WHO defined as essential drugs and medicines. Today that meant responding to a malaria outbreak in Angola and pestering her contacts at the major pharmaceutical companies to come up with the thousands of doses of the drugs needed to combat it.

With Hugo Luytens's last-minute donation, she'd surpassed her target.

Sliding closer to the desk, she sifted through the storm of papers until she found the one she was looking for. It was hard to get too enthusiastic. There were too many wildfires burning in Africa, Southeast Asia, and more and more in South America, too, to grow complacent. Just getting the WHO to act in a rapid manner was hard enough. To her mind, they spent too much time advising countries about what drugs they needed, how to distribute them, how to oversee the proper dosages, so on and so forth, and too little time procuring and supplying the drugs themselves.

Spinning in her chair, she stared out the window. A calm expanse of lawn rolled down to the shores of Lake Geneva. Water lapped at the sandy banks. A few sailboats were out on the lake, and she wished she could take a long lunch, maybe drive to Ouchy and sip a *balon* of the local rouge along with a *salade niçoise* on the terrace of the Beau Rivage. She had a ravenous appetite, but she was not allowed to eat too much. It was paramount that she remain thin.

Samuel's gleaming bald head rounded the doorway. 'Madame Charisse, I have Global Trans on the phone. They say there is a problem with the paperwork for some of the drugs. The Larythomine and Erythronex. They need your signature.'

'At the airport?'

'Yes.'

Claire grimaced. There was always such a hassle with the newer palliative drugs, many of which relied on radioactive isotope therapy to lessen the pain caused by rapidly growing tumors. The drugs wouldn't cure you, but they would make the last months of your life bearable. Anything, however, involving nuclear medicines raised eyebrows and demanded extra scrutiny.

'Tell them I'll be right out. And next time, we use DHL!'

Claire Charisse slowed long enough to open her desk drawer, grab a few cigarettes, and stuff them inside her purse. Camel with no filters. It was her bones, not her lungs, that were supposed to be the death of her. With a brief wave, she set out down the hallway. The headquarters of the WHO were as large as the Louvre. It took her ten minutes to negotiate the sterile hallways and cross the parking lot to her battered Ford. She'd wanted an Audi, but Glen insisted she drive American.

It was a straight shot on the highway to the airport. Midday traffic was light. Ten minutes later, she was nosing her car through the entry to the cargo terminal, rolling down her window, and extending her WHO pass to the security guard. Recognizing her, he waved her through. He was not so slack, however, as to neglect calling Global Trans to advise them of her arrival. She made it her business to notice such things.

Parking the Ford in front of the office, she nodded a frosty hello and walked through the door. 'Gentlemen, I trust there is a problem of mammoth proportions that requires my personal presence.'

Bill Masters, the British office manager, answered with a no-nonsense glare. 'Can't ship your Larythomine and Erythronex.'

'What do you mean?'

'New regs. Sorry.'

Claire planted herself on the desk. *'New regs, sorry?'* she repeated. 'We're talking about medicine that will prolong the lives of a good many boys and girls who are suffering from leukemia, myelogenous myeloma, Hodgkin's lymphoma, and about a dozen other diseases I can't even pronounce.'

'Terrible, I know, but look, you can read it yourself.'

Claire accepted the memorandum and eyed it cursorily. 'It's a crock of shit. Medicine is medicine. What? Does someone think the stuff is going to explode?'

Masters shrugged. 'Don't know, ma'am.'

'I don't want to be melodramatic, but lives are at stake.'

Masters lowered his eyes. 'Look, Claire, we just fly the stuff for you. We're already giving you a preferred rate. All it says is that you have to have a representative of the local government examine the cargo and sign off on it.'

'I'm with the WHO. The world's a helluva lot bigger than Switzerland. I'd say that's good enough.'

''Fraid not. We need a Swissie.'

'Where are the papers?'

Masters handed over a clipboard with a sheaf of forms attached.

Claire leafed through the pages, licking her thumb every so often. Finally, she snatched a pen from the desk and signed a name to the forms.

'Hey!' Masters protested, jumping out of his chair and taking the clipboard. He read the name. 'You are not Dr Robert Helfer.'

'You wanted a signature. I gave you one. Helfer's the local in charge. Who's going to know the difference?' She stepped close enough to Masters to see that he needed a shave and that he'd had more than orange juice for breakfast. 'Screw the regs,' she whispered through a conspiratorial smile.

Masters shook his head, laughing, then turned. 'Load it up, boys. There's a new boss in town, and her name's Claire.'

Claire Charisse stood on her tiptoes and gave Masters a peck on each cheek. 'Doesn't it feel nice to do something correct, instead of correctly?'

Chapter 34

George Gabriel walked briskly past the apartment building at 23 Rue Clemenceau. It was a modern structure with a floor-to-ceiling glass window running the length of the ground floor. Lawyers, doctors, the crème de la crème of professional Paris lived there. Instead of a concierge, the building had a doorman who spent the day sitting behind a desk reading the sporting gazette and sneaking out for cigarette breaks. His name was Henri, a Senegalese who talked often about bringing his family to Paris as soon as he had saved enough money. Raising a hand to his face, George glanced at the row of mail slots. The box for apartment 3B was still full.

He had been skulking around the neighborhood for an hour. He had eaten a Coupe Denmark at one café and ordered an egg frittata at another. Across the street there was a dingy bar he hadn't been in yet, but the thought of either eating or drinking anything more made him feel sicker than he already did. Worried about appearing conspicuous, he ducked into a corner kiosk and began browsing through the latest soccer mags. One eye glued to the apartment's entry, he skimmed stories on Ryan Giggs and Oliver Kahn. He would never be a pro now, he mused acidly. He'd been a fool to think he ever had a chance.

A clock behind the counter read 3:45. He had fifteen

minutes to wait. When the newsagent shot him a dirty look, he bought a pack of Mary Longs and returned to the magazines.

Fifteen minutes. The time stretched in front of him like a deserted highway.

George Gabriel was hardly recognizable as the young resident who had nearly murdered a female doctor at the Hôpital Salpetitpierre that morning. Fleeing the hospital, he had taken the Métro across town to Montmartre and lost himself in the crowded cobblestone alleys of La Goutte d'Or. There, he had slipped into one of the cheap fashion bazaars and bought a pair of baggy jeans, an oversize white T-shirt, a pair of Nike hightops, some wraparound sunglasses, and a New York Yankees baseball cap he wore bill backward. He was one more hip-hop punk among thousands. The lessons he had learned at camp about evading capture were depressingly useful.

From La Goutte d'Or, he had walked to the Opera, continuing on to the Tuileries. The gardens swarmed with tourists. For an hour, he had lost himself among them. He bought sweet popcorn. He sat beside one of the ponds and watched a small boy sail his boat. He took a ride on the Ferris wheel for the first time in his life.

Despite his anxiety and the near incapacitating fear that gripped him, he had been able to keep his mind focused on his most immediate concerns. Where could he hide? Where should he go? How could he escape? He had his passport and a plane ticket. If he wanted, he could go directly to the airport and get on the plane to Dubai. And then? Who would be waiting for him?

George had tried to reconstruct the police's actions, step by step. The pretty doctor and the American cop had seen him close up. George could count on an accurate description of him being passed to the gendarmerie; an order given to keep a lookout for a six-foot-two-inch man with a

Mediterranean complexion who had been too frightened to take a life.

No one would doubt but that Chapel was the target. The attempt on the American following yesterday's bombing would make the would-be murderer's apprehension a high priority, even if the police were scratching their heads wondering why he'd made such a mess of it; what reason there might have been for his failing to kill the woman.

It wasn't the police who worried him, so much as his father. The man had too many contacts in high places and too many friends in low ones. A city of four million inhabitants offered little security. His father would not forget. Nor would he give up until he had found him. George Gabriel had committed the ultimate sin. He had failed his father. Failed *the family*. There was no greater betrayal.

Drawn by the flocks of tourists and the promise of anonymity, George drifted toward the Louvre. Inside the museum, he traversed the long dusky tunnel to the Pavillon Richelieu and climbed the marble stairs past the Venus de Milo, past Winged Victory. Ambling from room to room, he felt safe in the *grandes salles* grainy light, a refugee sheltered by Rembrandt and Rubens, Vermeer and Van Dyck. The Romantics had always been his favorites, and after a half hour, he found himself glued to the floor in front of a giant canvas by Delacroix entitled 'Entry of the Crusaders into Constantinople.'

A team of mounted Saracens dressed in flowing robes and helmets, their banners crackling in the wind dominated the picture. The crusaders had taken the city, yet behind them the battle still raged. Turks and their women lay prostrate, begging to be spared. One captive was bound and tied to the commanding officer's horse. What would happen next? Would the crusaders kill all the survivors, women included? Would they free them? The lack of resolution fired his imagination.

But today, George found himself asking another question. One of a more personal bent. To which group did he, himself, belong? To the victorious, and (he was certain) benevolent crusaders whose faces spoke of reason, mercy, and strength? Or to the defeated, biblical Turks, whose long beards and impassioned countenances screamed fear, dogma, and fanaticism?

The answer came to him immediately. It required no introspection, no painful examination of his loyalties. By blood, he might be an Arab, but by nature, by temperament, by virtue of reason, he was a Westerner. He did not wish to reject Islam. In his heart, he was devout. He believed in the Prophet. He held his teachings dear. It was his head, however, that took exception. Islam's view of women as inferior, its impossible double-talk about paying them the ultimate respect by imprisoning them in the household angered him. Similarly, its ideas on punishment, revenge, and education were outdated. The world was moving forward, yet Islam remained rooted in the past.

That had been three hours ago.

Gabriel slipped the magazine back into the rack as a familiar red Mercedes turned the corner and continued down the street fifty meters before stopping. A door opened. A flash of blonde hair and a patch of denim crossed the sidewalk and disappeared inside the apartment building. George waited until the car had pulled away to leave the kiosk. Circling the block, he came upon the apartment from the rear, walking through the small alley that led into an expansive interior court. He had a key. He opened the garden entrance and slid inside the emergency stairwell. On the fourth floor, he cracked the door and slipped his head into the hallway. It was quiet.

'Who is it?' came a singsong voice, after he'd knocked.

'It's me. Open up.'

Claudine Cauzet opened the door. Her bright smile faded

as Gabriel shunted past her without a word. 'What is it?' she asked.

'I'm in trouble.'

He'd told her everything – at least everything he knew about his father's plans and his own place in them. He rattled on about Hijira, about the US agents tracking his cousin, Mohammed al-Taleel, about his misadventure in the hospital that morning and his failure to kill Adam Chapel. He'd left nothing out. It was one o'clock. He lay beside Claudine in her bed, the moon's silver light dancing on their faces as an unsteady breeze billowed the curtains.

'Now you know what it feels like to be me,' he said, feeling sorry for himself. 'I can't believe this is happening.'

'You did the right thing, George. I'm proud of you.'

'I let him down.'

'Let him down?' said Claudine disgustedly. 'I should think he'd be proud to have a son who can stand up to him, who can make his own decisions.'

'He's not your dad.'

'You can say that again.'

Claudine's parents, both doctors, were the model of progressive thinking. For the past week they'd been at their vacation home on the Spanish island of Ibiza, leaving her to fend for herself – something Gabriel's father would never allow.

George raised himself on an elbow, wanting her to understand. 'Family comes first. It's everything to us: who we were, who we are, who we're supposed to become. In Islam, family is the center of your life.'

'It is in Christianity, too,' Claudine retorted. 'That doesn't mean you can ask your son to kill for you. What if you'd been caught? What if you'd been killed? Or would that make you some kind of martyr who gets to go to heaven with however many vestal virgins and then it would be okay?'

'I wouldn't be a martyr, just a good son. That would be enough.'

'You are a good son. Just wait, he'll forgive you.'

'Never. He's been planning this for twenty years. Ever since his brother was killed.'

Claudine sat up, pulling a pillow onto her lap and hugging it. 'His brother deserved it,' she stated firmly. 'You cannot take that many people hostage and expect to get aw—'

'He let most of them go,' George interrupted. 'In the end, it was just him and the rebels.'

'And they all got killed.'

'Either in the raid or afterwards.'

'But . . .' Claudine appeared to struggle with the futility of the whole thing, just as George had done once himself. 'Did he really think he would succeed?'

'I don't know that it mattered to him. He was fed up with the hypocrisy. All the drinking, screwing, and living in sin, while pretending to be faithful. It was a lie. He just wanted people to stop and listen to what he had to say so that maybe they would open up their eyes and see for themselves.'

'And did they?'

'Probably not,' George admitted. 'I think he picked the wrong place to make his argument. Anyway, it was before CNN. No one was watching.'

'But you told me this whole thing with Hijira isn't even about religion.'

'I don't know if it is . . . maybe . . . no . . .' The problem was, there were so many ways to look at it. Part of it was about religion. But, it was also about power . . . about *controlling things*. All George knew was that he no longer wanted any part of it. 'So you'll come with me?'

Claudine smiled and pressed his hand to her bosom. 'I said I would. But I think it's better if we take an earlier train. You know, rush hour and all that. Besides, it will give us some extra time in Brussels before the plane leaves. There's only one flight a day to Ibiza.'

'Is it nice?'

'Ibiza?' Her eyes lit up. 'It's beautiful. The water is so blue and warm. There's a breeze that passes over the island at night that smells of wisteria and sage. It is heavenly. I'm not sure your father would approve, though. There are some wild parties down there. You don't have to drink, but you do have to dance.'

'I like to dance.'

'And I know you like girls,' she said, gliding her hand across his bare chest.

'Just one,' he said, suddenly feeling self-conscious. 'Very much.'

'You can stay as long as you like, even after Mama and Papa come home.'

'I don't know . . . I don't have so much money.'

'My parents left me six hundred euros for the week. The plane tickets will cost a bit more. I can't put them on my credit card.'

'Don't worry,' said George, remembering the ATM card in his wallet, the deposits and withdrawals he had made for his father the past year. 'I can get more before we go.'

Claudine tossed her pillow on the bed and pulled herself onto his body. 'Can I ask you one more thing?'

'Sure.'

'You really remembered the Diderot stent?'

Chapter 35

Midnight on the autobahn.

Sarah Churchill held the accelerator near the floor, her eye flicking to the speedometer and back to the road. At two hundred kilometers per hour, the world sped past in a silent roar. Road signs appeared, grew large, and vanished in a flash. A perilous infinity lurked beyond the eerie wash of the Mercedes's xenon headlights. They had been driving for an hour. Berlin lay behind them. So did Köln and Hannover. They were on a straight shot south. To the Rhine. To Zurich. To the truth of what lay behind Hijira.

'We have to tell someone,' she said, shaking her head because it was not the first time she'd argued the point. 'Glen's waiting for our news. We can't just disappear.'

'Why not?' protested Chapel. 'I'd say it's the safest proposition.'

'There's simply too much, that's why. All the names, the accounts. It's a treasure trove. What did you call it last night? A golden thread. We can't just sit on it. God knows there's enough to keep Glen and the boys at FTAT busy for a week. Let them work it from their end.'

'And then? Admiral Glendenning will pass on every tie to a French bank to Gadbois and ask him to look into it.'

'Why should Gadbois worry you?' Sarah looked at Chapel expectantly. 'You think Gadbois is the leak?'

'Hey, they let the Ayatollah camp out in their country for a year, didn't they?'

She laughed dryly. 'Don't be childish. You don't know the man.'

'And you do?'

'Well enough to know that the last thing he'd ever do is jump in bed with an Arab, a radical Muslim to boot. If Gadbois had his way, France would still be in Algeria. Anyway, you don't become chief of a spy agency by having a loose tongue. Calm down, Adam. You're over-reacting.'

'You didn't have someone waiting to kill you,' he said, knowing it sounded melodramatic. Surviving a blast was one thing. Having trained terrorists actively hunt you down was another. He had no experience with this kind of fear. 'Look, if someone is sharing my appointment book with Hijira, I think we can surmise that they're sharing a damn sight more than that. How many people knew I was to see Dr Bac at ten o'clock this morning? Answer me that, Sarah. Come on, let's figure it out.' Chapel held up his hand and counted on his fingers. 'First, there's you, me, and Dr Bac. I think it's safe to say we're innocent of all charges. Admiral Glendenning knew, and since Leclerc was so keen on my reaching the hospital safe and sound this morning, we can assume that Glendenning told Gadbois and Gadbois passed it along. I mentioned it to Allan Halsey, but he'd have to move pretty damn fast to get his operative into place in an hour's time.'

'Is that your rogues' gallery, then?'

'Unless you've got someone else you'd like to add.'

Sarah shook her head, indicating she did not. 'You've got to trust someone, Adam.'

But who? Chapel was in a world where lying, deception,

and treachery were skills to be honed and used at every possible instance. He knew no criteria by which he could judge any of his 'rogues' gallery.' He only had gut instinct to go on.

He reached an open hand towards her. 'I trust you.'

Sarah looked at the hand, then at Chapel. 'This is madness,' she whispered.

But a moment later, she grasped his hand and gave it a gentle, lasting squeeze.

It had started eight hours earlier when, armed with Judge Manfred Wiesel's signed warrant, they had been granted unrestricted access to the records of account 222.818E at the Deutsche International Bank, property of Claude François, Belgian national, born 1961, no photo attached. Seated inside yet another plush conference room, they had expected another dour official, another dry handshake and another folder full of account statements they were to sort through themselves. Instead, they received the full cooperation of the executive vice president in charge of private banking, his deputy, the banker who had personally overseen account 222.818E, and an escorted visit to the bank's back office, where for six and a half hours they studied a sum total of nearly two hundred pages of account records (saved to microfilm and transferred to CD) dating back nearly twenty years.

The number of wire transfers into and out of the account ran to the thousands, nearly one a week, sometimes more. The funds came from banks and brokerage houses of every stripe, both in Europe and the Americas. A rough sum of the incoming transfers totaled more than eighty million dollars. In turn, the money was wired to an equally diverse array of banks, congregated primarily in the Middle East: Dubai, Saudi Arabia, Jordan, Lebanon, even Israel. The Holy Land Charitable Trust counted as an exception. The charity's account at the Gemeinschaft Bank of Dresden had received over five million dollars.

While the information pertaining to the incoming funds listed only the bank's name and account number, nearly all the outgoing faxes included the beneficiary's name, as well. Sarah had railed about the necessity of warm bodies. Now she had them. Mr Abdul al Haq of Jidda, Saudi Arabia. Mr Hassan Daher of Abu Dhabi. Mr Ali Mustafa al-Faroukh of Cairo, Egypt. The list went on and on, numbering eighty-seven in all. If all these men counted themselves as members of Hijira, Sarah had been dead wrong about the organization having only six to eight operatives.

The last transfer was completed just hours after the Paris bombing. Two million euros to a brokerage account in the name of Albert Daudin at L.F. Rothschild in Johannesburg, South Africa.

Daudin, the self-same holder of the account at Bank Montparnasse, born 1961, Belgian national.

It was enough raw data to keep a team of investigators at FTAT and FinCEN busy for a month. Chapel had days, maybe just hours. So he chose to pursue a series of wires that stuck out from the blizzard of financial data like a sore thumb. Namely, five transfers of five hundred thousand dollars each that François had made over the last half year to a numbered account at the Bank Menz in Zurich. Three things about the transfers piqued his interest. First, it was the only time that money had been wired to a Swiss bank. Second, the regular timing of the payments indicated a contractually specified payoff. Last, there was the amount: five hundred thousand dollars. A sum identical to what Abu Sayeed wired to Royal Joailliers three days before.

There are no coincidences.

But when Chapel inquired if any of the bankers had made the acquaintance of Claude François, he came upon his first roadblock. No one currently at the Deutsche International

Bank had met or even seen him. A predecessor had opened the account. Tragically, he'd been killed in a one-car accident, driving home after a late dinner on the Kurfurstendamm. They were, however, pleased to provide the name of the Bank Menz's chairman, the eponymous Dr Otto Menz, as well as his private residential number.

Chapel dialed the number in Zurich immediately. Menz answered on the second ring. After the requisite introduction and apology for disturbing his evening, Chapel informed the banker of the American government's pressing interest in a certain account at his bank.

'Just give me the number,' Menz had answered irritably. 'Wait on the line. I'll phone my colleague to see if it rings a bell.'

Chapel gave him the account number, and a minute later, Menz returned. 'Mr Chapel? We'd be happy to discuss your concerns about the account.'

'You would?' Chapel was unable to conceal his surprise. It appeared that *Festung Schweiz* had a chink in its armor.

'Yes, but as it is a matter of some delicacy, we'd prefer to conduct our conversation in our offices. Do you have any objection to coming to Zurich?'

'Not at all.'

'Very good. Shall we say tomorrow morning in our offices? Seven A.M. We like to begin work at a decent hour. Oh, and Mr Chapel?'

'Yes?'

'What took you so long to get back in touch with us?'

The first-class lounge at Ezeiza International Airport in Buenos Aires was decorated in dark-hued tones of navy, black, and aubergine. Overstuffed leather chairs grouped in twos and threes beckoned the weary traveler. Dim lights added to the tone of a private retreat. A bank of televisions broadcast the evening news. Next to it, a well-stocked bar offered the finest scotches, vodkas, and rums from around the world. Laid out on a polished wooden credenza nearby was a selection of nuts, olives, and a platter of Las Pampas baby beef, an Argentinian speciality.

Though his stomach groaned with hunger, Marc Gabriel paid no attention to the enticing smells wafting from the generous buffet. Stopping only to pour himself a glass of water, he continued to a vacant desk where a small card advertised Internet connectivity. Sitting, he removed his cell phone and checked his voice mail. He'd asked George to leave a coded message to confirm that Adam Chapel was dead. Four words to seal the bond between father and son, and to ensure Hijira's success. 'I love you, Father.' He had checked several times during the day, only to find his mailbox empty. Once again, the operator's mechanical voice informed him that he had no messages.

Unzipping his overnight bag, Gabriel took out his Apple Powerbook and set it on the desk. In less than sixty seconds he was online. A check of the latest news headlines did nothing to ease his unrest. Nowhere could he find any mention of a murdered United States Treasury officer, a second terrorist attack in Paris. He checked AP, Reuters, then *Le Monde* and *Le Figaro*. Nothing. It was six P.M. in Buenos Aires. Eleven o'clock at home. Gabriel phoned his wife.

'He is out,' replied Amina.

'With the girl?'

'I don't know. He has been gone all day long. He looked very presentable when he left. Will you be home soon? Perhaps I can prepare somethi—'

Gabriel hung up. What business was it of hers when he would be home?

Returning his attention to his laptop, he typed in the address of his private server, and accessed his portfolio to mark-to-market the stocks he had shorted three days earlier.

The Dow Jones was down three percent on the day; the London 'footsie' three and a half. It had been a bad day for markets around the world. Lingering recessions. Political unrest in the Middle East. Rising oil prices. Continued epidemic in Asia. In general, a poor time to be long.

Over the past days, his stocks had lost an average of five percent of their value, leaving Gabriel a paper gain of forty million dollars. A tidy sum, but hardly what Hijira required. Switching over to financial modeling software, he ran through the scenarios projecting the gains in his portfolio accruing from a twenty, thirty, or forty percent decline in the value of the world's major financial markets. His best-case scenario left him a profit of four hundred million dollars. The worst-case, two hundred and forty million would barely meet his minimums.

The money was already allocated. Wire transfers were drafted and ready to be sent at the push of a button. One hundred million to the Bank of Riyadh. Sixty million to Emirates International. Fifty-five million to the Jordani Bank of Commerce. Each sum would be further broken down, earmarked for urgent purposes.

The list went on. The beneficiaries of Hijira's endowment.

Closing the programs, he logged on to a prominent American investment bank. He punched in the account number and the password. A moment later, the portfolio flashed onto the screen. Though the account did not belong to him, it showed a surprising similarity to his own. The same stocks had been shorted, if a day later and in vastly smaller quantities. It was no coincidence. He'd known for years that someone was 'piggybacking' his accounts – copying his every trade. In fact, he'd encouraged it.

Western intelligence had initiated surveillance on him shortly after he arrived in Paris twenty years earlier. He had tracked the surveillance to its source and laid his trap as surely as a fisherman sets his net. Spies were smart, ambitious, and underpaid. Gabriel had reasoned that if they were clever enough to keep tabs on him, they were clever enough to make some money from what they saw. When he felt the first tentative nibbles, he gave his prey ample line. Tips on shorting the British pound, buying AOL and Yahoo! Tips so good, they could not be ignored. The prey bit hard and Gabriel let him run deep, all the while keeping records of his every trade. When the time came, he reeled him in. Evidence was presented. An agreement made.

It was blackmail of an enlightened variety. Marc Gabriel conducted his business as he pleased. Richemond prospered. The victim rose through the ranks and grew wealthy. All he had to do was turn a blind eye and supply the occasional snippet of information. Of late, he had been particularly helpful.

'This is a first call for Air France, Flight 382 to Paris. All passengers are requested to proceed to Gate 66 for immediate boarding.'

Gabriel disconnected his laptop and slipped it into his case. Leaving the lounge, he accessed his voice mail a last time. Again there was no message. He was disappointed.

'George,' he whispered with silent anger. 'Have you failed me?'

But already, he was planning his revenge.

They drove.

Chapel surveyed Sarah from behind half-closed lids, secretly mapping every inch of her face, from the careless swell of her lower lip to the tense set of her eyes, from the sculpted chin to the warrior's scar that traced a jagged crescent on her cheekbone.

He'd never been able to get women right. He was no ladies' man, but he'd had his share of girlfriends. Somehow, though, they never turned out to be the people he thought they were when he met them. The shy ones turned into blurters. The loud ones suddenly shut up. The athletes were self-absorbed. The bookworms as nosy as a pew of spinsters. Did the women actually change, or was he just terrible at figuring them out?

The car passed beneath a streetlight. The halogen glow slashed Sarah's face and he was left with a vivid image of her.

Who are you? he wondered silently. *Beneath the uniform? Beneath the cocksuredness and the call to duty? Who are you when you take a bath and wash off the day's reality? Are you so deep inside your secret world that you've lost all trace of yourself and that you look for your job to tell you how to act, what you should feel, and who you ought to love?*

But in the end only one question mattered. *Are you the one? Is this the way I'm supposed to feel when I'm in love?*

'Look, Adam, it's late. Let's find a place to pull over and get some rest.'

'Keep going. I don't want to miss that meeting.'

She pulled off the road forty minutes later at an AGIP truck stop on the other side of the border from Basel. Guiding the car down the off ramp, Sarah threw her eyes to the Autobahn. A BMW 535i painted the green and white of the German police slid past, languid as a shark.

'Our escort?' said Chapel.

'You knew?'

'So much for keeping our destination hidden. The Swiss are probably waiting on the other side of the border. Glen's been keeping an eye on us all the way.'

'If he is, it's for our own safety. That's part of his job – to look after his own.'

If it is, in fact, Glen, Sarah added silently. She doubted it. Excusing herself from the conference room in the Deutsche International Bank, she'd phoned Owen Glendenning herself to let him know the extent, if not the details, of their discovery, and their plan to drive to Zurich. He had no need to follow them. Someone else had been keen to learn their destination. Who had alerted the police? The FBI? Judge Wiesel? Gadbois? She'd spotted the eyes, but she had no idea as to their ultimate allegiance.

The parking lot was half-full with big rigs, eighteen-wheel juggernauts, and RVs. Sarah pointed the car to a far corner of the lot, pushing the car over the curb and keeping the speed low as she crossed a wide meadow of waist-high grass.

'Where are we—'

'Patience, Mr Chapel. Patience . . . unless, that is, you'd like to wake up in an hour when every one of those trucks hits the road.'

The headlights played across a wide bank of trees fifty yards ahead. Rolling down the window, Sarah breathed in the cooling rush of fresh water. She killed the engine, and for a while they sat in silence, listening to the muted roar of a fast-flowing river.

'I won't ask how you knew about this.'

'I didn't. Just that there was a river in this direction. I figured it might be nice to relax somewhere more private than a truck stop. Call me a snob.'

She stepped out of the car. The night was warm and still. Crickets sawed restlessly while somewhere a motorbike puttered down a country road. She walked to the riverbank and stared at the moon's curdled reflection in the black water. Adam joined her a moment later. She looked at him. Though he was staring into the sky, she could sense his expectation, scent his desire.

'How's your shoulder?' Delicately, she ran a hand along the contours of his burn.

'Not bad,' he said, wincing. 'Actually, it hurts like hell.'

'Nothing I'm doing?'

'No,' he answered rapidly.

'Can you get it wet?'

'I'm not sure.'

'You have more meds, don't you?'

'Yeah. In the car.'

'Okay, then. We can't show up in Zurich smelling like swine.' Sarah stepped away from him, and raising her hands in the air, pulled off her tank top. She enjoyed the sweep of his eyes over her breasts, the near rabid hunger there. A year without a woman. Poor boy. Bending, she removed her slacks and panties. She lingered a moment, sure to erase any objection. 'Coming?'

They dried each other with their bodies. Sarah kissed his forehead, his cheeks, his neck, before allowing herself to taste him. He kissed her softly and she loved him for his restraint, knowing he wanted to devour her, as much as she wanted to devour him. His body was as she'd imagined, the muscles sculpted, the skin pale and taut, every ridge of his abdomen visible. She looked at the shoulder and felt a wave of genuine pity. 'My, my,' she said. 'You're braver than I thought. Third-degree?'

'Only a small patch of it.'

'We'll have to be very careful with you, Mr Chapel.'

'Not too careful,' he said.

Wrapping her arms around him, she lowered the both of them to the grass, silently ordering Adam to lie on his back. She ran her fingers across his body until he was rigid, his back arched, anxious. Only then did she climb on top of him. Suddenly, he paused. 'Sarah Anouska Churchill, right?'

'Cross my heart,' she said, gasping as he entered her.

Closing her eyes, she fought back the biting recrimination. She had no choice but to lie. She had to ensure that Adam trusted her. After all, it was her job.

Chapter 36

Bank Menz hid on the second floor of a sixteenth-century building on the Augustinergasse, a winding, cobblestoned alley just off the Bahnhofstrasse in downtown Zurich. If the exterior of the building remained unchanged but for periodic renovations since Father Zwingli's time, the interior was a state-of-the art mélange of halogen lights, plasma screens, and stainless steel. At seven in the morning, the office bristled with the urgency of a ship at flank speed. The staff was present, the corridors brightly lit and humming with what Chapel could only think of as 'Swiss efficiency,' the scent of freshly brewed coffee tickling the air.

'I hope the early hour didn't cause too much of a problem,' said Dr Otto Menz as he shepherded Chapel and Sarah Churchill through the warren of offices. 'We like to make a good start on things.'

'Not at all,' replied Chapel. 'We appreciate you seeing us at such short notice.'

'Short notice? We've been waiting six months to hear back from you.'

Menz was a spry, handsome seventy year old, his face tanned from weekends in the Alps, his white hair combed through with brilliantine, his blue eyes glinting with resolve. Directing his guests through the hallways, he never took his hand from Chapel's back, patting him all the way as if he were welcoming home a long-lost son. The banker was as far from a gnome as Chapel could imagine.

'Right this way,' said Menz, motioning towards an open door that led to a conference room.

A second man waited inside, business card at the ready. He was tall, dark, funereal, with oversize horn-rimmed glasses. 'Good morning,' he said in accented English. 'My name is Dr Irwin Senn. Corporate counsel.'

Chapel took the card and returned the firm handshake. The crisp professionalism of the place left him feeling distinctly underdressed. Khakis and a polo shirt didn't cut it when you were going up against tailored three-piece pinstripes. Even his Lobbs failed to stare down Menz's thousand-dollar ostrich skin lace-ups.

'Good morning,' said Sarah. 'The pleasure is ours.'

'Dr Irwin Senn,' the lawyer repeated, carefully selecting another business card from his billfold and offering it to her across the table. 'Corporate counsel.'

'Please, let us take our seats,' said Menz, and they all sat at once around the square glass table. 'Well, well, you're here at last. You were a bit vague last night. The security of the United States is a rather large statement.'

'We've come in connection with the bombing in Paris earlier this week,' explained Sarah. 'Our investigation into the identity of the culprit and his associates turned up some transfers made to an account at your bank.'

'Five transfers, to be exact,' continued Chapel, 'totaling two and one half million dollars that were made during the last half year.'

'Yes, yes, from the Deutsche International Bank,' said Otto Menz. 'I'm well aware of what you're talking about. We provided all pertinent information about the account to your good offices months ago.'

'You did?' Chapel had never heard of the Bank Menz until yesterday. Any reports of suspicious account activity –

especially activity of this magnitude – should have crossed his desk immediately. Why hadn't anyone at FTAT – Glendenning or Halsey, or whoever had caught the squelch, done something about it?

'You are with the Foreign Terrorist Asset Tracking Center?' Menz asked.

Chapel and Sarah said yes.

'Admiral Glendenning told us he was grateful for your assistance,' she added, lying with such grace and sincerity that for a moment even Chapel believed her. 'Unfortunately, when investigations move so rapidly, it's difficult for us to cull through past warnings.'

'You get a lot, do you?'

'Not enough,' said Sarah.

Menz raised an eyebrow. 'Any about nuclear physicists?' When neither Chapel nor Sarah answered, he continued. 'As I had suspected, the matter was potentially of vital importance. National security, you said.'

'Absolutely,' said Chapel.

'Well, then.' Folding his hands, Menz glanced at Dr Senn, who nodded curtly, as if to say that Menz had been discharged of his obligations of client confidentiality. 'The recipient of the funds is Dr Mordecai Kahn. Does the name mean anything to you?'

Sarah and Chapel indicated it did not.

'He is an Israeli. A nuclear physicist. At least, he wrote as much on his account documents. Also a professor. He came into our offices nine months ago asking to open a numbered account. Quite concerned about confidentiality, I've been told. He informed us up front that he would be receiving large sums from abroad.'

'Did that strike you as odd?'

'Not at all. Most of our clients wire in money from foreign banks. It was only later, when the money arrived, that we grew concerned. Two and half million dollars to a professor?

A modest man, by all appearances. What could it be for? Royalties? Speaking fees? An inheritance, perhaps, but in five equal sums? I think not.'

'You met him?'

'Of course not.' Menz dismissed the suggestion out of hand. He might as well have been accused of replacing the toilet paper in the public rest rooms. 'Our account officer took notes.' Menz consulted a sheet of paper. ' "Client poorly dressed. Digital watch. Tennis shoes. Nervous. In need of a shower." We like to be aware of these things.'

'Of course,' said Chapel, but something in his tone angered the older man.

'You see, Mr Chapel, one must either ask no questions or ask many,' Menz argued. 'There is no in-between. Willful ignorance is no longer tolerated.'

'What prompted you to contact us?' asked Sarah, touching Menz's arm. 'And may I say, we're ever so grateful.'

'It was later,' said Menz, calmer now, 'when we noticed the sums were coming from a dubious account. I can only say that this Claude François had raised some questions in the past. We bankers do talk. And, of course, there was the beneficiary: an Israeli scientist receiving money from a questionable account in Berlin. Why? For what reason? What services might he have performed? I was too frightened even to imagine. So I called you.'

So this was the new Switzerland, thought Chapel. The Swiss financial industry had undergone a sea change in the last six years. From impenetrable bastion of bank secrecy to an engaged, active, and cooperative partner in the international combat against money laundering and terrorist finance. Several factors had been responsible for the shift. First, the country had decided it was uncomfortable with its image as a partner of crooks and criminals. Second, many other countries had stepped up to challenge Switzerland as a fortress of secrecy. Luxembourg, the Cayman Islands, and a slew of stamp-sized republics in the South Pacific all promised to guard a client's secrecy against any and all intrusions. No longer did bank secrecy offer the Swiss banks a marketing advantage, a leg up on their opponents, as it were. It was this that decided the matter. Bank secrecy simply didn't pay anymore. It might even be costing the Swiss money.

'Has Dr Kahn withdrawn any money from the account?' Chapel asked.

'Seventy-seven thousand dollars wired to a BMW dealership in Vienna. That's all. Not a dime more.'

'And would you happen to have an address for him?'

'Naturally. I have all the particulars here.'

At his beckoning, Dr Senn passed copies of the documents to Chapel and Sarah. Kahn's address was listed as Jabotinsky Street in Tel Aviv. His profession as 'professor/research.' There was a home and work telephone. He'd named his wife as a beneficiary of the account. It all looked on the up-and-up. Except that a banker with forty years' experience had sniffed that something was wrong and had decided that a Jewish physicist wearing cheap clothing, a digital watch, who was in need of a shower and acting nervously could only be receiving large sums for illicit acts. *Well then*, as Menz might have said. That was the way the system was supposed to work. Why did it feel to Chapel like such a miracle that for once it had?

'May I ask you both one question?'

'Of course,' said Chapel.

Otto Menz came out of his chair an inch and leaned on his forearms. 'What has Kahn given them in exchange for the money?'

Sarah stood by the lake watching a majestic paddle-wheel steamer approach the dock. A freshening breeze raised a small chop. Swans and ducks bobbed on the surface. In the distance, like hovering ghosts, the outline of the Glarner Alps was visible.

'Hello Yossi,' she said into her cell phone. 'It's Meg from London.'

'Hello, Meg from London.'

'Need your help a bit. Got a sec?'

'Always a sec for Meg from London,' said Yossi, who was from Jerusalem, a mover and shaker in the Mossad, the Israeli intelligence service.

'I've run across one of your own in a little deal we're following. Mordecai Kahn. A physicist. Name ring a bell?'

'Kahn, you say. Not off the top of my head, but let me check.'

'Sure thing.'

Sarah looked at Chapel, who was on his own phone, booking them return flights to Paris. He was making things complicated. He loved her and she knew it. She'd encouraged it. And what about her? She had only to catch his eye to feel his longing. He was staring at her now. Something in his brown eyes stretched her loyalties in three different directions. She wrote it off to her sentimental side. A needy man always provoked her weaker emotions. But love? She dismissed it out of hand.

'Hey, Meg . . .'

'Yes?'

'Never heard of him.'

'Too bad,' she said, knowing better than to feel disappointed. 'Thanks for checking. I owe you.'

'Traffic goes both ways,' he said. 'Just in case I get something, where will you be?'

'*Just in case?*' Sarah hesitated a minute. Where would she be? Why, she'd be at the other end of her cell phone, that's where. Yossi knew that.

'Yeah, you know,' he said. 'If we need to get *in touch* with you.'

Oh, God, thought Sarah. *It can't be. It can't have come to this.* The intent of Kahn's payments was unmistakable. You only pay a nuclear physicist two million dollars for one thing these days and it wasn't to build a better mousetrap.

'Paris,' she said. 'Hotel Spendide. I'll even let you buy me a drink this time.'

But Yossi didn't respond, not with a laugh or even a good-bye. Without another word, the line went dead.

Chapter 37

Marc Gabriel made his way through the arrival hall at Charles-de-Gaulle airport, a hand in his jacket checking for his passport. He walked briskly, a man with somewhere to go. A man who would let nothing delay him. The boy had failed. Measures had to be taken. It was difficult to separate a father's disappointment from a commander's anger. Sidestepping, dodging, brushing past the relentless sea of tourists, he arrived at immigration control. He smiled perfunctorily for the passport officer, his fingers drumming the counter, itching to reclaim his documents.

'Welcome home, Mr François.'

'Thank you,' he replied, already past the booth, making a beeline for the taxi stand.

It had been a long flight from Buenos Aires. The movies and meals had done little to pass the time. Alone with his thoughts, he'd played out every possible scenario. George had been arrested. George had been killed. But in the end, he was left with only one possibility. George had failed. He was trying to flee. *Measures had to be taken.*

Outside, he raised his hand and whistled sharply. A silver Citroën docked at the curb. Gabriel climbed into the backseat. 'Rue Clemenceau.'

'Address?'

'Near the corner of Avenue Marseilles. I'll show you when we get there. And there's an extra twenty euros in it for you if you get me there inside an hour.'

Gabriel stared out the window, eyes glazed, unfocused. It could only be a lack of moral conviction, he told himself, trying to account for what had gone wrong. The rot had corroded his son's values. He himself was to blame. He had kept the family in Paris too long. So many years among the infidel, it was inevitable.

Islam was based on virtue; the word itself meant 'submission.' It was not a religion, not simply a set of beliefs, but an entire way of life. The Koran did not simply govern one's daily conduct, it extended to all aspects of society. To law and trade, war and peace, education and family. *Sharia* governed all.

By providing a sanctuary inside his home that valued these beliefs, he had hoped to mitigate the rot, but it had turned out to be too much. The temptations were constant and pervasive – the pounding amoral music, the lewd films, the relentless emphasis on sex, sex, sex. It was a form of intellectual colonization. Like syphilis, it entered the brain, eating away at it slowly, maddeningly, piece by piece, lobe by lobe, until there was nothing left but a hollowed-out rotten husk. There was no such thing as selective Westernization. You took all of it or none of it.

When the West had separated the realm of God from the realm of society, it had put itself on a collision course with Islam. It was a war, and either one side or the other would prevail. He'd felt certain that George knew all of this, that he believed it to the marrow of his bones. Yet, he'd been wrong.

It was the girl, of course. He'd known for quite some time that his son was seeing her. How could a father fail to notice when his boy had grown into a man? This, too, was his failure. He'd been slow to react. Soft.

Sentimental. He'd informed himself about the girl's family, where she lived, her record in school. She was *kuffar*, but a respectable child. A good student. A mature girl not given to childish fancy. Clearly, he'd missed something and he knew what that 'something' was. He'd committed every father's cardinal sin. He'd thought his son was different.

Marc Gabriel knew then that he, too, had succumbed to the rot.

The taxi dipped as it exited the freeway at the Porte de Clignancourt. Gabriel counted off the familiar sights, feeling calmer in the city he never wanted to see again. *Two days*, he said to himself. Two days until he was free of all of this. Until the desert wind seared his longing cheek.

'Rue Clemenceau,' called the cabbie over his shoulder as the taxi rounded a corner. 'Which building?'

'One more block. There, that's the one.' Gabriel pointed to a modern metal and glass apartment building halfway down the street. As the taxi braked, he closed his eyes and imagined a fist wrapped around his heart, clenched, constricting all emotion. George was his oldest, the firstborn, but he had six younger boys from his other wives. He would choose a successor from their ranks.

After paying the cabbie, he took his bag and walked up to the entrance.

'Ah, Henri,' he said, all camaraderie and good humor. 'Have you seen the boy?'

'Me?' answered the Senegalese doorman. 'No, sir.'

Gabriel couldn't help but pick up on the man's hesitation. Either Henri was a terrible liar or a first-rate con man. Snapping a hundred-euro note from his wallet, he pressed it into the doorman's hand. 'Our usual deal: a little something for your family, a little something for mine. The boy and I had a little disagreement. My wife is worried sick. You understand?'

Henri smiled sheepishly. 'Two of them leave 'bout thirty minutes ago.'

'Really?' Gabriel affected amusement at the news. 'Any idea of their destination?'

'Don't know, sir, but the girl, she had a bag.'

'A purse?'

'No, a traveling bag. Bigger than yours.'

'That right?' Gabriel peeled off another bill, and Henri's allegiance to his tenant, feeble to begin with, crumbled entirely.

'They cross the Pont d'Iéna, sir. Heading to the sixteenth, I think.' Suddenly, he smiled and his teeth shone like ivory. 'I say to her, with a bag like that you need a taxi. Claudine say what she need is money for a taxi. Would I lend her some? She always joking, that girl.'

'She must be quite funny,' said Gabriel as he left the building. 'I'd like to meet her one day.'

'Hurry up,' Claudine urged George Gabriel. 'You can walk faster than that.'

'I can, but I don't want to. We have plenty of time. No point in drawing attention to ourselves.'

'But everyone is walking fast—' Claudine caught herself. 'You're not thinking about your father? You said he only got back this morning.'

'His flight landed at seven-fifteen. That's an hour ago.'

'You checked?'

'Of course.'

Claudine shot him a look that said he was being ridiculous.

'By now, he'll know.'

'And then?'

Silently, George enumerated the possibilities. None was pleasant. 'I don't know.' Reaching for her hand, he brought it to his mouth and kissed it.

'Don't draw attention to us,' she chastised him.

'He doesn't know I have a girlfriend. You're my cover.'

George Gabriel squinted into the morning sun. He had never spent the entire night with Claudine. Holding her in his arms as he awoke, he'd tasted, if only for a few minutes, what the rest of his life might be like. He was looking forward to arriving in Ibiza. She'd told him about the farmhouse and the pond it overlooked and the warm waters of the Mediterranean. He knew exactly where he wished to be tomorrow morning, and whose eyes he wished to look into when he woke.

Seeing the ATM a half block ahead, he nudged Claudine and the two stopped walking. 'The code is 821985,' he said, handing her the bank card.

'Your birthday?'

'Just get the money and bring it back.'

'What else would I do?' Claudine rose on her tippy-toes and kissed him. 'Aren't you going to wish me luck?'

Marc Gabriel knew where his son would go. It had nothing to do with telepathy, premonition, or coincidence. It was a simple case of a father knowing his son.

Pointing to the nearest corner, Gabriel signaled the cabbie to stop. On the pavement, he set off down the block, an eye trained on the ATM cut into the wall of the Neuilly branch of the BLP. He'd given his son the bank card a year ago in April, when Gabriel had traveled to Israel to recruit the Professor and it was necessary for George to handle the weekly payments. The boy had done a competent job. Afterwards, Gabriel had allowed him to keep the card, advising him to use it only for emergencies. He'd never given George much allowance. When his son needed something, he came to his office, they discussed it, and most times, Gabriel agreed. In the past sixteen months, the boy hadn't made any unauthorized withdrawals, and

Gabriel had viewed his fiscal discipline as proof of his maturity.

Taking up a position in a recessed storefront of a men's boutique, Gabriel had an unobstructed view of the cash machine. Its current customer was an older man, wearing a black beret and leaning on a cane. Gabriel swept his eyes back and forth along the sidewalk for any sign of his son. Even among the throng of pedestrians, a man six feet two inches tall would be easy to notice.

It was a busy morning. Cars zipped back and forth on either side of the grassy median. Among them were a fair number of vans making their early deliveries. Dry cleaners, florists, caterers, cleaning services. An armored car lumbered to a halt in front of the bank, momentarily blocking his view. The rear doors opened. Two officers carrying gray twill sacks entered the bank.

Gabriel left his vantage point and advanced a few yards up the sidewalk. A woman had taken up position at the ATM. He looked past her, his eyes darting from man to man, seeking out his son's clean-shaven skull, the broad shoulders, the dark, smoldering gaze. He wondered if George might have gone to another machine. A second ATM was only three blocks away, but as it was situated across the street from the local police prefecture, Gabriel doubted that he would go there. Besides, it was that much farther from Claudine's building.

Claudine.

Gabriel returned his eyes to the woman at the ATM. For a moment, he'd forgotten that his son was traveling in a female's company. He took a closer look at her, catching the subtle tap-tap-tap of her heel, the deft looks to her right and left. Though he'd informed himself about Claudine's background, he'd never actually seen her. Could that be his son's Claudine? He dismissed the thought. He'd thought of Claudine as a girl, but this was a woman with full breasts, childbearing hips, and an assured dignity about her. She looked too old for his son, but then Western teenagers prided themselves on looking more mature than their age. The overt and sickening seduction of the male species began at the age of twelve these days. The bared midriffs, the exaggerated bosoms, the whorish makeup.

Then he saw it and his heart jumped.

The girl – the woman – *Claudine, yes it had to be her!* – looked to her left, and catching someone's eye, patted the air lightly with her hand as if to say, 'Calm down. I'll be right there.'

Gabriel turned to the left, trying to spot whom she'd signaled, but he saw no one. With a minimum of fuss, he made a U-turn on the sidewalk and began to walk back up the block. He hugged the concrete façades and slowed at the storefront windows, a hand brushing his hair, dabbing his sideburns, anything to conceal his features. And all the while his eyes scoured the opposite side of the street – the café, the kiosk, the boutique, the bakery.

Claudine had left the ATM and was folding a wad of bills and shoving them into her pocket. All he had to do was follow her to his son. She waved ever so slightly and nodded her head. A greeting of conspirators.

Gabriel's eye darted up the sidewalk and landed on a tall, rough-boned boy who had emerged from a public rest room. The boy was wearing baggy jeans, an oversize T-shirt bearing a scowling black youth's face above the words 'Fifty Cent,' and a baseball cap with its bill turned backwards. Sunglasses hid the boy's eyes, but there was no mistaking the face.

Marc Gabriel had found his son.

Chapter 38

'Miss Charisse, please come in. I'm Dr Ben-Ami.'

Claire Charisse passed from the waiting room into the doctor's suite of offices. 'Thank you for seeing me,' she said, ever her officious self. 'I know it was short notice.'

'Not at all,' said Maurice Ben-Ami, gesturing towards an empty examining room. 'I'm happy to help. I spoke with Hugo Luytens at Roche. He says you're making some real progress at the WHO. It's the least I could do, to see you.'

Claire put down her purse and took a seat on the raised bench, nervously adjusting her skirt beneath her legs.

'These are the latest?' he asked, accepting the manila envelope from her. He threw the X-rays on the light box as if he were dealing cards. 'Let's have a look, shall we?'

Sixty, sallow, with twenty-pound bags of coal under his eyes and a miner's fractured posture, Maurice Ben-Ami looked as if he hadn't left his offices in a year. His specialty was oncology, the branch of medicine concerned with the study and treatment of tumors. Staring at the X-rays, he saw three knotty masses attaching themselves to the elbow joint.

'Hmm,' he grunted. 'I had no idea the case was so advanced. Hugo didn't mention anything—'

'Hugo doesn't know. Our relationship is strictly professional. I strong-arm him into sending my patients drugs. He gets me doctor's appointments.'

'What I mean is that you look too healthy.'

'I'll take that as a compliment.'

'So you're familiar with the prognosis?'

'Intimately.'

'And how are you feeling?' he asked, sitting down on a rolling stool.

'Not great, or else I wouldn't be here.' Claire touched her elbow and winced.

'There, there.' Ben-Ami took her arm in his hands and gingerly worked the joint, his practiced fingers probing the afflicted area. 'You've started your second round of treatment?'

'Tuesday.'

'No nausea?'

Claire flashed him her survivor's grin. 'Nothing a cigarette won't cure.'

The strong, capable hands slid up the arm, massaging the biceps, the triceps. 'Your hair is staying with you.'

She lifted the three-thousand-dollar wig off her head. Clusters of brittle, gray-white hair clung to her scalp. 'Fooled you, didn't I?' she asked, before repositioning the hairpiece.

Ben-Ami smiled briefly, as if smiles were rationed. 'Loss of appetite?'

'I was never a big eater.'

Finished with his examination, Maurice Ben-Ami frowned. 'Strange. Usually, I can get some feel of the growths. Your arms feel strong. No deterioration in the muscle. The tumors seem to have shrunk.' He bent Claire's arm to her shoulder and she stifled a moan. 'I'm sorry.'

'It's all right,' she said, wiping at a tear. When she allowed her eyes to meet his, she appeared ashamed of her low tolerance for pain.

'One of the brave ones, eh? Good for you. It's important to put up a good fight. So many people, after a cancer metastasizes – when they have bone mets like you – they give in to the pain. They give up. It's a mistake. Our will to live is the strongest weapon we possess.'

Sighing, Ben-Ami rose from the stool and lumbered to the cupboard. He returned with two vials of clear liquid. 'This might do the trick. Metastron. The newest stuff we've got.'

'Will it help the pain?'

'Takes a few days to kick in, but I think you'll be happy. A third of my patients tell me they don't feel a thing. Of course, it's only palliative. It treats the pain, not the tumor, but it will add significantly to the quality of your life. Your appetite will come back. You'll be able to enjoy your wine. I always like Fendant this time of year, or maybe an Aigle Les Murailles.' He raised a finger in admonishment. 'But no more than a glass at dinner. Cut the cigarettes, too. They knock out your immune system.'

'And movement?'

'Your range of motion will improve. There's no reason why you shouldn't play tennis. Best of all, you should be able to sleep through the night.'

'Sounds wonderful,' said Claire.

Swabbing her arm, Ben Ami opened a vial and dosed a syringe. It wasn't a small syringe, the stuff of flu shots and tetanus vaccines. It was a large metal syringe, the needle a good three inches long, with the diameter of a ballpoint pen.

'You can expect some discomfort,' he said. 'It's necessary to administer the drug slowly.'

Claire winced as the needle entered her skin.

'This will only take a minute or two.'

'How does it work?' She already knew, but she needed him to talk, *anything* to distract her from the needle working its way into her muscle.

'Metastron? It tricks the bones into thinking it's calcium and gets sucked up into the tumor. The active agent is strontium. The radioactive isotopes bind with the tumor and lessen the friction against the bone. Hence less pain.'

'Strontium?' A look of horror passed across her face. 'Goodness, will I glow in the dark?'

'You're thinking of strontium ninety, which is a by-product of nuclear fission – the stuff we get comes from spent fuel rods, nuclear reactors, that kind of thing. Metastron uses strontium eighty-nine chloride. It's a different molecule.'

'But it *is* radioactive?'

'Mildly. All you need to worry about is that in five days most of your pain should have dissipated.'

Claire was more concerned about the shorter term. 'How long will it stay in my system?'

'The half-life of the active radioisotope is fifty-one days. You'll pass the debris by urination. The best part of it is that there are no side effects. You're getting your life back.' Ben-Ami removed the syringe and pressed a cotton ball to her arm. 'Dr Rosenblum told me that you'll be traveling soon.'

'Yes, this weekend. I'm flying to the States.'

'I'd like to schedule some X-rays. We can do them now, in fact. In the next office.'

'I'm afraid I can't this afternoon.'

'Tomorrow, then?' It was almost an order. 'I'll clear some time in the morning. Say, nine o'clock? I'm hoping to have some good news for you.'

'Can we say after the weekend? Monday morning?'

'Certainly. Anyhow, in the meantime, you may need this.' Ben-Ami scribbled a note on his drug pad. As to be expected, it was illegible.

'Thank you,' said Claire Charisse, rising from the bench. 'It's a great relief.'

Chapter 39

Leclerc sipped his coffee in the back-office operations center of the Banque de Londres et Paris. 'How many men have we got on the street?'

'Twenty-six,' answered Dominique Maison, chunky, ill-shaven, a twenty-year veteran of the Sûréte.

'What happened to the other four?'

'Reassigned. There was a double murder in the Bois last night.' Maison shrugged by way of apology. 'We need them to take statements.'

'We need them to watch these ATMs,' retorted Leclerc. 'These guys are on the run. Anytime, they might hit a machine for cash.'

He didn't believe it for a second. It had taken them all of two days to run through their leads. Rafi Boubilas's information about the Holy Land Charitable Trust hadn't yielded what Leclerc had hoped. He couldn't care less if the account had been frozen. He needed names. People to roust. Men to seek out and interrogate. In his mind, he played the digital videotape incessantly, including the section that Gadbois and Glendenning ordered to have edited out on the grounds that it would provoke too much worry and inhibit the investigators' proper functioning. The audio track had remained intact for a good fifteen seconds after the digital images had deteriorated. 'You will drown in a flood tide of blood,' the man in the red-checked *khaffiyeh* and mirrored sunglasses had said. 'Bodies will crowd the streets. Chaos will reign.'

As for Dupuy, the vaunted computer guru hadn't been able to pull anything more than a few pages of gobbledygook off Taleel's hard drive, though he was begging for more time to take apart an encrypted e-mail file he'd only just discovered. For all Chapel's faith in bank accounts, he hadn't come up with a damned thing that brought them a step closer to finding Santos Babtiste's killer and learning what in the world Hijira had up their sleeve.

Frustrated, Leclerc shook loose a cigarette from a crushed pack of Gauloises. 'All right, then, at least let's make sure our guys are in the right place.'

The map indicating the location of the most frequently used cash machines sat on a table in the center of the room. Lighting the cigarette, Leclerc moved his finger from point to point, inquiring whether the police had stationed a man at each spot. 'We need more men in the sixteenth arrondissement. Mr Chapel is convinced it's their base.'

'Chapel? The American? He's not even a real cop,' Maison snickered, and Leclerc cuffed him on the ear. 'Shut up,' he said. 'He's tougher than you, and a lot more fit. Just tell me who we have.'

Maison tapped a finger on the map. 'Sergeant de Castille is here and Officer Perez a few blocks away.'

'What about here?' asked Leclerc, laying a finger at the corner of Boulevard Victor Hugo and Rue Saint-Paul: the Neuilly branch of the BLP.

'No one.'

'No one? Well, get someone over there in a hurry.'

A buzzer sounded and Leclerc said, 'What the hell is that?'

All heads turned towards a technician seated at a console of small video screens.

'It's your man,' said the bank's director of technical services, eyes glued to the wall of glass screens. Most were dark. A few broadcast a line or two of text in fluorescent green letters. *Installation 212: down for repairs. Installation 9: cash needed.* 'Someone is accessing the restricted account. Installation number fifty-seven.'

'Where?' asked Leclerc, rushing to the console. 'Show me where!'

'Our branch on Rue Saint-Paul.' The technician hit a button and one of the video screens bloomed. 'There's your man,' he said, patching into the ATM's software, taking a look at just what 'their man' was up to. 'Withdrawing seven hundred euros. Transaction complete. Uh, no, trying to get more cash. Sorry, pal, seven hundred's the max for the account.' He adjusted a knob and the security camera zoomed in, showing not a man, but an attractive woman with fawn-colored hair pulled into a ponytail and wearing Ray-Bans. 'I didn't know you were looking for a girl.'

'We weren't.' Leclerc picked up a two-way radio and contacted Sergeant de Castille, who was three blocks away, ordering him to move his ass as quickly as possible to Rue Saint-Paul and to instigate surveillance on a blonde woman dressed in a navy T-shirt and a short white skirt. 'I don't know how tall she is,' he added, 'but she's got one helluva figure.'

A new voice squawked from Leclerc's radio. 'Captain, this is Michel Martin. I'm off shift, but I'm only a block away. Let me take a look.'

'Do it,' said Leclerc. 'And both of you keep your eyes open for a tall male she may be traveling with. Young guy, buzz cut, strong. Be careful.'

'You want us to take them down?'

Leclerc ran the palm of his hand over his cheek. It would take him at least fifteen minutes to get to Neuilly, maybe more. Surveillance hadn't turned out well last time they'd tried. He had little choice. 'If she's with the man, take them down. Otherwise just follow her. And okay, you are authorized to use deadly force – but, *les gars*, only if necessary.'

Marc Gabriel crossed the street, dodging the scattered traffic to take up position on the sidewalk twenty meters behind his son. No longer was he a father. He was a soldier, a warrior carrying out the Prophet's orders. There was no other way. He was not the only one looking for his son. The chances were simply too great that if captured, George would talk. And while George did not know the details of Hijira, he knew the fundamentals, the names of the bigger players. Perhaps most important, he knew that it was to happen this weekend.

Gabriel quickened his step. A hand delved into his pants pocket and came out with a gold Mont Blanc fountain pen. With his nail, he flicked off the cap, dropping it back in the pocket. Then he cupped the pen in his hand so that the nib rested in his curled palm. It would be unwise to nick himself. Instead of India ink, the pen contained a concentrated dose of Ricin, a deadly poison for which there was no antidote. How ironic, Gabriel thought: he'd always meant the pen for himself. He had no intention of falling into unfriendly hands.

Gabriel lengthened his stride. He stared at his son's garments. The baggy pants, the shirt with the black man's face, the American cap were all taboo in their household and served to fuel his rage. There would be no time for words. No need. His son was a traitor and he knew a traitor's fate. The jab would have to be quick. George had a mongoose's reflex. The neck would be best. The soft flesh just below the jaw.

Ricin acted instantly. Within a half second, the nerves became paralyzed. The heart stopped beating a moment later. George would be dead before he hit the ground.

Ten meters separated them.

He heard George laugh, and the laugh galvanized him. If he had harbored any doubt about his intentions, or his ability to carry them out, the laugh quashed them. Nothing could be so amusing as to warrant such a carefree chuckle – not when you'd let down your father; when you had broken a promise to your family; when you'd betrayed your destiny.

Marc Gabriel slid the pen forward in his hand so that the nib protruded and glinted in the sun like a warrior's blade. Fixing his jaw, he took a breath. His left hand rose before him like the arm of another man, a stranger, reaching towards his son's shoulder. He brought the pen up and felt his body tensing, readying itself to deliver the killing jab.

'*Hakim*.' He whispered his son's true name.

The boy stopped on a dime.

'*Stop! Police! Do not move!*'

Before Gabriel could lunge, he was knocked to the ground. A pair of plainclothes policemen swept past, tackling his son to the pavement. A third man hit the girl at the knees, swiping her legs from beneath her. She yelped, and Gabriel saw her eyes stretched in fright an instant before her skull struck the sidewalk. A fourth man fought his way in, a canister of pepper spray in hand, and as George struggled, the policeman aimed it at his eyes and fired a blast.

'You are under arrest! Do not struggle! Keep still!'

A siren wailed. Horns blared. Tires squealed.

Scuttling backwards on his hands and knees, Gabriel waited for the bite of the cuffs, the icy fire of the pepper spray. Incredibly, they ignored him. All eyes were on George. The police pulled the radios from their belts, talking feverishly to headquarters. One ran into the street to wave down the approaching squad cars. No one had the least idea who Gabriel was.

Suddenly, police were everywhere. Swarming like bees around their queen. More arriving every moment.

Brushing himself off, Gabriel rose and crossed the street with a host of his fellow Parisians, also eager to flee the crime scene. The pen was still in his hand. Carefully, he replaced it in his breast pocket. On the opposite sidewalk, he paused to take a final look. His last image was of the girl's blonde hair swimming in a pool of her own blood. He thought that they had probably killed her.

Chapter 40

Eventually all men talked.

That was the rule and that was why all members of Hijira had sworn to take their own lives before they could be captured. George, too, had known the rule, had sworn his allegiance, and Marc Gabriel had trusted his vow. Yet, within the past twenty-four hours his son had failed him twice. How long could he be counted on to resist the police's interrogation? Hours? Days? Was he talking even now? And what about the girl? How much did she know about Hijira?

All these thoughts raced through Marc Gabriel's mind as he unlocked the door of his office and marched to his desk. He knew he must proceed as if nothing was wrong. It was a footrace now. The finish line was in sight: Saturday night at eight-thirty when the newly crowned King of Saudi Arabia stepped into the blue room at the White House and toasted the American President as a prelude to ushering in a new era of goodwill between the two nations. He only needed to outrun the Americans.

Gabriel logged on to his computer. There were a few last things to be done. A trail to leave behind so there would be no doubt who was responsible. He tapped in the web address for the Gemeinschaft Bank of Dresden, then entered his account number and password. The twelve million dollars Gregorio had stolen from Inteltech would prove useful. It would be seen as a last-minute pay off, the investigators would say later. The irrefutable link between the bombers and the crazed Israeli physicist.

The screen blinked, and Gabriel was surprised to see that the bank was denying him access to his account. He tried again with the same result. Something was wrong. The denial was no coincidence. Calling the bank, he requested the account officer in charge of the Holy Land Charitable Trust.

'Reinhard.'

Reinhard? Gabriel stiffened, as if readying for the lash. Jurgen Reinhard was the bank's chairman. What trouble could have brought him to the phone? The day was shaping up to be a monumental disaster.

'Ali al-Maktoum speaking,' said Gabriel, adopting an Arabic accent. 'Chief administrative officer of the Holy Land Trust. I'm calling regarding our account. We are expecting a large transfer this afternoon. Twelve million dollars, to be precise. I would like to confirm its arrival. Then I shall ask you to make a further transfer of funds on our behalf.'

'I'm afraid that is impossible,' said Reinhard.

'Excuse me?'

'I said it is impossible. The account has been frozen by the United States government, pending an investigation into your organization's ties to a terrorist group. I have been instructed to ask you to contact the United States Treasury Department. A Mr Adam Chapel. I have his number here.'

Gabriel's heart caught in his throat. 'That won't be necessary,' he said, before hanging up.

Striding to the window, he looked down the block towards the spot where his son had been arrested fifteen minutes earlier. It was clear that the police had been waiting for someone to use the ATM. Gabriel required only a minute to piece together how they'd come up with the information. Taleel. The Cité Universitaire. Azema Immobilier. The

Banque de Londres et Paris. He considered how he might have done things differently, but was unable to come up with an answer. One had to pay rent by bank transfer or check. These days, cash was the vehicle of the poor and the dishonest, neither of which made desirable tenants. A trail was unavoidable.

But the Holy Land Charitable Trust was a different matter. Gabriel compartmentalized his operations to prevent authorities from using monetary data to link one entity to another. The Holy Land Charitable Trust operated as a legitimate enterprise. For years, Gabriel had set aside a portion of income generated by Richemond's portfolio for urgent pleas from those in need in Yemen, Palestine, Lebanon, and Saudi Arabia. He'd also used funds in the account to pay salaries to directors of the trust, including a hundred thousand euros a year to Abu Sayeed (under an alias) in a Pakistani bank, and a similar sum to Gabriel's younger sister, Noor, in a Swiss numbered account. Though Noor held a legitimate position, he could hardly expect her to survive on a bureaucrat's salary.

Gabriel was vexed. Nothing linked Taleel to the trust. It was impossible to mentally retrace all the deposits, payments, and transfers he had made into and out of its account. Yet, somehow they had found it. Then it came to him . . . *Rafi Boubilas*. A year earlier, Gabriel had asked him to wire the proceeds of a sale of two thousand carats of raw diamonds to the Trust's account. Despite assurances to the contrary, the owner of Royal Joailliers had talked.

And if the Americans had the Holy Land Trust's name, they had more. Inteltech. The Deutsche International Bank. Bank Montparnasse. Bank Menz. The web was endless.

The Americans.

Chapel.

Gabriel remained still a moment longer. His body grew rigid; his heart pounding inside his chest. Then, he could stand it no more. Grabbing his chair, he spun it in a wild circle and hurled it against the wall. This was too much. Taleel, Gregorio, George, and finally, the account in Dresden. His carefully constructed world was tumbling down on top of him. Twenty years of painstaking and meticulous effort. He wanted to calm himself, but calm was out of reach. He had only black emotions to console him. Hate, impatience, shame, and the will to revenge.

Yet, what had changed? he demanded. What really had changed?

The bulk of his money was situated neatly, ready to reap profits from the Dow's imminent plunge. Men stood ready to act, awaiting only his signal and the arrival of the large sums he had promised to them in their bank accounts. They were men in high positions at the ministries of the interior, finance, and defense; at the royal barracks, and inside the palace itself. The money was not a bribe, but an interim budget to assert their legitimacy as their country's new leaders. These were men who thought as he did; principled men who believed that power was to be treated responsibly, that wealth was no excuse for wanton behavior, and that whores, alcohol, and profligacy were the devil's hand-maidens and had no place inside the royal palace.

If he just thought clearly . . . if he separated his anxieties from the reality of the moment, he would see that everything remained as it had when he had awoken that morning.

It was a race, he reminded himself. He must simply run a little faster.

Breathing easier, Gabriel poured himself a glass of water and walked to the window. The Eiffel Tower shimmered in the morning sun. If someone could dream of building that, he could dream of retaking his country. Both were feats of engineering and the will to conquer.

His older brother's fault was that he had acted with passion. He had let blood rule him completely. What had he hoped to accomplish by storming the Grand Mosque at Mecca and seizing the Ka'aba? All his calls for a holy government, for reform, for simple fidelity to the Prophet's teachings as mandated by the country's constitution were drowned out by fears that he might destroy Islam's holiest site. He and his band of rebels had managed to hold out two weeks before royal troops had stormed the mosque, and with the help of their French advisors, overpowered them. The insurrection was over in minutes.

Bravery was to be admired, thought Gabriel, but intellect, planning, foresight were what one needed to win the day.

Inspired by his family's legacy, he picked up his chair and took his place in front of the computer. He would no longer react. He would act. He would prove to his older brother that his family's struggle was not in vain, that he had not frittered twenty years of his life away on some glorified pipe dream.

Adam Chapel was not the only man who knew how to follow a money trail. His colleagues both at the Foreign Terrorist Asset Tracking Center and at the Financial Crimes Enforcement Network were equally adept at scenting the odor of dirty money and tracing its path back to its origin. It was simply a question of giving them something to find.

Consulting his notes, Gabriel typed in the web address of a prominent financial institution whose headquarters were located in Washington, DC.

The game could be played both ways.

Live by the sword, Mr Chapel. Die by the sword.

Chapter 41

'You can't be serious,' Sarah said, darting an incredulous glance at Adam Chapel. Her cheeks had gone white with a small spear of red in their center. 'This isn't some juicy secret we can keep; not some nasty rumor that's best kept between you and me. I went along with you last night when you thought it best that we not call Glen. You were tired; you were scared. I can live with that. But this is something else entirely.'

They were driving beside the River Limmat, penned in behind a blue and white city tram. The river flowed to their right, the water a pleasant milk-glass green, boundaried by centuries-old buildings that rose in perpendicular harmony from the river's edge.

'No,' said Chapel. 'It stays with us. It's our problem. We discovered it. It's up to us to solve it.'

The tram slowed to a halt and Sarah braked late and hard. 'Our problem?' Palm open, she knocked her forehead and rolled her eyes. 'Cor, blimey, he's gone batty on us. Round the bend's our Mr Chapel. Never did have both feet on the ground. "Our problem?" Who are you to decide? May I remind you that somewhere in our cozy little European theater of operations, there may be a man in possession of a very nasty piece of equipment and he may very well intend to convey that equipment to Mr Albert

Daudin, or Claude François, or whatever the animal behind Hijira calls himself. Adam, we know now what the five hundred thousand dollars was for . . . it was for a bomb. Not for plutonium. Not for plans. Not for a trigger. For a bomb. *The bloody bomb*, for Christ's sake.'

'I understand,' he said, stiffening in his seat. Her gale-force onslaught left him feeling like a delinquent summoned to the principal. He knew full well what Sarah was talking about, and didn't think she was exaggerating in the least. He'd been sitting next to her when she'd called her pals on the Israeli desk at MI6 and asked them what they had on Mordecai Kahn, full-time nuclear physicist, part-time consort of international terrorists. 'Oh, yes, Mordy Kahn, well that's an easy one,' came the reply. 'Director of Israeli Nuclear Testing Laboratory, linchpin of their development efforts, one of the doers, hard science and all that. Takes the theory, sees if he can make a toy out of it. Clever chap.'

Chapel's hands wandered up and down his leg searching for something to do, and settled for fiddling with the air-conditioning vent. He wouldn't back down. It wasn't even a question of whether he wanted to or not. The issues involved might be bigger than him, but in the end it was as simple as telling the truth.

'You understand and you're still willing to keep this between us?' she demanded.

'I don't think we have any choice. Frankly, I'd say it's our responsibility to keep it between us.' When she didn't answer, he went on. 'We can't let things go south on us twice. We cannot let what happened in the Cité Universitaire with Taleel happen again. You know, find the guy, localize him, get ready to make the arrest, when bingo, Leclerc shows up with "le swat team" and all hell breaks loose. Only this time when the bad guy gets nervous and detonates his bag of tricks, he doesn't take four men with him, he takes four thousand or forty thousand, or even more, God help us.'

'You can't make that decision.'

'I don't have any choice in the matter. Knowing what we know ... what's happened in the last couple of days ... there's no other decision to make.'

'No, Adam—'

'Listen to me!' he exploded, bolting out of his seat, facing her. 'Someone tipped off Taleel. Someone tried to have me killed. Someone wants Hijira to succeed, and that someone is very close to us. One of us, Sarah. One of Blood Money. What are they going to do when they learn we know about Kahn? Hell, they just might tell him to blow up the bomb then and there. Forget about formalities. Any target's fine as long as there are a lot of "crusaders" around, even if crusaders are ten-year-old girls and their baby brothers who don't even know where the Middle East is, let alone why everyone over there hates us so much.'

Sarah took a breath and inclined her head as if it were time to bring a measure of rationality to the discussion. 'All well and good, Adam, but there are others better prepared to handle this kind of thing ... *professionals* well versed at dealing with any and all eventualities. They have technology to find these devices.'

'NEST teams?' Chapel scoffed. 'From what I understand, they don't work too well.'

'NEST' stood for Nuclear Emergency Search Team, and referred to teams of scientists and weapons specialists operating within the Department of Energy's Office of Emergency Operations who were trained to evaluate nuclear threats. After 9/11, NEST teams had fanned out around Washington, DC, and New York in anonymous vans equipped with the latest in radiation detection machinery to seek out rogue nuclear weapons. It was a decent enough idea, except that instead of finding any bombs, the teams ended up stopping every half block when the background radiation from the closest photo lab, pharmacy, or Circuit City set off their ultra-sensitive alarms. There were a million sources of radiation in any urban environment: TV sets, tobacco products, X-ray machines, smoke detectors, building materials . . . the list went on and on. After storming their umpteenth TJ Maxx only to discover a new delivery of digital watches (still in the box) equipped with luminous, and minutely radioactive, tritium dials, they packed it in. Next time, they would wait for a credible threat before mobilizing.

'It's not for us to decide that. We will alert Glen. We will tell him our suspicions about Kahn and ask him to keep it as quiet as possible for the time being. Kahn's gone walkabout, we'll say. Yossi as much as admitted it.'

'And Glen will call Gadbois, and the word will be all over Europe in ten minutes.'

'It's time we brought in the big guns. We're Laurel and Hardy.'

'We've gotten this far.'

'And that's as far as we're going to get. You're right, Adam. Your numbers are wonderful things. I'll admit that it's amazing the information you can get out of a set of figures. I'm a convert. Hallelujah and all that. Count me among your adoring faithful. But there is a time to call it quits.'

Chapel looked away, infuriated by her patronizing tone. Miss Churchill, the doyenne of the secret world, talking down to him as if he were some kind of well-educated rube, a circus act, massaging him with her belief in his theory of numbers. Turning his head, he caught her anxious glance and knew there was something else.

'You're afraid,' he said.

'Damn right, I'm afraid.'

'No, I don't mean afraid of the bomb. You're afraid of the responsibility. You can't stand it that the buck has stopped, and it's pointing at you and me.'

'It's too damn big, Adam,' she blurted. 'I'm a spy. Great title, but it's still just a job. Point me toward the bad guys, I'll go. Tell me to look and listen, I'm your gal. Tell me to shoot, you're getting on tougher ground. But I draw the line at taking personal responsibility for a hundred thousand innocent lives. No thank you. That's the general's job.'

The general. Sarah's all-knowing father, R.I.P.

'The general's dead.'

'Kahn could be headed anywhere,' she protested. 'Madrid, Tripoli, Helsinki, the South Pole . . . who knows?'

'Oh, I think we know where he's headed. You said it yourself at the embassy. There's a reason the money was sent to Paris. Now we know what it is. It's a payoff. Daudin or François, or whatever he calls himself, doesn't like to stray far from the city. I'm thinking he's got a business there, something that requires him to stay close to home. In Paris, he's invisible. Part of the city's fabric. On foreign turf, he sticks out. This guy's got a serious comfort factor. He's got his boys around him, his safe houses, his bank accounts spread around the city. Hundred to one, if Mordecai Kahn does have a bomb – if, in fact, he's selling it to Hijira for three million dollars – the deal is going down in Paris. You can bet on it.'

Sarah was nodding. He'd won her over, yet he still needed to explain himself. Skimming a hand along the back of her head, he said, 'I don't want this gig any more than you do. You know what I want? I want to go back to my desk in Virginia, put my feet up, crack open a can of Diet Coke, and get lost in my computer. I want my numbers. My sterile, safe numbers.'

The tram turned off the Limmat Quai at Centralplatz. Sarah floored the rental Mercedes, taking it around the large tram stop, through a series of tight streets, following the blue placards that showed the way to the Flughafen. They left the river and entered a tunnel.

'And so?' she asked. 'Where now?'

'Find Mr Claude François and we find Kahn,' he said.

'That simple?'

Chapel shrugged his shoulders. It wasn't simple at all, but there it was. 'Who do you trust?'

Sarah extended her hand and he took it. 'I trust you,' she said, squeezing it tightly.

They left the car in the Terminal A parking lot with the keys tucked beneath the visor. At the ticket counter, they purchased three seats on the twelve o'clock flight to Paris. One for Chapel. One for Sarah. And one for the three boxes of files they'd taken from the Deutsche International Bank.

Once through passport control, they walked the length of the terminal to their gate and bought coffee and a pair of sausages. 'Can't visit Switzerland without trying the bratwurst,' said Chapel, taking a seat on a leather banquette.

'What about the chocolate?'

'I'll get a bar to bring to Glen. A peace offering.'

'Sugar?' Sarah asked.

'No, and I take it black.'

'Suit yourself.' She opened three bags of Equal and dumped them into her paper cup.

'Nasty,' commented Chapel, grimacing.

'Terrible sweet tooth. Don't even get me started on toffee.'

'Bangers and mash?'

'Adore them.'

'Steak and kidney pie.'

'Lovely.'

'Fish and chips?'

'Yumm.'

'The Spice Girls?'

'Make me gag, but Robbie Williams is a cutie.'

'You are England's rose.'

'I take that as a compliment, sir.'

A minute passed as the two ate in silence. Their flight was called and they traded looks to say, let everyone else get on board first. Chapel felt that something had grown between them, something more than just a night together. It was a pleasant sensation. They watched the last stragglers disappear into the jetway.

'Shall we, Miss Churchill?'

'By all means, Mr Chapel.'

She stood, hefting the overnight bag onto her shoulder. Taking a step, she pressed her body against him and pecked him on the lips. 'So how do we find him?'

'I've got to sit down with all this info, run the account numbers and the beneficiaries through our database. Somewhere in here, we'll find a hint, a trail to follow. We'll start at the beginning. Daudin, or François back then, opened that account twenty years ago. He listed his date of birth as 1961. I'll wager he was a damn sight less cautious back then than he is now. There's a learning curve for terrorism, too.'

'What's your guess? Who is he?'

'François? He's a money man. A banker. A broker. Maybe a trader of some kind. Someone who knows the ins and outs of international finance. He's got to be a pro, the way he juggles those accounts.'

Sarah walked towards the gate. 'Takes one to know one, eh?'

'Something like—' Chapel's cell phone chirped. 'Hello.'

'*Allo, mon ami,*' said Leclerc. 'And where, might I ask, are you?'

Chapel stopped in his tracks. 'On the way to Paris.'

'I hope so. There's someone here I think you'll greatly enjoy meeting.'

'Who's that?'

'Right now, I'm calling him Charles François. Ring a bell? You two know each other already. I understand you bumped into him at the hospital the other day.'

It couldn't be, he thought. *Not so quickly*. 'How?'

'Poor guy needed some cash. We nabbed him at the ATM in Neuilly. The one with three dots on it. Blue, black, and red. *Felicitations*.' The map. Leclerc was talking about the map of the BLP's ATM locations.

'Where are you?'

'La Santé.'

La Santé. France's most notorious maximum security prison.

'Leclerc, do not lay a hand on him.' He exchanged the strident tone for one of dead earnestness. 'Please.'

'It's too late for that. This is my town. We do things my way.'

'We'll be there in two hours.'

Chapter 42

At the same time as Swiss International Airlines Flight 765 touched down in Paris, Marc Gabriel was standing in the center of his office, surveying the naked space. The last boxes had left a few minutes earlier. The desk, the computer hardware, the phones, the photos: everything was a memory. Gabriel was left alone with his view.

To his mind the last three days had stretched into one. Taleel's death. Ciudad del Este. George's treason. By all accounts, he should be exhausted, both physically and mentally. Instead, he felt refreshed, invigorated, and alive to the challenges that waited. Catching his reflection in the glass, he smoothed his white shirt and flirted with his Hermès cravat. If his expression did not convey the direness of his situation, it was because he had won. The footrace was as good as over. A single call had put his worries to rest.

'The city is more beautiful than I had expected,' Mordecai Kahn had said when he'd phoned an hour earlier.

'Summer is a kind season.'

'I take it you are free this evening?'

'Of course.'

'Say, eleven o'clock?'

'Eleven would be wonderful.'

Kahn gave Gabriel the name of the establishment where he proposed they meet.

'You're certain?' Gabriel asked, peeved at the choice.

'Neither of us can take any chances.'

Marc Gabriel had no intention of it. 'Very good, then. Till eleven.'

'Bilitis's Vineyard. It is on the third floor.'

'Bilitis's Vineyard,' Gabriel repeated.

The package had arrived.

Chapter 43

Narrow, dank, and dripping with limestone sweat, the corridors of La Santé maximum security prison stretched before Chapel like the decaying passages of an ancient tomb. Five steps inside the place, he'd felt the walls close in on him, and a grim weight fall on his shoulders. It was his first time inside a prison. He was a visitor, one of the good guys. Still, the place scared the hell out of him.

La Santé housed the worst of the worst. Murderers, rapists, terrorists. Carlos the Jackal was locked up somewhere inside its walls. Captain Dreyfus himself had spent a year here upon his return from Devil's Island.

Chapel walked beside Leclerc, with Sarah a step behind, while the Frenchman called out the particulars of the arrest.

'According to his passport, his name's Charles François. He had a ticket to Dubai, round trip in the same name.'

'Who paid for it?' Chapel asked.

'Credit card. Claude François.'

François. The same alias for twenty years.

'He hasn't talked?' asked Sarah.

'Not a peep,' said Leclerc. 'He's well trained, this one. Disciplined. He's got some scars on him. I'd say he's been to a camp. We ran the passport through immigration. All we got was a trip to Athens last summer.'

'Athens,' murmured Sarah. 'The great jumping-off point for voyages into the unknown.'

'We only keep track of the first leg out of the country,' continued Leclerc. 'He probably had a second ticket in a different name. He knows the tricks, this kid.'

Their steps had acquired a marching rhythm. They were an executioner's party on its way to carry out the sentence.

'The girl's still out?' Sarah asked.

'She woke an hour ago, but the doctors forbid us from speaking to her. They've got her doped up on steroids to stop her brain from swelling.'

'What did you do to her?' Chapel asked.

'The girl fell poorly. Hairline fracture of the skull. Ten stitches above the ear. She'll have a bad headache for a couple of weeks. Serves her right for hanging out with scum.'

Leclerc stopped in front of a broad, black iron door. Rivets the size of quarters studded the surface. Except for the modern lock winking from inside an ancient keyhole, it might have confined Edmond Dantes in his cell at the Chateau D'If. Sounds emanated from other floors of the prison. A metal cup ricocheted against the walls. Water coursed through the pipes in unpredictable surges. But most disturbing was an inmate's brief, excruciating howl, cut off mid-cry, as if the guillotine had done its work.

'You can listen from the next room,' said Leclerc, as he wrapped boxer's tape around his knuckles.

'You said he was a kid,' protested Chapel.

'That's no kid in there. Too bad you missed Dr Bac. She just left. You two could have held hands and said a prayer for the animal. Now it is time for him to talk.'

Chapel put a hand on Leclerc's chest. 'Let me talk to him.'

'How's your French?'

'He speaks English.'

'How do you know?' Leclerc pushed past Chapel, slipping the key into the lock.

'Call it a hunch.'

'*Desolé, mon pote.* No more time for hunches.'

Sarah leaned her shoulder against the door, lowering her face to Leclerc's. Sweat beaded his lip, and in the dim corridor, he looked ashen and ill. 'Come now, let Adam have a go.'

'What did you find in Zurich? Tell me that, then maybe I let your boyfriend go.'

Sarah looked at Chapel, then back again, as if choosing sides. 'More of the same,' she said. 'Another numbered account. Reams of documents. If it's of any interest, the account in Germany was opened by a Claude François.'

'We were talking about Switzerland. The Bank Menz. That was a quick trip to Zurich for nothing.'

'You know Adam,' she said. 'High hopes.'

High hopes. Leclerc's eyes narrowed in bewilderment. The naive and sentimental tripe of a naive and sentimental country. He considered Chapel, as if measuring him for a suit. 'Ten minutes,' he said, unlocking the cell door. 'I'm also in a hurry. Santos Babtiste's funeral begins at five o'clock. I'd like to pay my respects.'

'Is he cuffed?' Chapel asked.

'What do you think?'

Chapel held out his hand. Leclerc dropped a small key into his palm. 'Ten minutes. *Alors, bonne chance.*'

The door slammed shut. Chapel took a step and he was in the center of the room. It was a small, confined, frightening place. The walls were painted a glossy mint green. A naked bulb dangled from the ceiling. It was exceptionally clean, but for a skein of blood that decorated a wall like a furious exclamation point. The young man who had tackled him in the hallways of the Hôpital Salpetitpierre sat at a brutish wooden table, hands cuffed behind him, head lolling on his chest.

'Hello,' said Chapel, taking the opposite chair. 'I think we've met already. I wanted to say thank you, though. Personally. You know, for . . .' Chapel cleared his throat, searching for the right words. *For what? For not killing me? For behaving like a decent human being instead of a butcher with a holy cause?* He looked back at the door. Maybe it wasn't such a good idea to talk to the kid, after all – Leclerc was right about one thing: This was no kid, he was built like an NFL halfback.

Just then, the prisoner looked up, and Chapel got his first glimpse of his face. The right eye was swollen and purple. The capillaries on one side of the iris had burst, giving him a devilish look. His lip was cracked and bleeding. Chapel didn't know if the injuries were from the arrest or from Leclerc. It didn't matter. He felt offended and responsible. He couldn't allow Leclerc with his taped knuckles and raging inferiority to have a go at him. He held up the key, then circled behind the prisoner and unlocked the cuffs. The young man shook his arms to regain circulation, but offered no thanks, no acknowledgement whatsoever that Chapel was even in the room.

Taking a chair, Chapel put his hands on the table, fingers clasped. A familiar nagging tugged at his shoulders and he sat up straighter. Even inside a prison, he was the one who needed to measure up. 'You did a good job knocking the hell out of me. My shoulder's a complete mess. You did a real number on it.'

The young man shifted. He seemed bored and tense.

Chapel fought for something to say. He felt ill at ease, beyond his competence. 'So what's it all about?' he blurted. 'If you want to say anything, this would be a good time.'

It was no good. Chapel had about as much chance of reaching him as he did of finding Claude François. He was overcome with a sudden helplessness, a sinking feeling that made him want to pack it all in. Not just the interrogation, but the whole investigation. Let someone else have it. Maybe Sarah was right. It was too big for them. He studied the prisoner's shirt with its stencil of a rapper's leering face, capped teeth, and scornful eyes. Done in by the futility of it all, he was unable to suppress a laugh. 'Oh jeez,' he said. 'I bet that T-shirt really pisses off your dad.'

The prisoner's chin rose from his chest and Chapel saw he'd hit something. He remembered what he'd glimpsed in the hospital. As he lay on the floor with this hulk on top of him, there had been a moment when their eyes had met; a moment wedged between the kid's surprise at having run into the very man he was supposed to kill and his decision not to kill him; a moment when the curtain dropped, and Chapel was given a clear view into what drove this guy. What he saw was a teenager's frustration with his lot, a load of self-pity, and a dread resignation that said, 'I can't believe this shit.' It was like looking in the mirror when he was nineteen.

'Yeah, my father was a stickler, too,' he said. 'In my day it was glam rock and big hair. I was all over it. Whitesnake. Poison. Bon Jovi. *You give love a bad name . . . bad name.*' If Leclerc could sing, so could he. 'Didn't have the hair, though. Dad would have knocked the shit out of me. But, I had the T-shirts. You got Mr Fifty Cent there. I had RATT. Probably 'bout the same talent level. Minimal, if you know what I mean.'

No response. The kid wasn't even looking at him. Still, Chapel went on. What did he have to lose? If nothing else, he was giving the kid a few extra minutes to sort things out before Leclerc came in and beat the snot out of him.

'I know how you feel. There was no choice in my household, either. My dad had my career mapped out by the time I was nine. I took this test at school and it showed I was gifted. I had the highest IQ in my class. I couldn't have cared less. I was trying to make friends, get on the baseball team, learn how to play handball, anything to fit in. Dad said, "No way." I wasn't going to be like the other kids. I was too smart for that. He got me skipped two grades, and had me put in all kinds of enrichment classes. You know where I went in the summer? Math camp. Nine years old at math camp. And you know the scary part? I dug it. Or at least I thought I did. My dad loved it. I loved it. What was the difference? I was brainwashed. From then on, that's how it went. Dad said, "Jump!" I asked, "How high?" '

Chapel checked for some sign he was making a dent. A grunt. A nod. Anything. The young man across the table didn't register a word. He sat staring at his shoes. Brand-new Nike Air Force hightops. Chapel rapped on the table and stood up. 'All right then. Well, it's been a pleasure.'

For a second, he'd thought he was getting somewhere. Too bad. It had been a stupid idea. So much for his high hopes. 'By the way, Claudine . . . she's going to be fine. Her head's banged up, but I promise that she'll still remember you.'

He turned to the door.

'What happened?'

Chapel stopped dead, the muscles in his jaw and neck stiffening as a bolt of adrenaline ran the length of his spine. '*What happened?*' he asked, turning slowly. 'To me?'

The prisoner, Charles François, or whatever his name was, nodded.

'I went to Harvard and Harvard Business School on a full ride . . . you know, a scholarship. I got a job at an accounting firm. I worked my butt off and became a partner. I made a million dollars when I was twenty-eight years old. That's what happened. I did every single thing my dad wanted me to, and not a single thing for me.'

Chapel looked away, struck by a picture of his father, the

struggling shoe salesman damned by his own mediocrity, tortured by his dreams of wealth, means, and position. A man who forever expected more of himself than he was able to give. A man who decided it was better to live dissatisfied than to alter his expectations. Why? What was so damned terrible about being ordinary? Average used to mean happily in the middle. When had it started meaning perilously close to failure?

'I quit my job the day he died,' said Chapel, returning to the scuffed table. 'I never had the guts to stand up to him until then. Look at you. You're twice the man I was. I can't begin to imagine what it took to stand up to your dad.' He smiled appreciatively and extended his hand. 'I'm Adam Chapel.'

The prisoner, the would-be murderer, the boy in a man's body, looked away and Chapel thought he'd lost him. The ten minutes were up. It was time to hand him over to Leclerc. The taped knuckles could begin their grim, efficient work. Pain and anguish would overrule compassion and decency. Chapel stood up again. He was tired, but he knew there'd be no rest. His mind wandered ahead, already cataloguing the documents he'd need to start analysing.

And then he saw it: the arm rising above the table, the palm open, a big soft mitt, the prisoner gazing up at him with some sad mixture of hope and trepidation.

Chapel grabbed the hand. 'You are?'

'My name is George. George Gabriel. At least, that's my French name. Our family name is Utaybi. We're from Arabia. Never say "Saudi." The House of Saud is *kuffar*.' George knitted his brow with concern. 'Did your father really hit you?'

'No,' said Chapel. 'He never had to. I only talked back to him in my mind. I wasn't what you'd call a stand up kid.'

Gabriel took this in, eyes walking the room's perimeter: 'I think my father tried to kill me.'

'Your dad?' Chapel asked, uncertainly.

'Tell that French bastard that they just missed him. I heard him whisper my name on the street when the cops took me down. "Hakim," he said. It's my real name, though we're never allowed to use it here. I'm pretty sure I saw him getting the hell out of there.'

'You saw him? And you think he was going to kill you?'

'Crazy, huh?' George Gabriel tried to make it sound funny, an offbeat occurrence, but it was too much for him to pull off. The smile lost its mirth. The lips turned down and began to quiver. 'He had the pen out . . . It's poison . . . to kill . . .' He went on, his voice thick with emotion. 'I betrayed him. He always said that's what happened to traitors – even to his son.' Gabriel's shoulders caved in. Dropping his face, he began to cry. 'I want to tell him that I'm sorry, but I can't.'

Sarah listened in the next room with Leclerc and General Gadbois. Chapel's naive arrogance had at first amused the Frenchmen, then angered them, and now the two had pretty much shut up, so she guessed Adam had impressed them. He'd found the path to the truth. A little honesty and understanding had worked more quickly, and immensely more cleanly, than Leclerc's, or if she were to admit it, her own preferred methods might have.

'We let him go on?' asked Leclerc.

'Why not?' The question irritated Gadbois. 'He's doing our job for us. We should have him teach a class. An accountant. Maybe I'll have to start looking outside the army for my recruits. What do you think of that, Sarah?'

'By all means. Actually, I'm rather surprised, myself.'

A cell phone chirped and Sarah pulled the compact unit from her pocket. 'I'll take it outside.' Closing the door behind her, she stepped into the corridor. 'Hello?'

'This is your friend from Jerusaleum.'

'Hello, friend.'

'Any luck with your research?'

'Nothing yet. Still looking actually. You too?'

Yossi answered the question in his own oblique manner. 'He purchased a car in Vienna using the name John Herzfeld, his brother-in-law.'

'A BMW.'

A silence. 'Yes, Meg. A BMW.'

'The Swiss,' she explained.

'Ah. So that's who told you. A gold 750iL, in fact. We found it near Pale in Bosnia yesterday, along with four dead bodies. Robbery, hijacking . . . who knows? We have to assume that since he wasn't there, he's still on the move. He's coming in your direction.'

'I appreciate the information.'

'Is he talking yet?'

The question stunned Sarah, but only for a moment. 'A bit.'

'You know the rules.'

Sarah debated how far to go. 'We found a tape the other day in the wreckage of Taleel's apartment,' she said. 'Rather scary piece of footage: Couldn't let word get out. The target's the States. New York, DC, LA, we're not sure where. Forget Code Orange. This is Code Red all the way. We know it's happening now, but we don't know where.'

'Today?'

'Today, tomorrow, the weekend. What exactly did Kahn take from you?'

'Meg, this I cannot tell you.'

'Yossi . . . traffic goes two ways. We've got to know.'

'Just between us?'

'Cross my heart.'

'A neat little toy. One kiloton and fits in a cigar box. Some of the tough guys want to use it on the West Bank. Make Arafat disappear once and for all.'

'Jesus, Yossi, that small?'

'Wake up, Meg. Look at your phone. It can do everything but deliver a baby. We had it down to a suitcase thirty years ago. You think we gave up working in that area once Russia fell apart?'

Sarah leaned against the concrete wall, the cold and damp sobering her. She had a hundred questions she needed to ask: How? When? Who else knew? None of that mattered now.

'Between you and me,' Yossi went on. 'Find this guy, get our material back, and make him disappear. There's a place you might check. Something we found on Kahn's credit card. A hundred euros to an establishment called Cléopatre in Paris. We sent one of our boys over to have a look. It's a sex club. Open only at night. Some kind of porn thing. Ever heard of it?'

'No.'

'Probably nothing. He had strange charges from all over Europe. Prague, Berlin, Madrid. Setting up his escape. Still, you might want to check it out.'

Coming from Yossi that was an order to get the hell over there.

'Maybe,' she said. There was only so much honesty between spies and she'd used up her quotient.

Chapel waited until George Gabriel had regained his composure to continue. 'Your father's name is?'

'Omar al-Utaybi. He calls himself Marc Gabriel. He's an investor. His company's called Richemond Holdings.'

For the moment, Chapel wasn't interested in Gabriel's legitimate undertakings. 'What about Hijira?'

George Gabriel showed no surprise that Chapel knew the name. 'It's crazy,' he said. 'I mean, the whole thing.'

'What's the whole thing?'

'Nothing.' George Gabriel wiped at his eyes and took a few deep breaths. A stubborn stillness had settled over him.

Chapel could feel the resistance building. Gabriel had been caught out once, but that was that. His breakdown had shamed him and now he was intent on proving that he was made of tougher stuff. 'I'm a terrible son.'

'I'd say you're a good man.' Chapel put his elbows on the table and craned his neck forward. 'What exactly is your dad planning?'

George Gabriel crossed his arms over his chest and laughed to himself. 'You're good. You're very good. You made me feel sorry for you, as if you and I might have something in common. You are clever. I'll give that to you.'

'Listen, George . . . I can call you George?'

'Better than Hakim.'

'George, look . . . four of my friends died Monday afternoon. Good guys. Fathers—'

'Taleel was very brave,' George cut in, chin raised pridefully. 'He gave his life for my father.'

'He was a—' Chapel harnessed his anger at the last minute. Emotion was their tool. 'A lot more people are going to give their lives for your father whether they want to or not,' he explained as calmly as he could. 'I know that much about your father's plan. You couldn't kill Dr Bac. You couldn't kill me. You know what's right and wrong. Keeping quiet is no different than pulling a trigger. If your father succeeds in killing more people . . . I don't care how many – one, ten, a thousand . . . you are as responsible as he is. If that comes to pass – if you sit here without raising a finger to stop it, I can promise that you are going to spend the rest of your life in a room a lot less comfortable than the one we're in now. The rest of your life, George.'

George Gabriel squirmed, the boy in him now visible, protesting at such callous treatment. 'I didn't do anything.'

'But you know,' Chapel said painfully. 'You're part of it.' He pointed at the door. 'The French bastard out there is pretty sure you've been to a camp in the Middle East, and I don't mean a math camp. Dr Bac, she said you knew your way around a knife. You're not a regular kid, George. Just the fact that you went to that camp could land you in jail for twenty years. This isn't about your father anymore. It's about you. You've got to make choices to help yourself. And don't go shaking your head like that. Don't ask me for time to think about it. You and me both know that Hijira is happening now.'

Gabriel stared sullenly at the floor.

'Does the name Mordecai Kahn mean anything to you?'

'No.'

'A teacher. A scientist from Israel?'

'No.'

'You're sure? Maybe a professor.'

'A professor? No.'

Chapel bit back his disappointment. 'What can you tell me, then?'

'Get real,' said Gabriel. 'He kept everything secret. He told me what I needed to know, and that was all.'

'You're his son. He shared his dreams with you. I don't believe he kept it quiet.'

'All I know is that you were getting too close. That's why I had to kill you.'

'Why you? He has other men.'

'Does he? Then you know more than I do.'

'Bullshit!'

'I am his son,' Gabriel shouted back. 'It was a test. I failed it.'

'What's your father planning?'

'I don't know.'

'Tell me!'

'I don't know.'

Chapel reddened. Somehow, he managed to guard his calm. 'You'd better know or you're going to jail for the rest of your life. You may never leave this building again except for a ride to and from the courthouse for what I promise you will be a very short trial. Look around you. This is your life. *You* "get real." Let's try it again. What is he planning?'

'We're going home.'

'Where's home?'

'The desert. Saudi Arabia. Where do you think? We're Utaybis.'

'And that's his plan? To go home? I don't buy it. What's his plan?'

'I don't know.'

'Tell me!' Chapel slammed his fist on the table.

'Don't you see?' asked Gabriel, angry tears staining his cheeks. 'To get even! The plan is to get even!'

Chapter 44

Once in a while, even Bobby Freedman got tired. It wasn't something he liked to admit. Freedman was a former Marine, a four-year team leader of Force Recon who'd seen action in Panama and the secret war in Guatemala. He prided himself on his disdain for sleep, his ability to go hour after hour doing quality work while keeping his wits about him. But thirty-six hours at a desk was pushing the envelope.

Looking out the window of his third-floor office at the Financial Crimes Enforcement Network, Freedman admired the sun as it crept over the horizon and lit the rolling hills of northern Virginia. It was his second sunrise of the shift. Since Adam Chapel had called from Paris with the information about the Holy Land Charitable Trust, Freedman had only left his chair to shit, shower, and shave. The only thing keeping him going was the knowledge that Chapel was doing the same thing on his end.

Chapel. *The man was a maniac.*

Rubbing the fatigue from his eyes, Freedman turned back to the monitor. He was 'walking out' the accounts to whom the Holy Land Charitable Trust had sent money over the last twenty-four months. 'Walking out' simply meant feeding the numbers into the witches' cauldron – his pet name for the family of databases he regularly queried – and following each and every lead to its bitter end. He'd presorted the accounts by monetary value, investigating those that had received the most money first. In total, the Holy Land Charitable Trust had sent seven million dollars to fifty-six different accounts. So far, Freedman had looked at twelve of them.

Cracking the mini-fridge tucked beneath his desk, he retrieved an ice-cold Diet Coke and guzzled half of it in a go. 'Gentlemen, start your engines,' he said aloud, before burping monstrously. 'Bring on lucky thirteen.'

Freedman placed his ruler beneath the next account number on his list and banged the numbers into his computer. A quick jaunt through the Currency and Banking Retrieval System identified the account as belonging to the Beirut National Bank and nothing else. Beirut meant terrorism, drugs, and mayhem. On to NADDIS, the Narcotics and Dangerous Drugs Information System, and a reference to a joint FBI-Treasury CT investigation. But it was left to TECS, the Treasury Department's proprietary database, to spit out the name of the account holder as Yassir Ibrahim, a financial capo who specialized in raising funds for several well-known Pakistani *madrasas* – Islamic schools that advertised a virulently anti-Western curriculum.

Hijira was turning out to be a regular 'Terror, Inc.' They weren't so much a bunch of terrorists as they were financiers for nearly every radical Islamic cause within the Ummah. So far, he'd tracked monies flowing from the Holy Land Charitable Trust to the likes of Islamic Jihad, Resla Islaminiya, Hamas, Freedom Fighters of Palestine, FARC in Colombia, and the Al-Aqsa Martyrs Brigade.

As Freedman scrolled down the computer screen, ready to start walking out the next account, his eye caught an especially large transfer.

'Sixty-five thousand bucks,' he said aloud. 'No way!'

He couldn't have missed something as big as that. As if that weren't enough, he recognized the bank locator number as belonging to Hunts National Bank, a longtime DC institution. Looking back through the account history, he spotted four transfers over the past months to the account at Hunts totaling two hundred and sixty thousand dollars. He was mystified. It was as if the account information from the Gemeinschaft Bank of Dresden had updated itself.

Freedman shifted in his chair, fueled by an adrenaline rush. Two hundred and sixty grand to Hunts was some shot in the arm. The money constituted the first trace of Hijira's activity in the States. Halsey would shit his pants when he saw this. Glendenning would probably give him a friggin' medal.

Thirty minutes later, Freedman was decidedly less up-beat. After shepherding the account through all three tiers of databases – CBRS, all seven enforcement computer systems, including the IRS, INS, and even the Post Office, and LexisNexis, he had nada.

It was impossible. The account was dirty by default.

Snatching the phone to his ear, he hit the speed dial for Hunts.

'Hello, Jerry, this is Bobby Freedman over at FinCEN.'

'Oh no,' complained Jerry Oglethorpe, the bank's government liaison officer, only half in jest. 'What's up now? One of your subpoena hounds about to walk through my doors?'

'Give me more credit than that. You know I'd give you a heads-up if that were the case. This is different. Frankly, it's something that scares the heck out of me. I need a favor.'

Oglethorpe's mellow baritone regained its composure. 'What can Hunts do for its government today?'

'Got an account with you boys that looks mighty suspicious.'

'Can't say I like to hear that, but go ahead. What's bothering you?'

'It's got to do with the bombing in Paris on Monday. I've

traced some of the money from the sponsor group to your bank.'

There was a lengthy silence, and Freedman could feel Oglethorpe's angst. For the last two years, American banks tasked with scrutinizing their accounts had been on the lookout for the slightest indications of surreptitious activity. 'Know thy client' was the industry's clarion call. The discovery of a link to a murderous terrorist organization at this late date didn't portend well for the bank's reputation.

'Go on,' said Oglethorpe. 'I can't hold my breath forever.'

'It has to do with several transfers from the Gemeinschaft Bank of Dresden to your Georgetown branch.' Freedman read off the account number, the dates, and the values of each transfer.

Waiting for Oglethorpe to answer, he glanced out the window. Originally, he'd taken the job at FinCEN as a passport to bigger and better things – namely, a slot at one of the nation's elite enforcement agencies: FBI, Customs, Treasury. Somewhere along the way, though, he decided he liked being the custodian of so much information. He was in a unique position to assist the FBI, the CIA and the Secret Service, as well as state and local law enforcement agencies with their investigations. After six years, though, it was time for him to move up a level, to take possession of an assistant director's corner office and see what that Special Executive Service pay scale might buy.

A long, low whistle sounded in Freedman's ear. 'Hey, Bobby, if this stuff's right, it's not Hunts who's going to be in trouble. It's you guys.'

'Us?' Freedman rose from his chair, twisting the phone cord around his finger. 'What do you mean, us?'

'This guy's a federal employee. Worse than that, Bobby, he's one of your own. A Treasury agent.'

'Give me a name, Jerry. All I need is a name.'

'Got a pen?'

'Yeah,' said Freedman, scrambling to find a ballpoint. It was hardly necessary. Whatever the name, it would be indelibly engraved on his mind. 'Who is it?'

'Chapel,' came the response. 'Adam A.'

Chapter 45

The satchel contained fifty packets of one hundred dollar bills still bound by the bank's pink and white bands. Each packet was worth ten thousand dollars. Five hundred thousand dollars in all. Marc Gabriel set the satchel on his bed and removed the trim bundles, laying them side-by-side on the naked mattress. He derived a tactile satisfaction from handling the money. He brought a packet to his nose and fanned the bills with his thumb. The notes smelled clean and useful. He shook his head. It was a pity to destroy so much cash.

Once the satchel was empty, Gabriel placed both hands inside it and removed the false bottom. He had a space six inches wide and twenty-two inches long to work with. Carefully, he laid five rectangular bricks of Semtex across the bottom. Each brick weighed two hundred and fifty grams. It had taken less than half that amount to bring down Pan Am Flight 103 over Lockerbie, Scotland. The plastic explosive fit neatly, as if it had been measured and manufactured expressly for the task. A wad of tissue paper at either end ensured a snug fit.

Stepping away from the bed, he rolled up his sleeves and made sure to take a breath. He had not come to bomb-making easily. He was not by nature mechanically oriented. His hands were clumsy. His inclination to hurry posed a constant hazard. In truth, explosives made him uncommonly nervous. A bead of sweat rolled down his forehead. Irritated, he wiped it away. Handling Semtex posed no problem at all. The stuff was as safe as modeling clay. You could step on it, drop it, even shoot it without risking its detonation. Attaching a Skoda detonator was another thing entirely, and could pose a very large, very loud, and very messy problem if not done correctly.

Wiping his palms on the seat of his pants, he picked up the detonator and affixed the pressure plate to the false bottom he'd removed earlier. Using a small screwdriver, he calibrated the device to deliver its electrical charge if the weight upon it varied by more than five hundred grams, the equivalent of two bundles of notes. Uncrimping the red and green wires that led from the pressure plate to the det cord, he inserted the slim firing baton into the last slab of Semtex, which he then taped to the false bottom. Finally, he activated the device and replaced the false bottom into the satchel.

Then, one by one, he laid the packets inside the satchel, until the mattress was bare and the satchel nearly full.

When the device was armed, he closed the satchel and left its combination at '000.'

In the bathroom, he wiped his forehead with a washcloth. His shirt was soaked through. He would have to change it.

Just then, the house shuddered, as somewhere below him a piece of furniture collided with a wall. Rushing to the doorway, he sought the satchel. It stood on the bed, rocking slightly.

Gabriel ran down the stairs. He had a thing or two to say to the movers.

Chapter 46

'You are a member?' the woman inside the booth asked.

'Unfortunately, not,' said Marc Gabriel. 'But I've been told I may join.'

Gabriel stood inside the entry of a neatly maintained *maison de ville* in the third arrondissement. The third wasn't a part of the city he favored. It was where Paris earned its keep, a sprawling, colorless array of factories, warehouses, and rail yards. Here and there, quaint residential neighborhoods somehow managed to survive like grass sprouting in the cracks of the sidewalk.

'Perhaps,' she said. 'You are alone?'

'Yes.'

The woman rose from her seat and extended her head beyond the narrow transom that separated them. She was old and battle-weary, her hair dyed black, her cheeks fleshy and veined. She wore a twenty-year-old's silk dress that showcased a mottled, generous bosom. 'But, you are very handsome,' she sang, her eyes dancing over him. '*Tres BCBG*. You prefer women? Tell me now. If you favor boys, I will be happy to suggest an alternative location.'

Gabriel warmed her cold claw in his palm, raising it to his mouth and conferring upon it a kiss. 'I hope that serves as an answer.' He allowed his eyes to linger on hers. 'Surely, you do not work the entire evening?'

'Monsieur is too kind,' she admitted. 'Membership is one hundred euros. No smoking in the pleasure chambers. If you carry a cocktail with you – wine, champagne, whiskey – please bring a coaster. We've just had the furniture redone. When you've enjoyed yourself, please dispose of your protection in the receptacles. We are a respectable establishment.'

'Of that I have no doubt.'

The establishment in question was called 'Cléopatre,' and it was a come-one, come-all sex club dressed up as an Egyptian bordello. Gabriel paid his fee and passed through a beaded curtain into a salon decorated with an abundance of crimson velvet and smoked mirrors. Framed prints of Tutankhamen, Ramses, and Cleopatra decorated the walls, along with a poster of the pyramids at Giza. A corridor to his left led to a restaurant. The dining room was largely empty. A few couples dined lugubriously at their tables as a disco beat spilled from tinny speakers. *Dancing queen. Dancing queen. You are the dancing queen.* He walked back into the main salon, as a statuesque African woman emerged from a doorway.

'Good evening,' she said, swinging her broad hips. 'I am Véronique. You are familiar with Cléopatre?'

Véronique wore a gold lamé dress and looked like she weighed a hundred sixty pounds. Standing still, she teetered on her stiletto heels.

'Not entirely,' said Gabriel.

'We have several entertainment areas. There is the boutique upstairs, where you may buy something to wear this evening. Something to excite you. A ring. A collar. The boutique is also for watching. You may admire a lady from a two-way mirror. Don't be ashamed. Naturally, she knows you are enjoying her striptease. Maybe you would like to visit the piano bar? Anyone may play. And it is a fine place to meet a companion for the night while you enjoy a cocktail – wine, champagne, whiskey.'

'I'm interested in seeing Bilitis's Vineyard.'

Véronique's eyes narrowed as a sly smile entertained her lips. 'An adventurous gentleman,' she said. 'Follow me.'

She led the way up a flight of stairs and pointed to a door marked with a pharaoh's headdress. 'Attire is forbidden in Bilitis's Vineyard. You may remove your clothing and place it in a locker inside. Wear the key around your ankle or your wrist, as you please. I'll wait for you here.'

'That won't be necessary.'

Véronique ran a hand inside Gabriel's jacket. 'Perhaps monsieur would enjoy some company in the vineyard?'

'Thank you, no.'

Véronique shrugged and moved away. Nothing ventured, nothing gained. 'The vineyard is only for those who like to play. It is upstairs and to your right. Please don't linger. It makes the other members nervous. Some are quite shy. Their performance, you understand?'

'I wouldn't dream of it.'

'What is it with you men coming from work?' she asked in parting. 'Don't you leave your briefcases in the office?'

'It took place in November of 1979,' said Sarah Churchill. 'Juhayman al-Utaybi was a young officer in the Saudi Arabian National Guard. By all accounts he was a model soldier: charismatic, bright, tough as nails. He was also a devout Muslim. He came from a family of Wahabi clerics. The Wahabis practice a pure form of Islam. They're fundamentalists who follow Muhammed's teachings to the letter. No drinking, no smoking, no caffeine, prayer five times a day and no extramarital sex. Family comes first, and that's that. Good clean living by any standards. Well, you know all that . . .'

She and Chapel were headed across town to check out the premises of Cléopatre, the chichi sex club to which Kahn had purchased a membership six months earlier. Leclerc followed on his motorcycle, trailing a handful of his Action Service brethren. It was a long shot, but long shots were all they had.

'Go on,' said Chapel.

'A hundred years ago, the Saud family made a deal with their rival Ikhwan tribes to take control of what was then simply Arabia. Basically, they said, "You back us in our bid to unite the various tribes into a single kingdom, and we'll make Wahabism the kingdom's religion." The Ikhwans cared more about seeing a pure form of Islam practiced across the land than political power, agreed.

'Over the years, however, it became clear that the Saudi potentates – King Ibn Saud, Faisal, Fahd, and Abdullah, take your pick – didn't give two hoots for following the tenets of the religion. Oh, they put on a good show, but when the doors were closed, and sometimes when they weren't entirely, they liked to enjoy what you might call a Western lifestyle. Booze, women, and lots of both. This was fine as long as the behavior was limited to just the King and his retainers. Things changed when they started pumping oil big-time, and they really changed after the first oil embargo in 1973 when the price of that oil skyrocketed. The kingdom's revenues grew tenfold in a year. The royal treasury's coffers were overflowing with petrodollars. The King, being a good chap and very generous, spread the wealth to his sons. And to his nephews and cousins, and their sons and nephews, and so on, and so forth. Soon, there were hundreds of princes jet-setting all over Europe and America, drinking and screwing their way through billions of dollars. Talk about boys behaving badly.

'It was the era of the ugly Arab. Once in London, one of Faisal's sons, forty-fifth or something in line of succession, took over a floor of the Dorchester Hotel on Park Lane for a prolonged stay. Now, the Dorchester is swank as swank is. The prince, though, well in his cups, decided the hotel did not cater to his desert lifestyle. It was too civilized. Not at all in keeping with his Bedu roots. One day, he ran amok through Hyde Park, stole a dog, brought it back to the hotel, skinned it, and cooked it on a bonfire right smack in the corridor of the tenth floor. Word got back to the kingdom, along with umpteen hundred other stories about the Saudi predilection for call girls, coke, parties and the "good life." The Wahabis were not amused.'

'I can understand why,' agreed Chapel.

'Among them, Juhayman al-Utaybi was not amused,' Sarah continued. 'He decided he'd had enough of seeing his religion ridiculed by the very family that had sworn to uphold its principles. He was sick of watching the West's moral laxity undermine his country. Secretly, he gathered together a group of men who thought as he did. Soldiers, students, clerics. He proposed an audacious plan. They would take control of the Grand Mosque and force the House of Saud to change their ways. And he did it. On November the twentieth, Utaybi and a couple of hundred like-minded reformists took control of the mosque. For a week or two, he sent out letters decrying the Saud family, exposing their moral corruption. His version of Paul's letters to the Romans. "The rot," he called it. The Sauds weren't ones to take this standing still. They summoned their Western advisors – interestingly, the French, not the Americans – and after a decent interval stormed the Mosque. Utaybi didn't give up easily. The battle raged for days. Dozens of rebels were killed. No one knows how many soldiers died. Juhayman al-Utaybi was captured alive. He and sixty-seven of his cohorts were tried, convicted, and beheaded. "Chop-chop," the Saudis call it. Islamic justice at its finest.'

'And did the Sauds change?' Chapel asked.

'You tell me?'

'Not a lot.'

'What they did begin doing was financing a lot of radical Islamic groups to make it look like they took their promise of Wahabism seriously. They might not practice it, but they were certainly going to preach it.'

'And so we get Hijira,' said Chapel. 'I can see why Gabriel's family would be upset. But whom do they want to get even with? The Saudis for corrupting their religion in the first place? The French for helping put down the rebellion? The Americans for exporting their cultural drivel into their country?'

Sarah answered matter-of-factly. 'Why, all of them, of course.'

Mordecai Kahn picked his way among the nude bodies, lifting his feet gingerly, squinting to adjust to the amber-hued dark. He had no desire to observe these people engaged in the most intimate act, yet he couldn't help but look at them, if only so he would not stumble. There was little joy in their pursuits. The men moved brusquely, without tenderness or passion. The women bore an expression he could best describe as 'suffering for their art.' Groans came and went. Gasps. Occasionally, even something that might pass for pleasure. And always the piped-in dance music, the steady beat, the trebly vocals.

A hand clamped his leg, and he froze, horrified. The hand belonged to a recumbent woman. She was svelte and from what he could make out, attractive. Several men had gathered around her, masturbating. Her free hand aided first one, then another. Apparently, she desired one more. Kahn freed his leg and moved on without speaking.

It took some time, but he managed to find a dark recess where he could stand without peering at any active men or women. Like the others in the wandering suite of rooms they called 'Bilitis's Vineyard,' he was naked, except for the elastic wristband that held a key and a pendant engraved with the number forty-seven. One floor below in a rickety wooden locker he could pick with a paper clip, the package sat in a briefcase covered by his clothing.

He had made it. Tel Aviv to Paris. Three thousand miles in four days. He was tired, hungry, anxious, and elated, all at once. In a few minutes, he would receive the final payment, his salary for what remained of his life. It was a bargain for what lay inside the briefcase.

Kahn imagined the compact weapon. They had named it 'Salome,' after the biblical dancer who had asked for the head of John the Baptist on a plate. The neat stainless steel casing hardly larger than two packs of cigarettes contained fifty grams of plutonium-239 in a fissile core. Technically, it would be called a 'fusion-boosted fission weapon' utilizing an implosion design. A thin outer shell of plutonium would be driven inward by an explosive charge at a velocity of five kilometers per second. The impact of the outer shell on the center plutonium sphere would create two high-pressure shock waves, one traveling to the center of the shell, the other outward. The resulting pressure would compress the plutonium to four times its normal density. The collapse of the central sphere would crush the fusion fuel in its center. A chain reaction would ensue, resulting in a one-kiloton blast, the equivalent of ten tons of TNT. The design was hardly revolutionary. Similar bombs had been in production for thirty years. Kahn's genius was to create an explosive compound so powerful that only thirty grams were needed to initiate the chain reaction. This, along with the huge strides made in microchip technology that had reduced the components of the firing mechanism by a scale of ten, resulted in a significant miniaturization of the weapon.

Stealing the device had not proven difficult. It was merely a question of defeating the biometric security mechanisms governing entry and exit to and from the research and development laboratory. Only a small cadre of vetted scientists was allowed inside. A fingerprint scanner confirmed each scientist's identity. A scale recorded his weight and was calibrated to allow a variance of one pound from the time he entered to the time he left. Security was designed with a single goal: to prevent the theft of any of the devices being developed and constructed deep below the earth at the Eilbrun facility.

Kahn's challenge was to convince the scanner and the scale that he was another man. Someone who weighed exactly 4.3 pounds more than he. That man was his friend and colleague of twenty years, Dr Lev Meyerman. Meyerman who stood five foot five inches to Kahn's six foot two. Meyerman who weighed one hundred eighty-one pounds to Kahn's one hundred seventy-six. Eyeballing his friend's weight was not a possibility. Kahn was a man of science and approximation reeked of luck. The task demanded he take matters into his own hands, and if it was not science that supplied the answer, it was, at least, social engineering.

For months, Kahn pressed Meyerman to diet. Each day, he accompanied him on lunchtime walks around the complex's perimeter. Each day, he lectured him on the benefits of fruits and vegetables. Together, they monitored the shorter, huskier man's weight as it dropped from two hundred pounds to one hundred ninety, one hundred eighty-five, and finally, to one hundred eighty-one pounds.

Beating the fingerprint scanner demanded less finesse. Kahn lifted latent prints of the man's index finger from Meyerman's morning bottle of Perrier. Using cyanoacrylate adhesive fumes, more commonly known as Krazy Glue, he enhanced the fingerprints and photographed them with a digital camera. Adobe PhotoShop sharpened the contrast of every ridge and whorl. When printed onto a transparent sheet, the resulting reproduction was impeccable.

Using a photosensitive circuit board he'd purchased at

Radio Shack in Tel Aviv and the transparency, Kahn etched the fingerprint into the copper board, effectively creating a mold.

As for the 'finger,' he'd had the ingredients all along. Five Gummy Bears melted on a Bunsen burner provided the gelatin with which to shape the last joint of an index finger. As the 'finger' cooled, he pressed its tip against the circuit board. The impression was perfect. Lifelike. The scanner, which did not measure body heat, was fooled. In the end, Kahn walked out of the laboratory with Salome inside his jacket and a nonfunctional prototype left behind in the vault.

Kilotons. Plutonium. Fissile material.

The words scalded Kahn's tongue. Tomorrow, he would be free of this devil's lexicon. His duty – as an Israeli, a Zionist, and a father – fulfilled, he would fly south to Madrid, then on to Cape Town. The city housed a prominent colony of Jews: seekers, strivers, pioneers like him. He would fit in nicely. He hoped for a teaching post. High school physics would suit him, as would chemistry, or even Hebrew. It was time to give back.

A hand touched his shoulder and Kahn flinched uncomfortably. Who was it now? Another pot-bellied Romeo? A saggy-breasted matron seeking gratification from a skinny old Jew? Turning, he found himself looking at the man with the smiling eyes.

'Good evening, friend,' said Marc Gabriel. 'You are a long way from home.'

Chapter 47

Admiral Owen Glendenning stared in disbelief at the print-out of Adam Chapel's monthly account activity at the Hunts Bank. 'When did you discover this?' he asked Bobby Freedman.

Allan Halsey answered in his subordinate's stead. 'Bobby came across the info a little more than an hour ago,' he began. 'He was—'

'I believe I asked Mr Freedman,' Glendenning interrupted.

'Yes sir.'

The three men were standing at the back of the Foreign Terrorist Asset Tracking center's operations room at CIA Headquarters in Langley. An uncharacteristic calm hung over the auditorium. Glendenning was bleary-eyed and scruffy. He'd slept ten hours since Blood Money had begun its search for Hijira. 'Well, Mr Freedman, I'm waiting.'

Bobby Freedman looked from his boss to the CIA's deputy director of operations. 'Like Mr Halsey said, I was walking out the Holy Land Charitable Trust's transfers when I came across these four. Sixty-five thousand dollars each to an account at an American bank. At first, I'd thought it was a mistake. I didn't see them the first time around. And if you'll excuse me, sir, it isn't like me to miss something like this. I thought maybe it was a mis—'

'Go on, Mr Freedman.' Glendenning had folded his arms

and was physically leaning toward the beefy analyst in an effort to make him hurry up.

'Well, sir, as I was saying, I was curious. If the Holy Land Trust is, in fact, a front for Hijira, then the transfers would constitute the first evidence of an American connection. Proof that they're operating on home soil.'

Glendenning raised a hand for Freedman to shut up. 'And, who exactly did you see about getting a warrant to look into these accounts?' he asked, sniffing as if he detected an unpleasant odor.

'Jerry Oglethorpe at Hunts.'

'Is that "Judge" Jerry Oglethorpe, or just your good buddy, Jerry?'

'Mr Oglethorpe is in charge of government relations at Hunts, where Chapel kept his account. I recognized the ABA number so I gave him a call and asked if he might do me a favor.'

'The favor being to illegally obtain a US citizen's private banking records.'

'Yes sir,' agreed Freedman, who looked like he was catching a whiff of the same lousy brew.

'Allan, get on to legal posthaste. Have them issue me a warrant for Chapel's accounts at Hunts and make sure it's stamped twenty-four hours ago. See Judge McManus about it. He's one of the good guys.'

Halsey made a gesture like he was throwing in the towel. 'Glen, please, that's not—'

'*Allan*. Remember. If we're not stepping on somebody's rights, we're not doing our job.'

Swallowing hard, Halsey lowered his head and moved a few steps away to contact the judge.

Glendenning returned his attention to Bobby Freedman. 'Now then, Mr Freedman, am I to believe that this fount of information is wholly the product of some below-the-table cooperation?'

'Yes, Admiral.'

Glendenning chuckled, his face brightening. 'Call me Glen,' he said, clapping a hand on Freedman's shoulder before leading him to a glassed-in office at the rear of the room. 'I'm glad somebody around here realizes this is a goddamned war we're fighting. You know what happens to the nice guys in a war? The ones who swear by the rules of engagement and won't open fire until they get the four star's go ahead? Do you? They get slaughtered, Robert. *Slaughtered,*' he said, banging his cane for emphasis. 'Now, Robert, I want you to blastfax Chapel's social security number to every bank in the United States and all the others with whom we maintain any kind of cordial relations. Feed his every particular into your database, your witches' cauldron – isn't that what you call it?'

'How'd you—'

'Feed everything you have on Chapel into that,' continued Glendenning. 'Driver's license, home address, passport – all of it. Let's have a look and see where he might have turned up before. I want to see every transaction Chapel has made in the last five years. I want to know where he earned his every last red cent. Once you get that, I want you to walk out every transfer Chapel made to another bank. If he's got some co-conspirators running around, I want to know who they are. And pronto. Am I clear?'

'What about a warrant?'

'I'll have a warrant on your desk ready to read to those banks in two hours. This is a section three-fourteen-A case, if ever there was one.'

Glendenning was referring to subsection 314 (a) of the Patriot Act, which allowed members of the law enforcement community access to all of an individual's most private records if deemed to be vital to the protection of the nation.

Freedman nodded uneasily. 'Come on, sir,' he complained, shifting his heavy shoulders. 'Don't you think this whole thing kind of stinks? I mean, this is Chapel we're talking about.'

Glendenning was careful not to dismiss the comment too easily. 'I understand your concerns, Robert,' he said solemnly. 'I can't divulge too many elements of the case history, but please know this: from the beginning it was clear that task force Blood Money had been penetrated. I am as shocked as you are to learn it was Adam Chapel. Still, it had to be somebody. Betrayal always wears a human face.'

Freedman nodded, but Glendenning could sense his hesitance, his distrust. It wouldn't do. 'Who said numbers don't lie?'

'Chapel, sir. It's his favorite expression.'

'Thank you, Robert. Now, get on out of here, and get me my facts.'

Allan Halsey snapped his cell phone closed and returned to Glendenning's side. 'Judge McManus is on it. He just needs the account info and he'll have the warrant taken care of in an hour.'

'Sonuvabitch's been leading us by the nose for a week,' said Glendenning, allowing his anger to show now that it was only he and Halsey. He rubbed his face, sighing. 'We've got to keep this quiet. Another mole, now? The public won't accept it. Is Chapel still in Paris with Sarah Churchill?'

'Yes.'

'Call Neff at the embassy over there. Arrest him.'

Chapter 48

Sarah Churchill turned down a street and craned her neck to read the addresses. 'We're looking for number sixteen.'

'Two . . . four,' said Chapel, calling out the numbers. 'It's still a couple blocks up.'

Sarah hit the accelerator as the Cyclops lamp of Leclerc's motorcycle trailed in the rearview mirror.

'Just the three of you go,' General Gadbois had said, after Chapel had finished with George Gabriel and Sarah had revealed the crux of her conversation with 'Yossi,' better known as Colonel Yigal Blum, chief of the Mossad's European Intelligence Directorate. 'Take a look. Ask some questions. If you find our men, back off. We'll send over some boys from the Action Service to lend a hand. We can't risk the same clusterfuck that killed Santos Babtiste. This one stays with us.'

Leclerc had caught Chapel's accusing glare. 'Still think it was us who blew the whistle?' he asked. 'Think again. Leaks are an American specialty. Maybe you should look closer to home.'

'Enough,' Gadbois had barked, adding in a pussycat's growl, '*Allez maintenant. Mais doucement.*'

If he could be accused of not taking the threat of a rogue nuclear weapon in his jurisdiction as seriously as he might, it was because he had been deceived. Sarah had neglected to mention the stolen weapon. Kahn was on the run, she'd said, but he was carrying plans, nothing more.

Entering the next block, Chapel resumed his search for addresses. He spotted number eight. Number ten. All were three-story town houses with short flights of stairs leading from the street to large front doors, and narrow alleys between them. The façades were identical: sandblasted granite, dark shutters, steep mansard roofs.

'By the way, you were very impressive back there,' Sarah said.

'Yeah, we had a moment, didn't we?'

Chapel felt winded by his victory; a sprinter who against all odds had come from nowhere to capture the race. George Gabriel had opened up. He had talked. The problem was that he hadn't answered the hard questions. Who? What? When? How? To say his father wanted to 'get even' got them precisely nowhere. 'Getting even' wasn't enough. Not from a son who lived under the same roof as the architect of a plan that 'would bring a floodtide of blood' to the United States.

George Gabriel had offered other nuggets, but they had confirmed what Chapel and Sarah had already pieced together. His father had flown to Buenos Aires two days earlier. A check of flight logs showed one Claude François, first-class passenger, continuing to Asuncion, Paraguay, returning to Charles-de-Gaulle early this morning. The mention of the name Inteltech provoked a positive response from the prisoner.

Even as the interrogation continued, the Gabriel home in Neuilly was raided and found deserted, picked as clean as if a swarm of locusts had been through the place. A team of Leclerc's colleagues was currently examining the phone records to determine if Gabriel had slipped and phoned one of his coconspirators on the landline. Chapel doubted that he had.

The offices of Richemond Holdings, likewise, were discovered to be empty. It would take months, if not years, to track down the firm's investments. A corporation was a different beast than an individual. Financial institutions were less likely to succumb to the type of arm-twisting that had opened the door for Chapel and Sarah earlier in the week when it was a fellow investment house being investigated.

One of Leclerc's buddies was with George Gabriel now. Another man who taped his knuckles and got them bloody before he began asking questions. Did Gabriel know more? Chapel wasn't the one to answer. It was a serious game they were playing. He didn't think any of his friends' widows would object if things got rough. In the end, they simply had to know whether George Gabriel was holding anything back. Chapel had learned the cardinal rule of interrogation. No one finished talking until they told you what you wanted to hear.

In the absence of hard facts, they had Marc Gabriel's actions to console them.

He was in Paris. His decision to kill his son rather than risk his exposing what he knew spoke volumes about the immediacy of the plan. Or had he, as George claimed, tried to kill him to exact his own brand of justice? If nothing else, George Gabriel had been able to confirm that his father's plan was under way – *that he had gone tactical*.

Hijira was happening now.

'Here we are,' said Sarah, pulling the car to the curb. 'Sixteen Boulevard des Italiens. It's the house two up.'

On the sidewalk, Chapel, Sarah and Leclerc formed a tight circle. 'Follow my lead,' she said. 'My guess is Kahn wants to be as anonymous as the other clients. That's the way I'd play it.' She shook her head. 'Thousand to one he's not even there.'

'What do you think he got the membership for?' Chapel asked.

'A sex club's a private place,' said Sarah, who had assumed the leader's role. 'Not a lot of room to carry a piece if you're starkers. Perfect spot for a handover.'

'Doesn't sound like he trusts Gabriel.'

'Smart of him,' said Sarah. 'Kahn's way out there on the political fringe, as far right as right will go. A former officer. Lost both his children to the Intifada. I don't see him selling anything to an Arab.'

'Neither do I,' said Leclerc. 'It's probably a false flag operation. Gabriel made himself out to be someone he wasn't. A South African. An American. Most likely, a Jew.'

Chapel felt the presence of others nearby, but when he looked behind Leclerc he caught only shadows. The street was too quiet. It bothered Chapel. It was the still before an earthquake.

'Shall we, gentlemen?' said Sarah. 'And boys, remember, we're a jolly trio. No squabbling.'

'I take it we exchange keys,' Gabriel said.

'Simple, but effective,' replied Kahn.

Gabriel had forgotten how haunted the man looked, how frightened by his chosen responsibility, how serious. He had aged ten years in the months since they'd last met. 'You must learn to trust,' he said in a voice suggesting sincerity and good fellowship.

'I have the rest of my life for that.'

Gabriel slid the elastic band off his wrist and handed it to Mordecai Kahn. 'You'll find it all there. I think it best if we retrieve our goods separately.'

Kahn stepped uncomfortably close to Gabriel, given their state of dress and the establishment. At this distance, the man smelled rancid. It was obvious that he had not bathed since leaving Tel Aviv.

'The device can be detonated in four ways,' said Kahn. 'A proximity fuse, a velocity switch, a timer, or manually. It is not my business to pry, but it would be better if you let me know which method you find the most interesting.'

'A patriot will deliver the weapon.'

'It would be best if I showed you personally, however, I do not think either of us can take the risk. I can only explain.' Kahn set out in three precise steps how to access the bomb's CPU and detonate the device. 'Rather simple, actually.'

'So then,' said Gabriel, extending an open palm. He'd been in the club too long. Years of survival had taught him that his presence in foreign environments was to be limited. He noticed an odd man eyeing them from the next room. He was pale and slender with ginger hair and girlish hips, and – Gabriel could not help but notice – an insignificant manhood.

'There is one more thing,' said Kahn.

'Oh?' Gabriel sensed a wrench tumbling into the works.

'You will need a code to unlock the CPU.'

'What is it?'

Kahn smiled regretfully. 'You will have to wait until tomorrow to receive it. Think of it as my fail-safe.'

Gabriel stood rooted to the spot. He thought of the satchel in his locker, the neatly bunched packets of hundred-dollar bills sitting atop a half kilo of Semtex. There would be no tomorrow for Mr Kahn. The thought crossed his mind that the Israeli had outsmarted him. *A code.* Gabriel should have imagined as much. He would have done the same.

'The deal is off,' he said, snatching the key out of Kahn's hand. He brushed past Kahn and found the stairs, never once looking back. There was only one way to play this game. Full-throttle or not at all.

He made it down three steps before he heard the scientist padding next to him. 'Please, stop,' Kahn panted. 'I was wrong. It was foolish of me. Stop. Please!'

Gabriel ignored the entreaties a few seconds longer. 'It was worse than foolish!' he spat, pushing Kahn against the staircase wall. A passing couple recoiled in fear. 'It was dishonest. Ask someone else to strike freedom's blow on your behalf. My people can wait.'

'Really, I apologize. It is difficult to trust in this day and age.'

Gabriel huffed angrily, then relented. 'The code?'

'One, twenty-two, two thousand and one. The day my David was killed.'

At the entry, Sarah spoke for the three of them. 'Good evening. Is a girl permitted to bring two boyfriends?'

A washed-out brunette replied with brittle alacrity, 'But, of course. You are members?'

'Not yet.'

'One hundred fifty euros for a couple. One hundred for single men.'

'But we're an extended family,' pleaded Sarah in a loopy voice. She was the playing the drunken slut, a personality the club couldn't get enough of. Always too many pegs and not enough slots.

'All right, then. Two hundred euros for all of you. And no more bargaining, or you can get lost.'

Chapel set the money on the transom.

'Actually, we're looking for a friend,' confided Sarah, leaning into the smoky cubby-hole as she suppressed a giggle. 'A foreign gentleman. Tall, grayish hair, very serious.' She had a picture with her, but to show it was as good as announcing themselves as the police.

And Gabriel? Chapel wanted to remind her. *Ask if he's here, too.* George's description of his father would do nicely: forty-five years old, black hair worn short, brown eyes, handsome. But the woman answered before Chapel could protest.

'You're late, honey,' she rasped. 'He came in an hour ago. A *vieux* like him. He's already exhausted.' Standing, she raised a hand in the air and snapped her fingers. 'Véronique will show you the way.'

Chapel climbed the stairs eagerly, another sex-starved exhibitionist on the way to an illicit assignation. The holster chafed his ribs, the square butt of a French-issue Beretta nine millimeter pressed against his arm. He was finished with the legwork, done being Chapel the accountant, Chapel the dogged bookworm. This was the other part of his training. To enforce and apprehend. This was the part he had no practice at, except to lunge at the flailing feet of a fleeing terrorist and miss.

Leclerc had called Gadbois to alert him of Kahn's presence. The hard boys from the Action Service had secured the perimeter. Agents waited at every door, discreetly hidden submachine guns at the ready. It was to be a silent arrest. No sirens. No shouts. A raid that never happened. A bomb that didn't exist.

'You can't set it off at the drop of a hat,' Sarah had whispered. 'But be careful. He won't be taken alive.'

It wasn't Kahn she was talking about. It was Gabriel. He was here, too. Leclerc had asked, and the woman had had enough experience with *les flics* in her lifetime to know a cop when she heard one, and to know when it was time to tell the truth.

The tinkling of a piano drifted to him from the second-floor landing. Chapel headed towards the music, his eyes adjusting to the dim lighting. He entered the lounge shyly, as if unsure he was in the right place. An older man sat on the piano bench, his right hand noodling the melody of 'It's Impossible.' Chapel was relieved to note that he was wearing clothes. A pall of cigarette smoke hung in the air. Several men and women circled the baby grand, making small talk and nursing colorful cocktails with umbrellas. Were they getting up the nerve? Chapel wondered. Or dissecting their performances? He searched their starchy, bored faces, but knew immediately that neither Kahn nor Gabriel was among them. Neither had come for the advertised specials.

Across the landing was a boutique selling the usual embarrassing accessories and undergarments. Leather bustiers, rubber corsets, an entire wall devoted to whips, chains, handcuffs, and hoods. Chapel was surprised to see the boutique had a second room. He went inside, eyes strictly on the merchandise. Another few steps brought him to the hard stuff, the toys that he had always found more ridiculous than repulsive. The boutique's customers had gathered at the far side of the room, their eyes glued to a dusky mirror. As Chapel approached, the mirror grew transparent. A thin, gangly woman ten years past her prime stood on the other side of the mirror, trying on a bra and a pair of panties. It took Chapel a moment to notice that she was moving in time to music. Her exaggerated motions were the tip-off: the coquettish swirl of the hair, the methodical removal of the brassiere. She knew she was being watched.

More amused than disgusted, Chapel turned to leave. A shadow flitted at the corner of his eye. A man dressed in business attire moving quickly, athletically. Turning back, Chapel stared past the woman at the slim, dark man moving across the room on the other side of the glass. Chapel put his hand to the glass and looked closer. He saw Marc Gabriel nudging his shoulder against an emergency exit. Mid-forties, short black hair, fit, handsome. Who else would be carrying a leather briefcase in a sicko's pleasure palace? Gabriel pushed again, but the door didn't budge.

Chapel dashed from the boutique. In the corridor, a naked man hairier than a Canadian grizzly stared at him, gasped, and backed away. It was the gun. *Didn't expect to see one of those in here, did you, pal?* Chapel was running now. He was in a plush maroon tunnel. Framed prints of Egyptian motifs traded places with black-and-white photos of engorged human appendages. A hall appeared to his left. He ducked into it, slowing, pistol raised in his hand, safety off, round chambered. His training was coming back to him. But training had never been the problem. Shooting was. He couldn't hit a barn door outside of ten feet.

Leclerc was upstairs checking the fuck rooms. Sarah was making a sweep of the restaurant and kitchen. *He's here,* Chapel felt like yelling. *Get your asses to the second floor.*

Chapel spotted the emergency exit, obstructed by a potted Kentia palm. Gabriel was gone. Chapel tried the door. Locked. In the changing room, the woman was finishing up her striptease, strapping on a pair of three-inch pumps with her sad, bony bottom pressed against the window. No other hallways issued from the corridor. It was a dead end. Chapel looked left and right.

Gabriel had disappeared.

Chapter 49

Mordecai Kahn sat on the bench in the changing room, staring at the scuffed leather satchel between his legs as a profound relief poured over him. There. It was done. For the first time in his life, he'd acted. He'd formed his opinions and given them weight. Most men begged to have a chance to affect the course of history. Offered that chance, he had taken it. He had made his mark. Kahn slipped on his shoes, then dropped a hand to the satchel. Carefully, he sprang the lock and looked inside. Packets of one hundred dollar bills winked at him.

Strangely, he felt no elation at seeing the money. True, it would make things easier. If it cheapened his motives, he could live with that, too. The Sayeret would never give up until they had found and punished him. In the spy's game, he was a marked man. Three million dollars would keep him ahead of the pack for a while. Months? Years? He didn't care to guess.

Selecting a packet of bills, he slapped it against his knee, then fanned the currency against his thumb, just like in the movies. He would buy himself an extravagant meal. He would check into a five-star hotel, have a long bath, purchase some new clothes, and set out for a night on the town. It was only eleven-thirty. In Paris, the night was still young.

'*Bonsoir*, Dr Kahn.'

Turning his head, Kahn looked at the slight, sallow face of the man who had called his name, and he knew he would never have any of it.

'*Bienvenu à Paris.*'

Leclerc drew his pistol and stepped inside the changing room. 'Did you have a nice trip?' he asked.

Kahn said nothing. Dropping his hand to his lap, he simply sighed.

Leclerc was looking at the satchel. To his mind, it was the same satchel that Taleel had carried halfway across town on his martyr's last mission. It was the satchel that had killed Santos Babtiste and the Americans. It was the satchel that should have killed him.

'Stand up,' he said.

Kahn stood.

Leclerc took a step back. He wanted to get out of there. It was a bomb. He knew it. Just like he'd known the other satchel was a bomb. He wasn't a coward. It was not fear that had prevented him from rushing like a hero into Taleel's apartment. It was instinct. Survival. Something had told him that Taleel possessed a bomb. It was nature's private warning that he had no business entering a confined space with a suicidal maniac. And this satchel held a bomb, too.

'Move away from the bag.'

'You don't want some?' Kahn asked, as if astonished. He raised the packet of one hundred dollar bills, fluttering the notes.

'I said move away.'

'You're too late, actually. It's the other thing you want. I'm afraid he's gone.'

The door opened behind Leclerc. It was Sarah Churchill. 'Get back,' he warned her. 'Clear the building.'

'What is it?'

'Clear the building!' He swallowed and fought to keep

THE DEVIL'S BANKER 371

from blinking. He sounded scared. He had to watch that. He nodded, and her head disappeared.

Leclerc envisioned himself inside the gloomy hallway at the Cité Universitaire. He had always disliked small spaces. A premonition, he knew. He had wanted to follow Babtiste. He had ordered himself to chase after Chapel and the others, but his legs had refused the command. He'd stood there nailed to the ground, wondering which idiot had called the police. It was probably Gadbois, despite his protests to the contrary. Gadbois and his distrust of the Americans. 'Wheels within wheels,' he liked to say. There was always something Leclerc didn't know.

'Come on, then,' he barked, liking the sound of his voice this time. 'Move away. Don't make me ask you again.'

Kahn buried his head in his hands. 'All this money,' he pleaded. 'Please. We can come to an agreement. I'll help you find him. I will. It's yours – all of it. Take it, please.'

Leclerc advanced a step, then another, his heart beating wildly. A voice told him to turn around, to get out, to grab Sarah and Chapel, and flee the building as quickly as possible. It was Taleel's satchel. A small space. Remember the premonition. *No*, he answered. He wouldn't run again. This was his stand. It was his arrest to make. Rising on his tiptoes, he glanced into the satchel. He relaxed. It was just money, after all.

'Okay,' he said, his voice regaining its natural pique. 'Just keep your hands where I can see them.'

But something in Leclerc's voice had sparked hope in Kahn. The Israeli physicist dropped his hands into the satchel. 'We can come to an agreement,' he cried. 'Here—'

And he lifted two of the slim green packets and thrust them towards Leclerc.

Chapel ran back through the corridors and down the stairs. Gabriel was in the building. Chapel had to alert Sarah, to warn Leclerc. Kahn might be here as well. His mind was a mess, his powers of logic and rational thought as frayed as a cut rope. Hitting the ground floor, he glanced to his right and left. Four men he didn't know but who looked somehow familiar were marching toward him. All wore blue suits and white shirts.

'Mr Chapel,' one said. It was Neff, the FBI legal attaché. The starched-collar bureaucrat who'd ferried him from the hospital to the meeting with Owen Glendenning. 'Mr Chapel, we'd like you to give us your weapon please.'

Chapel looked to his right hand and realized he'd been waving the gun like an idiot. 'He's here,' he said feverishly, lowering the gun to his side. 'Gabriel is here. I mean Utaybi. Upstairs. I saw him for a moment, then he moved away. Tell the Action Service to block the exits. He's here!'

Neff had his gun out, too, a snub-nosed thirty-eight police special, and he was aiming it at Chapel. 'Lay the gun on the floor.'

'Are you listening to me?' Chapel exclaimed. 'Gabriel is in the building. Now!'

'*Drop – your – weapon!*' Neff shouted so loudly, so sternly, that Chapel did as he was told. The Beretta landed on the floor with a thud, and a second later, Neff and his three thugs were all over him, pinning his arms behind his back, cuffing his hands, and shoving him towards the exit.

'What's going on?' Chapel protested, asking one man, then the next, getting no answer from any of them. He'd never been cuffed in his life. He was too shocked to fight. He was certain this was a foolish mistake and that given an opportunity, he could explain his way out of it – whatever 'it' was. 'He's here,' Chapel repeated. 'Are you guys deaf? The man we've been looking for is inside that building. I spotted him on the second floor less than a minute ago.'

Neff led him outside into the warm night air past a picket of Action Service men. A convoy of black Fords was parked in the middle of the road. Wooden trestles had been erected at both ends of the street. Uniformed police cordoned off the sidewalks.

'Neff,' Chapel began, then remembering his first name, used that. Lesson number one of the Dale Carnegie course he'd been asked to take after joining Price Waterhouse and his interpersonal skills had been found wanting. 'Frank, hold on a second.'

They'd reached the sidewalk and Neff shoved Chapel against the car. 'No, you hold on, you piece of shit. "What's going on?" Is that what you want to know, Chapel? Why don't you tell me, bin Lad—'

Before Neff could finish, a tremendous explosion rocked the night. A violent clap of thunder boxed Chapel's ears. A flash of orange blinded his corneas as a gust of heat singed his cheeks. Fragments of mortar, wood, and glass pummeled the car and rained down on the street. A quarter of a second later, the blast hit him, a wave that lifted him off of his feet and tossed him bodily over the hood of the car and onto the street. He was unconscious for a second, maybe two. When he came to, he saw a black curtain of smoke seething from the building.

And there was Neff, sitting up on the ground next to him, stunned, picking shards of glass out of his bloodied cotton shirt and calmly flicking them away.

The last man had been brought out of the building ten minutes earlier. Sitting upright on a gurney, covered from head to foot in ash, he resembled a shrouded mummy with an oxygen mask clasped to his mouth. Chapel heard a paramedic say that he'd been found at the rear of the building beneath a collapsed spar. A chef on his midnight break.

One of the firemen started back up the steps to continue the rescue effort. A colleague coming the other way shook his head, and together they returned to the sidewalk, taking up position a few feet from where Adam Chapel sat, cuffed in the backseat of a Ford.

'You can't stop yet,' Chapel implored them silently. 'If you found the chef, you'll find her, too. Go on, now! Keep looking!'

For the past two hours, the living and the dead had been escorted past his window. Chapel had searched the faces of the survivors, checked the clothing of the dead, hoping for a sign of her.

The blast had eviscerated the second story of the building and ignited a fire that had rapidly engulfed the upper floors. Within minutes the building was a raging inferno. All the survivors had been pulled from the ground floor, or the east side of the second floor. Everyone else had perished. Smoke. Fire. The blast itself. They hadn't stood a chance.

At three-thirty, Frank Neff slid into the front seat of the car. He was wearing a fireman's stained canvas jacket, and he wiped the dust from his eyes with a damp towel. 'Nice work,' he said, directing his comments over his shoulder. 'Seventeen dead. Thirty-three injured, most of 'em with burns that'll never heal properly. Five are critical, not expected to make it. If you want to cheer, go ahead. Tell me, Chapel, was it worth it?'

Chapel ignored the question. Denials, explanations, apologies: nothing concerned him except her. 'Sarah,' he said. 'Have they found her?'

Neff threw an arm over the center rest and stared at Chapel. 'No luck, bud. She didn't make it out.'

Chapter 50

'Clearer, baby. Just a little bit clearer. Come to Daddy. That's right, sharpen up. Looking good. Looking very, very good!'

Perched over an ocular lens, Sam Spencer fiddled with the focus of his Leica magnified videoscope. The face grew clearer. The chin firmed, the lips solidified, full and firm. He had no problem with the hair. A dark mane parted in the middle and cut to the shoulders. No, the hair was not the problem. It was the eyes and nose that eluded him. The center of the face was still a blur.

'Darn it!' Spencer muttered, raising his head from the eyepiece and pushing himself back from the desk. Until he could define these all-important pixels, he would not be able to submit the picture to the Identix software for a match. He wouldn't go to Owen Glendenning with anything less. A picture without a name was no good to anyone.

Sam Spencer, age thirty-seven and one day, director of the FBI's forensic audio, video, and image analysis unit, had been enhancing the final seconds of the digital tape rescued from Mohammed al-Taleel's apartment for thirty-six hours running. What had begun as a top-secret rush job had continued into the night and plowed right through his birthday. He didn't mind missing the celebration dinner with his wife and parents. He did mind the yellow packages piling up outside his door. Spencer was conscientious about his responsibilities to a fault. At this rate, he'd have to motor through the weekend to clear the backlog.

Working out of an air-conditioned bungalow on the grounds of the FBI Academy in Quantico, Virginia, Spencer assisted not only the FBI, but also state, local, and international law enforcement agencies with the examination of recorded audio, video, and photographic media. Jobs varied from converting a tape from NTSC to PAL to repairing shot-up video cameras. Most of his enhancement work came from ATM security cameras and involved getting a clear shot of the robber's, and sometimes, the eventual murderer's, face. It was critical work and he loved it.

Never, though, had he been tasked with such an important project. *Top Secret. Eyes Only. Utmost national priority.* The urgency of the mission had been drummed into him ad infinitum. And the calls. Every hour on the hour the deputy director for operations of the CIA called for an update on his progress, always ending their conversations with the same terse warning not to share the information with anyone.

A box of See's candies was in easy reach. Snapping up the Birthday Sampler, Spencer hunted for his favorite – a dark chocolate ganache. He was pretty sure he'd eaten the last one, but it paid to look twice. A finger poked under the gold crenelated paper and blindly surveyed the bottom tray. His conscience stopped him cold. It was cheating to start on the bottom tray until you'd finished the top. Spotting a pecan caramel, he popped it into his mouth. The chocolates weren't a luxury. They were a necessity. Fuel.

Chewing the delicious confection, Spencer crossed the room to a humming white machine, the size of a refrigerator. Slipping on a pair of surgeon's gloves, he ran the original tape through the Canon X3 Digital Enhancer one more time. The X3 broke down the picture into individual pixels, then using an artificial intelligence program, compared each to the pixels surrounding it, and either sharpened, or flattened, the image. It was the same process the human eye performed in concert with the brain when it looked at Monet's cathedrals. Each step you took away from the painting rendered the cathedral in clearer focus.

So far, Spencer had run the image through the enhancer five times. What had started as a speck on the mirrored sunglasses had evolved into a slender brunette wearing ivory pants and a matching sleeveless T. Model material all the way. But that fact and ten cents still wouldn't buy him a cup of coffee. He needed a face. The problem was that the machine was at the end of its tether. There was only so much the A.I. could manipulate the pixels without the result boomeranging. This was the last go-round.

Wiping a lock of hair out of his eyes, Spencer retook his place on his red stool and rolled up to the X3.

'Clearer, baby. Just a little bit clearer.'

Chapter 51

They would be waiting for him at the border, thought Marc Gabriel as he guided the year-old Mercedes S-class with Berne license plates along the curving country roads. It was an hour before daylight. Hills thick with heather, fields ripe with wheat, and glades of summer pines lay asleep beside him, but in his mind he was dreaming of yellow sand and blue skies, of the graceful curve of a windswept dune and the razor hush of an approaching storm.

By now, he could be sure George had talked. Genteel approaches had yielded to older, trusted methods. At the least, they had a description of him. Perhaps even a photograph, if George had been stupid enough to carry one. But what else? Gabriel had been meticulous in compartmentalizing information and sharing with each contact only that which he required to complete his assignment. George, like the others, knew only what he needed to know, and in his case, the basics.

He had not told them about Kahn or the meeting at Cléopatre. Gabriel could only guess that somehow, somewhere Kahn had slipped and that the Americans had gleaned the information from the Israelis.

The sun rose as he passed through Besançon, fifty kilometers from the Swiss border. The terrain grew mountainous. The road bordered gaping chasms and roaring cataracts. The dashboard clock read 6:55 as he spotted the red and white flag flapping in the morning breeze. Two lanes slimmed to one and led to a steel and glass booth sitting astride the highway. A black and white striped pole was raised to allow cars to pass. Five vehicles filled the lane ahead of him.

Gabriel turned off the radio and drummed his fingers against the wheel.

If they were waiting for him, it would be here.

Nonchalantly, he checked the rearview mirror. A Peugeot nosed close behind him, then a Volkswagen Combi. Traffic leaving Switzerland was sparse, but steady. He saw no vehicles parked near the booth, or in the examination lanes beside it, that shouldn't be there.

A guard left his post and began strolling down the line of vehicles. A longtime veteran; fifty, gray, serious. Not one of the young lions doing their annual military service.

Gabriel busied himself with formalities. He gathered his registration, driver's license, and passport. He was a Belgian businessman returning to his home in Berne after a week-long stay in Brussels. He rehearsed his home phone number, his address. Both would check out if confirmed. If they were looking for Omar al-Utaybi, they would be disappointed.

The guard met his eyes and motioned for him to roll down the window.

Gabriel's spine stiffened.

They had him.

Rolling down his window, he extended his passport. 'Morning,' he said, as if bored.

The guard did not return the greeting. 'Front tire needs air,' he said, not bothering to look at the passport.

'*Vielen Dank,*' said Gabriel, but the guard was out of earshot, pointing a finger at the driver of the VW Combi and motioning him into the inspection lane.

A horn blared at Gabriel.

Ahead, a second guard was waving traffic through.

Raising an acknowledging hand, Gabriel shifted into drive and pumped the accelerator with a little muscle.

He was in Switzerland.

They met on the third floor of the parking structure at Geneva Cointrin Airport. They had not seen each other for over a year, but they did not kiss, offer to hug, or even shake hands. He was her controller, nothing more. He opened the trunk and lifted the panel to the spare tire. A compact titanium box lined with lead held the package.

'So small?' she asked, accepting the weapon, assaying its weight.

'Incredible, no?'

'Maybe the rot is not as pronounced as we believed.'

Gabriel's instinct was to slap her, but he knew her too well. 'Maybe not,' he agreed, and together they laughed.

The woman straightened and sighed. 'I must go.'

'Yes,' he said, and lifting his hand, he touched her cheek. 'Good-bye, sister.'

'Good-bye, brother.'

In the changing room of Terminal B, Marc Gabriel removed his jacket, pants, shirt, and tie for the last time. Opening his overnight bag, he withdrew the long white cotton shirt-dress known to Arabians as the *dishdasha* and slipped it over his head. The *bisht* came next, a loose-fitting black silk robe with a gold shawl collar and piping on the sleeves. He'd had the clothing tailor made for him at Harrisons off the Etoile. Finally, he folded the red and white checked *ghutra*, or *khaffiyeh*, in a triangle and arranged it on his head, securing it in place with a sleek black *agal*, or headband, made from tightly woven goat hair and sheep's wool. He spent a moment adjusting the clothing, enjoying the generous fit. When he looked in the mirror, he gasped. After twenty years, he was looking at his true self.

Emirates Flight 645 to Dubai was on final call when he presented his boarding pass to the stewardess. 'Seat 2A,' the pleasant woman said. Something in his expression stirred her concern. 'Has it been a long trip, sir?'

Omar al-Utaybi shrugged tiredly. 'You have no idea.'

Chapter 52

Adam Chapel was running. His stride was fast and loose, his legs fresh, with no sign of cramping. His breath came easily. His arms, tucked at his side, pumped with short, efficient strokes. It was his habit to keep his eyes trained on the twenty feet of pavement in front of him, to disappear inside his mind to a tranquil place he had prepared in advance, a quiet corner where he'd set aside his treasured memories. But today, his mind was a crowded, chaotic place, and he let his eyes meander from the pavement towards the vast expanse of ocean that spread to his right. Over the great blue Pacific. Over the whitecaps cresting the late afternoon chop. Over the dolphins jumping in great arcs and the seagulls wheeling and diving into the sea.

'It will be over soon,' Chapel repeated to himself.

The swim and the bike were behind him. The wind was at his back. Thirteen miles along the superheated roadway of the Kilauea Highway would carry him across the finish line. The pavement stretched like a silver ribbon across the black pumice stone and the red volcanic ash. His body had weathered eight hours of constant physical strain. It could endure two more hours of abject misery. Time, effort, discipline and the will to survive would see him through.

'How much longer can you take it, Chapel?'

It was not his voice that demanded he give in, but the corrugated baritone of General Guy Gadbois. 'Eight hours. It's a record.'

Chapel squeezed his eyelids tighter, as if blackness would block out the voice. He knelt upright on the cold concrete floor of an interrogation cell at Mortier Caserne. Handcuffs pinned his hands behind his back. A round three-inch-diameter pole nestled in the craw of his knees. If he sat up, the kneecaps dug harder into the unyielding floor. If he sat back, the pole cut all circulation to his feet. Either position promised an excruciating result.

'Twenty-one dead in a week,' Gadbois continued as he circled Chapel, his toad's head lowered to seek out the prisoner's eyes. 'That's good work for anyone. A record to be proud of. Come now, Mr Chapel. It is time to rest on your laurels. To pass on the baton to someone else.'

'Sarah,' Chapel muttered. 'I want to see Sarah.'

'But you can't. Whatever remains of her is back in the building you and your colleagues saw fit to blow up.'

'No. She isn't dead.' When the pain had grown too intense, and the world had dissolved in a freakish kaleidoscope of white noise and unbearable sensation, he had seized upon the idea that she was still alive. The notion of her waiting for him somewhere, after this was over, was the only thing keeping him going. He had not seen her body, therefore she was alive.

'Perhaps you should have taken your feeling for her into account before embarking on such rash actions? Or did you have a choice? Did Marc Gabriel order you to lead us into Cléopatre in order to kill us off, just as he ordered you to lead my men into the Cité Universitaire?' Gadbois put a foot on the pole and allowed his full weight to rest on it. 'Santos Baptiste deserves an answer! Herbert Leclerc deserves an answer! Sarah Churchill deserves an answer. Tell me now,

Chapel. Clear your conscience. You loved the girl. Tell me, for her sake!'

Chapel moaned as the blood left his feet. His flesh was slowly dying. Every cell screamed for oxygen, the nerves firing off their emergency flares. He was kneeling on razors. Sweat beaded his forehead. He began to shake.

'No,' he said. 'No.'

He'd already given his answers. He'd sworn his innocence. No one had paid him two hundred sixty thousand dollars. If it was in his account, it was a setup; more of Marc Gabriel's handiwork. Chapel began to shake his head violently. No, he had not tipped off the police. No, he had not sent George Gabriel to the Hôpital Salpetitpierre to boost his own credibility. No, he had not warned off Dr Mordecai Kahn.

'The problem, Mr Chapel, as you know, is that as lead investigator on this case it was you who determined which directions we were to follow. It was you who led us every step of the way. It was you who told us what was black and what was white. We simply have no way of knowing what was clean and what was dirty. You leave us no choice but to believe that this whole thing has been nothing but an elaborate wild-goose chase. From bank to bank we hopped, but what did we find? Names? Addresses? Any live person who might bring us one step closer to figuring out what Gabriel was discussing on the tape? That was him, wasn't it? You see, we've come up with some photos of the man, and I've been told he hasn't aged a day. We found exactly nothing.'

'Kahn,' said Chapel. 'We found Kahn. We found the Holy Land Trust. We found François's account in Berlin.'

'Window dressing,' complained Gadbois. 'Diversions. I called the Mossad myself, and they deny ever talking to Miss Churchill. "Bomb?" they say. "There's no bomb. Kahn is still at work in Tel Aviv." He released his weight from the stick. 'Come now, Chapel, let's be gentlemen about this. Tell me what you know – everything from A to Z – and I'll take you down to the officer's mess and buy you a *steak frites* and a glass of beer. Hmm? What do you say? I told you that I'm impressed. Eight hours. I've never had anyone hold out on me like this. You're a tough bastard. I could've used more like you in Algeria.'

Chapel continued to shake his head, the steady rhythmic motion comforting him, transporting him. It was a denial of his complicity, a refusal to acknowledge his plight. It was a dying heart's plea to bring Sarah back. Yet, even as he fought the pain, he freed a corner of his mind to unravel the insanity of his predicament. Gabriel's sleight of hand did not interest him. Cybercrimes were a trivial menace. Hacking into commercial bank's accounts was a daily occurrence. The crime could be uncovered in hours.

What bothered Chapel was his colleagues' lightning access to his account at the Hunts National Bank. They had no right to pry into his personal affairs without a court order. Evidence suggesting that Chapel had been receiving money from a known or suspected terrorist was to be brought before a federal magistrate; a warrant obtained. If they'd just given him an opportunity to explain, he would have happily presented his monthly statements showing the receipts of his federal paycheck and nothing else. If they wanted to look at his assets, he'd let them see that, too. Two million dollars tied up in government bonds and a fifty-acre lot on the slopes of Mount Haleakala on the island of Maui. Nowhere would they have found Gabriel's black money. By subverting Chapel's chance to defend himself, the US government had become one more of Marc Gabriel's dupes, blind pawns in Hijira's network.

You know what they say: if you're not violating a few rights, you're not doing your job. It was Glendenning's favorite joke, and Chapel was the prime offender. When he wanted information, he wanted it right away. He'd never given a rat's ass about rights and the issues of personal freedoms. Chapel decried his hypocrisy. What court had he spoken with to obtain access to Taleel's accounts? How else had he explained his exasperation at Manfred Wiesel's refusal to force the Deutsche International Bank to reveal their client's records?

'You leave us no choice but to return to the young Gabriel,' declared Gadbois, starting towards the door. 'We are pressed for time. I'm afraid he'll receive a rougher brand of treatment than you. Then again, he's neither a French nor an American national, so who gives a damn? Just a bloody wog. Isn't that what Miss Churchill might have said?'

Chapel strained at his bonds. 'He isn't involved,' he pleaded. 'He was manipulated by his father.'

'Just like you? What a merry duo you two make.'

Gadbois approached with a cobra's speed and slammed his heel onto the rod.

'What is Hijira's plan?' he shouted when Chapel had finished screaming.

'A bomb . . . they're going to detonate a bomb.'

'Where are they going to strike?'

'I don't know.'

'When?'

'Soon.'

'How soon?'

'I don—' Chapel's mouth froze, his teeth bared, muscles constricted by the pain. The light faded. He was drifting over a blue sea, back to the highway on the Big Island. *Faster*, he told himself. *Faster*. He lunged for the tape and fell into darkness.

Chapter 53

The weekly shipment to the Philadelphia offices of the World Health Organization included three hundred cartons of Atabrine; four hundred fifteen boxes of Z-Pacs, the five day course of zithromycin; and four hundred thousand aspirin tablets. A total of eight hundred thousand individual doses of medicine that had passed its expiration date and was to be returned to its manufacturers for immediate destruction. The traffic in expired drugs by certain dubious distributors to the impoverished nations of the third world had grown from a trickle five years earlier to a torrent. Measures had to be taken to protect innocent victims, and Claire Charisse was at the forefront of the effort.

'Paperwork in order today, Bill?' she asked, standing in the Global Trans offices on the grounds of Geneva Cointrin Airport.

'A-OK. Just sign off and we'll get the stuff airborne.'

Claire scribbled a signature on the paperwork and tore off her copy. Looking out the window, she could see the pallet of medicine being loaded by forklift into a Global Trans container. From there, the container would pass through a cursory security check before being put aboard the morning flight to Philadelphia. Normally, all containers being shipped into the United States were made to pass through VACIS, the vehicle and cargo inspection system.

The VACIS system used gamma rays emitted by cesium or cobalt and hundreds of advanced sensors to detect anomalies in density within the container and create an X-ray–like photo of the object inside. However, as the medicines were preclassified as radioactive and the property of a nongovernmental organization, they would forego VACIS and pass directly to a US Customs inspector, whose job was simply to verify that all medicines were accounted for.

'Look at you,' Bill Masters said. 'You're all spiffed up for a Saturday. What do you got going?'

'I'm taking a trip,' Claire answered crisply.

'You? Leaving Geneva? Who'll man the offices? They'll be lost without you.'

'I'm sure they'll find someone to replace me.'

A concerned look darkened Masters's face. 'You're leaving for good?'

Suddenly, Claire Charisse found it very hard to speak. Without answering, she turned and rushed from the office.

'Hey!' shouted Masters after her. 'You didn't give me a chance to say good-bye.' He looked at Doherty, his assistant. 'I liked that gal. She had guts.'

Chapter 54

The lock groaned as a key was inserted. Tumblers fell. Adam Chapel huddled against the bone-cold wall, knees drawn to his chest, chin tucked in as if he was expecting a good pummeling and was determined to absorb the blows. He'd known they would return. As best he could, he steeled himself for another round of their stubborn, futile questioning. He willed his rational mind dead. He divorced his extremities. He withdrew to a black corner where a heartbeat signaled his survival and pain did not exist.

A few hours ago, they'd chucked in a soggy, moth-eaten mattress, and he'd collapsed onto it. His last thoughts before he fell into a dead sleep had been about what he could tell them that might draw them off. What precious salve he could offer to prove his innocence once and for all, and secure his immediate freedom. Some all-purpose solvent to erase the stain on his name. Gabriel's stain. But no answer came. How could he combat evidence he'd never seen? What did words matter when no one was listening?

The door swung open, banging against the wall. Squinting, he raised a hand to shield his eyes and waited for the first impossible request.

'Been tough on you, have they?'

Chapel raised his head. The voice . . . the dry English

accent . . . its promise of affection and sympathy and a return to sanity. 'Not exactly the Plaza.'

Her arms engulfed him. He smelled her hair, and a current of relief rushed over him. Sarah was alive. She'd made it out of Cléopatre, after all. He wanted to smile, but he knew that if he did, he would break, so he held her hands and tried to gather his breath.

'How?' he began. 'What hap—'

A finger silenced his lips. 'Ssshhh. Have something to eat. Then we'll get you showered and shaved.'

A soldier followed close behind and set down a tray of steaming food on the bench. Spaghetti bolognaise. Steamed spinach. Bread and butter. Two bottles of Orangina. The rich smells awoke a gnawing hunger. Ripping off a chunk of bread, he doused it in meat sauce and chewed contentedly.

'I saw him,' he said after he'd caught his breath. 'On the second floor. He was trying to get out of a fire exit but it was locked.'

'So did I,' said Sarah.

'He got out.'

'Yes, I know. Now eat up. We've got to go.'

'We're leaving?' Already he could feel a change in her manner.

'Oh yes,' she responded, as if it had been planned all along. 'Air France's noon flight out of Roissy. We're flying home, Adam. Back to DC.'

The plane was full, every seat, every luggage bin, every square inch of available space taken by the usual summer bandits. They sat in the rear of the aircraft and talked as mothers and infants strolled the aisles and restless children climbed the seats and the cabin lights were extinguished and the second-rate movies played one after the other.

'It was Leclerc,' she explained after they'd eaten their plastic dinners and purchased a Courvoisier to get the taste out of their mouths. 'He took the hard drive that was found in Taleel's apartment to a friend of his. Name doesn't matter. A pro on the outs with the service. The hard drive was a mess, shattered into three pieces, but he was able to dredge up the ghost of some e-mails. There was the usual coded garble. You know, "going to beach tomorrow. Meet for ice cream." Chatter. Stuff we could decode, but it would take us weeks. And then there was something more personal. Something that was sent "in the clear." Correspondence between Taleel and a woman named "Noor." ' Sarah polished off the last drops of cognac and set down her glass. 'Ready for this?'

'Shoot.'

'Noor was Gabriel's younger sister. Taleel and she were in a relationship. A regular Romeo and Juliet. Seems Taleel was Gabriel's cousin. Bad enough having an operative diddling your sis, isn't it? Imagine if he's your cousin, too. Gabriel would not have been pleased.'

'Was she in on it, too?'

'Noor? Given the Arab prejudices against women, I doubt it. But she knew something was going on. Noor mentioned that her brother was leaving this weekend. She said she would never see him again.'

'That fits with what George told us, the apartment being deserted. Gabriel's doing the dirty deed himself.'

Sarah nodded. 'Taleel was supposed to accompany him. In one of his letters, he talked about needing to buy a ticket to go along. He was pleased that he didn't need a visa to go to America. Noor was upset and tried to talk him out of it.'

'Ah, dissension in the ranks.'

'Love,' said Sarah pointedly, as if dismissing a bad habit.

Chapel reached out for her hand, but she was staring out the window and couldn't be bothered. He had the feeling that they weren't really partners in this; that they would never be. Sarah was always a step ahead, playing all the angles, while he worked with his feet planted firmly on the ground.

'Sarah, what happened to you back there?'

'I saw Leclerc in the dressing room,' she said, her eyes fixed on some faraway target. 'He was with Kahn. There was a case on the bench between them. A satchel. Leclerc told me to get out. To clear the building. He knew it was a bomb. I closed the door. I didn't want to leave without you, so I went upstairs. Gabriel was coming out of one of the sex rooms. He fitted George's description to a T. I knew it was him. They'd made the exchange. I realize that now. He had whatever Kahn had sold him.' Anger tightened her eyes, puckered her mouth. 'It was so easy, Adam,' she said, imploring him to forgive her. 'All I had to do was shoot him. He was right there, ten feet away. But I froze. I hesitated. I don't know what I was thinking. And then, just as I was gathering my wits, the place went up. It was Semtex again, if you didn't know. Same signature as Taleel used, just more of it. They're saying two pounds of the stuff. The next thing I knew, I was sitting on the ground floor with the whole building on fire around me. Not a scratch. I took a step out the front door, and that's when I saw you, all bundled up like Jean Valjean on the way to doing his twenty years. I got the hell out of there. Time to make my own queries, if you know what I mean. All that nonsense you'd been spewing about moles and spies got to me. Wheels within wheels, Adam. I was scared. I'll admit it.'

'What happened?' said Chapel. 'I mean, what did you do to get me out? Did you talk to Glen? Did you explain that it had to be Gabriel who framed me?'

Sarah answered with her Cheshire cat's grin. 'Something like that.'

'So who's waiting?' he went on. He was already working out the next steps. Word that a terrorist was trying to enter the United States in possession of a rogue nuclear weapon – whatever the size – would have local, state, and federal law enforcement agencies on maximum alert. Manpower at all major points of entry would be strengthened. Photographs of Gabriel, or rather, of Omar al-Utaybi, would be printed and circulated. The Nuclear Emergency Search Teams (NEST) would be out in full-force.

Chapel had his own plans. George Gabriel had spoken of his father's trip to South America earlier in the week. A check of the flight manifests had, indeed, shown a first-class passenger, Claude François, Belgian national. It was crucial that Chapel forward the passport number to the Immigration and Naturalization Service to put a watch alert on François. If Gabriel had traveled to the States before under the same name, there was a good chance that somewhere there was a record of his arrival, perhaps even a mention of where he stayed.

'Who's waiting on the other end?' he asked again. 'Halsey? Glen? I'll need a ride to FinCEN right away. In fact, I'd like to call ahead.'

'No one,' Sarah responded.

For a moment, Chapel thought she was joking. 'No, really? Who'd you call?'

'No one,' she repeated.

'That can't be. I mean, I'd rank this situation as fairly urgent. You mean to tell me that Admiral Glendenning isn't pulling out all the stops right now?'

'As far as Glen is concerned, you're still at Mortier Caserne.'

Chapel unbuckled his seat belt and began to stand. 'They have a phone in the back. I'll call him myself.'

'I wouldn't do that if I were you.'

It was a new tone of voice. Earnest, uncomplicated, and frighteningly honest. It was the real Sarah. Sarah before the intelligence services had gotten ahold of her. Sarah the teenage watcher. Sarah stripped clean of her hard-earned artifice.

Chapel settled in his seat and listened as she unburdened herself of her suspicions.

Chapter 55

His name was Michael Fitzgerald, and as special agent in charge of the Secret Service's White House Division, it was his job to vet all guests gaining proximity to the President of the United States during visits to 1600 Pennsylvania Avenue. Fitzgerald's immediate concern this muggy Saturday morning was to run through the guest list for the State Dinner being given Sunday night in honor of the newly crowned King of Saudi Arabia.

One hundred thirty-three names stood on the list. Twenty-five belonged to members of the administration: the secretary of state and his wife, the attorney general, the secretary of commerce and his partner. Most were regular visitors to the Oval Office and merited no further examination.

Another twenty names belonged to members of the Saudi King's retinue: the minister of finance, minister of defense, chief of the armed forces, the Saudi ambassador to the United States, as well as five of the King's wives. Mike Fitzgerald shook his head, smirking. He didn't approve of queerbaits and polygamists in general, and the thought of them rubbing elbows with the most powerful man on the planet turned his stomach. Sometimes he doubted whether civilization would survive much longer. But what did he know? He was just a crusty old Catholic from Southie who liked his bottle of sour mash after Saturday mass, his French fries with mustard, and was still madly in love with the only woman he'd slept with, his wife of thirty-seven years, Bea.

The approximately eighty names that remained on the list were a diverse group: governors, senators, civic leaders, academicians, sports stars, actors, and big money 'friends of the President.' All had already been nominally cleared. Their names had been run through the National Crime Information Center and come back clean. Not a felon, crook, or convict among them. In theory, Fitzgerald's brief was completed. To the best of his knowledge, there was no one on the guest list who might wish to physically harm the President. But the commander-in-chief had asked him to do a little extra digging. He didn't want any Johnny Chungs sneaking on the guest list, snake oil salesmen eager to get their two minutes with the President. 'Buckskin,' the Secret Service's designation for the President of the United States, did not sell coffee klatches in the Oval Office to finance his reelection, or seats to a state dinner. If there was dirt, it was Mike Fitzgerald's job to find it. Already, Fitzgerald had had to scratch a prominent Arab-American actor who, unbeknownst to Hollywood, not to mention his wife, was keeping an underage party boy on the side.

Fitzgerald skimmed over the last few names. One in particular caught his suspicious eye. Picking up the phone, he called Blake Godsey, who'd done the actual case-by-case gruntwork. 'Charisse, Claire M,' he said. 'What the hell's a Frenchie doing attached to Owen Glendenning?'

'She's his girlfriend,' answered Godsey. 'Whatdya think, Fitz?'

'What happened to *Mrs Glendenning*?'

'Divorce. Pretty acrimonious, from what I gather. This is Glen's first public soirée with his new squeeze.'

'What's her story?'

'Midlevel bureaucrat at the WHO. Works out of Geneva. A real do-gooder. In charge of Drug Action Program. Don't worry, Fitz. I checked her out. Nothing recorded against. Oh yeah, one thing . . . she's sick. Cancer.'

'Cancer?' Fitzgerald rocked in his chair, watching the fan turn slowly above his head. He'd made his bones as a homicide detective working out of the Ninth Precinct in Boston. Suspicion was as much a part of him as the lingering limp from a childhood bout of polio. 'How bad?'

'That I can't tell you. Admiral Glendenning made a point of informing me that she's taking chemotherapy.' Godsey read off the drugs. 'Didn't want any embarrassing moments. I think he was present when Mrs Hersh had her . . . um, you know, *her thing.*'

'Yeah, I know.' Fitzgerald would never forget Mrs Hersh's 'thing.'

Mrs Hersh was in fact, Mrs Sidney M. Hersh, wife of the chairman of Hersh Industries, and the single largest contributor to the Republican Party. Three months earlier, the Hershes had been the President's guests at a state dinner given in honor of the Israeli prime minister. Mrs Hersh was being treated for cancer, too – Stage III non-Hodgkins lymphoma, as it turned out – but Mr Hersh had forgotten to inform the Secret Service of her illness. Passing through the doorway to the Blue Room, where predinner cocktails were being served, the radioactive isotopes present in the drugs in her bloodstream set off one of several Geiger counters that were hidden in key locations around the White House. The alarm was hellacious. Bells clanging, lights flashing, agents beating it like hell to her location. Naturally, one of the younger guys got a little overzealous and took down Mrs Hersh, all five-foot-nothing, ninety-one pounds of her, like she was a tackling dummy for the Ohio State football team. Worse, her wig came off in the fall. When she stood up, the first thing she saw in the mirror was her bald scalp, and about fifty guests staring at her in horror. Not only was she a suspected nuclear terrorist, she was a bald nuclear terrorist. That was that. Good-bye, Mr and Mrs Hersh. Good-bye to all future donations to the Republican Party.

'Get her oncologist's number,' said Fitzgerald. 'Call him up and verify. Otherwise, she's good to go. Who's handling the door tomorrow?'

'Cappelletti and Malloy.'

'I'll have a word with them to make certain we don't unnecessarily embarrass Miss Charisse.'

'You bet, Fitz.'

But Mike Fitzgerald made a mental note to greet Miss Charisse personally. He had a motto that had gotten him through 'Nam, homicide, and for the last twenty-some odd years, the Secret Service. *Take nothing for granted.*

'Let's move on, then,' he said, dreaming of French fries and mustard and a glass of sour mash. 'What do we know about this LA lawyer, Amir somethingorother? Looks like he's been consorting with some pretty flakey types . . .'

Chapter 56

It always came back to the money, thought Chapel. If Hijira was running a cell out of the United States, it had to finance and support their clandestine operations. They had to rent an apartment, purchase a car, have a phone connected, utilities hooked up, water, gas, electricity. Each iteration demanded proof of identification, credit history, bank accounts, deposits. Gabriel had been planning his act of revenge for twenty years. He would not set up an operation on American soil without having a man on the ground. And so, inevitably, he had left a trail.

Follow the money and you find the man. It was as simple, and as difficult, as that.

Chapel swiped his credit card through the cellular pay phone next to the aft lavatory and dialed the private extension of a certain senior analyst at the Financial Crimes Enforcement Network. The phone rang five times before a tired voice answered.

'Freedman.'

'Bobby, this is Adam. Listen up for a second and don't say a word. This whole thing is a setup. Marc Gabriel, the man we were looking for in Paris, hacked into the Hunts mainframe and took control of their system. He fudged my account. Get last month's tapes from Oglethorpe. Look at the bal—'

'Already got 'em,' Freedman cut in. 'You? Hijira? It stank from the git-go. Man, you don't have time to be involved in anything like that. You're here twenty-four seven. I already called Glen and told him that I found proof that the system had been hacked.'

'You did what?' Chapel grimaced.

'I was the one that gave him the original information. I'm sorry, Adam. I was stunned, too. I know I should have waited, done some double-checking, but the heat of the moment, man. You know how it is.'

Yes, Chapel, answered silently, he knew how it was.

'He's on his way over to collect the stuff now,' Freedman was saying. 'I figured I got you into the trouble, I had better get you out of it.'

'Admiral Glendenning is coming there?'

'Yeah. He was excited about the news. Just for the record, he told me he never bought into the fact that you were a mole either. You're lucky to have a guy like him going to bat for you.'

'Tell him you were wrong.'

'Tell him I was what?'

'Tell him you were wrong, Bobby. Tell him that I'm guilty.'

'What are you saying? I never make mistakes. That's what set me off in the first place. I saw that—'

'Shut up, Bobby!'

A stewardess eyed Chapel warily and motioned for him to keep it down. He was scaring the other passengers. Turning to face the rear hatch, he said, 'When is the admiral due there?'

'Now. Actually, he's five minutes late. What's going on, Adam? What's the big deal?'

Chapel weighed how much he might tell Freedman.

'It wasn't Leclerc who called the police Monday and blew your surveillance on Taleel,' Sarah had whispered to him in the confines of *Mortier Caserne. 'Not General Gadbois, either.'*

'How do you know?'

'I know. It was the same man who delayed the A-team from getting to me in the Smugglers' Bazaar. The same man who ordered Frank Neff to arrest you. The same man who told Gadbois to keep you locked up until Monday. The same man who thinks I'm dead.'

Hours later, Chapel bridled at the suggestion. Her suspicions were too circumstantial . . . too crazy. 'I need a favor,' he said, 'and if Admiral Glendenning's coming your way, I need it quick.'

'Hey, Adam, you're freaking me out a little.'

'Just go with me, Bobby. Are you at your terminal?'

'Yes, I am.'

'Log on to INS.'

A moment passed. 'I'm there.'

Chapel read off the passport number Gabriel had used under the name of Claude François to open the account at the Deutsche International Bank, and more recently, to fly to Paraguay, and asked that he check if François had entered the United States anytime in the past five years.

'Five years?' moaned Freedman. 'You know how many people come into the States in one year? The INS's system isn't up to singling out a passport number. Give me something else, a date, a flight number, an address he's staying at in the States. I need at least two identifiers or else we're going to be here all day.'

Chapel closed his eyes. The joys of Boolean logic. 'June last year.' The words came automatically. He'd never been quite able to get his mind around the series of urgent withdrawals made by Taleel from the Bank Montparnasse that were the subject of the suspicious activity reports he'd discovered at Tracfin. What had prompted Taleel to so flagrantly break with procedure? The defection from normal conduct was all the more glaring now that he knew what kind of man Gabriel was and the degree of discipline he demanded from his ranks. 'Scratch François. Look under

the name Albert Daudin.' He read off the passport number
from his notes.

'Nothing.'

'Okay, then. Log on to Customs. Check under the CMIRs.'
CMIR stood for Currency and Monetary Instrument Reports.
Any visitor traveling to the United States was obliged to
inform the US Customs if he was carrying more than ten
thousand dollars in currency. Gabriel was a finance man.
He was meticulous. He was exacting. He would know that
declaring cash on arrival to the States did not sound any
alarms or precipitate any actions. The information was filed
in a bin to be entered into the Customs database at some
future time, and most probably to be ignored. On the other
hand, were Gabriel or any member of Hijira to be caught
bringing in a large sum of cash, he would be arrested and
his name, photograph, and (false) identity would be forever
known to US law enforcement.

Again, 'Nothing,' said Freedman.

Frustrated, Chapel sighed. Without some record of
Gabriel's entry into the United States, he had nowhere else
to look. Chapel studied the information on his notepad:
Gabriel's passport numbers, his addresses, phone numbers,
all of them false. Flipping the pages back and forth, he locked
on two pairs of numbers. It was only then that he noticed
that Claude François and Albert Daudin possessed sequen-
tially numbered Belgian passports.

Belgian passports had long been a favorite of smugglers
and terrorists due to the ease with which they could be
stolen. In Belgium, the issuance of passports was not the
domain of any single federal agency, as was the case in
nearly every Western country, but the responsibility of over
five hundred local *mairies*, or municipalities. As such, blank
passports were often kept in less-than-secure locations: filing
cabinets, wall safes, even simple desk drawers. On more
than one occasion, thieves had simply helped themselves to

a portable safe, choosing to crack it and take the contents at their leisure. Worse still was the laxity (until 9/11) with which authorities reported the thefts.

If Gabriel had two Belgian passports, why not more?

Chapel read off a third passport number to Freedman, raising the final digit from a seven to an eight. Amid the pitter pat of Freedman working the keyboard, Chapel heard him murmur, 'Here's the big kahuna, now.'

Chapel jumped at the words. 'Who? Is Glen there?'

'Just pulled into the lot. Analysts get to look at asphalt all day. You big shots get the Galleria. I gotta run in a sec—' Without warning, Freedman's voice dropped an octave. 'Oh man . . . whoa, got it! Two years ago. June twenty-first. Mr Gérard Moreau arriving passenger, Geneva to JFK, declared cash amount forty thousand dollars.'

'Where'd he stay?'

'Hotel Richemond, New York.'

'It's a fake,' said Chapel. 'That's the name of his investment company. He knew we wouldn't check. What does he list as his home address?'

Freedman recited Taleel's address in the Cité Universitaire. 'So where do we go from here?'

'Run the name through the CBRS. Check for SARs and CTRs. Let's see if Moreau's got an account.'

'That's a negative,' said Freedman after an agonizing silence.

'Try the IRS. That much cash must be burning a hole in his pants. See if there are any eighty-three-hundreds filled out in his name.' Merchants were required to fill out a Form 8300 for cash purchases totaling more than ten thousand dollars. Another tool in the fight against money laundering.

'Just a sec . . .' Chapel heard Freedman speaking on another line. 'Yes sir. I'll be right over.' Then to Chapel: 'It's Glen. He's at the entrance. I've got to sign him in.'

'Don't go.'

'Adam, I'm not keeping the deputy director of operations of the Central Intelligence Agency waiting . . . oh, wow, look at this – you are the maestro, Chapel. Amazing!'

'What is it?'

'Moreau put down twenty-two thousand dollars at a BMW dealership in Falls Church, Virginia.'

'Who's the registered owner of the car? If the dealership filed an eighty-three-hundred, they had to list a vehicle identification number.'

'Let me check, um, hold on . . .' Freedman's voice developed an eerie whine. 'No, no, this can't be. What is this, some kind of joke?'

'Tell me, Bobby.'

'Gabriel's some kind of wiz if he can do this.'

'What is it?'

'The car is registered to Thirty-three oh three Chain Bridge Road. It belongs to Owen Glendenning.'

'Get out of the building, Bobby. Now!'

Chapter 57

It was thirty-seven years ago to the day that Admiral Owen Glendenning had led the action that resulted in his being awarded the Congressional Medal of Honor. Standing in the bedroom of his modest home in McClean, Virginia, he held the framed award, and in the day's dying light, read the citation, trying to reconcile the amoral, duplicitous man he had become with the guileless warrior he had been.

'For conspicuous gallantry and intrepidity at the risk of his life above and beyond the call of duty while serving as a SEAL team leader during action against enemy aggressor (Viet Cong) forces. Acting in response to reliable intelligence, Lt. (jg.) Glendenning led his SEAL team on a mission to capture important members of the enemy's area political cadre known to be located on an island in the bay of Nha Trang. In order to surprise the enemy, he and his team scaled a 350-foot sheer cliff to place themselves above the ledge on which the enemy was located. Splitting his team into two elements and coordinating both, Lt. (jg.) Glendenning led his men in the treacherous downward descent to the enemy's camp. As they neared the end of their descent, intense enemy fire was directed at them, and Lt. (jg.) Glendenning received massive injuries from a grenade that exploded at his feet and threw him backward onto the jagged rocks. Although bleeding profusely and suffering debilitating pain, he displayed outstanding courage and presence

of mind in immediately directing his element's fire into the heart of the enemy camp. Utilizing his radio, Lt. (jg.) Glendenning called in the second element's fire support which caught the confused Viet Cong in a devastating crossfire. After successfully suppressing the enemy's fire, and although immobilized by his multiple wounds, he continued to maintain calm, superlative control as he ordered his team to secure and defend an extraction site. Lt. (jg.) Glendenning resolutely directed his men, despite his near unconscious state, until he was eventually evacuated by helicopter. The havoc brought to the enemy by this successful mission cannot be overestimated. The enemy soldiers who were captured provided critical intelligence to the allied effort. Lt. (jg.) Glendenning's courageous and inspiring leadership, valiant fighting spirit, and tenacious devotion to duty in the face of almost overwhelming opposition sustain and enhance the finest traditions of the US Naval Service.'

After the war, the medal had guaranteed a swift ascent through the naval ranks. He hit all the good billets: two stints at the Pentagon, commander of BUD/S School in San Diego, naval attaché to the Kingdom of Saudi Arabia, a year as a White House fellow, and finally, a posting as director of Naval Intelligence. By the age of forty, he was a rear admiral, and all his efforts, his gilded connections and sheer moxie, couldn't budge him a rung higher.

The lateral swing to the CIA was a natural. He welcomed the new responsibilities and the higher salary, but already the gnawing dissatisfaction that would come to plague him was making itself known. The early 1980s were a heady time. The economy was rumbling back to life, having survived a bare-knuckled, knock-down-drag-out with inflation and unemployment. Up in New York, people were making barrels of money and flaunting it. This irked Glendenning. He didn't like coming up short on the material side of things compared to his cronies in lobbying, law, and defense. Men who were less intelligent than he and didn't possess his capacity for work, earned five times as much as he did. A salary of eighty grand a year didn't go far in the rarefied air of Virginia hunt country.

At first, a rapid series of promotions stemmed his envy. He moved from regional director to deputy director of operations within five years. But the same stasis that ended his naval career shadowed him at Langley. Year after year, he guarded his post as deputy director of operations. Four directors came and went. Not once was he mentioned as a candidate. It was his time as a SEAL that did it. You simply could not have a proven assassin at the helm of a major government agency. The American people would not stand for it.

Resentment of the hypocrisy festered inside Glendenning, rankling him more with each passing year, and with every change of regime. The lack of generous pay spurred his ill will. There was no reason serving your country shouldn't be a profitable endeavor. He viewed this as a structural flaw and decided he had every right to address it.

Omar al-Utaybi, or Marc Gabriel, as he called himself, provided the means.

He'd been watching Gabriel practically since the day the man had set up shop in Paris. He'd had a good reason, of course. During his posting to Riyadh, he'd come in contact with Gabriel's older brother, Juhayman, then a headstrong lieutenant in the national guard making waves with his calls for religious reform. When Juhayman took over the Grand Mosque, Captain Owen Glendenning advised the King on tactics to storm the sacred area and overwhelm the rebels. Juhayman was captured and executed. The remainder of the Utabyi family was exiled shortly thereafter.

At first, he took only a professional interest in Gabriel's activities. Gabriel's contacts with radical elements in Saudi Arabia left no doubt that he wished to see his brother's plans come to fruition. Gabriel was building a shadow government to be run by men from the armed forces, national guard, and foreign ministry. To finance their activities, he was playing the market, making equity investments and trading in currencies with extraordinary success. It soon became clear that Gabriel had a knack not only for fomenting a coup, but for value investing.

With careful planning and forethought, Glendenning began copying the Saudi's trades. If Gabriel bought ten thousand shares in Coca Cola, Glendenning bought a hundred. If Gabriel purchased call options on IBM, Glendenning did the same. 'Piggybacking' it was called in the business. Profits were in the hundreds, not thousands. But over time, the sums added up. His investments increased and so did his profits. After a few years, Glendenning boasted a hefty account at one of the more discreet offshore banks that the Agency liked to patronize.

He had made the decision to retire from the Company when Marc Gabriel called him.

It was blackmail pure and simple, and Glendenning couldn't say no. Gabriel had known for some time about Glendenning's activities. He, too, had friends in corner offices, and he was able to present Glendenning with a catalogue of his misdeeds. The sheer lack of options made Glendenning's complicity an easy matter for his conscience to swallow. Gabriel didn't ask for anything much, just that Glendenning keep an eye on the intelligence community and make sure no one got too close. It was a domestic matter, he promised. Strictly an internal Saudi affair.

But the events of September 11, 2001, magnified the scope and intensity of the intelligence world's interest in Middle Eastern affairs one-hundred-fold. When Sarah Churchill had phoned from London saying she'd identified a new group calling itself Hijira, Glendenning could do little to impede her investigations without provoking questions about his commitment to stamp out terrorism in all its forms.

Warnings that he'd sent had been largely ignored by Gabriel's field operatives. But Gabriel pressed for more. During the past week, he had been relentless, demanding information about the inner workings of Blood Money, threatening to expose him to Gadbois, to frame him for the deaths of the three treasury agents, if he refused to comply.

Anyway, it was through between them. Glendenning had done the man his last favor. Gabriel had his bomb. He could blow up half of Saudi Arabia as far as the admiral was concerned.

Slipping on his dinner jacket, Glendenning grabbed his walking sticks and hobbled to the stairs. The first thing he'd do when he retired was build himself an elevator, he mused as he made his way to the bar and fixed himself a cocktail. He poured a liberal dose of Russian vodka into a highball glass, threw in a few ice cubes, and added a twist of lemon.

'Claire,' he called out. 'Ready, love? It's time we got moving. Can't keep the president waiting.'

A whiff of perfume drifted from the bathroom where she was changing, and he thought of the ways his life had changed since he'd met her. The decision to cast off a cloying wife and end a loveless marriage had been a vote for his future. He looked forward to helping Claire through her illness. After, they would marry. He would retire to an island in the Caribbean where Gabriel would be just a bad dream, and life a series of golden sunsets and passionate nights.

'Claire,' he called again. One thing was the same about all women. They took a helluva long time to get themselves pretty. Taking a long sip, he set the glass down on his coffee table, only to pick it right back up and search for a coaster. How many times had he heard about moisture rings on the antique Williamsburg table?

The doorbell rang.

Glendenning froze, caught between looking for a confounded coaster and answering the door. His eye fell on the invitation to the state dinner. Snatching it in his fingers, he laid it on the table and put his drink down on it. 'There now, you happy?' he called to the shadow of his soon-to-be ex-wife. Walking to the door, he checked his watch. It was nearly seven. He wasn't expecting a visitor.

'Yes?' said Owen Glendenning, opening the door. It was Sam Spencer, the eternally youthful technician who ran the FBI's videotape enhancement unit.

'I've got it, Admiral,' the man blurted, waving a small cassette in his hand. 'The woman in the videotape. I've identified her.'

'Have you? That's wonderful news. Come in.'

'She's a Saudi,' said Spencer. 'From one of the ruling families.'

'That much I could have told you myself. Marc Gabriel, er . . . Omar al-Utaybi, the man we're looking for in Paris, is also a Saudi. Get you a drink, Spencer? A thank you for all your hard work.'

'A beer would be great, sir.'

'Sure thing.' Glendenning took a step towards the hall. 'Claire, let's go, sweetheart!' He smiled at Spencer. 'State dinner at the White House. You couldn't get me into this monkey suit for anything less. Come on in, then. Don't be shy.'

As Spencer advanced into the foyer, there came the sound of a faucet being shut off. A door opened beneath the staircase, and a slim woman with thick black hair and fine features stepped from the bathroom. She was dressed in a black taffeta ball gown and white brocade evening jacket. At her neck she wore a stunning set of black pearls, but it was the bejeweled belt that captured Spencer's attention. A rectangular buckle the size of two packs of cigarettes laid end to end and dusted with sparkling pavé diamonds.

'Here I am, Glen,' she said, then seeing Spencer: 'Oh, I didn't realize we had company.'

Spencer froze, his gaze jumping between Glendenning and the woman. 'Admiral—' he said haltingly.

Glendenning turned, the open beer in his hand. 'What is it, Spencer?'

The FBI agent stood as if nailed to the spot, his eyes unblinking. 'Admiral, that's her. That woman is Noor al-Utaybi. She's the lady on the tape.'

Glendenning glanced at Claire. 'Don't be ridiculous. This is Miss Charisse from the World Health Organization. Miss Charisse is my date for this evening. Claire, say hello to Sam Spencer.'

'No sir,' said Spencer, shaking his head, and it was clear that he would not be convinced otherwise. Stepping forward, he handed Glendenning the mini-cassette. 'You'll want to look at the tape.'

'Claire?' said Glendenning unsurely. Why wasn't she denying it? Why wasn't she smiling and telling Spencer in her lovely singsong voice that he was mistaken. Why was she just standing there looking every bit as scared as he felt? 'Claire,' he said again, less certainly. 'Is this true?' His throat tightened as the realization took hold. Spencer was right. Claire was Marc Gabriel's sister.

Yet, even as Glendenning began to have the first inkling of why, the bottle of beer shattered in his hand. Struck in the chest by a blunt, immensely powerful force, he staggered backward and collapsed to the floor.

Noor al-Utaybi turned and fired a single shot into Sam Spencer's uncomprehending face.

She would be certain to express the admiral's apologies to the President of the United States herself.

Chapter 58

Adam Chapel had been gone barely a week, but already he'd forgotten the oppressive, richly scented cloak that was a Virginia's summer eve. At six-forty, the sky blushed with the first hint of night. Crickets sawed frantically. Farther off, a lawn mower coughed sporadically. The thermometer attached to the rearview mirror read ninety-seven degrees.

'Park up the block,' said Sarah as they passed Owen Glendenning's home and noted the Ford Taurus parked in the driveway. 'I want to have a look around before we enact the Chapel Doctrine.'

'When did it become a doctrine?' he asked. 'A few minutes ago, you were calling it a "cheeky gambit." '

The Chapel Doctrine was the equivalent of a frontal military assault. He had decided to confront Admiral Owen Glendenning with the chain of evidence linking him to Marc Gabriel, in hopes of making him reveal Gabriel's plan. There was a corollary to the Doctrine, which he might call the Churchill Defense. While he was speaking with Glendenning, Sarah would gain entrance to his home through a back door or window and search the premises for concrete evidence of his complicity, and, Chapel hoped, be ready to lend a hand in case Glendenning was less than cooperative.

Chapel continued on a hundred yards, then pulled the

Ford Explorer to the curb and killed the engine. Sarah climbed out and shook out her legs. 'Let me have a quick look-see,' she said, and before he could protest, she jogged across a grassy knoll towards the thick beech forest that backed all the houses on Chain Bridge Road.

The suburb of McClean, Virginia looked as if it hadn't changed in fifty years, he thought, as he eyed the redbrick colonials set back from the road on leafy, rolling two-acre parcels. The phone lines had been laid underground, but otherwise, McClean had been spared the indignities of modernization. There were no corner 7-Elevens, no gas stations and mini-marts, no stoplights within miles. The boys and girls madly pedaling their bicycles might have been hurrying home to eat their usual Saturday supper of fried chicken and okra before sitting down to watch Buffalo Bob and Howdy Doody on their fifteen-inch black-and-white televisions.

Sarah arrived back at the car, her face flushed, but her breathing as calm as if she'd only gone for an evening stroll. 'Didn't see him,' she reported. 'Lights are on and I can hear some music. There's a second car parked up the driveway that might interest you.'

'A Beemer?'

'M3 Cabriolet. Very snazzy set of wheels for a man on a government salary.'

'Alright then, let's go have a chat with the good admiral.'

'Adam, be careful. You're going to shock the hell out of him. There's no telling what he's capable of.'

'I'll have you "watching my six," right? Isn't that what they teach you to say in spy school?'

'I think we preferred "covering my ass." ' She took a breath. 'Give me a minute to get round the back.'

As she started to leave, he clutched her hand and pulled her toward him. 'Sarah,' he asked. 'Mortier Caserne. I want to know how you got me out of there.' He had other questions, but if she answered the big one, she'd answer them all. How had she convinced Gadbois to free him and not keep his bosom buddy, Owen Glendenning, in the loop? How had she known about Leclerc's private contacts?

'Later,' she said. 'When we have more time.'

And then she was gone, running like a doe seeking the safer confines of the forest.

Chapel rang the doorbell and took a step back, clasping his hands over his stomach. The sound of light jazz tickled his ear. Waiting for Glendenning, he rehearsed his words. 'Admiral, I believe we have a problem,' he would say calmly. The heat, the jet travel, the enduring lack of sleep had robbed him of his anger. He didn't favor dramatics, just a straight-forward recounting of the facts. Glendenning would realize that if Chapel knew this much, so would others. The past week's stress had to have been playing on the man. 'It's time for this to stop,' Chapel would say. 'Enough men had—'

Just then, Chapel heard a moan coming from inside the house.

Rushing forward, he put his ear to the door. Hearing nothing more, he trampled the flower beds in his haste to peer through the front window. Lace curtains obscured his view. He could see the outline of furniture, but no sign of a man or woman.

'Sarah!' he yelled, moving back to the walk.

Just then, the door opened. 'Come in,' she said soberly.

Stepping into the foyer, Chapel was struck by the acrid scent of spent cordite, and then something else . . . something brash and metallic. He saw the bodies sprawled on the floor, the bamboo walking sticks lying askew, the pools of blood.

'No sign of forced entry,' said Sarah. 'No struggle, either. He knew whoever it was who killed him.'

Chapel was too stunned to speak.

'Stay here,' she commanded. 'Don't touch a thing. I need to look around.'

She was back in three minutes, holding a crumpled plane ticket and a battered pink sheet of paper. 'Claire Charisse signed for a pallet of expired pharmaceuticals this afternoon in Philadelphia. Here's her plane ticket. Point of embarkation: Geneva. Return portion unused.' She looked at Chapel. 'Taleel wasn't planning on accompanying Gabriel to the States. He was planning on accompanying Claire Charisse.'

'How's that?'

'Claire Charisse is Gabriel's sister, Noor.'

Chapel examined the discarded airline ticket. 'I don't think she's planning on going home.'

Sarah read over the shipping forms, mumbling the words of the different drugs. 'Half these medicines contain radio-active isotopes. It's here, Adam. The bomb is in the city. She got it in with the drugs.'

Chapel let his eyes fall to Glendenning's corpse. It was hard not to stare at the shirt. Blood had dyed the entire chest a deep crimson and pooled on the carpet around him. Sarah knelt next to the other body. It belonged to a man, with very little of his face remaining.

Sarah found his wallet and removed the identification. 'FBI,' she said. 'Spencer, Samuel A. Director, videotape unit.' She replaced the ID. 'He'd come to tell Glendenning who he'd found on the digital tape.'

'Noor?'

Sarah looked for the tape on their bodies, but found nothing, 'Maybe,' she said. 'Doesn't matter now. We know it's her. Where's he going, Adam? Where was Glendenning headed all dolled-up like this?'

From the corner of his eye, Chapel noticed a glimmer of gold. A flash from the coffee table. Carefully, he lifted the highball glass and picked up the invitation beneath it. The eagle of the presidential seal sparkled beneath beads of moisture. 'The White House,' he said. 'Eight o'clock.'

Sarah was on the phone three seconds later. Chapel watched as she dialed a Washington number, followed by four digits, and a moment after that, another two.

'*Bonjour, Jean-Paul, c'est moi . . . oui, il est la . . . Monsieur l'Ambassadeur, il est chez vous? . . . bien, écoutes . . . il me faut un smoking,*' she lowered the phone and asked Chapel, 'What's your jacket size?'

'Forty long.'

'*Quarante longue,*' she continued. '*T'as quelque chose pour moi? . . . Formidable . . . alors, trente minutes.*'

Chapel stared at her as she put down the phone. 'Who are you?' he asked.

Chapter 59

It took him five minutes to reach the crest of the highest dune near to the camp. Looking north, Omar al-Utaybi surveyed the sweeping, undulant expanse of the Rub-al-Khali. The Empty Quarter. Sand. Rock. Parched herbage. It was a landscape of despair. Yet, no other vista could thrill him as this one did.

In less than twelve hours, he would begin executing the plan to make it his own.

'Sheikh,' came a young boy's cry. 'The council is waiting.'

Utaybi waved to his second son from his second wife. 'I shall come at once.'

Taking a last look at the sweeping sands, he started down the dune to the mobile encampment that was home to the government in exile. It was more a small, vibrant town than a camp. Eighty-four persons in all. Fourteen Land Cruisers. Seven trailers modified for desert travel. Eleven four-wheel all-terrain vehicles. Sixteen all-weather tents. Four portable generators capable of providing enough electricity to power a state-of-the-art communications facility, a mobile refrigeration unit, and a pair of Liebert air conditioners to keep the all-important servers, mainframes, and laptops that comprised the nerve center of any invading army at a perfect sixty degrees Fahrenheit.

Omar al-Utaybi had ordered camp to be established at

the leeward base of a great dune. The cusp of the dune, and the dunes around it, all rising eighty feet or more, provided a natural bowl that deflected electronic surveillance measures and made it difficult for eyes on high to penetrate. A two-square-acre web of camouflage netting interwoven with the advanced reflective composites used in the construction of Stealth fighter aircraft helped nature with the task.

Utaybi threw back the flap to the communications tent and entered. As one, the ten men present bolted from their consoles and stood at rigid attention. All wore the starched white *dishdasha* and the red-checked *khaffiyeh* of his country's ruling classes. Sweeping off his headdress, he motioned for them to sit.

'Let us begin our review with the armed forces,' he said. 'Colonel Farouk, if you please.'

Farouk was stocky and taciturn, a thirty-year veteran who had been passed over for promotion because of his fierce fundamentalist beliefs. On Utaybi's cue, he began a recitation of the events that would unspool upon the death of the Saudi chief of staff and his deputy, both guests of the King during his four-day state visit to America. A liquidation squad in place in Riyadh and Jidda would target the remaining army leaders loyal to the King. Farouk's men would replace them and storm the palace compound. Martial law would be declared until Omar al-Utaybi reached the city and imposed his clan as the new and rightful ruler of Arabia. The cost of Farouk's complicity came to one hundred million dollars.

One hundred million dollars to the Bank of Riyadh.

'Finance,' Utaybi called out.

'World markets are down on average five percent since the shorts were put on. Market-to-market, our positions show a profit of seventy million dollars. Authorized wire transfers have been submitted to all our brokers. We are anticipating a first day's decline of between twenty and thirty-five percent, more on the volatile Asian exchanges.'

Sixty million dollars to the Jordani Bank of Commerce? Treasury had been bought for sixty million.

Utaybi listened intently, while his mind imagined the havoc the bomb would wreak.

The detonation of a one-kiloton nuclear device inside the White House would obliterate every building within a two-square-block radius. The explosion, the equivalent of one thousand tons of TNT would vaporize the White House including the West Wing, the Old Executive Office Building, the Treasury Building and the Treasury Annex and leave behind a crater two hundred feet across and forty feet deep. Everyone inside these buildings would die instantly and painlessly, as the initial gamma ray blast would literally erase every trace of their bodies before the electrical signals from their sensory organs could reach their brain. The expanding shockwaves would level the Veteran's Administration Building, the Commerce and Interior Departments, the headquarters of the American Red Cross, and every building around them. If lucky, the force of the blast might even topple the Washington Monument, though it was not prudent to hope for so much.

As the blast spread outward it would create winds upward of one hundred miles an hour, wreaking severe structural damage on all buildings within a two-mile radius and shattering windows up to five miles away. The narrow corridors of the Federal Triangle would become a killing zone as shards of metal, concrete, and glass rocketed through the air at near supersonic speeds. The intense heat generated by the explosion would melt the asphalt streets before causing them to burst into flame, and ignite a firestorm engulfing everything in its wake. The hurricane force winds would feed and enlarge a mushroom cloud, pushing it a mile into the night sky.

While the American system of democracy was capable of marching on with hardly a stutter in its step, the deaths of the King, his ministers of finance and education, and his chief of armed forces, would leave Utaybi's oil-rich homeland paralyzed and open to new, more capable leadership. Evidence linking certain Saudi princes to Hijira would prove the final straw.

Though espousing a return to the fundamental values of the Koran, Gabriel would not sever relations with the Americans. He was already realizing that his earlier plans to return Arabia to its pure Wahabi roots might prove unwise. He would limit 'the rot.' Oil workers would be forbidden from visiting the larger cities. American troops would be expelled. Yet, he would wield a carrot as deftly as a stick. He would break with OPEC. He would lower prices. He would increase twofold his oil production. No one would threaten such a proponent of economic growth. The US would move quickly to recognize the new regime. The House of Utaybi's reign would be assured.

'Education,' Utaybi called, and discreetly he checked his gold Piaget wristwatch.

Chapter 60

The couples passed through the front door of the White House, the men in tuxedos, the women in gowns. Upon entering, each presented their engraved invitation to the social secretary, who in turn read the name to one of the younger, handsomer agents assigned to the White House detail. The agent checked the name against the list of invitees and nodded his approval that they enter. Heightened security demanded that all handbags be passed through a metal detector, neatly disguised to resemble a polished oak hutch. Vapor detectors designed to sniff out conventional explosives, and radiation sensors remained hidden.

Michael Fitzgerald kept his distance from the arriving guests. For most, attending a state dinner was the invitation of a lifetime. It was to be an elegant affair, and security, though rigorous, was to be invisible.

'Hey, Fitz,' came a voice in his earpiece. 'The Frenchie's here. Black dress, white jacket, pearls. She's a looker.'

'She got Glendenning in tow?'

'Don't see him yet.'

'Hold her,' said Fitzgerald. 'I'll be right there.'

Fitzgerald moved out of the shadows and approached Claire Charisse. She was a dazzler, he thought. Those flashing brown eyes were capable of luring the most faithful husband away from his wife. He was more concerned, however, about Glendenning's absence. Putting on his diplomat's smile, he took the woman's arm.

'Excuse me, Miss Charisse, but would you mind coming with me?'

A broad smile greeted him. 'Certainly.'

'You are the guest of Admiral Glendenning?'

'I'm afraid Glen's been delayed. Work.'

'Will he be arriving soon?'

'Frankly, I do not know. It concerns the terrorists in Paris. One of his men has been arrested.'

Zee terrorrr-eeests. The accent was a little too strong for Fitzgerald's ear. He wondered if she was pouring it on for his behalf.

He steered her towards the doorway that permitted access to the elevators that would take the guests upstairs. A knot of guests were backed up at the checkpoint, cheerfully presenting their handbags for inspection, allowing his agents to run metal detectors over their bodies. He thought he'd clear her through security and have her take a seat until Glendenning arrived. Just then, he remembered that she was ill and receiving radioisotope therapy. His deputy had spoken with her doctor in Geneva and confirmed her course of treatment. Metastron. Doxorubicin. Cyclophosphamide. She was a walking radioactive cocktail. The moment she got near one of the Investigator Radiation Screeners embedded in the wall, the alarm would start screaming like a banshee. Fitzgerald changed direction. He had no intention of causing a scene. Safer to take her up the back way. He'd screen her himself.

'Would you mind if I phoned him to confirm?' he asked.

'Not at all.' Claire rattled off his work number at the CIA. 'If there's any problem at all, I'd be happy to stay with you until he comes. To tell you the truth, I'm not quite up to such a radiant affair. Glen insisted. Perhaps I can sit down while you call.'

'Certainly, ma'am.' Fitzgerald had to catch himself. He'd almost addressed her as 'madame.' He led her up two stairs to a bank of Louis XV chairs set against the main stairwell. 'If you please . . . oh, and watch your step. The carpet's come up a bit—'

It was too late. As soon as he uttered the warning, she caught her heel on a bulge in the carpet. Fitzgerald reached for her arm a second late and could only bear witness as her ankle turned beneath her and she collapsed to one knee. The woman let out a pathetic cry.

'Miss Charisse, please allow me to . . .' Then he saw it, and he knew he had to get her out of the entry hall PDQ. The wig. 'Excuse me, ma'am.'

She was holding her ankle and her cheeks had grown taut and pale. 'I'm so sorry,' she said, dazed. 'I'm so clumsy these days.'

Christ, thought Fitzgerald, *how do you tell a sick dame her wig's coming off?* 'Ma'am, please excuse me for saying it, but your hair . . . it's uh . . .'

The woman's hands flew to her head. Appalled, he could see her eyes dashing from one guest to the next, anticipating their impolite stares. She tried to stand, but fell back again. He heard an angry sniff, and he thought, *No, not on my watch*. He wasn't going to have another Mrs Hersh start bawling in the main entrance of the White House with fifty of the country's most important movers and shakers on their way to what was supposed to be the dinner of their lives.

Gently, he lifted her by the arm and guided her past the brace of agents blocking access to the stairs, around the maroon velvet rope behind them, and directly upstairs to a private bathroom off the Blue Room restricted for 'Buckskin' himself. When she emerged a few minutes later, Fitzgerald had forgotten all about phoning Admiral Owen Glendenning. He was thinking that it had been a stupid idea even to question the woman. She worked at the World

Health Organization. A do-gooder. And Glendenning? The man was a medal winner. *The* goddamned medal. As close a thing to a hero as they minted these days.

'Enjoy yourself, ma'am,' said Fitzgerald, all but doffing an invisible cap as he escorted her into the throng of guests enjoying predinner cocktails and the music of the Marine Band in the Blue Room. 'If you need anything, just ask for me. Michael Fitzgerald. The boys all know me.'

'You're most kind, Mr Fitzgerald.'

Fitzgerald watched her until she'd disappeared into the crowd. *Quick recovery*, he thought. She barely had a limp.

Chapter 61

The White House shone like an ornament against the burnt orange dusk. Lights blazed beneath the massive portico and beamed from the lawn. The mansion was as magisterial as a democracy would allow.

'How long?' asked Chapel as he and Sarah walked past St. John's Church. Across the street, a steady stream of elegantly attired men and women passed through the wrought iron gates along Pennsylvania Avenue and strolled purposefully up the wide, curving driveway towards the modest door that offered entry to the presidential mansion.

'Does it matter?' asked Sarah, and when she saw his jaw set firmly, his eye blazing with hurt, she added, 'Since the beginning. I didn't change horses midstream.'

'But they're our allies.'

'Allies are for wartime. In peacetime, it's every man for himself. National interest comes first. Has to, really. It's a country's job to protect itself. America's the number one practitioner of that policy. Why is it that you're always so convinced that what's good for you is good for the rest of us? France is the only country trying to go it alone these days. For God's sake, look at Britain. A hundred years ago we ruled the seas. Now we can't even commit a soldier anywhere outside our borders without America's consent.

All in the name of the special relationship. Nelson must be turning in his grave.'

'You can't believe that?'

'Can't I? I'd say I voted with my feet.'

'What did it?'

Sarah stopped walking and confronted him with a disdainful smirk. 'Something had to do it?'

Chapel refused to be cowed. He'd had it with her sidestepping the truth, her polite silences and clever delays. 'Yes,' he answered emphatically. 'The daughter of a British general doesn't just go trotting across the lines because the cuisine is better.'

Sarah shrugged, but the defiant tone remained. 'You already know. It was Daddy.'

'What about him?'

'They abandoned him. Left him to die like a soldier, I suppose they might say. I sat by his side watching the cancer consume him, holding his hand as he grew weaker every day. What did the army do? Put him in a ward with ten others and refused to try every experimental drug I brought to their attention – including Gleevec, which turned out to have an eighty percent survival rate over five years – because the drugs were too expensive or not proven.' Sarah put her hands on her hips, her cheeks taut with anger. 'They did nothing to help a man who'd given his country forty-four years of his life. Put me in a bad mood at the right time.'

'When you were a student at the Sorbonne?'

'So you were listening.'

Of course he'd been listening. He hadn't forgotten a word she'd said to him.

'Gadbois found me. Asked if I might lend a hand. I asked how. He said he thought MI6 would like to have a look at me. Told me to join up. Keep an eye open, an ear to the ground. I signed on.' She added lightly, 'I've always been a sucker for French culture.'

But Chapel was in no mood for her whimsy. 'You're a spy.' He meant it in the old-fashioned sense. A traitor. Against us. Against the good guys. Someone they take out and shoot at dawn.

'I am a double, Adam,' she said coldly. 'A double agent. I don't hurt Mother England. I just do what I can to help France. And if one day I find someone else who I think could use a hand, I hope I have the courage to help them, too.'

Chapel had nothing to say.

'You think I could go to my controller at MI6 with this?' Sarah demanded, and it hurt him more that she was trying to explain. 'He'd have had Glendenning on the phone lickety-split. "What's this about you tipping off the French police? I told Sarah it was nonsense, you know the girl, she's got a mind of her own. And oh, yes, she mentioned you'd arrested one of your own men before hearing him out, seen to it the French gave him a good beating, too." It would have been us back there on the floor instead of Glendenning and poor Mr Spencer. Right now, you should be counting your blessings the French *don't* trust us implicitly.'

She pursed her lips, and a great shudder passed over her body. As she closed her eyes, he could sense her shame, though if it was for her actions, or her need to confess them, Chapel couldn't tell. When she opened them, he could see she was done with her confession. A smile stretched her lips, and she spent a few seconds arranging his bow tie, brushing a few specks of lint off the lapels of his tuxedo. 'By the way, you look smashing for a man who's slept five hours in the last four days and had a rather unpleasant course in "torture lite." ' She leaned over and pecked him on the cheek. 'I'm sorry for that. General Gadbois had to know for himself that I was telling the truth.'

'He didn't *trust you?*'

'Darling,' she said, giving his hand a squeeze. 'It doesn't do to trust a double.'

Chapel knew the advice was directed at him, not Gadbois.

He took her in, this new Sarah, his fairy-tale princess dressed for the ball. She wore a black satin gown that hugged her bosom and fell to the knee. Her hair was arranged in a chignon, and pinned high. At the French Embassy, one of her unnamed associates offered a plastic composite stiletto as an accessory to hold the elegant bun in place, something that wouldn't set off the metal detectors. Sarah had turned him down with a cryptic smile. She didn't need a weapon, the smile had said. She was capable of handling things herself. Midnight eyeliner and mascara amplified the depth of her eyes. To catch her gaze was to lose your breath.

Looking at her, he felt a stab of desperation. She was in another league altogether. Essentially another man's woman.

Slipping the invitation out of his pocket, he took Sarah's hand and they crossed Pennsylvania Avenue and joined the partygoers on their promenade past the cordon of Secret Service agents, up the driveway to the brightly lit portico, where they both nodded to the Marine guards bracketing the front door.

'The Honorable Mr Dominique Villefort and Mrs Villefort,' said a blonde woman in a white gown who accepted their invitation. Villefort was the second secretary at the French Embassy. A name, but not a face. 'We're so pleased you could attend.'

'It is our pleasure,' answered Sarah, a Gallic demiglaze sweetening her words.

A Secret Service agent approached and asked Sarah if she had a handbag. Sarah said she did not, and the agent directed them to an elevator that would carry them to the Blue Room where, he informed them, the cocktail hour was drawing to a conclusion. Upstairs, the crowd was a hundred strong, and by the sound of the raised, convivial voices, in rare spirits. Chapel recognized the secretary of state, the chairman of the joint chiefs of staff, and the attorney general. It was an A-list affair. The Marine Band played Sinatra and they were very good.

'She'll be alone,' Sarah said. 'She has to have the device on her body.'

'What am I looking for?'

'Something small. Eight inches long, four inches wide. It might not be visible. Let's split up. If you sense something suspicious, you're probably right.'

Sarah disappeared into the crowd, leaving Chapel on his own. A bar was set up on a table in the far corner. Liveried waiters circulated, taking orders. He was struck by how familiar it all was. Hardly different from a 'do' at the Four Seasons. His eye wandered from face to face, appraising but not lingering. Was he supposed to rule out every white-haired woman over fifty? Every African-American? Every Asian? It was a dinner for the Saudi King. Every other person in the room fit at least half the profile, that is, a woman of Middle Eastern extraction.

A waiter spotted his empty hands and asked what he would like. 'Water,' answered Chapel, but thinking of what Sarah called 'cover,' he changed his order to a Jack Daniel's on the rocks. Right about now, a rebel's courage would do him right.

The band stopped playing. A hush spread over the crowd. Double doors that he had not previously noticed swung open. A stout, silver-haired man threw out his chest and bellowed, 'Ladies and gentlemen, the President of the United States and His Royal Highness, the King of Saudi Arabia.'

The two men entered in deep discussion. The First Lady followed with one of the King's older wives. Behind them trailed the King's retinue, ten men clad, like the King, in traditional Saudi garb – *dishdashas, khaffiyehs*, and the male's requisite mustache and goatee.

'Everyone's here,' thought Chapel nervously. 'Now's the time. If you're going to do it, do it while your blood's running hot, before your doubts get the better of you.'

His own palms were moist and he felt flushed, jittery. He searched for Sarah and couldn't find her. Discreetly, he pushed his way to the edge of the crowd. The guests had formed a crescent and the President and the King were working their ways to opposite ends of the line, doing their mandatory 'meet and greet.'

By now, Chapel had developed a routine for examining each person. He would start at the shoes and move north to the head. There wasn't an American cobbler represented in the room. It was Blahniks, Ferragamos, and Chanels all around. The woman rubbing his elbow was red-haired and Irish. Next to her stood the commandant of the Marine Corps. Count those two out. A chubby Arabian woman gazed adoringly at the President, her smile stretched to cracking, but dripping with such obvious goodwill that Chapel dismissed her, too. Next to her stood a svelte, severe brunette in a fluted black ball gown, and if the diamonds were real, a million-dollar belt. *Definite donor material there*, thought Chapel.

The King was approaching him, shaking hands with all the guests, looking decidedly bored. Chapel looked at the slim woman again. She was standing stiffly, her eyes locked on the King. Chapel gave her the once-over. She wore low black pumps with white toe caps. Hardly enough heel for the gown. A dot of blood graced the piping at her heel. Chapel stepped closer. It was then that he got a better look at her eyes, the unflinching stare directed at the King. It was Taleel's gaze, the otherworldly view of a soul already departed. She was trembling. He noticed that her hands were fiddling with the belt buckle, her fingers pressing at either end.

Something small, Sarah had said. *Eight inches long, four inches wide.*

By then, he was moving, imagining how he would grab her – if he should throw her to the floor, or pinion her arms behind her back. It was her turn to greet the King. She took a step forward, her hands locked on the belt. But even as Chapel shoved the Marine commandant aside, there came the crash of a porcelain vase splintering on the wooden floor. As one, the guests craned their heads behind them to look. Chapel reached for the woman, rising on his tiptoes. He diverted his gaze for a second – less, even. He felt rather than saw her. A rustle of black silk, a shadow out of the corner of his eye. He heard a second crack, this one crisper, muted but distinct, like the snapping of a brittle twig. And Sarah was cradling the woman in her arms as the King ignored the two and passed down the line, as if causing women to faint was an everyday occurrence.

Everything happened very quickly then, so it was only later, when Adam Chapel was alone and his world had changed forever, that he was able to play it back and set the events in their proper order. A flurry of Secret Service agents appeared, as they so often do, as if out of thin air. Chapel tried to help, but Sarah warned him off with her eyes. The woman was dead. No head could loll at such an unnatural angle. A trickle of blood rolled from her mouth, but one of the agents dabbed it off before it could drip onto the carpet.

And then they were gone. Sarah still supporting the woman, being led with the help of five or six agents through the double doors.

The President guided the King into the dining room. The crowd followed. In a minute, the Blue Room was empty. Chapel kept expecting something else to happen, but he didn't know what. Everyone acted as if nothing had occurred, and he realized that, of course, nothing had. No mention of the event would reach the papers. No bomb had been stolen from the Israeli arsenal. Hijira was simply one more ill-planned, ill-funded assembly of crackpots who wanted the world to conform to their demands or else! Gabriel was still out there, but as a threat, he was neutralized. The intelligence authorities knew his name, had by now dug up several photographs of him. His son was cooperating fully to assemble a complete picture of his activities. The Saudi monarchy was as stable, or unstable, as ever.

Chapel waited until dinner was served for Sarah to return, then asked to speak with the agent in charge, the tall, white-haired man with a ruddy drinker's complexion he'd seen usher Sarah out of the Blue Room. Not possible, came the answer. Perhaps the gentleman would care to take his seat and enjoy his dinner. The chef had prepared a fine meal: potato galettes, roasted squab, a medley of summer squash. And for dessert, at the King's request, a hot fudge sundae. He even let slip that the Saudi potentate had asked for vodka in his water glass. If the gentleman would care for the same, it would be a pleasure.

Chapel waited outside the White House until the last of the guests had filed past him. They had done it. Together, he and Sarah had stopped Marc Gabriel's plan. They had thwarted Hijira. Yet why did he feel so empty? Slowly, he made his way through the silent streets to the car. It was parked where he'd left it, but he realized that Sarah had the keys. He looked around, eyes darting up and down the street. Searching. Wondering. Hoping. He caught sight of a shadow and raised himself onto his toes. But it was only a homeless man adjusting a blanket around his shoulders. He knew then that she wasn't coming and that he would never see her again.

Still, he would not go. Eyes locked on the White House, he stood by the car until the exterior lights had dimmed, and night cloaked the portico in its forgiving shade, and he heard a bell toll midnight.

Chapter 62

A soft, steady wind swept across the sand, driving the gnarled strands of dried acacia before it, singing the tremulous song of a coming storm. Omar al-Utaybi wrapped the tail of his *khaffiyeh* over his nose and mouth and hiked the last few steps to the crest of the southernmost dune. The sky was still dark, an effervescent canopy of stars. As he stared to the east, the sun's first rays fired the horizon. A reaper's blade sliced the world into two. Another day had begun. He shivered at the drama.

Utaybi had not slept the entire night. Televisions tuned to CNN, Al-Jazeera, and the BBC still burned in the command tent. As yet, there was no news on any of the stations, nor on any of a half-dozen radio frequencies being monitored, of an attack in the American capital.

It was nine P.M. in Washington DC. By now, Noor was to have completed her task. Her instructions had been precise. She was to wait until the Saudi impostor entered the White House and then detonate the device. If for any reason she was denied access or threatened with capture, she was to immediately sacrifice herself. If any other eventuality ensued, she was to position herself as close to the White House as possible and set off the weapon.

Noor had phoned two hours earlier in jubilant spirits. Glendenning was dead. She was proceeding to the White

House. She foresaw no difficulties. In parting, she had wished him a prosperous life and many more children, and said she hoped to see him in a better world. There was no question of her will. He could not imagine what had happened.

Closing his eyes, Utaybi offered a silent prayer for his youngest sister. Yet even as he completed his blessing, his phone rang.

'Noor,' he cried, recognizing her number on his phone's digital screen. 'What has happened? I have no word of the attack.'

'Noor is dead,' said the emotionless voice of an English female.

'Who is this?'

'We have the bomb. You failed.'

'What do you want?'

'This is your wake-up call, Omar al-Utaybi. Time to go to hell.'

Desperately, Utaybi tried to turn off his phone. He could not. Somewhere high in the sky a satellite had acquired the signal and was jamming his frequency. It was too late. He knew the technology. They had triangulated his position. His fate was cast.

Dropping the phone, he turned to run down the hill. He had only covered a hundred yards when he caught the cruise missile's silver streak, its blazing black orange flame rushing at him.

The sun, he thought, reflecting off a limestone bluff.

The Runner

Christopher Reich

July 1945. For Germany the war is over. But in POW Camp 8 on the outskirts of Garmisch, one man refuses to believe his duty to the Fatherland is finished. Erich Seyss, once one of Germany's greatest Olympic sprinters, now awaits trial for war crimes committed as a fanatical officer in Hitler's SS. But he has no intention of facing his accusers. Instead, he is determined to run one last race for Germany.

Given only seven days to track Seyss down, Devlin Judge, a lawyer with the International Military Tribunal set up to try Nazi war criminals, faces an almost impossible task. Not only must he outwit an elite killer trained to operate behind enemy lines, but he must also fathom the extraordinary conspiracy to which Seyss is the key. A conspiracy that could change the face of Europe forever.

'Wonderful . . . a sophisticated story of conspiracy, treachery and intrigue' Nelson DeMille

'Wonderful' *New York Times*

'Brilliant' James Patterson

'Astonishingly powerful' *Daily Telegraph*

0 7472 6624 7

headline

The First Billion

Christopher Reich

'Mr Reich deserves the Grisham mantle. The plot is so suspenseful, the dialogue so believable and the characters so finely drawn' *New York Times*

John 'Jett' Gavallan, a former fighter pilot, now the high-flying CEO of Black Jet Securities, is banking on the riskiest gamble of his dazzling career. In exactly six days, he will take Mercury Broadband, Russia's leading media company, public on the New York Stock Exchange. Billions are at stake, but rumours that the company is a fraud place the deal on a knife-edge and when his number-two man disappears in Moscow, Gavallan fears that deception may turn into murder.

Plunging into a desperate search for his best friend, Jett finds himself trapped in a conspiracy that could shatter the delicate balance between nations and plunge the global economy into chaos. Hunted by the F.B.I. and a band of elite killers, Jett races from Palm Beach to Zurich to Moscow in his search for answers. But the truth will come at a terrible price . . .

'Engrossing . . . destined for a big readership' *Wall Street Journal*

0 7472 6623 9

headline

Now you can buy any of these other bestselling Headline titles from your bookshop or *direct from the publisher*.

FREE P&P AND UK DELIVERY
(Overseas and Ireland £3.50 per book)

Something Wild	Linda Davies	£6.99
Mandrake	Paul Eddy	£6.99
American Gods	Neil Gaiman	£6.99
Stone Kiss	Faye Kellerman	£5.99
Flesh and Blood	Jonathan Kellerman	£6.99
One Door Away from Heaven	Dean Koontz	£6.99
The Oath	John Lescroart	£6.99
The Jury	Steve Martini	£6.99
Long Lost	David Morrell	£6.99
2nd Chance	James Patterson	£6.99
Violets are Blue	James Patterson	£6.99
The Runner	Christopher Reich	£5.99
No Good Deed	Manda Scott	£5.99

TO ORDER SIMPLY CALL THIS NUMBER

01235 400 414

or visit our website: www.madaboutbooks.com

Prices and availability subject to change without notice.